A NOVEL

THE GIFTS OF CUTTER COUNTY

AUDREY ZAJAC

Despite the setting taking place near the Three Mile Island nuclear power plant, *The Gifts of Cutter County* is purely a work of fiction.

Paperback ISBN 978-1-960007-51-3
eBook ISBN 978-1-960007-52-0

Published by
Orison Publishers, Inc.
PO Box 188
Grantham, PA 17027
www.OrisonPublishers.com

DEDICATION

To my beloved cat, Puffin,
in whose memory I will donate a portion of book proceeds
to Pennsylvania animal-rescue groups and charities.

PROLOGUE

Dauphin County, Pennsylvania, 2026

Christie Cutter inhales a whisper of smoke as she ascends the stairwell of the operations building at the Three Mile Island nuclear power plant outside Harrisburg, Pennsylvania. The roar as the building shook a moment ago still echoes through her head. Was that an earthquake? Or did a truck slam through the glass doors of the main entrance? *Explosion* was not among her first thoughts, because it was nearly impossible for the reactor to explode, everyone said. *Nearly* impossible.

The other two security guards are scouring the grounds around the reactor building, checking for damage. Christie is the only one inside; the only one who can't see what is going on out there.

Then her boss's voice crackles over her radio. "Cutter, the operations building is on fire! Check the Control Room, then get out!"

"Copy that." Christie is panting as she reaches the top of the stairwell, barely able to hear him over the blaring fire alarm. "What's going on out there?"

"Debris everywhere. Reactor is intact, though. Mitch is flying in from the east, I think. I can hear his chopper. Can't see him through all the smoke, though."

A wave of relief washes over her. Her husband is on his way in his security helicopter, ready to rescue her coworkers. Hopefully, the reactor will be okay. She can handle a burning building. But not a burning building during a nuclear meltdown.

She had thought being a security guard at the newly functioning nuclear power plant would be a good deal. She'd struggled through four years on the Harrisburg police force but had seen too many shootings and drug overdoses by her thirtieth birthday to make it a career. Yet, she didn't want to give up the life entirely, and her husband, Mitch, encouraged her to apply to be a security guard where he works at Three Mile Island.

The Control Room hall is shrouded in smoke and darkness. There are no visible flames. Christie covers her mouth with her sleeve and trains her flashlight beam down the murky corridor. "Jim, where is the fire, exactly? I'm at the Control Room."

Jim's response is a string of garbled words and static. Christie will have to worry about the fire later. Right now she needs to get the Control Room door open. The power went out with the explosion, and opening the door won't be as easy as swiping a key card.

As she eyes the smoke billowing from a crack under the door, Christie's stomach twists at the thought of what she might find. She touches the metal door. It is still cool. She pounds on it. "Hello! Can anyone hear me?" she screams, sweat dripping into her eyes.

"Christie! Oh, thank God!" Her best friend, Karen, screams from the other side. "Our key cards don't work! We can't get out!"

"I know, the backup generators must have shut down. How much smoke is in there? Can you cover your faces with cloth or something? And stay on the floor!"

"We're doing that!" Karen calls back through a coughing fit.

Suddenly another explosion rocks the building. This one seems closer than the first, or maybe bigger. Christie is momentarily knocked off her feet, and she wonders if *that* was the reactor. She knows an attack on the nuclear facility is essentially impossible, and there are so many safeguards in place that a meltdown should never happen, but she can't help thinking the worst.

Choking on smoke, she fumbles with the fire axe she grabbed from the stairwell. Raising the axe high overhead, she screams, "Stand back! I'm going to break the door with an axe!"

"Okay, ready!" Karen calls.

Christie heaves the axe into the door, relieved as the metal crumples much more easily than she expected. A huge plume of smoke wafts out of the hole, and she ducks toward the floor to avoid it. Her eyes sting.

She swings the axe again and this time manages to make a hole wide enough to allow her twelve captive coworkers to escape to freedom…or at least to a smokey stairwell that may soon be annihilated in a radiation cloud.

"Cutter, you brilliant piece of work!" says Dave, the lead operator, as he practically pushes Karen through the hole and grabs another of his colleagues behind him. They all tumble out to the relative safety of the hallway.

"Just doing my job, Dave," Christie replies with a false sense of confidence. She has only been a security guard at Three Mile Island for four months and is definitely not prepared for a rescue mission of this magnitude.

"Christie, where's Mitch?" Karen refers to Christie's husband as they flee to the stairwell.

"He's in the chopper." She activates her radio. "Mitch, which chopper pad? I have everyone from the Control Room."

Mitch's voice is clear enough for Christie to understand through the static. "Christie! Thank God you're all right … Pad 2. Touching down now. Watch yourself out here. There's smoke and debris everywhere. My God, I can barely see the ground!" Mitch's voice shakes. Christie hears the thundering propeller as he opens the door of his security helicopter.

It must be bad out there; Mitch is the bravest man she knows. She can picture him jumping down from the chopper, ready to greet her and her coworkers and fly them all to safety.

"Dave, is your entire team here?" Christie calls to him at the front of the group.

Dave turns and surveys his colleagues. Christie also silently counts the small group of people as they rush through the doorway. There should be twelve people from the Control Room, but she is unsure how many other people may be in the building. She counts again, not liking her total.

"Where's Ricky?" Dave asks grimly.

"Everyone, get to Pad 2! Mitch will get you out! Good luck!" Christie yells as she holds the door open for Karen, the last to scurry outside. "Karen ... tell Mitch I love him."

Karen turns and locks eyes with Christie. They nod to one another, a look of understanding passing between friends.

"Cutter?" Dave addresses Christie. He has taken the door from her, holding it open for Christie to join them outside.

"Dave ..." Karen's voice is low and stern. "Come on, Dave." She takes his hand, and they turn together from the doorway. Christie doesn't watch them run toward Mitch's chopper.

She covers her nose and mouth with her arm, axe still in hand, and sprints back up the stairs, intent on searching for survivors.

Her radio crackles again. She knows it is Mitch even before his voice blares from it. "Christie!" he screams at her. "Where are you?"

"I have a duty to search the building, Mitch. You know that."

"The bomb squad is here. They can do that! Get out here now!"

"Take off, Mitch! Who knows if there will be a meltdown? Don't kill the people I just saved!"

There is silence, and Christie wonders if the connection has been lost. Then Mitch says softly, "Christie ... I love—"

"Tell me later, over dinner. I'm heading out the back door to the parking lot. I can see my car. It's closer than your chopper." She clicks off her radio, running deeper into the doomed building.

✳✳✳

Cutter County, 28 Miles South of Three Mile Island, 2033

Seven years later, Scott Givins sits in his sixth-grade history class one October day, daydreaming about his family's trip to Disney World the week before. It was fantastic. His parents are rich, and they paid off the park staff so he and his little brother could jump to the head of the lines. Best vacation ever. But now it's over, and he is back in school, bored out of his mind.

He gazes out the window. The leafy trees are ablaze with fall color, but Scott doesn't care about foliage. Things like trees are extremely uninteresting, compared with private jets and fishing on his father's yacht on Chesapeake Bay.

He leans away from his computer, resting his eyes, not even able to remember the name of the book the class is reading today. Something about the Radiation Zone, but it isn't the interesting stuff, like the huge explosions, the deaths and mass destruction, or the radiation leak. It is mostly about Christie Cutter, the local heroine security guard who sacrificed herself to save her coworkers.

Scott's glazed eyes skim the computer screen. He has heard about Christie, the meltdown at Three Mile Island, and the Radiation Zone since he was a little kid. It's all boring. It has no impact on his life. The Rad Zone is a toxic wasteland of nuclear activity, and it is dangerous—even fatal—to go in there, so people simply ignore it now. Out of sight, out of mind. Other than knowing that the county where he lives was renamed in honor of Christie Cutter for her heroism or whatever, Scott's brain can't soak up any more information. So she died doing her job. So what? He wants to be out fishing with his father. He rubs his eyes and rests his head on his desk, pretending to be finished with the reading assignment.

***

Washington, DC, 2033

At that moment, about a hundred miles south of Scott's school in Cutter County, Pennsylvania, Scott's father, Sen. Roger Givins, is climbing into Senator Joseph Starling's limousine outside their offices in Washington, DC.

"Hey, Roger, how have you been?" Senator Starling gives his friend a hearty handshake, sliding over in the seat.

"Not bad, Joe. Good to see you." Senator Givins sighs as he loosens his tie and settles into the back seat. "I'm glad this week is over ... but I have to say, I'm not looking forward to the Switch next week. I know we're friends and all, but I did *not* vote for it," he says good-naturedly.

"Ahh." Senator Starling waves his hand nonchalantly, brushing off his friend's remark. "We have nothing to worry about. You and I are two of the good ones."

"Humph." Senator Givins disagrees, staring out the window at the Washington Monument. "I can't believe you convinced a majority to vote for it."

"It just shows how much people need a change. They are at wit's end with the way things are going," Senator Starling says, pouring a Scotch from his limo's mini fridge. He hands it to Givins and pours one for himself. "They all just need to behave themselves, and, really, nothing will be different for them. This is meant to help the country, not its leaders."

"Well, that's the problem, isn't it?"

Senator Starling shrugs in reply, sipping his drink.

The Switch is the brainchild of a small group of senators, including Starling, who have been fed up with the corruption and debauchery of politicians as a whole for years. But not everyone is on board with the new plan for the country's political leaders.

"You do know you have death threats against you, don't you?" Givins asks, always impressed with how Joe Starling can take things like potential assassination in stride.

"Oh, yeah."

"Have you told Mary Ann?"

"Oh, God, no," Starling scoffs, draining his glass. He stretches his arms above his head, relaxing in the seat, and changes the subject. "Got any weekend plans?"

"I'm taking the wife and kids fishing," Givins replies, thinking about his yacht, moored on the Chesapeake Bay. "You?"

Senator Starling sighs and refills their glasses. "I need to have a little talk with Sam, and I'm not looking forward to it." He closes his eyes, thinking of his nine-year-old son.

"Hmm, trouble at school again?"

"Yeah." Starling runs his hand through his wavy blond hair. "And at home. He is really getting to be a handful ... mouthing off to Mary Ann ... sometimes getting so wound up we don't know what to do with him. Other times, he gets in these moods where he won't even come out of his room. I think I'm to blame. ... I can't spend as much time with him as I would like."

"And you'll have even less time when the baby comes," Givins says sympathetically, thinking of his own two boys at home, Scott and Blaze.

"Yeah, well, we'll get it figured out," Starling says as his driver pulls up in front of his hotel, where he'll spend the evening meeting with the California delegation before flying home in the morning. He drains his glass, opens the car door, and steps out. "Hey, enjoy the limo. Take care of her for me this weekend."

"Thanks for the loan," Givins says with a grin. "I can't believe how long it's taking to fix mine. Who knew a deer could do so much damage?" Givins gives his friend a quick wave as he pulls the door closed. Then he flashes a thumbs up to Starling's driver, who eases the car back into traffic.

Givins stretches out in the back seat, eager to get home to his family. Little does he know, as he watches the cityscape glide by en route to the interstate on ramp, that he will not make it out to his yacht this weekend. He won't make it home, either. Because Senator Starling's limo will erupt in a fiery explosion thirty minutes later, on the way north to Cutter County.

CHAPTER 1

Jessie

Cutter County , March 2040
"Aw, man, are you kidding me?" Jessie Cox mutters under her breath as she sleepily opens her eyes and looks at the clock. It's 9:07 on a Saturday morning. Way too early to be so rudely disturbed by her cat, Puffin, who has knocked a flower vase off the kitchen countertop, shattering glass and spilling water all over the floor. No, Jessie isn't sleeping in the kitchen. She can't even see the wreckage from her cozy bed. Puffin is telling her about it as he leaps onto her feet. He tells her he is sorry, but only a little bit. He is mostly bored, and also kind of hungry. As usual.

"Sometimes I hate you, Puffin," she says sleepily as her cat purrs at her side. Jessie absently scratches him behind his ears. She'll get up and clean his mess in a minute, then get her homework finished for the weekend. That way she won't have to worry about it.

Jessie has two assignments due Monday. The first one will be easy: a three-page essay on her career choice for her college-prep writing course. She has wanted to be a veterinarian since she was a kid, long before she became Gifted with hearing the thoughts of animals. Her father, the mayor of New Harrisburg in Cutter County, had prodded her toward a life in politics. But Jessie had quickly pivoted away from a political career when Senator Givins was senselessly murdered by a car bomb a few years ago. Also, with the Switch in place, politics are too daunting for Jessie to even consider.

"Other ear, please," Puffin says inside her brain, pressing his fuzzy head into her hand. Jessie obliges and scratches his left ear, then turns her thoughts back to her homework.

The second assignment won't be much fun. It is a five-page essay on the ecological effects of radiation poisoning for her environmental science class. She is generally aware of what damage can be done by radiation, having heard for years about the meltdown at Three Mile Island in 2026. The problem with the essay is that there were never any studies done on the environmental and ecological impacts in the local Radiation Zone, a restricted area that stretches outward from Three Mile Island in a twenty-five-mile radius. Jessie will have to spend a few hours doing some general research on the topic.

I'll just research Chernobyl, Jessie decides as she rolls out of bed, Puffin bounding along at her heels. She wishes she could write about her personal hero, Christie Cutter, instead. That would be easy to write. There are numerous Internet resources with information about the local heroine.

She walks down the hallway to the bright kitchen to survey Puffin's damage. Her mother is coming up the stairs.

"What was that noise?" Mom asks.

"Puffin broke something. ... I'm sorry; I'll clean it up," Jessie answers, grabbing a cloth off the marble countertop and sopping up the water on the floor, carefully sifting through shards of glass. Puffin isn't hurt. If he had cut his paws on the glass, the news would have been apparent to Jessie immediately. She can read that cat from fifty feet away.

Bright morning sunlight streams through the skylights, highlighting the destruction. Her mother's flowers are strewn everywhere, some stems obviously chewed.

"Too bad lilacs aren't poisonous to cats!" Jessie yells to the big black-and-white cat, who is now insistently bumping his head into her ankles, obviously in an advanced state of extreme starvation. She hugs him, squishing his warm head against her cheek. He is her favorite thing in the world—if you don't include actual human family members. She's not actually mad at Puffin, but she likes pretending to be.

"Hi ... food ... now, please." Puffin purrs and pushes his head into her chin. (Actually, Jessie adds the "please" in her own mind. She needs to believe that Puffin is polite, and not just a small and cute nuisance that constantly barrages her for food and attention.)

"Okay, fine! Here's your food!" she mutters under her breath, grabbing a handful of kibbles and throwing them down the stairwell, making Puffin "hunt" them.

"Yay, yay ... food ... yay!" Puffin yowls happily as he tumbles down the stairs after his prey. Jessie feels a slight twinge of guilt as he utters a soft, "Yikes!" and cowers at the sound of a motorcycle roaring away on the street.

It's heartbreaking knowing how many times animals get scared in their day-to-day lives. Jessie had realized this sad fact the very first day she heard the thoughts of animals stream through her own mind. Lots of things intimidate Puffin—loud cars, people shouting across the street, and sometimes even loud noises from the TV. All these things bother him, at least to some degree.

Other than sharing in these brief and occasional moments of fright, Jessie usually finds solace in the minds of animals. She sometimes loses herself in their thoughts, simple thoughts based on instinct and whatever immediate need they have to fill—warmth, water, food, companionship. She has been blessed with a truly amazing Gift.

After cleaning up Puffin's mess, Jessie wanders down the hallway to her bedroom and fishes her computer tablet from her bag. Once she finishes these assignments, she can relax for the rest of the weekend. She is sixteen years old and currently a junior in high school; only three more months until those college applications will fill her every waking moment. She is dreading it.

Puffin bounds onto her bed. "Sunspot ... warm," he purrs, curling into a ball in the sunlight near the head of the bed. He is asleep within a few minutes, his thoughts quieting to a soft murmur, a soothing white noise.

Jessie starts her research on the environmental effects of nuclear radiation. A quick Internet search of the "Radiation Zone" turns up nothing, except the facts she already knows. "Fifty-mile wide federally restricted region in south central Pennsylvania that was created due to the meltdown at the Three Mile Island Nuclear Energy facility in 2026." She skims the page. No one has ventured back in the Rad Zone in the past fourteen years to do any kind of testing. Not helpful for her homework assignment.

A few minutes later, her brother's bedroom door squeaks, and she hears plodding footsteps coming down the hall. He appears in her doorway, sulks over to her bed without looking at her, and flops down next to Puffin.

"My spot," the cat says groggily before his thoughts shift back into quiet sleep.

"Good morning, Alex. What's up with you?" Jessie asks, turning to her little brother. He is sprawled over the bed, his feet hanging off the end. He is a small kid for his age—nearly fifteen—and thin and wiry. He has always enjoyed playing sports but never seems to get more muscular. He is all knees and elbows with a bunch of curly dark hair. Jessie has been secretly wondering if staying small and young-looking is his Gift, and no one knows it yet.

Alex massages his temples as though he has a bad headache. He glances at his sister, barely opening his hazel eyes. She squints at him, concerned. It is very unlike him to be this melancholy, especially on a Saturday morning.

"What's wrong? Are you sick?" By this time, Jessie is half out of the chair, ready to put a hand on his forehead to check for a fever.

"Blaze got his Gift today. He just texted me and Sam," he answers glumly, turning his head away so she can't feel his forehead. He closes his eyes again, still massaging his temples.

"Ah," she says knowingly, situating herself back in the chair and placing her tablet on the desk to give Alex her full attention. Alex and his two best friends, Blaze Givins and Sam Starling, have been pals since elementary school. They are all in the same grade, though Sam is older by a year because he had to repeat the fourth grade after breaking both legs in a biking accident. (That's another story, and Jessie doesn't have all the details. To this day, Sam has kept pretty quiet about it.)

The three boys had all been Normal until today. Like most kids in Cutter County, Alex and Blaze have been worried they will not become Gifted. Jessie isn't quite sure what Sam thinks about the whole thing, but unlike Alex, Sam seems way too cool and self-assured to care whether he ever becomes Gifted or not.

Poor Alex has been dreading for weeks that he will remain Normal forever. His fifteenth birthday is only a few days away, and the pressure is on. Jessie got her Gift the day after her fifteenth birthday, and she knows Alex is jealous. His only consolation had been that his friends were all Normal, too, up until today.

Jessie knows better than to ask immediately what Blaze's newly bestowed Gift is, though it is always exciting to have another Gifted member in the county. Sometimes it's just good to know that you have a better Gift than someone else. There will always be some good-natured rivalry, though you can't control what you get.

Finally, Jessie asks her brother as gently as she can, "So, you wanna talk about it?"

He has always been good about letting her help him with any problems he has. They are usually open with each other, considering she's his older sister and he probably doesn't think she's cool enough for him or whatever.

Alex rests his hands on his forehead, his skinny elbows pointing toward the ceiling. He moans dismally and says, "I don't know ..." His arms flop down, causing Puffin to jump up and glare at him. "I mean, there's really nothing to talk about. ... I guess I'm gonna be Normal forever. I can't change it."

Jessie shifts her gaze from her troubled brother to her cat and watches as Puffin turns in a tight circle and settles down again, shifting slightly to remain in his sunspot, his thoughts going from sudden alarm to peaceful quiet within a few seconds.

She stands up. "Come on, let's go to the park. It looks like a beautiful day. We can get some ice cream. Paul's is opening early today to start the season." She takes Alex's limp hand and pulls him to a seated position, pushing his curly dark hair out of his eyes and tousling it a bit, knowing he hates it when she does that. He shakes his head, allowing his hair to flop down over his forehead. "I'll buy," Jessie says encouragingly.

"Not gonna argue with that." He follows her into the hallway, walking with more enthusiasm, but stops after only a few steps and looks back toward his bedroom.

"You okay?" Jessie turns around.

"Yeah ... yeah, I feel like ..." Alex answers uncertainly, eyebrows knitted together and lips slightly parted. "I feel like I have to do something really important, and now I can't remember what it is. That's weird."

"Homework?"

"Seriously?" He rolls his eyes and follows Jessie down the hallway again.

"Well, you'll remember eventually."

"Give me a minute to grab my fishing stuff."

"Grab a jacket, too." Jessie pulls her phone out of her jeans pocket to see if her best friend, Hannah, wants to meet at the park to go bird-watching, then runs back to her room to get binoculars. She yells to her mother that she and Alex are going to the park and not to expect them home anytime soon.

Jessie steps out the front door, pulling her fleece jacket over her sweater. The March morning is chilly.

Alex runs out of the garage with his fishing pole and tackle box swinging from his hands.

"I said grab a jacket," Jessie patiently reminds him.

"Yes, Mother." Alex rolls his eyes and careens back into the garage without breaking stride. Within a minute, he runs out again with a red windbreaker slung over his arm.

"I meant put it on."

"You said, 'Grab a jacket!' So I grabbed it!" Alex sighs in mock exasperation, sets down his pole and tackle box, and makes a show of pulling the jacket on and zipping it all the way up to his chin. "Happy now?" He sticks out his lower lip at his sister, pouting playfully.

"You better be careful, kiddo. You're starting to sound like Sam."

They amble across the wide expanse of sprouting lawn toward the sidewalk, the new spring grass showing small patches of bright green.

Jessie hears the birds in the trees chattering away about nesting materials. There is a grumpy squirrel who is mad that the robins are building a nest on his favorite tree branch. *Warmth, water, food, companionship.* The words echo through her head daily, the constant background thoughts of every creature around her.

They cross the quiet suburban street, walking in silence toward the ice cream stand near the community park. Jessie will wait for Alex to start talking—if he even wants to. Sometimes he broods for hours, not speaking to anyone, lost in thought. But usually, he either snaps out of his mood or opens up to her for advice about whatever is bothering him. She is used to his fleeting episodes of sullenness, and it doesn't really phase her. Alex is a good kid, a hard-working student, and a loyal friend. Whatever the issue, he eventually finds the right way to handle it, whether he asks his sister for help or not.

Suddenly a sharp whistle pierces the cool air behind them. Alex lifts his chin toward the sky and closes his eyes. "Damn it," he mutters, shaking his head.

"Language," Jessie says, somewhat sternly.

"You say it," her brother gives her an accusatory glance out of the corner of his eye and turns around to look for the source of the whistle, though they both know perfectly well what, and who, it is.

"Yeah, well, when you're sixteen you can use those words, too. Just not in front of Mom, okay?" She doesn't need her mother getting on her case about allowing Alex to swear once in a while.

They look back up the sidewalk and see one of Alex's friends, Sam Starling, careening toward them on a red scooter. He isn't wearing a helmet, of course. After breaking both legs as a kid and living to tell the tale, Sam doesn't ever seem to worry too much about getting hurt again.

"He's not wearing a jacket," Alex grumbles, spying his friend.

"Sam is also not known for making good choices," Jessie replies, pulling her own jacket closer around her. The March morning can't be more than 45 degrees. "Hey, Pigeon! Can't you fly? Why do you need those silly wheels?" Jessie calls to Sam, only sort of smiling at him. The joke is old and worn out, and she no longer finds it funny. It is just a habit now, calling Sam by any bird name other than *starling*. Sam gives her a devious grin and hops off the scooter to walk with them.

"When are you going to get some new material?" he asks, running his hand through his white-blond hair. He is pretty tall for a kid, slightly taller than Jessie, and is kind of good-looking, in Jessie's opinion, though she would never tell him that. His hair glints in the morning sun, and he pushes his scooter along with one tanned hand, the other hand pushing Alex ahead of him to avoid running into the smaller boy's plodding heels.

Jessie finds herself involuntarily staring at Sam's hands. He recently returned from a beach vacation in Cancun, while everyone else was freezing up in Pennsylvania. Perks of being a senator's son; jetting off to exotic, warm destinations even during the school year.

But really, Jessie can't complain. She and Alex don't have it too rough either, being the children of the mayor of Cutter County, but their family always takes a vacation in the summer, which is just as well. It always makes Jessie anxious to miss even one day of school. How will she ever get into college if she misses classes? She will never understand how Sam is able to catch up on homework after missing a week of class. On the other hand, he really isn't the world's best student. Maybe he doesn't catch up.

"Can you please wear your helmet when you ride that thing?" Jessie asks Sam as he falls into step beside her.

"You're not my mom," Sam teases. He can never be serious, but also never has a bad attitude. Sometimes he is just really annoying.

"It *is* the law, you know," she reminds him.

"So arrest me." He gives her a sidelong glance, and his lip twitches up.

Jessie sighs. "You are *such* an idiot." There is no point trying to convince Sam to wear a helmet. He will do what he wants to do, without worrying about consequences. But she mostly worries he will teach Alex his bad habits. "What are you up to today?"

"Eh, whatever trouble I can find. Apparently, I was already too obnoxious for Mom this morning. She told me to get outside and not come back until curfew, and you know me: I *always* listen to my mother." Sam smirks.

Jessie scoffs. "Yeah, sure. When did that start?"

"Umm ..." Sam runs a hand through his hair. "Like, two minutes ago."

"Mm-hmm," Jessie barely responds, then changes topics. "So, how was your vacation?"

"Awesome," Sam replies happily. "The surfing was great! I did some scuba diving, saw some sea turtles ... and wow, there are some hot beach babes down there! I saw this one girl who was wearing—" Sam glances at her quickly and seems to suddenly realize he is not with a group of guys. "Oh, hey, did I mention the turtles?" He trails off in a falsely innocent voice and flashes another devious grin. Jessie shakes her head, trying to convey disapproval, but not really concerned about the girls. She just doesn't want Alex asking what Sam meant. At least not in front of her. He's still a kid!

Turning his gaze forward, Sam says casually to Alex, "Move along, move along," and slows his long stride to avoid walking into Alex, who is too dismal to walk any faster. "Where are you two going?" Sam inches his scooter off the sidewalk and into the lawn along the edge of the concrete to keep from running into his friend.

"Paul's for some consolation ice cream," Jessie whispers, discreetly waving her hand at Alex's back.

"Mmm ... bad day already?" Sam raises his eyebrows, again catching her eye.

Alex turns around at that. "What do you think, moron? Just because you don't give a damn doesn't mean I don't!"

"Language," Jessie repeats, only halfheartedly this time, as Alex turns forward and walks faster. Jessie knows Alex has every right to be upset. Watching his younger friend become Gifted without him is heart wrenching.

"Whoa, whoa, whoa, what did I do?" Sam asks innocently, his blue eyes wide, staring at Alex's back. He glances at Jessie, then reaches out and pushes Alex gently again on the shoulder, this time only playing, the wheel of his scooter nowhere near Alex's feet.

"Stop pushing me!" Alex turns and shoves the scooter's handlebars into Sam's ribs. Sam utters a soft "oof," a puzzled look on his tanned face.

Jessie feels only a little sorry for Sam. She knows he doesn't care much about becoming Gifted, and he most likely can't understand why this situation is bothering Alex. But can't Sam see that Alex is in no mood to be teased? How inconsiderate can he get? Jessie wants to yell at him, *"Why can't you leave him alone? Not everyone can be as carefree as you!*" But she doesn't say anything. It isn't her place to intrude on their spat.

On the other hand, Alex is being a bit unnecessarily rude to Sam. After all, Sam himself remains unGifted, too.

Jessie stays silent, letting the boys' argument unfold. She really only ever had to step in once before, years ago now, to break up an argument when Sam was relentlessly daring Alex to jump off the top of the sliding board at his pool as if it were a high dive. Sam had shut up pretty quickly when Jessie pointed out that he hadn't jumped off it, either.

She suppresses the urge to roll her eyes, remembering that Sam's response at the time had been, "Well, I don't want to be a show-off." Funny how that sentiment never stopped him from doing any other stupid stunt over the years.

"What? What did I do?" Sam asks defensively, massaging his ribs where the handlebar had dug into him.

"You don't even care!" Alex takes a step toward him, hands in the air, completely exasperated and out of patience with his friend. "How can you not care that you aren't Gifted yet? You'll be sixteen next week! Our younger friends are all getting their Gifts. What if we don't?" Alex is on the verge of tears.

"I care … sorta," Sam says unconvincingly. "I just don't take it as hard as you."

"Are you calling me a sissy?"

"Okay, that is definitely not what I said."

"That's what you meant," Alex retorts. "Please, let's just go."

Sam raises both hands in mock surrender. "You're the one who stopped," he says under his breath. Alex doesn't hear him, but Jessie does. She gives Sam a partially apologetic look, still feeling like he should have taken it easier on her brother.

Jessie and Sam have always gotten along well, especially when she began babysitting him and Alex. They had all grown up together, though they didn't officially meet until Jessie was ten years old. Sam had been in fourth grade, the year between Alex and her, and had never really hung out with them until he was held back that year in school.

They share similar backgrounds, all enjoying the perks of living in luxury, Alex and Jessie being the children of the New Harrisburg mayor,

Marshall Cox, and Sam being the son of Sen. Joseph Starling. The families are fairly close, often traveling in the same political circles and attending dinners and charity functions together a few times a year.

While Jessie was babysitting him all those years, Sam never *really* gave her any trouble; he was mostly loud, sarcastic, and usually too wound up to ever go to bed on time, which was extremely annoying when she was banking on a few hours' quiet time to finish homework while waiting for the Starlings to return.

Though Sam is not very good in school, his humor is usually clever and not *too* immature, and Jessie has enjoyed some corny banter with him over the years. They tried to come up with silly nicknames to use on him, different puns and word plays revolving around his last name. Last year, Jessie learned a few of the scientific names of common birds. Sam had been "Leucocephalus" for the entire summer, in reference to the bald eagle. Jessie liked that it means "white headed" in Latin, which is very fitting since Sam has the palest hair in the school.

Jessie realizes she is still staring at Sam's blue eyes and is about to tear her gaze away when he gives her a shrug and tips his chin toward Alex, silently asking, "What's his problem?" Jessie gives him a small shake of her head, hoping he will understand that he needs to drop the subject. He will never understand how Alex feels.

A short time later, they turn onto the pathway to Paul's Patio, the local hangout for kids, both Gifted and Normal alike. There is always a jubilant atmosphere around Paul's, with young children climbing on the life-sized cow in the play area, the teenagers bunched together on the brightly colored tables and chairs, actually talking to each other and not looking at their phones.

Jessie has always loved coming here with her family. She has spent hours here and at the community park across the street every summer with her best friend, Hannah. They used to play on the swings all day and race each other back and forth to the duck pond. Their parents always valued outdoor activities over being glued to a computer screen.

The owner of Paul's Patio also valued outdoor activity over digital entertainment and declared his establishment a "device-free zone" in 2030, when he saw his customers sitting with heads bent over their phones, forgotten ice cream dripping down their arms and forgotten friends becoming more distant. That was ten years ago, and everyone still honors the tradition.

Today is opening day at the Patio, and there is a long line already. Jessie stands behind the boys, her big sister/babysitter instincts kicking in. She always keeps a close eye on them. Alex is a good kid, but Sam has a way of talking him into mischievous activities. The absolute worst infraction (that Jessie knows about) happened last summer when Sam and Alex rode their bikes to the border of the forbidden Radiation Zone. They didn't actually get caught *inside* the Rad Zone (it's almost impossible to get in, considering there is an eight-foot-wide moat around it) but they went right up to the moat, throwing stones into the water below. Alex said it was his idea to explore near the border, but Jessie was skeptical. That stunt had Sam Starling written all over it.

Jessie thinks about her homework assignment again. The original nuclear power plant was shut down in September 2019, but a private corporation bought it a few years later, revamping it to produce nuclear energy on a smaller scale. Then, in 2026, explosions at the plant killed 247 people, including many of the employees and most of the residents within a mile of the plant. Above-normal radiation levels were detected as far out as fourteen miles from the plant, and the government forced a permanent shutdown and evacuation of Harrisburg and surrounding towns. The new state capital, New Harrisburg, was moved farther south, and Cutter County was formed.

Jessie was too young to remember the incident, but she has learned a lot over the years. Everyone at school is required to take classes about the health risks of radiation exposure. It has been drilled into them to stay away from the Radiation Zone at all costs.

No one knows who planted the three bombs that caused the meltdown. A suspect and motive have never been discovered. Sam always jokes the bomber was an employee who just wanted a day off. Jessie reprimands him when he jokes about that, which, thankfully, isn't often. She sometimes has to remind him to show some respect. Seriously, people died.

The nuclear meltdown is what most people believe instigated the Change that occurred throughout much of the surrounding area, most prominently in Cutter County. The Change is what is bestowing the

Gifts on the new generation of children born here. So far, at least in these first few years, the Change does not seem to be a side effect of a toxin or something sinister that grows like a cancer. It actually seems more like evolution, offering unusually beneficial traits to a few random individuals.

Awareness of the Change was slow at first, as evolution tends to be, with random and weird stories appearing in the headlines every few months, when someone would suddenly find that they had an unusual power. In the past year or two, though, Jessie has known many students who were Changed within the same month, almost always near a birthday.

The Change never bestows a superpower; it is usually something that makes day-to-day life a little easier. A kid, usually a teenager, will suddenly know how to speak every language in the world, without ever hearing them or studying them before. Another kid will have the unique ability to always find a great parking spot, no matter how crowded the lots or streets. Some of the abilities, or Gifts, as they have come to be called, can be overall unhelpful. There was one senior boy in Jessie's school who always had a writing utensil when he needed it, but almost everything is done by computer nowadays, so that was kind of a useless Gift. On the other hand, some Gifts are absolutely amazing. (Jessie thinks her Gift of hearing the thoughts of animals is the best one out there, but she's a bit biased).

As Sam parks his scooter at the bike rack, Jessie's thoughts wander back to Alex and his friends. It really would be horrible if Alex doesn't get a Gift. He feels *so* left out. As a whole, only about 25 percent of the new generation has become Gifted so far, but most kids feel like outcasts if they remain Normal, especially if their friends are all Gifted. Jessie remembers the relief she felt when she realized she was Gifted. Her best friend, Hannah, had gotten her Gift nearly eighteen months earlier, when she turned fourteen. Those eighteen months of waiting were interminable, but it all worked out well for both of them.

Jessie gazes at her brother, who has a sullen look on his face. She slides her arm around his skinny shoulders and gives him a gentle squeeze, which he only allows for about two and a half seconds before sidestepping away, his fishing gear jangling.

The boys stand in line for ice cream, their previous argument apparently forgotten. Sam scrolls through his phone, ignoring the time-honored tradition of not using phones at Paul's. He lets out a quick chuckle and says to Alex, "Oh, man, look at this," and sidles up to him, turning the screen around.

"Hey, Raven, what part of 'device-free' don't you understand?" Jessie teases, slightly exasperated. There are literally three signs around Paul's Patio stating "Device-Free Zone—Fun, Food, and Family Allowed."

"Free what now?" Sam teases back in a goofy voice. He does put his phone in his pocket, though, and crosses his arms over his chest, immediately adding, "Well, this is boring," with an exaggerated sigh.

Jessie laughs and playfully pushes Sam's elbow, something she has done for years as a way of getting his attention when he is being particularly obnoxious, which is frequently. Sam feigns losing his balance and sidesteps.

"Wow, I am taking all kinds of abuse today from you two."

"Well, you're kind of a good sport about it," Jessie replies.

"Yes, yes, I am," Sam boasts, puffing out his chest as though he is the most important person in the world. "I'm also extremely modest, which makes me really great."

Jessie rolls her eyes. "You're an idiot."

"Thanks, it's a gift."

"Oh, my God, what if that *is* your Gift?" Alex pipes up and stares at Sam.

Sam's response is a casual shrug and an offhand, "I'd be okay with that," as he absently pulls his phone out of his jeans pocket again. Jessie grabs it from him and puts it in her own pocket.

"My goodness, more abuse," he says, smiling his crooked smile at her. She shakes her head and turns away, facing the front of the line.

"Do you two know what you want?" she asks, preparing to order.

"Hot fudge sundae!" Alex responds happily.

"I don't know. Surprise me," Sam replies. "You know I'll eat anything."

"How about a salad?" Jessie jokes. She has been teasing Sam for years that he needs to lose weight after he had eaten an entire pizza by himself and still asked for dessert, then ate twice as much ice cream as everyone else.

"Man, that's harsh. Hey, how about you 'lettuce' order what we want?" he quips. She rolls her eyes at him, and he sticks his tongue out at her.

"Why did you have to come here with us?" Jessie asks, sighing.

"So the two of you could enjoy the glory of my company. Really, you should be thanking me. You're welcome."

"Oh, my God, please stop talking," she teases but laughs at his silliness. Sam gives her a small smile, settling back into line and making a motion of zipping his mouth and locking it with an imaginary key. "Please lose that key," Jessie says seriously to him.

Sam bursts out laughing, then whines, "This never would have happened if you hadn't taken my phone away. I'm *bored*."

Right before ordering, Sam fidgets and pats the pockets of his jeans. "Darn," he says, "I don't have any money. Alex, can you spare a few bucks?"

"Sure," Alex replies. Jessie has always wondered how many hundreds of dollars Alex has "spared" Sam in the last few years. Sam's parents had allowed him access to his online account a while ago, but after he bought thousands of dollars of computer gaming equipment without permission, they decided he wasn't quite ready.

"I can give you some money, Bluebird, but I don't think I brought enough for all three of us," Jessie inserts. She orders ice cream for them, then fumbles in her pockets for cash. Her parents discourage her from paying for things electronically, if possible.

"Maybe I can get away on my good looks," Sam says confidently, pushing his hair out of his right eye with a practiced flick of his hand.

"Dubious," Jessie replies flatly.

"That will be $18.75," the cashier says. Jessie only has $15 with her, and Alex reaches into his pocket and comes up with $3.75 without even looking.

"What the heck kind of magic trick was that?" Sam asks, narrowing his eyes at Alex suspiciously.

"What do you mean?" Alex replies, confused.

"You just happened to have, like, exact change?"

"Oh, yeah, I guess. I don't know." Alex shrugs, taking his sundae from the window.

"Unlike you," Jessie says to Sam in a falsely stern voice, "my brother has a very good grasp of responsible money-handling and knows exactly what he has with him."

"Listen, buddy," Sam scoffs at her. "I *did* know exactly how much I had. It just happened to be nothing."

Jessie shakes her head and hands him his cone.

"He has a point there, Jessie," Alex chimes in.

"Don't you dare take his side," Jessie mutters, but Alex knows she's kidding.

"Come on," Sam says, pushing his solid shoulder into Jessie as they walk toward the picnic area. "You know you love me." He sprawls on a bench while Jessie and Alex take a table.

"You do not live in reality," Jessie replies flatly.

"Then how do you explain this awesome tan?" He laughs at his own stupid joke. Jessie sighs and looks at Alex, who is focused on his sundae. He raises his eyebrows at his sister as if to apologize for being friends with Sam.

After savoring their sugary treats, they meander to the back of the park to watch the ducks in the pond. The mallards and geese swim over, curious, asking if they have food.

"Sorry, cuties; I'm out of money," Jessie replies, knowing they can't understand her. She feels guilty. She always feeds the ducks at the pond. "Maybe tomorrow."

"Here," Alex says, holding out a quarter for the food pellet dispenser.

"Wow, Mr. Moneybags," Sam laughs. "Hey, are you ready to fish? I guess I can be your cheerleader or whatever."

"Yeah, sure," Alex replies. "Do you want to go home and get your pole?"

"Nah, I actually only have about an hour ... then I gotta split."

"Ha! That would have been great if you had a banana split," Jessie teases.

"Aw, man. Missed opportunity," Sam says, shaking his head, then adds, "And now I want a banana split. But I guess it's back to my kale shakes and celery sticks for the rest of the week." He smirks at Jessie, patting his flat stomach.

Alex ignores their banter and says to his sister, "Jessie, will you tell us where the fish are good?"

"Fine." She sighs, feeling squirmy inside. She used to love fishing. Now it is like being trapped inside a nightmare. "Don't you find it takes the fun out of it when I tell you?"

"Nah," Sam replies. "I mean, how long can you really wait for a fish to randomly show up? It gets boring."

"Whatever. You're bored by everything," she mumbles disagreeably.

"It's not that I'm bored by everything. I just need constant mental and physical stimulation." His smile broadens as he spies something over Jessie's shoulder. He calls in a singsong voice, "Hey there, girlfriend!"

Jessie turns to see her best friend, Hannah Buckley, striding toward them. Jessie gives her a wave. Hannah half-heartedly waves back, her hands invisible as she tucks them inside the sleeves of her jacket, fending off the cold.

"Shut up, loser," Hannah says in greeting to Sam as she walks up to them, no trace of humor in her voice. She has never really liked Sam. He is always such a hotheaded pain in the butt, talks way too much, and never cares about anyone but himself. And she hates him now more than usual because some kids at school mentioned that Sam and Hannah would make a great couple, both being tall, blond, and athletically inclined. Sam had caught wind of that conversation and has been blowing kisses and batting his eyelashes at her in the hallways at school for the past two weeks. Hannah finds it all extremely annoying and juvenile and secretly hopes she won't have to deal with any of this nonsense in college. High school graduation cannot get here fast enough.

Sam flashes his sly smile at Hannah, who folds her arms and looks away from him. It's too early and too cold to even bother with his inane babble. He turns his attention back to Jessie, getting down to serious business. "Okay, where we goin'?"

"I can't believe you find this fun," Jessie replies, lowering her gaze, reminiscing about her childhood, when she would spend entire days fishing, always waiting patiently for the fish to bite, never really knowing where they were. "The fish are mostly over there," she says, gesturing to a spot about thirty feet to the right. "But there are some big ones circling around on the other side, near the hemlock trees." She points across the water.

Jessie isn't able to communicate with all the fish in the pond simultaneously; it is too large for that, but she can usually survey about a quarter of the area, giving the boys a bit of an edge. She has admitted to Hannah that she toys with the idea of lying and making them work for their sport but could never do that to Alex. Sam would deserve it, though.

The boys decide to walk around for the bigger fish, which is good news for Jessie. She will be out of range soon enough.

Jessie turns her attention back to her best friend. "Thanks for coming, Hannah," she says happily. "I see you brought your binoculars!"

"Mm-hmm," Hannah responds, wishing she was back in her warm bed. She likes spending time with Jessie, but not this early on a cold Saturday morning. "You are turning me into a good little bird-watcher."

Bird-watching has overall become much more enjoyable for Jessie since she became Gifted, but her first hobby as a kid had been fishing. She and her father would wake up early on weekends, sometimes driving an hour to the best fishing holes. Jessie loved being outside on those crisp mornings, drinking in the peacefulness of nature. But the last time she held a pole was the day she got her Gift.

The day had started like any other June day, clear and cool but with the promise of soaring temperatures later. Jessie had wandered down to the duck pond, alone and elated to have so much summer vacation ahead to fish and hang out with Hannah. Her fifteenth birthday had been the previous day, and she was eager to try out her new fishing pole.

She cast her line and watched the vapor rise off the calm pond. The ducks were at the far end that morning, crowding around the early visitors, who fed them corn and pellets. There was an almost imperceptible tug on the line, and she slowly reeled in, finessing the line through her fingers. Then she felt a more insistent jerk as the fish tried desperately to escape.

Jessie smiled, but suddenly heard someone yelling nearby as though they were being attacked. Startled, she almost dropped the pole as she peered into the dense stand of trees behind her. Maybe a jogger had fallen on the running path in the woods? Maybe a small child fell off a swing? The sound stopped, and her fishing line simultaneously went slack.

She couldn't find the source of the sound and continued reeling in. She would investigate after this fish was out of the water. The sound started again, a high-pitched wail that chilled her bones. Jessie could see her fish struggling and bucking against the line. Suddenly the fish popped out of the water, and she reached forward to grab it. Then she recoiled and fell onto her backside, dropping the pole into the water with a soft splash. She absolutely could not believe what was happening.

The tiny silver fish at the end of the line was screaming.

***

The girls disappear into the wooded area beyond the pond, the tall trees displaying the first buds of spring. The running trail winds a circuitous route through the trees and provides a great place to watch birds, which are in full spring singing mode. Jessie easily picks out eight different songs and calls. Hannah is still struggling with recognizing bird calls. They all kind of sound the same to her. They watch the wrens, cardinals, and blue jays for a while, Hannah trying to identify as many as she can.

Hannah thinks it would be creepy to hear the thoughts of animals, but overall, Jessie seems to do well with it. It's a good thing Jessie wants to be a veterinarian. Her Gift will be extremely helpful. Hannah possesses the fortunate Gift of having a decreased sensation of pain. She isn't especially fast or strong, but she tires slowly, making her a good athlete on the high school cross-country team. Actually, she's not allowed to compete, due to her unfair advantage, but she still has fun.

She asks Jessie for help identifying a red-bellied woodpecker, and they watch the bird hitch its way up a tree trunk.

Their conversation turns to events at school, homework, and plans for the summer. Their families, including the Starlings, to Hannah's dismay, are all planning to take a beach vacation together in July.

"I'm not super thrilled about going on vacation with Sam," Hannah admits dismally. Jessie knows Hannah doesn't much care for the kid. "I feel like he is going to ruin it."

"He isn't too bad with his parents around. I'm hoping we will all keep pretty busy, so he doesn't have time to get into trouble," Jessie says, trying to console her friend.

"Well, I guess we'll see what happens," Hannah says skeptically. "Nothing we can do about it." She launches into an excited monologue about other summer plans. "Did I tell you I'm applying for a summer internship at the hospital where my father works in Baltimore? I'm so excited!" Her father is a thoracic surgeon, and Hannah desperately wants to follow in his footsteps. Her mother is the governor of Pennsylvania, and Hannah, like Jessie, has absolutely no interest in politics.

"Wow, Hannah, that's great!" Jessie says.

Jessie is hearing of Hannah's summer plans for the first time, and Hannah is sure she is feeling somewhat inadequate. "You should look into volunteering at the animal shelter or vet clinic or something," Hannah prods.

"Yeah, that's a good idea. I'll look into that. ... I can't believe we have to start applying to colleges this summer. I'm dreading it."

"Oh, you'll do fine." Hannah tries to reassure her, but Jessie has a penchant for anxiety that Hannah doesn't quite understand. Sometimes she feels like Jessie worries about everything.

They continue walking down the path, the trees and shadows becoming denser. There is no one else on the trail this morning, which is how the girls prefer it. When it is too busy, the birds hole up in silence.

"Alex said Blaze Givins got his Gift today," Jessie says, changing the subject as she focuses her binoculars on a bright-red cardinal.

"Oh, yeah? Do you know what it is?"

"No," Jessie replies, shaking her head. "I didn't have the heart to ask. Poor Alex is taking it kind of hard. He's hoping any day now he'll get his Gift. He's really feeling left out."

"Yeah, but he's still only going to be fifteen. That isn't too old yet. And why should he feel left out? Sam's almost sixteen and isn't Gifted."

"Well, I think Alex is trying not to compare himself with Sam. With pretty much everything."

"Oh ... yeah, that's a very good idea." Hannah nods vigorously.

"Sam doesn't exactly feel the same way everyone else feels about getting a Gift. And it doesn't help that he makes fun of Alex for worrying about it so much. They were practically fighting about it this morning. I haven't seen them argue in years."

"Well, that doesn't surprise me. I don't know Sam as well as you do, but man, he doesn't know when to lay off sometimes. It's like everything is a huge joke to him." Hannah shakes her head, her long blond hair falling around her face. She tucks her hair into her hood and thinks about what a nuisance Sam has been at school lately. "I swear, if he blows one more kiss at me, I will slap him in the face."

"He would actually probably love that, knowing him." Jessie stops and holds her binoculars to her eyes, scanning the bare treetops. A crisp breeze ruffles her dark hair. She shivers and pulls her hood up.

"It's funny he and Alex are such good friends. They are total opposites." Hannah focuses on a small black-and-white chickadee to her left.

"Maybe that's why they *are* such good friends. Don't opposites attract?"

"I guess. But don't you worry that Sam is going to get Alex into serious trouble some day? I feel like he is gonna steal a car or something just to see if he can get away with it."

Jessie sighs. "Yeah, I worry about that sometimes. I mean, I don't really *think* Sam would do something like that. ... I know he doesn't always use his brain, but he isn't a criminal. I practically grew up with him. He isn't that bad, at least not so much anymore. He hasn't done any stupid stunts or gotten into any fights at school lately. But I do worry Alex might start picking up his bad habits. Mostly, I feel like Sam is just kind of full of himself, I guess."

"Okay, maybe," Hannah replies, unconvinced. "Why was he doing court-ordered community service last September?"

"I don't know ..." Jessie's thought trails off uncertainly. "I guess I was kind of hoping he was lying about that. Doesn't he pretty much lie about everything?"

"No idea, Jessie. He's your friend."

They continue down the trail in silence, stopping to look at a pileated woodpecker. They have only seen the crow-sized bird twice before, and Jessie always gets excited when she spots it. The woodpecker stares at them and then quickly flies away in a flurry of black-and-white wings.

Hannah lowers her binoculars, watching the bird as it is swallowed up in the tree branches. Jessie still has her binoculars up to her eyes.

"Now I see a white-breasted nuthatch on this tree right—Oww!" Jessie drops her binoculars as Hannah simultaneously feels a large insect sting her right shoulder—even through her sweatshirt and jacket. That must be a huge insect!

"What was th—?" Hannah tries to yell, but she can't finish her sentence. She can no longer hear her own voice and can't tell if she is actually speaking.

Hannah whirls around, suddenly aware of two men behind her on the walking path. Or, more accurately, two man-shaped figures. She barely has time to register the black masks covering their faces, their thick winter jackets zipped all the way up, before her vision gets blurry. One figure is tall and broad, the other is shorter and more lanky, perhaps younger.

Hannah has no time to react as the larger man grabs her around the shoulders and covers her mouth with a thick-gloved hand as she tries to scream. Another strange sting jabs her on the right shoulder, and she manages to gasp, "What are you doing? Get away from us!" although she doubts anyone could understand her words with the rough fabric of the work glove smashed against her lips.

Tears spring to her eyes. *Is this really happening? Are we really being attacked in the middle of the park?* Her thoughts slide out of focus as if half her brain is partially stuck in the slow-churning wisps of a dream.

The masked man raises a black bag to her face. Hannah sees Jessie falling next to her, her dark-brown hair billowing around her shoulders. The smaller masked man is throwing a hood over Jessie's head. Hannah feels something slide over her head, a soft blanket caressing her skin, and everything goes black. Her head is heavy, her legs are weak.

"Give her another one! She should have gone down by now!" The larger man says gruffly. There is a third sting on her arm. *How many drugs are they going to give me? They are going to kill me!*

Hannah loses her balance and falls to the ground, palms skidding and chafing over the packed dirt, knees slamming onto cold gravel. Her head swims, but she maintains partial consciousness. She tries screaming for help but can't move her jaw. She moans and tries thrashing against the strong hands restraining her, but her efforts are futile. Her legs don't move at all, though she is *very* willing to kick them toward the man to try to disable him. But she can't. She is completely paralyzed.

The man drags her by her arms, and more lucid thoughts work their way into her brain as she judders across the ground. *What do these men want? Who are they? Where are they taking us? Is Jessie still here? Are we being taken somewhere together? Are the boys okay?*

She is dropped on the ground, her hands falling limply to her sides; she is staring at nothing but blackness. The soft cloth over her head fills her mouth each time she gasps for air. She tries kicking her legs again, but as far as she can tell, nothing happens.

Hannah vaguely wonders what drug has been pumped into her arm. Three times. Whatever it is, it works crazy fast, at least the paralysis part. It looked like Jessie was completely unconscious before she even hit the ground. *I bet my Gift is making me more resistant to the drugs.*

The men pat down her khakis. Her phone is lifted from her pocket, and her watch is unbuckled from her wrist. *Is this all for a robbery?* Strong hands pull her upright and her head lolls forward. She is certain she *should* have passed out by now. Her Gift is keeping her awake, but barely. *Should I play dead? I can't fight back, I can't scream ... I can't ... can't ...* Her thoughts jumble as she loses focus.

Muffled huffing breaths and a loud clunking noise nearby jolt her out of her semiconscious state. She is pulled up by her armpits and feet, then is suspended in the air for a few seconds as the attackers' hands let her go. She lands hard, thudding onto something that feels and sounds like smooth metal.

She lies motionless, thinking it might be best to pretend to be asleep. Two car doors slam, and an old truck engine roars to life, too loud to be electric, seemingly right in her ears. The humming of the motor is white noise lulling her off to sleep; she is helpless to resist the strong pull of the drugs any longer. *This is all a nightmare. I'll wake up in bed ...*

Hannah doesn't know it at the time, but she passes out next to her friends in the back of a pickup truck stealthily making its way north from Cutter County, the two masked attackers in the front seat on a mission to change the course of their unfortunate lives.

CHAPTER 2

Hannah

After an unknown length of time, maybe minutes, maybe hours, Hannah's head begins to clear, and she wonders at first why her normally comfortable bed feels so ... bouncy. *What the ...?* She groggily raises her hands to her face to rub her eyes and is momentarily shocked to feel the material of the bag there. She quickly pulls it off and gasps, not even aware she had been oxygen-deprived.

The cold air feels good in her lungs and quickly rejuvenates her sluggish brain. Hannah remembers what happened.

She is not in bed. A woodpecker had sailed off into the forest, and then there was something on her arm. She remembers the stinging sensation of the sedative ... being dragged over the ground ... the rapid paralysis.

Her heart nearly thuds out of her chest as she remains immobilized, not sure if from paralysis or fear. She doesn't seem to be hurt, only a little cold. There is a loud roaring in her ears, and she eventually identifies it as high-speed traffic.

After another few minutes (or a few hours), Hannah manages to raise her head and take in her surroundings, the black bag clenched in her hand, forgotten. She is in a truck bed that has been fitted with a brown canvas tarp tied to the top of the cab, the tarp hanging over the back window, making it impossible to see who her captors are. But the men are also unable to see she is awake. *Oh, crap, are there cameras in here? Ah, screw it ...*

Hannah groggily rolls onto her side, her legs heavy and lifeless, and sees Alex, Sam, and Jessie all in various sprawled positions, all with matching black bags over their heads. "Guys!" she tries to whisper loudly, but not too loudly. Her voice is hoarse, making it impossible to speak any louder even if she wants to, which she really doesn't want to do.

Oh, my God, what is going on? She decides not to speak again, fearing their captors will hear her. They probably aren't expecting any of them to be awake yet. Her Gift has mitigated the effects of the sedative somewhat, but who knows how long she was supposed to stay asleep? Everyone else is still out cold.

She stares at her friends, her brain fuzzy again as she slips in and out of semiconsciousness. Her arms and legs are numb, and she concentrates on moving her fingers and toes, her mind clearing as she focuses on their problem. How can she get them out of here? *Can I somehow use my Gift? My sedatives didn't last very long, but what do I do now?*

Hannah isn't sure what to do. She is stuck in the back of a truck with three comatose friends, held captive by at least two men, speeding off to who knows where.

Her thoughts wander back to last year when she had surgery to remove her wisdom teeth. The anesthetist was only able to achieve a light sedation for a few seconds; Hannah was still able to move and respond to the questions they asked her. Finally, after giving her three times the normal amount of sedative, the surgeon decided to try using only local anesthetic (also in large doses) to remove her teeth. She had felt minimal pain and recovered with no complications. Drugs don't last long in her Gifted system. *But that still doesn't really help me get out of here ...*

Inching her way slowly toward Jessie, who is closest to her at the back of the truck bed, Hannah whispers in her ear, "Jessie, can you hear me?" and pulls the cloth bag off her friend's head. Jessie's long hair cascades around her face, and Hannah clearly remembers Jessie falling in the woods; her hair was the last thing Hannah saw before the black bag blinded her.

Jessie doesn't respond but is alive and seems unhurt, her chest gently rising and falling with steady breaths. Hannah edges around to the boys, who are in similar states. Alex is crumpled on his side and Hannah gently eases him onto his back, straightening his bent wrist. He makes no sound and does not even stir.

Feeling somewhat relieved that no one appears hurt (or dead), her thoughts turn back to escape. *God, I need to think!* She wriggles around to Jessie at the back of the truck bed, where the heavy canvas tarp is tied down. Luckily, there is no tailgate, only the tarp tied to the bottom corners of the bed. *If I can just untie it …*

She glances toward the cab to make sure there is no way her captors can spy on her. Unless there are cameras. *Nah, the driver would have stopped by now.* The back window is completely covered by the tarp. She can move in secrecy.

She stretches her hands toward the rope and unties the knot in the heavy twine, her hands shaking. The corner of the canvas eases up, creating a tiny peephole to the outside world, through which she sees a yellow-lined, two-lane, country road.

Nothing looks familiar. There are no houses, no road signs; only forest and an occasional field breaking up the swatches of bare trees. The landscape appears bleaker and more desolate than Cutter County. *Are we still in Pennsylvania?* She has no idea in which direction they traveled from home, but she guesses north, judging by the gray slush on the side of the road and the even grayer wispy tree branches. Could be in New York by now. No clue.

There's really no point in checking her friends' pockets for their phones; Hannah is sure they suffered a similar blow. This predicament gives a whole new meaning to the term "device-free." Her parents always reprimanded her when she scrolled through her phone at dinnertime. "Not having your phone for ten minutes won't kill you," they had scolded. Well …

Hannah tucks the canvas down and tries to think, her brain buzzing with fear and adrenaline. The sedatives have definitely worn off entirely, and the full force of this situation is hitting her.

She wishes her friends, especially Jessie, would wake up. Maybe they could hatch a plan together. She rubs her eyes vigorously, wiping away the tears that have trickled down her cheeks.

The truck's engine suddenly shifts from its high-pitched, melodic hum to a lower, grating sound. They make a left turn, bouncing through a dip when turning onto the new road. The bed shakes and rattles.

Hannah peeks out the flap again. They are still in the woods, though the trees are much bigger and denser. It looks like they are on a dirt and gravel track now. She glances down the road to see if anyone is following them—maybe she can wave her hand for help while staying mostly hidden under the tarp. Unfortunately, the landscape is devoid of life.

She huddles next to Jessie and waits for inspiration to strike. She's not sure what will happen when the men find her awake. Will they be angry? Should she put the cloth bags over everyone's heads, including her own, and pretend to be asleep? Tie the corner of the tarp back down and pretend she didn't do anything? She stays frozen for an indeterminate time, her body shuddering with every bounce of the truck as fear paralyzes her.

It is a long time, with a lot of jostling around, before she finally gets up the nerve to make a move. *Okay, I need to do something. Can I just jump out and run? Run where?*

Gathering her courage, she edges toward the back of the bed again and peeks out the flap. She looks toward the cab. If anyone glances out the passenger mirror, they might see her peeking around, but it's a risk she must take. It's time to do something. *Anything.*

She sits up and holds onto the side of the truck near the taillights. The forest is dense here, with a lot of large trees and some gigantic rocks near the road. *Should I just start running?* No, she decides, dismissing the idea quickly. There is no way she is leaving her friends. She has no idea where this road leads and may never find the truck or her friends again. And when the men realize she is missing, what fate will befall the others? That's definitely a risk she is *not* willing to take.

She peers around the side of the truck, terrified of being seen, and spies a squat brown structure coming up on the right side of the road. It looks like a large garden shed set a few feet back from the gravel track.

Without really formulating a plan, Hannah reaches back and grabs Alex by his arms, dragging the small boy backward quickly, the aluminum bottom of the bed offering almost no resistance as his windbreaker and jeans slide easily. She positions Alex's immobile form as close to the end of the bed as possible and edges herself backward over the bumper. Her feet drop to the ground.

Hannah ducks low against the truck frame and pulls Alex down with her, cradling him as they both fall onto the unforgiving gravel. She braces for the impact, but her Gift allows her to be more resistant to the jarring pain. Standing quickly, she silently congratulates herself; she is only a few feet from the brown structure. It is a restroom facility, like the kind at the community park, except this one appears abandoned.

Hannah heaves Alex to the side of the restroom, out of view of the driver if he happens to look in the passenger-side mirror. She momentarily stops breathing, heart racing, waiting for the driver to realize two of his unwilling passengers have escaped. But the truck doesn't stop; it continues slowly plodding deeper into the forest. *Thank God.*

She props Alex against the wall, his head lolling, and runs a hand through his wavy hair like Jessie does. How he hates it when Jessie plays with his hair. He always shakes his head and moves away from her, shooting her an offended glare.

Tears creep into Hannah's eyes. Alex has been like a kid brother to her, too, and she often feels that Jessie and Alex are her siblings. She and Jessie have always tried to protect Alex, to keep him safe from this big, scary world. *Did I do the right thing by pulling you out of the truck? Will I be failing you by leaving you here all alone in this unknown forest?*

Alex remains completely knocked out, head slumped on his chest, legs splayed, narrow shoulders propped awkwardly against the painted cinder blocks of the wall. Hannah surveys his fragile form, praying she's not leaving him here to die.

She ducks low and runs directly behind the truck to catch up with it. It only takes about ten seconds of hard running to catch up. Leaping back into the truck, trying to land silently, she squirms under the canvas and quickly notes that Sam and Jessie still appear to be dead, in the same positions in which she had left them.

She waits a full minute. Maybe longer. Her heart and head are pounding, eyes and teeth throbbing with every thud. She vaguely wonders if this is a side effect of the drugs.

The truck continues picking its way across the unkempt gravel track. Their captors so far haven't noticed that their cargo is a bit lighter, but Hannah knows it is only a matter of time before they reach their destination, wherever that is, and discover that she set Alex free.

Hannah pulls Jessie to the back of the truck. She edges over the bumper and runs along with the truck for a few seconds, then grabs Jessie under her arms, holding on tightly as the truck pulls away. Jessie's heels will hit the ground hard, but there is nothing Hannah can do about that.

Alex was small enough that she had been able to curl around him as they fell, keeping him more or less in her arms, but Jessie is almost as tall as Hannah is, though not as muscular. Hannah isn't sure if she will be able to move Sam at all. He's a thin kid, but tall for his age and well-muscled. She always had a feeling that Sam doesn't wear jackets even in cold weather just so he can show off his biceps.

With a skidding and tumbling bounce, she and Jessie come to a stop in the gravel. Hannah pulls Jessie quickly to the edge of the road, leaving her behind a large boulder. "Be safe," she whispers, tears blurring her vision as she runs back to the truck. She feels better about leaving Jessie; she is a sharp girl and will probably figure some way to get herself out of this mess. This is what Hannah tells herself to keep from completely breaking down into hysterical sobs as she leaves her best friend to an unknown fate.

Luckily, Hannah feels her usual sure-footed athleticism return, all traces of sedatives gone, as she jumps into the truck and wriggles under the tarp again. She grabs Sam under his thick arms, heaving him toward the back. She wastes no time now, waiting to see if the men in the cab catch onto her plan. They need to get out of here.

Sam is definitely not moving as easily as the smaller kids did, and Hannah realizes the bare skin of his arms is creating too much friction, whereas the smooth fabric of Alex and Jessie's jackets allowed them to slide. *You had to be a tough guy, didn't you, you dumb kid,* she scolds Sam silently. *God, you are such an annoying brat. Maybe I'll just leave you here. Ha, can you smooth talk your way out of this?*

She smiles a little at the thought of leaving Sam here to fend for himself and then redoubles her efforts to get a better grip under his arms.

Thankfully, Sam stirs, and Hannah speaks directly into his ear. "Sam, can you hear me?" She slaps his face gently, and he moans quietly. *If he says, "Five more minutes," I will slap him harder.* "Sam! Please wake up!" *Oh, God, please just wake up so I'm not alone.*

He doesn't make another sound, and Hannah pulls him toward the back. It takes a while, his bulk proving much more difficult to move, but she eventually slides him inch by agonizing inch to the bumper. They tumble onto the ground, both landing hard. Hannah's teeth clatter as she skids to a halt in the gravel, head and heart pounding in unison. She has the urge to vomit and kneels in the dirt, but the sensation passes quickly. She turns her attention back to Sam.

The fall has roused him slightly, and she pats his face and shakes his head from side to side by grabbing his chin. His white-blond hair falls over his right eye as she jostles his head. She has no desire to push his hair up like she had done for Alex. Part of her still wants to leave him here and go back to Jessie and Alex on her own. *Nah, I can't do that, not even to Sam. ... It would be kind of funny, though.*

She crouches low over him, keeping one eye on the slow-moving pickup truck. *Please don't stop, please don't stop, please don't stop!*

She moves to Sam's broad shoulders and lifts him a few inches off the ground, struggling against his solid weight. Before she can drag him to the cover of the rocks and brambles by the side of the road, he opens his eyes a crack and gazes placidly at the sky. A zing of hope shudders down Hannah's spine. Maybe he will be aware enough to move to the side of the road himself, and they can get out of here fast. She really doesn't care for his cockiness, but any company is better than facing this nightmare alone. Also, Hannah doubts Sam will have too many stupid comments in *this* situation.

"Sam, please wake up. We have to get out of here!" She shakes his shoulders vigorously. He doesn't seem to care too much and closes his eyes, arms and legs sprawled in the gravel, hair falling back over his head.

Sam groans, unable to form words.

"Sam, open your eyes! Can you sit up? We have to get out of here! I don't know if I can move you ... please, please, Sam, please wake up!" She glances desperately toward the receding truck. There is a turn in the road ahead. After rounding that bend, the truck will be out of sight. She silently prays the driver won't be stopping anytime soon to check on his cargo.

"God, Sam, please ..." Hannah sobs, hovering over him, trying to shake him awake. She pushes his shoulders into the loose gravel, not caring if she hurts him. He's tough, he'll get over it. "Come on! Sam, please!" Hannah's voice cracks, and her words catch in her throat.

"Hannah?" Sam's eyelids flutter, and he looks bleary-eyed and confused, his voice wavering.

"Oh, thank God!" Hannah breathes a sigh of relief and wipes her tears. She stands up to give him some room to move. He sits up slowly, rubbing his eyes like he is waking up to a long weekend and is in no particular hurry to go to no particular place. He even turns from side to side to crack his back. "Are you freaking kidding me?" Hannah mutters under her breath as she gazes down at him.

He squints his blue eyes against the sun. "Why do I feel like absolute garbage?" he mumbles, barely audible. "Oh, man, am I hungover? Again?"

Good God. Seriously? Hannah rolls her eyes out of habit and realizes she isn't the least bit surprised that Sam has been hungover at some point. *What a moron. I can't believe I'm stranded out in the woods with this idiot.*

Finally, she screams at him, "Stand up and run!" and grabs his bare arms, pulling him roughly to his feet.

Sam groans and stumbles forward, falling into the thick underbrush at the side of the road, cursing as he hits the ground heavily on his palms. "Oww, Hannah! What is your problem?" His voice breaks as it gradually dawns on him that something is terribly wrong.

"Go! Just keep going! Get away from the road! We've been kidnapped! Jessie and Alex are ... okay." She knows they aren't exactly okay, but she can't worry about that now. She pushes Sam forward, both stumbling over rocks and tree roots.

Sam falls again but manages to get up without help. He looks back over his shoulder, his bloodshot eyes registering a look Hannah has never seen there before: sheer terror.

"Keep going!" she shrieks at him, putting a hand on his shoulder to guide him further into the woods.

"Hannah? What is going on?" Sam's voice wavers as he passes a trembling hand across his eyes. He has a pounding headache.

"I don't know exactly ... keep going! We've been kidnapped. The four of us were in a truck, and I got us out." Hannah is panting, pushing Sam ahead of her. Her fear is overpowering her Gift. Her legs are getting weak. "I left Jessie and Alex further down the road." She wraps her right arm around his shoulders, guiding him as best she can through the underbrush. He is still really unsteady.

Sam's foot catches on a downed branch, and he falls forward onto his stomach, arms and legs splaying in the dirt and dry leaves. Hannah winces as she watches him go down. He's probably going to be hurting after this.

"I can't ... I can't see well," he mumbles as he tries unsuccessfully to unhook his foot from the ensnaring branch. His muscular arms work at the dirt, trying to find a handhold and pull himself up.

"I know. We were given some kind of sedative. It took my eyes a minute to clear, but you'll be okay soon." Hannah frees his foot from the branch, and he rests on his hands and knees, swaying slightly, head hanging limply. He lets out a soft moan.

"I guess there's no chance we still have our phones, huh?" he says grimly.

"Nope," comes Hannah's equally grim reply. She is about to reach for his arms again to pull him upright when she hears what she has been dreading: the whine of the pickup truck's engine, getting louder and louder, coming closer. The driver has discovered his prey has disappeared. He is hunting them.

Hannah screams at Sam to keep running, to get as far from the road as possible as he gingerly stands up and lurches a few steps on wobbly legs. She turns back to the road to intercept the truck. She can't let their captors find Jessie and Alex. She hopes her friends are both awake by now and can start running out of here. It occurs to her that they won't know which way is out (Hannah is not sure she knows at this point either), but she hopes they will at least be able to hide somewhere.

Then it occurs to her that they might go running toward the truck, thinking the driver is someone who can save them. Feelings of doubt and regret crash over her in waves. Their captors will collect them all again, one by one. *Oh, God, what have I done? This is the stupidest thing I could have done!*

She can't let that happen. She will stop the truck, allowing herself to get kidnapped, this time alone. Maybe she can hold them off, if only for a short time, while her friends regain consciousness.

She looks back for Sam and sees he has fallen again and isn't moving, but he is about thirty feet into the dense underbrush. She almost turns back for him, but she realizes he is actually well hidden from the road. She can see a thin ridge of his blue jeans peeking over a fallen log. He *shouldn't* be visible from the road, but Hannah can't be sure.

She bursts out from the tree line, her feet slamming the hard gravel as the truck careens around the bend toward her. She prays the driver didn't see where she exited the woods. That would make Sam an easy target. Her legs pump faster and faster. *This is just another Saturday afternoon training session for cross-country. No big deal, right? I can totally do this.* The pep talk is not as helpful as she had hoped. Her heart thuds as the truck's whine gets louder. Gravel kicks up behind the tires. The driver sees her.

Should I run back into the woods? Maybe I can outrun them through the trees and get back to Jessie and Alex while they are looking for me ... A million thoughts race through her mind as she runs the fastest quarter mile of her life. She stays on the road, too scared to run for the cover of the trees. Her mind is blank.

In a few seconds, the truck is on her, screaming in her ears. She finally turns into the woods, but the rocks and downed branches are too dense; she falls almost immediately. "Damn it!" she says under her breath.

The truck stops, and heavy footsteps sound on the gravel, then on crunching leaves. A man is close behind Hannah. She leaps up, but strong hands grab her shoulders, and a needle sinks into the flesh of her arm for the fourth time today.

Hannah again wavers for an unknown length of time on the edge of consciousness. Eventually, she finds herself sitting in the cab of a pickup truck, not sure if it is the same truck as before, her head leaning against the headrest. The truck is not moving. There is something rough and tight around her hands; it isn't painful, but the pressure makes her wince when she tries to pull her hands apart. She can't. Her wrists are bound by thick, coarse rope.

Fear jolts her spine. They hadn't been tied up before. Any tiny hope of another escape is rapidly fading.

Her long, blond hair falls into her eyes as she strains against the ropes. She tosses her head back to clear her vision and sees someone out of the corner of her eye, standing right outside the cab of the truck. Startled, she jerks away, but the seat belt prevents almost all movement. The tight strap digs into her hip as she squirms toward the center of the bench seat, trying to get as far from her captor as possible.

"There's my girl," the man says softly when she catches sight of him. She shivers. His voice is low and gravelly. She can't tell how old he is. He is still wearing a ski mask and heavy coat. He is holding a thick but short tree branch and is slowly pulling strips of bark off it. *Is he going to hit me? They didn't hurt us before. ... Of course that was before I totally screwed up the plan, whatever it was ...*

"What do you want?" Hannah's voice wavers as she tries unsuccessfully to wriggle further away from him.

"Look at me," the man says in a low voice. Hannah peers out of the truck cab through half-open eyelids. She is terrified and nauseous. The truck's engine is still running, and the exhaust billows over her through the open passenger door. Her headache is worse than ever; she isn't sure if it is from fear, the exhaust fumes, or all the sedatives coursing through her body.

The man says, "We're going to have some fun, you and me, sweetheart. I need you to do exactly what I say, okay? Then you and your little friends won't get hurt."

Hannah struggles against her makeshift handcuffs at the mention of her friends, but the rope doesn't budge. Where are they? Did they get away? Did her plan work? Or are they all tied up too, being threatened with clubs? She swallows the saliva welling in her mouth, willing herself not to vomit.

The man waves his tree branch at her. "You are going to do exactly as you are told. If you don't, you get this club right in that pretty face of yours. Understood?"

Hannah nods, tears flowing unhindered down her cheeks. She is not really afraid of being beaten (too much) since she knows it won't hurt quite as much as if she were Normal, but still, there are far worse things this man can do to her than smash her face in. She hopes Jessie is okay.

It occurs to her that there were two men previously, and now there is only one. Where is the other man? Is he out torturing her friends?

"We're going to have another chat with your mother."

Hannah's tears flow faster at the mention of her mother. She can't even imagine what their parents must be going through right now.

"You see, your parents have been lying to me. All of them. I'm asking all your parents for $20 million. Should be pocket change for rich, entitled politicians like them, right? But apparently, you kids don't mean *anything* to them. They tell me there is no money. I need you to get on the phone and convince your mother otherwise. Easy enough, right? We'll have this whole thing sorted out in less than two minutes." He lets out a low, wheezing laugh that lacks all traces of humanity, and Hannah knows this man will have no problem killing her.

And killing her is a distinct possibility because he will not be getting his ransom money. Their parents are telling the truth. There *is* no money. They have no more money than what they need for their day-to-day essentials, like groceries, utilities, and some entertainment. It is a facade that politicians are rich. They are "given" their life of luxury as a reward for "good behavior." And of course, bad behavior must be punished. If there is scandal or even the slightest hint of corruption, the news story breaks that a political leader has "lost everything," and he or she is banished to poverty.

It has been like this for the last seven years or so; Hannah is old enough to remember when the Switch, as it is called in political circles, occurred. Her parents, she believes, are overall morally upright people, and the Switch didn't really change their daily lives. Until now ...

The Switch is society's way of keeping the country's leaders honest. Politicians understand that they need to earn what they get, knowing it can all be gone after one mistake, one moment of debauchery or giving in to immoral tendencies. But that is all kept secret from the public.

Hannah trembles as the full realization of the situation hits her. There is no ransom money. There is nothing anyone can do to help her and her friends now. They are completely on their own.

"Now listen carefully, sweetheart," the man says in a raspy voice close to her ear. "I'm getting your mom on the phone. You need to convince her that your life is worth $20 million."

A jolt of hope surges through Hannah's stomach. Maybe she can give her mother a clue as to where she is, before this man hits her with his club. *But I don't know where I am. ... How can I give Mom a hint?*

The man pulls out a generic-looking phone. Hannah guesses the number is untraceable. She has watched enough crime dramas to know some of the tricks. He is also wearing gloves, a thick coat, and a ski mask. No chance of him leaving fingerprints, and she sees really no possible way of getting a piece of his hair or skin for DNA analysis.

She desperately looks around, trying to find something that can help her determine where she is. But there is literally nothing. Lots of trees and rocks ... and more trees. The road is nondescript, a winding, gravel, one-lane path through the woods. She can't even remember seeing any signs when they were out on the paved road. She is completely lost.

The man pushes the phone roughly to her ear. "Listen, sweetheart. You cooperate and you'll be out of here." His voice sounds like he swallows razor blades with his morning coffee or something. *Maybe he is using some kind of voice-altering device to hide his identity.* She shudders, tears springing to her eyes.

The phone rings. Suddenly Hannah hears her mother's concerned but dignified voice. "This is Governor Buckley."

Hannah starts sobbing. She can barely breathe. To her surprise, the crazy, creepy man patiently waits for her to calm down, holding the phone up for her to speak. His patience and unmoving hand are even more eerie than watching him fashion a club.

Finally, Hannah manages a croaking and stuttering, "Hello? M-mom?" She hastily wipes her eyes and nose with her bound hands.

"Hannah?" Governor Buckley's voice is frantic but clear. She was definitely not expecting her daughter's voice on the line. Hannah pictures her mother in her stately office with her Secret Service people around her, trying desperately to trace the phone call.

"I'm here, Mom." Hannah's voice breaks as she sobs even harder, which she didn't think was possible.

"Oh, my God, are you hurt? Where are you? Do you know who kidnapped you?"

"I don't ... I'm not hurt ... I don't know where I am ... I don't know ..." She squeezes her eyes shut, her mind racing, trying to think of some clue without tipping off Crazy Creepy Guy.

The man pulls the phone from Hannah's ear before she can say anything else. "Happy now, Governor? She's alive. Now get me $20 million, or she dies."

"I told you: we don't have it!" Governor Buckley says sternly, but Hannah catches a slight waver. "You don't understand! It's not what you think! None of us has that kind of money! Not even pooled. If we can discuss this like rational human beings, I'm sure we can come to an understanding." Her voice becomes stronger, like she is making a speech outside the new Capitol, something Hannah has heard her do a hundred times over the years.

"Yeah, yeah, you keep telling me that," the man says fiercely. "I'm sick of your lies!" He stalks away from the truck.

Hannah cranes her neck out of the cab to listen. The man isn't looking at her anymore. He is staring off into the woods, his back rigid. She glances behind the truck to make sure no one else is out there. She's not sure how many people are in on this kidnapping. At least two. *Should I unbuckle the seat belt and make a run for it? Mom can't help me now. ... I'm pretty sure our conversation is over.*

She is about to reach for the belt buckle when the man turns around and stalks back. Her last glimmer of hope quickly fades, and she lets out a breath she hadn't realized she was holding.

Hannah hears the tremor in her mother's voice. She knows there is no way the families can scrape together $20 million.

"I told you; we can raise $7.8 million, combined, from the three families. If you give us more time, we can get the rest … we can absolutely get the rest. … But we need more time! You have to understand. Please, let the kids go! They have nothing to do with this!"

"They have everything to do with this! They don't deserve the lives they have! Everything has been handed to these kids their whole lives!" The man is wild now, his voice rising as he waves his arms as though he is conducting an orchestra that is just as crazy as he is.

"Hannah! Can you still hear me?" Her mother's voice echoes from the phone. "We are so sorry! Your father and I … no one ever imagined something like this happening! We are so sorry! We love you!"

"I know, Mom, I know about the money. I understand." Hannah sobs. "I love—" Her voice is cut off as she is pulled roughly by her right arm out of the truck cab. The man doesn't try to break her fall, doesn't try to make her stand up. He simply pulls her right off the seat and lets her hit the ground as though she is as light and disposable as a paper bag. She can't get her bound hands underneath her to break her fall.

The wind is knocked out of her as her shoulder hits the ground, hard. Then her feet go over backward as the man grabs her legs, still partially inside the cab, and flings her away from the truck. Her feet land with a crunch in the gravel, both ankles twisting painfully.

"To hell with all you politicians!" The man shrieks as Hannah gasps for breath, every part of her body screaming in pain. He must have *really* thrown her on the ground with some major force to cause this much pain. "You better hope I never find your friends. All of you will be beaten into bear food."

The last thing Hannah sees is the thick club coming down toward her head.

CHAPTER 3

Jessie

Ahh, the warm sunshine feels so good. Jessie stretches out in the grass near the duck pond, her hands behind her head, enjoying the bright sunlight on her face. She had fallen asleep next to Hannah after they had finished their bird walk. The boys are somewhere nearby; Jessie hears them chattering about gathering food, the warm sun and ... nesting material. *Wait ... what are they talking about?*

Jessie slowly opens her eyes, shielding them against the sunlight. She is suddenly aware that she is definitely *not* sitting on the soft, grassy bank of the pond, but on hard ground strewn with small pebbles, leaves, and sticks. She is propped up against a very large boulder covered by dry remnants of last year's moss and lichen. Jessie looks up at this unfamiliar rock, not entirely sure if she's dreaming. The wide smooth face of the stone is dappled in sunlight, a few tree branches caress its top. It's pretty nice … and peaceful … *but seriously, where am I?*

She inspects her surroundings from where she sits, too dazed to even think about moving. There are no boulders this large in the community park … or trees this huge.

Finally, she sits up gingerly, a weird twinge in her back jolting her brain back to reality. Or whatever this is.

The chattering voices are not those of Alex and Sam, but instead belong to two mourning doves flitting in the trees above. The mourning doves calm her growing unease as she loses herself in their thoughts.

"Hannah?" Jessie's voice wavers as she gathers strength to move. She unsteadily raises her hands and pulls desiccated leaves and sticks from her long hair. *Wow, my head hurts. Why does my head hurt? Did I fall?*

She holds her head, trying to ease the throbbing, then bends her legs and steadies herself by leaning against the boulder. It is warm and comforting in the sunshine. "Alex, are you here?" she calls softly, not sure yet if other people are nearby, and if so, whether they are enemies or friends.

After another minute, she walks slowly around the boulder, which is close to a gravel road. She looks left and right and sees nothing but trees on either side of the road in both directions.

A light breeze tickles her face; the fresh scent of early spring is in the air. There is a dampness in these woods, but also the scent of new life, new growth. Normally Jessie would relish this. But right now, not so much.

With a jolt of uncontrollable fear, she begins running as fast as she can, having some difficulty getting her legs to work. She's not really sure why she is so unsteady, or why she has this horrible headache. All she knows is she has to *move*, get away from here, and find her friends.

She had randomly turned right onto the road, not sure why she had chosen that direction. Suppressing the urge to scream, she slows her pace, mainly because her entire body hurts and her lungs are heaving, but also because she has no idea where she is going. She takes a few deep breaths, but it feels like her throat is closing. She is on the edge of a panic attack.

Her feet slow to a stop and she presses her palms into her eyes. Rational thought weaves its way into her panicked brain. The last thing she remembers is walking through the community park with Hannah, talking about summer vacation. ... *Did that happen? Or was that a dream? Is this a dream? Where are Hannah and the boys?*

She is pretty sure she remembers Hannah yelling at someone, and then a blanket was thrown over her head or something. *Is someone playing a trick on me? We don't usually go to this level to prank one another. ... Maybe we've been kidnapped!*

She blindly runs up the road again, fear jolting her into action, but soon begins gasping, her head pounding with every step. Suddenly, she hears a loud roar in the distance. She skids to a halt in the loose gravel and listens. A vehicle is coming down the road! Hurray! Help is on the way! She runs to meet her savior, much steadier this time. Then she has the sinking realization that maybe it is the captors who are coming back for her. Maybe they left her by the rock, a landmark of sorts, on purpose, so she would be easy to find again. Maybe she isn't supposed to be awake yet.

She freezes in the middle of the road. She knows this feeling all too well from the hundreds of squirrels and rabbits she has heard as they become immobile, her parents' car barreling down the road toward them. Those helpless creatures didn't always run, didn't always escape. Jessie cried in her room for two days the first time she felt and heard in her own brain the unwelcome terror of an animal seconds before it became roadkill.

This feeling now is all too familiar. The gut-wrenching indecision; the mind racing in a hundred directions, but the body glued to the ground, unsure how to react when faced with unknown danger.

At the last second, not knowing how she even came to a conclusion, she decides to stay out of sight. Terrified, she dives off the road and into the trees, crawling on hands and knees to keep low. Her hands scrape over dried leaves and twigs, her knees dig painfully into the rocky ground.

She glances over her shoulder and sees the silver glint of a pickup truck's grill bouncing down the road. She hides her head in her hands and prays she's well hidden.

After a minute, the truck passes, speeding away. Jessie breathes a sigh of relief. The relief is short-lived though, as she fears she may have passed up her one opportunity of rescue. *What if they were here to help me? Well, that was dumb ... but why were they driving so fast? That was weird, right? Didn't seem like a rescue party.*

She looks up at the gently swaying pine branches. *There is nothing out here ... only me. ... Oh, my God, am I going to die out here?*

She decides to stay off the road and walks farther into the woods, finding something that resembles a trail, maybe a little-used deer path. She runs along the leaf-strewn trail for a minute before fully realizing she still has no idea where she's going. She had chosen to go a certain way, this time, turning left, to stay somewhat parallel with the road, but she really has no idea which way is correct. Is there even a correct way?

The forest is eerily silent, with only a faint whisper of wind rustling the brown leaves on the ground, those that hadn't disintegrated under the chill of winter. The sun is watery but still providing some warmth. She knows it will be close to freezing in a few more hours, and she needs to figure out some way to make a fire or find some other source of warmth before nightfall. Or would making a fire give her position away to her captors? She glances behind her, making sure no one is following.

Panic bubbles in her throat. *Okay. Think. How do people die in the woods? Exposure to the elements? Or dehydration? Oh, my God, are there still mountain lions in this part of the country? Wait, in what part of the country? Is this still Cutter County?*

She laughs bitterly when she thinks of mountain lions. She will hear their thoughts, intent on murdering her, as she is stalked. She will know the mountain lion's exact plan and watch it all unfold inside her own head before her throat is ripped out.

So that's super fun to think about. She notices the eerie silence again. Other than those two mourning doves, there doesn't seem to be any animal life at all.

Another terrifying thought suddenly strikes her. *Was I abandoned inside the Radiation Zone? Is it silent because hardly anything can live in here? Maybe there are no animals left here and very few birds, because they can fly over the moat. ... Or maybe the radiation, if there is any left, has deactivated my Gift! Maybe there are animals all around, but I can't hear them.* Her thoughts spin out of control. *But I heard those doves ... that was only a few minutes ago, right? How long have I been going?*

A full-blown panic sweeps over her. She could conceivably be in the dreaded Radiation Zone. How long can she stay in the Rad Zone before getting sick? What was all that stuff about half-lives she learned in school? Why didn't she pay better attention in history class when she learned about Three Mile Island? How long will the Rad Zone supposedly be "uninhabitable" or whatever?

Suddenly, a harsh chatter breaks Jessie from her frenzied thoughts, and a scared voice squeaks, "Intruder! Intruder!" She is ready to hit the dirt in absolute terror until she realizes a fat gray squirrel had jumped from a sugar maple to a white pine, alerting his family of the potential danger. Two smaller squirrels chase the first one out of her range of perception, and she is once again completely alone.

It is comforting to know her Gift still works, and Jessie wills herself to assess her situation more thoroughly. She speaks slowly out loud.

"Okay, back to basics. I don't seem to be hurt ... other than this headache. No one is chasing me at the moment ..." She turns in a cautious circle to make darn sure no one is sneaking up behind her. She shudders. This is spooky.

She desperately hopes she doesn't have a ransom on her head. She knows her parents don't make much money in their government positions. She knows how the system works and is old enough to remember when the Switch took effect, though she didn't know what was going on at the time. She really only remembers her parents sitting her down one day and explaining she needed to be an exemplary student and citizen at school, out in public, and at home. Her future, and the future of her family, depended on it.

She tries to think of an explanation other than money for being in this crazy situation.

"Okay, let's see, why else do people get kidnapped? Maybe to force the governor to pardon someone in jail?" She again speaks out loud, finding it keeps her whirling thoughts from racing out of control (too much). She also hopes speaking will deter predators from bothering her. She is not entirely convinced there *aren't* mountain lions out here. This place seems pretty wild.

She wonders if anyone was ever legally wronged by her family and is now in jail or something. Suddenly her brain switches gears, and she remembers the old board game Monopoly, with the players making trades and swapping brightly colored money for glossy property cards. *I'll trade you one sixteen-year-old girl for my brother to get out of jail free ... Oh, no! Alex!* She had momentarily forgotten about her brother. *Where are you?*

Hot tears spring to her eyes, her head pounding with a renewed vengeance, and for the first time since she was a kid, she sobs hysterically. This quickly progresses to hyperventilating, falling to the ground, and scratching her fingernails into the unforgiving dirt. It isn't pretty. She crinkles the dry leaves in her hands, turning them to powder, grinding them into nothing. *I'm going to die. Just like these leaves. Probably within the next twenty-four hours.*

Then, without consciously thinking about it, the words "warmth, water, food, companionship" echo in her head. She has heard it a million times, one way or another, from every animal that has ever spoken to her. She has eavesdropped for countless hours in the minds of Puffin, squirrels, birds, fish, and wild rabbits.

"Warmth, water, food, companionship. Warmth, water, food, companionship," Jessie whispers over and over until she isn't sure if it is her own thought anymore or if she is hearing a woodland creature now.

Sometimes the mind of an animal melds so perfectly with hers that she has trouble discerning her own thoughts. "Warmth, water, food, companionship." The mantra calms her significantly, and she dries her eyes on the sleeve of her jacket, resting her forehead on the cool dirt.

She lies still, then rolls onto her back and squints at the sky. It is still fairly light; she guesses there is about an hour or two before nightfall to figure out what to do about warmth and water. She stretches out her arms and legs until she resembles a starfish. *This is some kind of yoga pose, right? Hannah would know.*

She smiles when she thinks of Hannah. Will they ever see each other again? Will they ever do yoga together again? Write secret codes to each other at school again?

With what she thinks is a very cleansing breath, Jessie sits up and resets her resolve to take stock of her situation. It doesn't matter why she isn't dead or why she was left here alone. All that matters is getting out of here alive.

She stands up and brushes off her jeans and jacket, looking down the trail the way she had come. No one. Another gray squirrel, or maybe one from earlier, is watching her intently. "Intruder, intruder," it chatters.

"*You're* intruding on *me,*" Jessie says softly as the squirrel's thoughts stream with hers.

She takes off her jacket and ties the sleeves around her waist, watching the squirrel as it wiggles its whiskers. He calmly but authoritatively tells his family to seek cover from this strange upright creature that dares venture so close to their home. The squirrel gives a final chatter in her direction and bounds out of her range.

Jessie turns away from the squirrel and becomes acutely aware of the silence again. This is really creepy. Back home, there are always birds or rabbits intruding on her brain waves. Things are weirdly quiet here.

As she walks, she tries to channel the courage of her personal hero, Christie Cutter. She knows it is corny, but she has always admired Christie, ever since she learned about her in second grade. Christie was so brave and selfless the day she died, sacrificing her own life to save her coworkers.

The attack on Three Mile Island in 2026 will probably never be fully understood. The people who survived the bombings never really had much information to tell the authorities. One minute, everyone was at work on a regular day, and the next minute, the buildings were on fire.

The first explosion blew up the main building, the one Christie was in, and she searched the building until she found everyone inside and got them out. She single-handedly saved everyone in the main operations room and then rescued another four people who were trapped in a partially collapsed stairwell. They all made it out safely that day, thanks to Christie and her husband, Mitch, the helicopter pilot who flew them to safety before the reactor melted down.

Unfortunately, not everyone on Three Mile Island survived. Two more bombs exploded at the nuclear plant, including one that had been placed in the pipeline that provided cooling water to the reactor. And once the water was cut off, the reactor overheated, causing the extreme devastation that resulted in the Radiation Zone.

To this day, no one knows who planted the bombs. No one knows why there were three bombs, and not just the one in the pipeline. That one would have done all the same damage. There are theories that the culprit wanted to cause as much fear and confusion as possible before completely annihilating the area. Or maybe that person even watched the buildings burn for a while, knowing what was to come. No one ever confessed, and the investigation turned up nothing. Some say the mastermind behind the destruction died along with the victims that day—by accident or suicide is anyone's guess.

Jessie walks along the trail, trying to be brave, but keeping her ears alert and eyes peeled for anything that looks useful or dangerous (well, mostly dangerous, to be totally honest). *What would Christie do,* she wonders. *What would Christie do?*

Her brain latches onto the thoughts of some insects in a nearby tree, but their chatter quickly dissolves into a low buzz. She has never really been able to get full sentences out of insects. It is always more of a whispered word that she barely catches before it fades away. She's not sure why insects are so difficult to understand, but it's actually a good thing, since she would never have a silent moment and would probably eventually go crazy. Insects are everywhere.

She presses onward to cover as much distance as possible, knowing full well she may be going in the wrong direction. Another squirrel squeaks in alarm, warning the others that there is an intruder in their midst. This time, the high-pitched voice gets louder and louder as Jessie walks. She quickly spots the new squirrel, his puffy tail erect, a billowing gray warning flag. The squirrel is running toward her, yammering, "Intruder, intruder!" to his friends. He suddenly stops his circus act of graceful leaps among the branches and stares at her, his tiny black nose quivering. He shifts back on his haunches, and with his front feet turned inward, it looks as if he's praying. He bolts to his left, away from

Jessie, and sounds his verbal warning again. He soon disappears from her range, swallowed up by a sea of bare branches.

She continues on the path, listening for the squirrel, and hears another two or three go on the alert in various locations around her. The word is spreading that she is here. "Intruders, intruders ..."

Fear rises inside her, and she stops in the middle of the trail. *Intruders. Plural.* The squirrel had been coming toward her, alerting his friends of only one intruder. It was only *after* the squirrel had seen Jessie that the message changed. Someone else is out here with her.

CHAPTER 4

Alex

Alex finds himself half-propped up and half-slumped down the side wall of a little brown building, barely able to open his eyes. His neck hurts from his head lolling on his chest. After a minute, he can pick up his head and glance around. He recognizes exactly none of his surroundings.

He tries calling for his sister, but his voice is only a harsh whisper scratching along his windpipe and throwing him into a horrible coughing fit. He hunches over in the dirt, retching and choking, trying hard not to vomit.

A soft breeze rustles the tree branches. Birds are chirping, though Alex can't identify the species. Jessie would know. She can identify any bird by sight or sound. *Where is Jessie?*

He manages to sit up and leans back against the wall, vaguely watching those swaying branches. *What is going on? How did I get here?*

He dully ponders these questions, trying to calm his roiling stomach, the words taking an uncomfortably long time to form in his head. His brain is sluggish and fuzzy.

Fat, silent tears trickle down his cheeks, and he hides his head in the dirt and gravel next to the wall, sucking in deep breaths, inhaling the scent of the earth. He wants to scream and run, fly away and not look back. But there is nowhere to go. The surrounding trees look pretty scary, with unknown dangers lurking just beyond the low branches.

Alex kneels in the dirt, forehead on the ground, back arched and arms tucked between his knees. He breathes deeply for two straight minutes, heart thudding in his ears.

Suddenly, a new sound rises over the chirping birds and his thundering heart. It fills his aching ears, and he gradually realizes it is an engine, maybe an old car or truck that still uses gasoline. Maybe it is a rescue party! He wobbles to his feet and leans against the wall, trying not to pass out from his excruciating headache.

He takes a few halting steps into the road near the building. The engine is getting closer!

"Hello?" he calls uncertainly, though he is pretty sure no one is close by. He squints up the road that meanders into the trees. Then a terrifying thought strikes him. What if whoever is coming is *not* here to rescue him but instead means him harm? His mind reels. How can he possibly know? Clearly something bad has happened to him already.

What the hell is going on? I mean, "heck," he thinks, automatically correcting his bad language. *Where is Jessie?* He feels the urge to hide.

Without wasting another precious second, he wheels around and moves behind the building. But now he feels too exposed next to this bare wall. There is a wide tract of dirt and gravel around the building, no tree branches offering any cover at all. The forest looks much more inviting now, the dark shadows offering some form of refuge from ... whatever is coming.

Alex has always preferred to stay quiet and hidden, especially when he was a little kid. It always felt safer. Even in school, he seeks refuge at the back of the classroom, hardly ever speaking, sitting quietly and diligently completing his work. *Stay out of trouble and don't make waves.* That plan has worked well for him so far.

He decides to stick with it. Stay out of sight and hope nothing goes wrong. He ducks low to maneuver under the tree branches and cowers behind a large rock that is mostly cast in shadow.

The vehicle rumbles past, kicking up gravel, engine whining. Then it skids to a halt and backs up to the brown structure. Alex can barely see a man in a thick work coat and ski mask jump out and run around the tiny building, scanning the ground and nearby trees, obviously searching for something, or someone. Alex holds his breath, though he would not be able to breathe even if he tried. The blood whizzes through his vessels, a buzzing wave threatening to explode out his ears.

The man disappears around the front of the building, and Alex hears him grunting with effort, trying to tug open the doors to search inside. After what feels like an hour, the man finally jumps back in his truck and drives away.

Alex fights the bile rising in his throat and pushes his fists against his mouth. He curls up behind the rock, not moving for hours, his brain not comprehending what had happened to him. He is vaguely aware of the time passing as he watches a patch of sunlight slowly march across the forest floor.

When darkness shrouds the forest, the temperature drops. There is no way he is sleeping out here alone all night. He sneaks out from behind the rock and listens intently, then darts to the side of the building. He hugs the wall and inches his way to the front, peering out onto the gravel road. It is empty. *Now what? Start walking? Which way?*

He zips his jacket against the gathering chill. *Best to stay here, I guess. Hopefully, I will hear that guy coming again if he comes back. Who the hell—I mean, heck—was that, anyway?*

Taking one last look along the road in both directions, hoping to see Jessie, he sighs and turns to face the front of the building. This is probably the safest and least exposed place to spend the night.

He inspects the structure. It is an old, abandoned restroom, with a door on either side of the front facade. An aluminum awning shields a small patch of concrete from most of the elements. He quickly tries to open one of the doors, but it is rusted shut. A worn, faded sign on the door designates it as the women's room. He tries the men's room door, which opens just enough for him to squeeze his narrow, lanky frame through.

The bottom of the door stops dead on the corrugated concrete, the door having settled a few millimeters over the years as the rusty hinges weakened. Alex takes some comfort in this. The door is not easy to open, and most likely no animal will try to get inside. Anything big, like a bear or mountain lion, definitely won't be able to fit through. He's not sure exactly how big bears or mountain lions are, but he chooses to believe they are too large to squeeze through this narrow opening.

The restroom has clearly been abandoned for years. The last remnants of evening light filter through the dirty windows, and Alex inspects the interior. He finds a few rolls of toilet paper and an unopened package of paper towels near the rusted and dust-covered sinks. He turns the faucets on, not daring to hope any water will actually spring forth. Still worth a try. He opens the bag of towels and scatters them in the cleanest corner he can find, creating a somewhat soft bed for himself. He gathers all the toilet paper and unfurls the rolls, throwing the billowing sheets over his body. It proves to be an effective blanket against the evening chill.

Alex cries for a while, huddled in his nest of toilet paper, not fully understanding this new predicament. If Jessie were here, they could pretend they are on a camping trip or something. They had gone camping quite often as a family when they were younger, telling stories around the campfire and toasting marshmallows. It was great fun, but Alex couldn't help feeling a twinge of fear, a slight tug to his nerves, even when wrapped in his father's arms in his sleeping bag. There was that ever-present, nagging sensation that he was being watched by some bloodthirsty creature with large eyes and even larger teeth.

That is a terrible thought to have now, while he is completely alone in these woods, terrified in a dark corner under old toilet paper. *Why do I have to think about something eating me? Why do I always think about the worst-case scenario?*

He suddenly wishes Sam were here. He would tell Alex a funny story or brag that he could fight off anything that came through the door. Sam could fight a bear, or so he claims.

Alex thinks back to the first time he officially met Sam, almost exactly six years ago. Alex had frequently seen him at school, but Sam was in the grade ahead of Alex, and they had no classes together. They would occasionally see each other at boring political functions and banquets, both having politicians for parents, but Alex would usually only see him from across the room, looking dapper in his suit and tie, flashing his smile at the politicians and even fist-bumping some of them.

Alex has always wished he could be that comfortable in those situations, but mostly they are really boring and kind of overwhelmingly crowded. He tends to sit at his assigned table, not mingling or making eye contact with any of the grown-ups.

He is pulled from his reverie by a screeching wail right outside the door. Alex jumps up, toilet paper cascading to the floor. He wishes he could see. But it is completely dark, and he can't even discern the outline of the white ceramic sinks against the wall. His heart thuds. The scream comes again, further away, and he creeps toward the door. *Maybe it's a screech owl?*

Feeling relieved, he slowly makes his way back to his nest, secretly elated that Jessie possesses the nerdy hobby of bird-watching. Some of those bird calls she studies have wormed their way into his brain. *Yeah, that definitely sounded familiar. Definitely an owl ... but it sounded like someone being murdered! Oh, great. Now I'm thinking about being murdered again. Okay, I need to think about something else ... bears ... darn it!*

He fluffs up his makeshift bed and tries to calm his racing thoughts. This proves to be impossible. He forces his brain to return to happy thoughts of his sister and his friends, and he again thinks about the day he and Sam officially met. Which isn't really the *happiest* of memories, but they became best friends because of that day.

Alex had decided to take the long way home from school on a particularly beautiful April day, six years ago. Instead of taking the sidewalks and streets all the way home, he cut behind the school near the baseball field to take the short track that connects to the community park. He planned to stop and feed the ducks, then work his way home from there. He made sure to text Jessie that this would be his route in case something happened to him. He was always careful to let someone know where he was.

He rounded the chain-link fence at the baseball field and started down the track in the woods when he saw three other boys slowly walking along the path. The sound of Alex's footsteps caught the boys' attention, and they all turned around in unison like a pack of hungry hyenas, identical ugly and threatening expressions on their faces. Alex's heart started pounding when he saw who they were. Of course he would run into his number one enemy out there in the woods, off the school grounds, all alone.

"Hey, wimp, is your mommy coming to take you home? Where's your mommy?" Chris Alder took a menacing step toward Alex, blocking the path. "Did you cry yourself to sleep last night? Did your mommy have to tuck you in so you wouldn't have nightmares?"

Alex immediately felt hot tears sting the corners of his eyes, and his lips trembled. He wished he were tougher, wished he could tell off those jerks, put them in their place. But he had never been able to do that. Those boys were the worst bullies in the school, always picking on the smaller kids—most recently, Alex.

Chris and his sidekick, Justin, had been teasing Alex for the past six months, ever since his mother had to come get him from school when he wasn't feeling well. Chris had been within earshot when Alex said into his phone, "I don't feel well, Mommy; please come get me." Ever since then, Alex had been Chris's target.

Alex eyed the third boy, Scott Givins, who was quite a bit older than the other boys and was standing behind Chris and Justin like their bodyguard. Alex thought that was odd, as he hadn't known the three of them were friends, but he figured that bullies must stick together.

He turned his attention back to Chris, who was leering at him. Alex so badly wanted to punch Chris in the face, but he knew he would never win a fight against him. Chris was quite a bit bigger than Alex, with beefy arms and huge hands that he imagined could easily wrap around his throat. Chris had always been chubby and was never shy about throwing his weight around to bully the smaller kids, which was practically everyone. Unfortunately, Alex was the smallest and most timid boy in their third-grade class.

Scott piped up from behind Chris and Justin. "Hey, Chris, I won't say anything if you beat up this loser ... but he is Blaze's friend." A wave of relief flooded through Alex. Scott was his best friend's older brother.

There was *no way* Scott would allow anyone to beat Alex up. But to Alex's dismay, Scott continued gruffly, "On the other hand, I can't tattle about something I never saw." He clapped Chris on the shoulder and sneered at Alex. "Have fun, Chris." Scott ambled away, giving Chris and Justin permission to beat up his little brother's friend.

Alex stared open-mouthed, not believing what Scott was doing. He was *walking away.* How could he be so cruel? Alex didn't have much time to ponder the older boy's actions.

Chris pushed him hard on the shoulder. "You hear that? No one is gonna save you now."

"Stop bothering me," Alex said through gritted teeth, trying to sound tough but also trying to keep from crying. The tears were threatening to spill over the edges of his lower eyelids, and he was determined to keep them there.

"Aww, but you didn't say the magic word. Your mommy will be so disappointed," Chris made a pouting face, sticking his fat lower lip out and furrowing his brow. Justin snickered appreciatively, as if Chris had made a profound statement.

"Please," Alex automatically responded and immediately wished he hadn't said anything at all. His pitiful response to Chris's taunts caused Chris to roar with laughter, and Alex lost all the remaining resolve he had. Which wasn't much. "Please stop!" Alex bleated in a high voice, hiding his head in his hands.

He turned away from Chris, only to be met by Justin, who was Chris's sidekick in every sense of the word. Justin had stealthily slipped behind Alex, who accidentally trod on Justin's shoes.

Justin grabbed Alex by both wrists and swung him effortlessly around to face Chris, who was still shaking with laughter, his right hand cupping his chin, his left arm slung across his wide belly as he gazed at Alex with ruthless mirth.

Alex hated him. Hated his cold gray eyes, his slick red hair, the few freckles spattered across his nose. He longed to punch Chris's fat pink face and watch the shock register in that cruel boy's eyes as he finally summoned the courage to do something totally out of character.

But he would not have the satisfaction that day. Justin was holding Alex's wrists high above his head, keeping his feet slightly off the ground, a rabbit dangling from a snare. There was no way Alex was getting out of that hold. And really, even if he could get out of Justin's clamp-like hands, what was he really going to do? Chris was huge.

"Do you want to punch him while I hold?" Justin asked, tightening his grip on Alex's slight wrists.

"Oh, yes, *please!* That would be lovely," Chris replied, mocking Alex and drawing out the word "please." He took a step backward and pulled his fist back, preparing to land it squarely on Alex's tear-streaked face. Alex made one last futile attempt to squirm away, his arms still wrenched securely behind his back in Justin's unforgiving hold.

"Oh, my God, can you all *please* just shut up?" A new voice rose over the dying laughter, doing a fantastic impression of Chris, also mocking the word "please." Alex thought the voice sounded vaguely familiar. Maybe Scott was coming back to rescue him!

The new boy spoke again. "Let him go, freak show; you're not impressing anyone."

Alex felt Justin's strong, callused hands drop his wrists instantly. "Go to your leader, like a good little sidekick. Who's a good little sidekick?" the boy teased in a baby-like coo as if he were speaking to a cute puppy. Alex saw out of the corner of his eye that the new boy had pushed Justin toward Chris, which Justin didn't like at all.

"Don't push me, you spoiled, rich brat," Justin retorted, spinning around. He stayed close to Chris, though, even taking half a step behind him, clearly wanting his leader to protect him.

Alex felt a tug on the back of his polo shirt as the newcomer gently pulled him away from his tormentors. He took an awkward step back but still couldn't see the new boy.

"Ooh, ow, that one hurt," the new boy moaned sarcastically. "You really got me there. How will I ever recover from the barbs of your quick-witted repartee?"

Chris and Justin exchanged puzzled looks, giving Alex a moment to turn around and identify this smooth-talking angel who had saved his face from certain death.

He immediately recognized Sam Starling, who stood with his right hand rubbing the front of his left shoulder as if he had been stabbed there. "Yeah ... that's definitely gonna leave a mark," Sam said. He looked over at Chris and flashed a crooked and somewhat cruel grin. "Wanna go a few rounds? I could use the exercise. You look like you could, too."

"Shut up. You talk way too much," Chris said, taking a menacing step toward Sam, immediately forgetting that Alex had been his previous target. Chris had a new quarry. "And I can flatten you like a bug without even trying. A spoiled ... rich ... bug." Chris poked Sam in the chest as he drew out his words. "You think you're so special. The son of a senator. Well, guess what? No one here thinks you're special. No one here is going to help you. This wimp isn't going to do anything about it. He's too scared to tell anyone about us, anyway. Hold him," he directed Justin.

Justin grabbed Alex's wrists again and held them tightly behind his back. Alex sighed. This was getting ridiculous. He wanted the fight to start already so it would all be over faster.

Sam laughed. "I think our wimp is getting bored with you. So am I, actually. This is the lamest fight I've ever been in. And I've been in a good number of fights. ... Hey, did you hear about the time I fought off that black bear that came into the school? That was epic! There was like, national news coverage and stuff. Oh, never mind. You don't look like the type who would understand the news."

"I told you to shut the hell up!" Chris's red face became even redder, but Alex saw his eyes flicker at Sam, and Alex knew that Chris was wondering if this kid really did fight off a bear. Alex had never heard that story and didn't think he would have missed something like that. But whatever, if Sam were willing to fight Chris, Alex would believe anything Sam said.

Alex watched intently as the two boys glared at each other, Sam's bright blue eyes boring into Chris's cold gray ones. Chris was about six inches shorter than Sam, but much wider. Alex thought both boys could easily beat up a bear, probably without help.

Sam stood eerily still and blinked slowly at Chris, his eyes glinting in the sunlight. Alex could tell that Chris was becoming unnerved by this newcomer's steady gaze, as no one had ever dared look Chris in the eye for that long before. The two boys stared at one another for a solid ten seconds, Sam taking deep, even breaths while Chris fidgeted and glanced at Justin.

Finally, Chris looked back at Sam. "Why are you just standing there?" he demanded. He was thoroughly confused and a little annoyed. "Say something!"

"Oh, come on. Make up your mind," Sam muttered, rolling his eyes. He took a step back and shrugged his shoulders in a questioning gesture. "First you tell me to ... oh, darn, what was your elegant phrasing? Oh, yeah, 'shut the hell up.' And now you want me to speak. What do you want?"

"I want you to leave us alone. This has nothing to do with you!" Chris replied.

"Why don't you leave this kid alone? He did nothing to hurt you ... at least, I'm sure, not physically. What, did he permanently damage your tender ego or something?"

Chris had no reply for that but took half a step toward Sam and said slowly through gritted teeth, "Get out of here before I hurt you."

Sam smirked and took a step back, raising both hands in surrender. "Fine," he agreed. "This is boring anyway. Plus, I'm late for my skydiving lesson." He pushed his pale blond hair out of his eyes with a careless flick of his hand and looked up at the cloudless sky. "Perfect day for it, too. You can see for miles from my plane. All the way across the Radiation Zone." He turned to leave and addressed Alex. "You're coming this time, right? I know last time you ditched me because it conflicted with your BMX championship. Congratulations, by the way. Those stunts you did were amazing! Come on," Sam waved his hand at Alex, motioning for the younger boy to follow him.

As he glanced back, Alex was sure Sam caught the dumbfounded stares and open-mouthed expressions on all their faces, including Alex's. *Skydiving? BMX championship?* How could Sam lie so easily? He had completely stumped all of them.

Alex quickly realized he had been given the opportunity to get out of there.

"Right! Skydiving lessons! I'm supposed to move to intermediate level tonight!" Alex said, picking up on Sam's cue. He rushed forward to catch up with him, looking back to stick his tongue out at Chris and Justin.

Once they were out of the woods and no longer within sight of the bullies, Alex punched Sam hard on the shoulder, causing Sam to stop and turn around, a hurt and confused expression plastered on his smooth face.

"Dude, what the heck?" Sam asked, rubbing his shoulder.

"Why did you tell them that? They can see online that I didn't ride in a BMX championship! Now they will pick on me worse than before!" Alex whined, exasperated.

"Oh, don't stress over it." Sam nonchalantly waved his hand as if he were getting rid of a pesky fly. "I mean, seriously, are they really the type who will actually research stuff? They'll forget all about it by Monday." Sam pushed open the gate to the baseball diamond and entered the field. "Wanna throw a ball around for a while?"

"Umm ... I don't know," Alex replied tentatively. He wasn't sure if he really wanted to hang out with this kid. He vaguely knew who Sam was and knew he had a reputation for being a bit of a troublemaker. Alex remembered that Sam had gotten into a few fights at school over the past year or so, usually pushing kids on the playground or something stupid like that. And only a few months ago, he had tried to walk off school property during gym class. There was even talk that Sam might get expelled over that stunt. Alex did not need that kind of stress in his life.

Alex hung back at the gate while Sam walked toward the pitching mound.

"It's okay. I promise I don't bite," Sam said, sliding a leather baseball glove over his left hand, flexing the fingers. He tossed another glove to Alex. It was too big, and he uncertainly slid it over his slim hand. "My father was supposed to play with me tonight, but he had to work late ... again." Sam looked at the ground as he spoke, then gave Alex a half-hearted shrug. "If you see those stupid kids coming, let me know and we can hide under the bleachers or something."

"Oh, so you're not gonna be all tough and tell them off again?" Alex responded, confused by Sam's sudden change in tactics. Why would he hide now after he already successfully put them in their place?

"Well, they think we're skydiving right now. We can't show them we were bluffing and lose all credibility, can we?"

Alex immediately felt stupid and didn't reply.

Sam rolled the baseball against his glove and tossed it gently to Alex, who caught it and threw it back.

"Nice arm, kid." Sam tossed the ball again and took a few steps backward so Alex could throw farther.

"Thanks, but really, I don't need a bodyguard."

"Mmm, okay, I see." Sam caught the ball, and they threw it a few more times, falling into a smooth and perfect rhythm, as if they had been playing catch together their entire lives. "Then how about a friend?"

Alex pondered that proposition. Did he really want to be friends with this kid? Rather than answer Sam's question, he asked one of his own. "Did you really fight off a bear?" His nine-year-old brain wrestled with whether that story was true or not.

"Oh, heck no," Sam scoffed, throwing the ball again. "That would be insane."

"But you get into a lot of fights?"

"Not with bears." Sam's lips curled into a mischievous grin.

"Why did you help me get away from those guys?" Alex asked, missing the ball and running backward a few steps.

"Can't I do a good deed?" Sam asked, also missing the ball. "My father told me to do ten good deeds every month."

"Why ten?"

"That's how old I am. He says you should do good deeds according to your age. That way, the older you get, the better you become." He flashed a friendly smile this time.

Sam's explanation of his courtesy threw Alex off guard. It didn't match Sam's reputation at all. He tentatively asked, "Are you Sam Starling?"

"That's me." Sam threw the ball higher, causing Alex to miss it again. Alex fumbled with the ball for a second, hoping Sam wasn't getting bored with him, and threw it smoothly back to Sam, who also missed it again, thankfully.

"You're the son of Senator Starling?"

"Me again."

"My dad is the mayor of New Harrisburg."

"Yeah, I know. I've seen you with him at some of those stupid dinners we're all required to attend." Sam said this with a slight eyeroll, clearly indicating that he thought those dinners were the most boring things in the world. Alex had to agree there. "I don't know your name, though."

"Oh, sorry. ... I'm Alex."

"Nice to officially meet you, Alex."

"Yeah ... you, too," Alex replied, still tentative. He missed the ball for the third time but quickly grabbed it and threw it back. He was glad to see that Sam, who seemed so agile and athletic, also missed the ball. Alex realized he didn't feel *too* self-conscious and awkward.

Maybe it wouldn't be so bad having this kid as a friend (and, if truth be told, a handy bodyguard), even if all they did was throw a ball around once in a while. They had similar family backgrounds, which was something that Alex's other friends lacked. His other friends sometimes made fun of him because he was a "spoiled rich kid," despite his best efforts not to flaunt that fact. And here Sam really *was* another spoiled rich kid, though you couldn't tell that by looking at him. He basically looked like any other student at school, with his slightly worn jeans and faded T-shirt.

Alex looked down at his own clothes—wrinkled khakis and a light-blue polo shirt with a small tear in the seam near his right hip. He remembered with a pang of dread that Chris had grabbed him in the hallway at school the month before and had ripped that shirt. Yeah, maybe Sam would be kind of handy to have around. Who was Alex kidding? He definitely needed a bodyguard.

"Is your family rich?" Alex asked, catching the ball.

"Oh, heck yeah. It's awesome," Sam responded without a trace of modesty. "Yours?"

"Um, yeah, I guess. I mean, sometimes I hate it, though, because the other kids make fun of me."

"Yeah, I get that too, sometimes ... as you just saw with Chris."

"You mean other kids make fun of you, too?" Alex stared at him, incredulous, not able to fathom who else would have the nerve to tease Sam Starling. Even Chris had lost his cool.

"Yeah, sometimes. Not so much anymore, but when I was your age and younger. People don't like people who are different from them. ... That's just the way it is. I mean, look at these kids who are getting these weird superpower things or whatever they are. That's some crazy stuff. No one understands it, so people are kind of avoiding them." Sam caught the ball in his bare hand and smoothly threw it back to Alex without missing a beat. He continued, "Some kids don't like me because of who my father is, I think. ... I don't know, I think he's made some enemies through his work. But I don't really know for sure. He doesn't actually tell me stuff like that. I barely see him, anyway."

"Why not?" Alex asked nervously. He could not envision a world where he didn't see his father every day.

"He works in Washington, DC. Sometimes he only comes home for a Saturday night and Sunday morning, then goes back to his office for the week. He was supposed to come home tonight, which is why I brought my baseball stuff here. He was supposed to meet me after school, and we were going to play for a while. He called me and said he isn't coming home at all this weekend. Too busy at work. ..." Sam's chatter trailed off, and Alex got the impression that he felt silly for talking so much about something so personal.

"That sounds like it kind of sucks," Alex said.

Sam shrugged. "I'm sort of used to it by now. It's been this way for years. Basically, I know I can't rely on him for anything. So I don't."

Alex had no reply for that but realized he felt a bit sorry for Sam.

"Well, I should get home," Sam said. "I need to get better at doing my homework and chores. I really suck at that. ... Do you want to meet me here Sunday afternoon?"

"Um, okay." Alex was still uncertain about befriending Sam. They walked toward the gate of the baseball field, where Alex saw Jessie leaning over the fence, watching the boys. "Oh, hey, Jessie. How long have you been here?"

Jessie shrugged, her long, dark-brown hair rippling. "About five minutes. It was nice watching you play. ... I thought you would be around here somewhere when you weren't home yet. Why didn't you answer my texts?"

Alex quickly pulled his silenced phone from his pocket. "Oh, sorry ..." he said guiltily, seeing the four missed texts and two missed calls from Jessie.

"Who's your friend?" Jessie asked, though she knew exactly who Sam Starling was and wasn't exactly happy to see her innocent little brother getting so chummy with him.

"This is Sam Starling. He helped me get away from some kids who were teasing me," Alex said, beaming up at Sam. "Sam, this is my sister,

Jessie," he dutifully continued, making polite introductions the way his parents had taught him.

To Alex's surprise, Sam very maturely stuck out his right hand toward Jessie, who tentatively shook it.

"Nice to meet you, Jessie. I hope you don't mind that we kept you waiting. Your brother is a formidable opponent when it comes to playing catch. I lost track of time trying to keep up with him." Sam released her hand but held eye contact for what Alex thought was an uncomfortably long time. He was getting an uneasy feeling about Sam, like he was up to something. He also wasn't sure what a "formidable opponent" was, but it sounded kind of scary.

Sam took a step away from Jessie but kept his eyes on her, as though sizing her up for a fight. Alex got the sudden urge to grab his sister's hand and pull her toward home without looking back.

"Come on, Jessie. Let's go home," he said, squeezing out of the partially open gate.

"What's your hurry, kid?" Sam asked, staying inside the playing field and casually crossing his arms over the top of the chain-link fence, still gazing at Jessie. "I just invited Alex to meet me Sunday afternoon to continue our game here. Wanna join us?"

"Um ... not sure. I'll have to check with our parents," Jessie replied, turning toward Alex to shuffle him back home. Alex immediately regretted his sister's words. They made him sound like a complete baby. *Check with our parents. Jeez.*

"Well, whether you want to join me or not, I'll be here at two o'clock. But remember, Alex, even I have trouble being pitcher *and* catcher," Sam said, a hint of practiced arrogance in his voice.

Alex saw Jessie roll her eyes at that remark, but he replied, "Okay, yeah, I'll definitely try to be here." He tagged along behind his sister into the fading light. Little did he know that he would be sitting in the bleachers alone on Sunday while his new friend and savior was lying motionless in the hospital with two broken legs.

CHAPTER 5

Sam

Sam just had the strangest dream. Hannah Buckley had pulled him out of his nice, warm bed, and they'd landed on a gravel road after being kidnapped or something. She kept screaming at him that he needed to move.

Weird. She needs to calm down. She's even uptight in my dreams. Ah, well, whatever. ... Not my problem. Sam stretches his arms over his head and yawns, drifting back into a light sleep.

A semilucid thought works its way into his sluggish brain. *I vaguely remember saying something about not having my phone ... what a weird dream. I've gotta stop watching scary movies at bedtime. ... Nah ... that was fun. ... Wait, why is my mattress so uncomfortable?*

Sam's fingertips explore the space behind his head and touch something that is definitely *not* his pillow. He jolts upright and peers around at a bunch of trees and rocks and stuff.

"What the heck?" he mumbles as he massages his neck with one hand, leaning back on his other palm. He glances around uncertainly and finally stares at the dirt, not comprehending his situation at all. "Huh ... this is really weird ..." His voice trails off as he surveys the thick bed of dry leaves and sticks entangling his feet and hands.

"Hello? Hannah? Anybody?" he calls out, his voice harsh and scratchy, as he slowly disentangles his feet from a snarl of twisted vines. His left ankle is sore and scraped up, and he sort of remembers getting his foot caught on something in his dream ... and Hannah helping him. She kept screaming at him. ... Was that real?

He inspects his ankle vaguely, as if it doesn't really belong to him, his hair falling into his eyes. There are thin, linear gouges on both of his palms and bits of gravel and dirt ground into the pink flesh of his hands.

He gently rubs the debris out of his palms, trying to think, but his thoughts are slow and muddled. *Did I take a bunch of my sleeping pills? I don't remember that. ... I haven't taken my pills in years ... and I usually don't feel this trashed from them. Okay, what is going on with my hands? Weren't we just fishing? Or was I dreaming that? No, Jessie and Alex were here ... and Hannah ... but then Hannah and I were on a ... a road?*

He pats the pockets of his jeans in a desperate search for his phone, thoughts whirling, feeling nothing except his cigarette lighter against his thigh. *Well, this is a first.* He always has his phone. He scans the ground nearby, sifting through the bunches of dry leaves he's sitting in, remembering that his trusty phone had survived even his bike accident and had saved his life. Well, that was actually three phones ago, but still, he always has it with him. *Darn, I really liked that phone. And it had that awesome photo of Jessie at the beach last summer. ... Always back up your photos, kids. They don't need to be kept secret ... usually.*

"Jeez, focus, Sam. Okay, seriously. ... What is going on?" he whispers to himself, sifting through another bunch of leaves but having no luck finding his phone.

Groaning, he stands up slowly and leans against a tree trunk, arms and legs heavy and stiff. He rests his head against the rough bark and massages his throbbing eyes.

"Did I take a bunch of sleeping pills or something? What the heck did I *do?*" His mind races, searching for any reason why he should feel this badly and how he ended up here. He is starting to think he must've done something *really* stupid but has no idea what. He has done some dumb things, but nothing where he can't remember whole *hours.* Except for that one time he got totally wasted on his father's Scotch.

After another minute of unproductive thinking, Sam hesitantly winds his way through the underbrush and downed branches, scanning the ground, hoping to spot his phone. His brain is still fuzzy, the remnants of a headache lingering behind his eyes. This might be the weirdest situation he has ever been in. ... Where is everyone? He glances up to survey the empty forest, not at all sure what to do.

He leans against another tree, surprised to find he's a little out of breath after walking literally just ten steps. He's seriously considering simply lying down again and seeing if he wakes up at home. Maybe he'll get a whole do-over on this thing. And he's really thirsty—and starting to get hungry, too.

What time is it? He glances up at the sky, but the sun hurts his aching eyes. He casts his gaze to the ground, and his eyes eventually wander to the road. He instantly recognizes it from his dream. *Okay ... so I wasn't dreaming. I definitely woke up here, with Hannah screaming at me.*

"Man, this is ... just ... crazy ..." he mutters under his breath, baffled. A light breeze ruffles his hair, and he shivers, though he isn't cold. Everything is alarmingly quiet, like there are no other humans within a hundred miles. *Wait a second! Am I the last living thing left on Earth? Okay, maybe that's a little ridiculous.*

His brain is clearly grasping onto random doomsday storylines from the action movies he binge-watches.

Without really knowing why, maybe because he thinks Hannah screamed to stay away from the road, he quickly crosses the gravel track and finds a narrow trail meandering into the woods. He must have been here before; it is all a bit vaguely (and eerily) familiar. But when? On a family camping trip when he was a kid?

Instinctively, he picks up the narrow, worn trail and jogs slowly, the sluggishness in his limbs dissipating as he moves.

He doesn't seem to be hurt in any way, other than this headache that is worsening with every footfall. His brain is still foggy, and he realizes he must have been drugged—and probably not with sleeping pills. His right hand unconsciously massages his left arm, and he slowly becomes aware that something like a needle had been stuck there. *Hmm ... yeah. Alex and I were fishing, and then ... there was this pinch on my arm, and ... I don't know. I wonder where Alex is? Was he drugged and dumped in the woods somewhere around here, too? Weird.*

As he jogs, Sam carefully picks his way around rocks and pushes aside tree branches, thinking about this new situation but finding he can't make much sense of it. Eventually, as the final cobwebs clear and somewhat rational thought takes over, a niggling tendril of fear creeps in on the outskirts of his brain. So that's new.

Okay, I bet this is some kind of joke. ... Yeah, I'm gonna go with that ...

He has to keep moving. He has never been very good at staying still anyway. Moving makes him feel like he is doing something productive, though he usually isn't. It gives him something to do. *I'm totally okay, right? I've been in worse scrapes than this. No broken bones ... yet ... so, yeah, totally fine ...*

As he continues his easy jog, not entirely sure where he's going, his mind involuntarily wanders back to one of the worst days of his life. Way worse than this, at least so far. Almost exactly six years ago. ...

✳✳✳

There had been a lot of trouble at home, six years ago. Sam had just turned ten a few weeks prior, and his sister, Violet, was only three months old. His parents were overwhelmed with work and taking care of two kids, and they seemed to be in crisis mode 24/7. Sam didn't quite know what was going on at the time; he just knew his mom spent an awful lot of time with his new baby sister, sometimes taking her out of town overnight to faraway cities like Philadelphia or Baltimore, leaving him with a babysitter, whom he never liked.

And Sam's father, when he did occasionally come home, was always in a bad mood. He and Sam never played catch anymore. When his dad was home, his parents spent hours poring over their computers, talking about things like "side effects" and "prognosis." Sam always figured it had something to do with the Radiation Zone, an enigmatic off-limits wasteland that had intrigued him since the first time he heard about it. His parents had been telling him for years, "Don't ever go there. People have died there." This made the Rad Zone all the more alluring to him. Don't tell Sam Starling he can't do something. Especially if an explosion and dead people and stuff were involved. *Cool.*

Anyway, Sam was having a particularly bad Saturday, the day after he met Alex Cox in the woods behind the school. That had been fun. He liked telling off losers like Chris Alder and his moronic sidekick. He hoped he and Alex would become friends. The kid seemed all right. And oh, man, Alex's sister? Sam *really* wanted her to be his friend. He had seen Jessie from a distance over the years and always thought she was pretty. But up close, she was stunning. He loved her wavy, dark hair and those amazing hazel eyes. They were big and gentle, but Sam had seen a wariness there. He knew he had a reputation as a troublemaker, and he guessed Jessie was not happy to see her brother palling around with the likes of him. He would have to change her mind somehow.

He had been pedaling his bike along the edge of the school property, intent on taking the forested track to the community park, his mind wandering to his chance meeting with Alex and Jessie in almost that exact spot the previous day.

He rounded the corner of the baseball field fence, taking the curve at a good speed and tipping his bike sideways, skidding the back tire and rutting the spring mud. He glanced into the baseball diamond and caught sight of two people in the bleachers. A jolt of pleasure shot up his spine. Oh, goody! Chris and Justin were sprawled lazily across the seats. Sam slowed his bike as they sat up like cobras sizing up their prey.

"Well, well, well. Look who it is," Chris rubbed his meaty hands together as if warming them by a fire. "I was hoping you would show up." He lumbered off the stands toward the gate.

"Oh, really? Did you finally decipher our conversation from yesterday? That must be a new record for you," Sam retorted. He stopped his bike by the gate and had a vision of Jessie standing right there yesterday, her slender arms resting on the top of the fence as she watched him.

He straddled his bike, arms crossed over his chest, feet planted, while the two boys ambled closer to him, Chris in the lead, of course. Sam tried to give him his most indifferent gaze but was actually looking forward to some more witty banter. Well, witty banter on his part.

Chris was usually too busy wiping the drool off his chin to engage in highly evolved activities like speaking.

Suddenly, the boys heard a deep voice call, "Hey! Is he bothering you?"

Chris's lips curled into an evil smile, his gray eyes glinting in the late-afternoon light. Scott Givins was rounding the back corner of the baseball field, the way Sam had come, stalking toward them. Sam glanced back and watched as Scott closed the gap between them alarmingly fast. Scott was two years older than Sam, but Sam knew him well by reputation. Scott's father was also a Pennsylvania senator, like Sam's father. The only difference was that Scott's father was dead.

"No, we're fine," Sam said, gripping his handlebars.

"I wasn't talking to you, punk." Scott snarled at Sam. He shoved him on the shoulder, unseating him for a second. Scott stood right behind Chris, crossing his muscular arms over his broad chest.

"So, what are you doing, Chris?" Sam taunted. "Did you hire this goon to be your bodyguard or whatever? How much are you paying him?"

Chris ignored Sam's remark and said, "I heard some bad things about your daddy."

Sam was momentarily taken aback. He had not expected Chris to go after his father, at least not so soon.

After getting no response from Sam, Chris continued, menacingly pounding one fist into his other hand as he spoke. "Apparently your daddy likes to screw with us regular, honest people, and steals money from hard-working taxpayers. My parents are furious. They say all politicians are crooks. The last good one was Senator Givins." Chris hitched his thumb over his shoulder at Scott. "Dad says we need to start over with people who *aren't* entitled ... spoiled ... rich ... bugs." Chris repeated his taunt from yesterday and again poked Sam hard in the chest as he said each word.

"Okay, you need to get a few things straight." Sam steadied himself on his bike, gripping the handlebars and shuffling his feet on the ground. Chris's pokes had unseated him, mostly because he was not expecting him to get right up in his face. Chris was much braver with Scott behind him. Sam had never even realized Scott and Chris were friends, as there was a three-year age gap between them. But strength in numbers or whatever.

Even with Scott towering above him, Sam wasn't going to back down. He needed to put Chris in his place, especially after Chris insulted his father. Unacceptable. Sam was going to try his best to let the air out of him with words, rather than get into a physical altercation. Chris was pretty darn big, and Sam really didn't *want* to fight him. And Scott wasn't exactly small, being twelve years old and in good shape.

Sam gazed steadily at Chris and said, "First of all, I'm really impressed you watch the news. Or at least understand what your parents say about it. Good for you. Very mature. Second, my father did *not* steal money. That was Senator Walker, from like, Indiana or something. That wasn't even a Pennsylvania senator."

"It doesn't matter. They are all the same," Chris sneered.

This remark made Sam angrier than he thought possible. How dare this kid lump *his father* in with all the other senators and politicians? Chris obviously didn't know how amazing his father was, how he *always* fought for the citizens, and *never* did anything immoral.

"Please stop talking about my father." Sam tried to speak steadily through gritted teeth. "You can make fun of me all you want but leave my father alone."

"Oh, how adorable. You sound like your little buddy, Alex. '*Please* stop picking on me. I'm just a spoiled, rich wimp and can't handle being teased,'" Chris's voice was high and taunting. "You rich brats are all the same. ... What do you think about this rich brat, Scott?"

Sam saw the older boy's features twist from smugness to rage.

"It should have been your father," Scott whispered in a deadly low voice, his lips pulled back over his teeth, giving him a wild, feral look.

Suddenly, Sam was sailing through the air, his bike falling away. Scott had punched him square in the jaw while Chris had punched him in the stomach. He hit the ground, hard, his head snapping back. He was glad for the first time in his life that he was wearing his bike helmet. He felt agonizing pain on the left side of his face, in his stomach, and in both legs, as all three boys punched and kicked him at the same time, like a well-rehearsed dance. The solid weight of his beloved bike fell on him; one of the boys had picked it up and thrown it. *If they hurt my bike, I will seriously kill them,* Sam thought savagely as he slowly brought one hand up to turn the handlebars out of his face, massaging his bruised ribs with the other.

"Aww, what's the matter? No snappy comeback? You're not so tough now, are you?" Chris kicked Sam's leg again.

"Three against one is hardly a fair fight, you moron." Sam's voice was steady, but he was fighting very hard to hold back the tears. He had never been beaten in a fight before and had certainly never been thrown to the ground. That was definitely a first. He tried to get up but was actually too stunned to move.

"Hey, no one said it would be fair. No one asked you to butt in yesterday. Maybe this will teach you to mind your own business." Chris stooped down, picked up a handful of loose gravel, and threw it at Sam's face.

When Sam shielded his eyes, Scott leaped at him and hauled the bike off him, exposing him on the ground. Suddenly Scott was straddling Sam's chest, knocking all the air out of the younger boy.

"Scott ..." Sam gasped. "Please ... I can't bre—"

Scott pulled back his fist and punched Sam in the head, over and over again, until blood ran in rivulets through Sam's eyes, and he could no longer see. "It should have been your father!" Scott screamed into Sam's face.

"Scott! Stop!" Chris and Justin jumped at the raging boy, trying to pull his arms back to get him off Sam.

"It should have been your father!" Tears streamed down Scott's face. "I hate you! I hate you!" He got in one last punch on Sam's jaw before he fell back, exhausted, Chris and Justin pulling him away, all three panting heavily.

"Stop, Scott! You're gonna kill him!" Chris shrieked in a high voice. His steely gray eyes were wide, his perfect hair sticking out in all directions. He doubled over, gasping and clutching his stomach.

"Crap, someone's coming!" Justin piped up as he disentangled himself from Scott's arms. "Run!" Justin took off, his long lanky legs pumping through the mud into the woods, toward the community park. Chris waddled after him as fast as he could.

Scott towered over Sam's nearly lifeless form, then bent down and grabbed the front of Sam's shirt, forcing him to partially sit up. Scott straightened and pulled Sam up so that he was kneeling, head lolling forward, blood streaming from numerous cuts on his face. Scott put his lips close to Sam's ear and whispered, "If you breathe a word of this to anyone, I will kill you. I have nothing to lose. ... Don't think I'm kidding."

Sam got the distinct impression that Scott was definitely not kidding.

"Understand?" Scott cupped Sam's chin and forced his head up to look at him. He gave Sam a satisfied smirk, knowing he had won.

Sam's brain was swimming, and he was only vaguely aware that Scott had let go of his shirt and he had fallen back into the dirt, his bike falling on top of him again as Scott heaved it, the handlebar digging painfully into his stomach. He was too weak and ashamed to care, though, and lay there for half an hour, tears rolling down his cheeks, his chest rising and falling with wracking sobs. *This is gonna be all over school on Monday. ... Maybe I can just be home-schooled from now on.* He turned his head and spit out a mouthful of blood.

Justin had called out a false alarm. No one came to help. Sam was completely alone. At some point, his fingers fumbled with the chin strap of his bike helmet, and he pulled it off, allowing his head to rest back in the dirt and grass. His mind was buzzing but with no clear thought. All he could feel were the hot, sticky trails of blood and tears running down his face. Attractive.

His first coherent thought was that he hated everything. Really *hated* everything. Hated Scott and Chris ... hated school ... hated his new baby sister and how his parents seemed so upset ever since she had been born a few months ago ... hated his father for having a job where he could be assassinated any day ...

Sam vividly remembered when Senator Givins was killed in a fiery car explosion as he was driving home to Cutter County for the weekend last October. Sam had been terrified that his father would be next. Every time his mother's phone rang, he was sure it was someone calling to tell them his father was dead. For the past few months, he had been having nightmares of his father being blown to bits or getting fatally shot or meeting some other gruesome death.

Sam lay on his back, gazing at the sky, the pain in his jaw finally easing to a dull throb. His thoughts turned to revenge. He was going to get Scott back someday, but he needed to figure out how. It needed to be something clever, something he would be remembered for. Merely beating him up was not going to be good enough. And after that day, he doubted he actually *could* beat him up. Scott had essentially lifted Sam off the ground with one arm. There was no way Sam could take him in a fight.

He pondered the past few months while lying on the ground, mainly because he still couldn't move and had nothing better to do. How had things gotten so bad? His family was a wreck over something he didn't quite understand, but he worried it was all his fault. He wasn't doing too great in school and had failed his last math test. His parents were extremely unhappy about that. And now he had gotten beaten up for the first time ever. *What next?*

A groan escaped Sam's lips as he pushed the bike away and rolled onto his side, vaguely wondering if he had cracked a rib. He was really trying hard not to cry, but every inch of him hurt, including his pride.

He peeled up the front of his T-shirt and wiped his face, not entirely surprised to see quite a bit of blood come away on it. Attractive. He didn't want to go home feeling this angry and ashamed. He needed to go someplace serene and try to calm down. He slowly stood up and inspected his bike. It seemed to be in working order, thank goodness. Too unsteady to ride, he pushed the bike into the woods along the trail toward the park, but he didn't feel like going to the park. Not looking like that. Not *feeling* like that. There would be too many people there he knew.

Pale sunlight dappled the woods, and he could see a narrow trail, probably a deer trail, leading away from the park, deeper into the dense trees. A thought struck him. *The Rad Zone is this way, right?*

He pictured the maps he had studied in history class. The Rad Zone was maybe three or four miles away from the school property, at the northern edge of Cutter County. He had always wanted to explore the Rad Zone. And now seemed like the perfect time to do it. He needed to be alone, and where better to seek solitude than in a barren wasteland of toxic radiation? Seemed like as good a plan as any. He pushed his bike along with a new purpose.

The Rad Zone had always intrigued Sam. Apparently there was a moat around it, but that wouldn't deter him. He was a good swimmer and he imagined he would be able to swim across and pull himself up the other side. He had to at least check it out and see what all the fuss was about. And that day seemed like a fine day to break some rules or federal trespassing laws—whatever—since things really couldn't get much worse.

Tantalized by this adventurous prospect, he straddled his bike and pedaled down the deer path. His pain was subsiding with this new distraction, this new goal, on his mind. He was going to explore the Rad Zone. And he would be the only person ever to do it.

He quickly checked his pocket for his phone; he would need photographic evidence that he had, in fact, been in the Rad Zone. This would be the story all over school on Monday. Sam Starling had trespassed into a restricted area full of toxic waste. No one would even care that some kids had beaten him up an hour before this epic adventure.

The trail headed straight into the woods, away from the school. Sam's sense of direction had always been decent, and he knew he should keep the sun to his left to head north at that time of day. That was something his father had taught him on one of their camping trips, before life got so ... difficult. That was way before Violet was in the picture. But ever since she had been born, it was like Sam didn't even exist. His father barely said hello to him before rushing off to see Violet in the nursery. They almost never played catch anymore, and if they did it was only for a few minutes, and his father always seemed distracted. Sam had been wondering for months what he had done wrong to make his father ignore him like that. He couldn't figure it out.

After about forty minutes of fast pedaling, Sam came to a wide dirt track that looked to have been well used at one time but now was overgrown with weeds. Last year's weeds were all dead though, and the new spring growth was sparse and straggly, making the track easy to navigate on the bike. He looked up and down the road. There was a sign facing away to the right. He pedaled over to read it. It was a large brown, wooden sign with faded red lettering that appeared to be hand painted. "DANGER! Radiation Zone 100 Yards Ahead. KEEP OUT."

A thrill shot down Sam's spine. He made it! He was there! The dreaded Radiation Zone! He quickly took a photo of the sign and pedaled back up the track the way he had come. Not much further now.

The track became muddier closer to the moat. There were fewer rocks on that section of road, and large ruts seemed to be permanently gouged into the earth. Sam navigated around them and stood up on the pedals to get through the mud. Some parts were deep, and the tires squelched along slowly. Suddenly, the front tire hit something hard but smooth and then bounced off into the mud again. Sam looked down. A long wooden plank was half buried. It looked like a 2 x 6 board, maybe something that was left behind when the moat was built.

He rounded the final curve in the dirt track and stopped the bike, taking in the scene before him. It was extremely ... anticlimactic. Thick trees lined both sides of the road but did not extend all the way to the edge of the moat, which was an eight-foot-wide ditch delineating the Radiation Zone. The moat stretched away in both directions as far as he could see, a monotonous, muddy, brown canal with a shimmer of water in the bottom.

The bank on the near side was almost all mud, with only a few shriveled shrubs dotting the land. The Radiation Zone itself looked like a marsh, with no trees or vegetation topping out over ten feet or so. Dried-up brown reeds and tendrils of old cattails waved gently in the early April breeze. Only a few short, scrubby pine trees with sparse needles and some deciduous trees with a hint of small spring buds glinted in the late-afternoon light. It looked like there may have been an abundance of low vegetation at one time, miles and miles of tangled brush and vines, but it was all brown and dried up at that time of year.

This is it? This is so ... like, boring, Sam thought, disappointed. There was nothing sinister about it at all. It was a bland-looking, typical, early spring scene. But it was quiet and peaceful, something he needed to calm his fiery temper.

His anger suddenly flared again. This sucked! No one was going to believe this was the Radiation Zone from a stupid photo! He whipped his bike around, furious that he really had no proof he had been there, other than the photo of the dumb sign. He'd hoped there would be a huge black char in the ground, something that showed there had been an *explosion* there at one time. *This is just a stupid marsh!*

He pedaled fast down the dirt track, full of angry adrenaline. The bike tire hit the wooden board again, and a thought struck him. It was a stupid thought, but a thought, nonetheless. He glanced into the woods for a rock. ... Yes!

Sam hopped off his bike and ran to the tree line, heaving a large rock with one flat side onto his shoulder, feeling a surge of excitement rather than anger. This was going to be an epic day, after all.

After working for a few minutes, he mounted his bike again and faced the moat. Taking a deep breath, he steadied his hands on the well-worn rubber grips of the handlebars, surprised that his nerves were jangling, his throat was dry, and there was the slightest hint of perspiration on his palms. He wiped his hands over the knees of his jeans, then pulled up the front of his T-shirt to mop his forehead. More blood stained the cloth, mingling with the sweat.

The early spring day was cool, and he hadn't been exerting himself. Why was he sweating? Why was his heart thudding so fast? Surely, he wasn't that scared to jump over the moat! He had jumped his bike nearly as far in his yard last fall when he had set up a plank of wood over a cinder block to fly into a leaf pile. This was only a little farther, right?

His enthusiasm began shrinking, shriveling and wrinkling like a balloon losing air. Even if he did jump the moat, no one would believe him. He toyed with the idea of setting up his phone to record the jump, but realized he would be on the other side without his phone, and that simply would not do. He had never been without his phone. No way was he leaving it there while he explored the Rad Zone. What if he saw a two-headed beaver or something?

A light breeze rustled the tendrils of hair peeking from under his helmet. He squinted into the setting sun and looked across the drab, desolate wasteland of the Rad Zone. It was actually kind of pretty, the slanted rays of the afternoon sun giving the landscape a soothing glow. It wasn't nearly as scary and intimidating as his parents had made it sound.

Hot, unwelcome tears suddenly stung the corners of Sam's eyes as he thought of his parents. A pang of guilt surged through him. He knew he was making things difficult for them but didn't know how to stop it. *Mom and Dad definitely won't be too thrilled if they find out I explored the Rad Zone.*

A tear slid down his cheek, and he quickly brushed it away. He had seen his mother cry occasionally, though it seemed more often since Violet was born, usually because Sam had failed a test or had "mouthed off" to her, as she called it. Sam caught his father crying once, though he wasn't supposed to have seen it. It was a few months ago, when Sam had been peeking into his father's home office late at night when he couldn't sleep. Sam's plan was to ask his father to read him a story, but he stopped short and hid in the hallway when he saw his father crumpled over his desk, sobbing and shaking quietly.

That scene had rattled Sam more than he ever thought possible. What was going on? His father had always been practically a superhero, always impeccably dressed in expensive, tailored suits, shaking hands with the country's other important leaders with a confident and easy smile. Sam was confused and scared after seeing his father that night.

His parents argued frequently about how much time Senator Starling spent at work, and Sam could hear them whispering harshly in the home office, long after Sam was supposed to be sleeping. He would creep silently out of his bedroom to eavesdrop. Mrs. Starling would accuse her husband of not helping her enough with the house and family and complain that Sam was getting to be too stubborn for her to handle on her own. "He needs a father more than a few hours on the weekends!" she would hiss. Sam's father would reply with a deep sigh, ice clinking in a glass as he swirled his drink.

Sam could never actually see his parents as he listened to their midnight arguments, as he was securely tucked in his bedroom doorway down the hall, but he could easily picture them in his mind, his father reclining in the soft leather desk chair, his long legs maybe propped up on one of the drawers, his drink nestled against his chest. Mom would be standing, hands on hips, squared off against him.

It was nights like those when Sam heard his mother crying alone in their bedroom, his father staying in his office until the early hours of the morning. Sam would listen intently from his room, huddled in a blanket near the doorway, praying his father would not peek in as he walked downstairs to sleep on the couch and fearing he would get in trouble for not being asleep yet. Sometimes, though, he wished his father *would* find him alone and trembling on the floor and answer the questions racing through his young mind. *Why are you fighting? Is it about me? I promise I'll be good! Why can't you come home more? Can we play catch tomorrow? Or do you have to spend the whole day on the phone again? Are you mad I failed my math test?*

His thoughts spun out of control the more his parents fought, for Sam was certain they fought because of him—the tests he failed, the curfews he missed, the chores he forgot to do. But he didn't know how to correct those shortcomings. He didn't know how to be smarter, how to be more responsible, or how to pay better attention in class. He was at a complete loss.

Just once he wanted his father to wrap him in a big hug and say that he loved him and was proud of him. But that never happened.

Sam wiped away his tears and looked far into the Rad Zone, pushing the thoughts of his parents away. *Okay, enough of this garbage, back to this moat thing. ... Stop being a baby,* he scolded himself.

With that final thought, he grabbed the handlebars, drew both feet onto the pedals, and burst away from the woods. The ground was hard there, the gravel packed down from the construction vehicles rolling back and forth while building the moat. The solid ground allowed for a fast takeoff, and the makeshift ramp came up sooner than he anticipated.

He had no time to think, no time to back out or change his mind. The front tire of the bike careened up the wooden plank. This was it! He was doing this!

As the bike sailed up the narrow ramp, Sam leaned forward over the handlebars, high on adrenaline, all thoughts of his parents and of stupid Scott and his even stupider accusations wiped from his mind. He only had one thing left to do, and that was to jump that moat. Then he would be the most popular kid in school, and everyone would know he wasn't a wimp or a spoiled rich kid or whatever.

He was airborne, literally flying weightless, for a few seconds. From that perspective high in the air, the bottom of the moat resembled a tiny river with trees of rotted reeds dotting its banks, a miniature village in the middle of nowhere. There were clumps of decayed and slimy leaves bunched up in some areas, while other areas contained pools of clear undisturbed water.

The water flashed by quickly, though, and he realized he should be looking ahead, lining the bike up with the far bank, not getting mesmerized by the water. Fear jolted through him as he began to drop.

With a wave of relief, he saw that the front tire would land on the far bank with a few inches to spare. He had done it. He had jumped the eight-foot-wide moat into the dreaded Radiation Zone.

But what Sam didn't know, couldn't possibly have known, was that the ground on the far bank of the Rad Zone had been essentially untouched for hundreds of years. Before the nuclear explosion, that particular spot of earth had not been built upon, and no vehicles had ever needed to go onto the far side of the moat during its construction. The silt was soft and loose, undisturbed, with no tree roots to build a strong foundation underground, and no rocks or gravel to make a sturdy landing strip on top.

The front tire of the bike hit the ground hard, sinking four inches into the damp earth. It held fast. Sam catapulted over the handlebars, wheeling toward the earth like a kite caught in a downdraft. Acting on instinct, he held onto the handlebars as long as he could, bringing the bike around in a semicircle as his legs hurtled over his head. His body twisted as a jolt of terror shot down his spine.

Well, I'm gonna die, he thought rather confidently as the brown and green of the earth and trees whirled into one blended color. *And this is really gonna seriously hurt.*

He ended up being half right. He did not die, but it really did seriously hurt. He landed sideways, both of his feet crashing into the ground almost simultaneously, the left leg hitting the dirt a fraction of a second before the right. His young, growing bones splintered upon impact.

If there had been observers there that day, they would have heard a blood-curdling scream that Sam was not real proud of as he lay broken and defeated on the bank of the Radiation Zone, facedown, both legs bent at unnatural angles, hands buried in the loose silt, writhing in pain. The edges of his vision blurred, and the afternoon seemed to suddenly fall away to dusk, the bright blues and pinks of the sky turning to deep purple.

Maybe I am dying, he thought resignedly, and it briefly crossed his mind that if his phone broke in the fall, he could be out there for weeks or months before someone found his body.

Only about ten seconds had passed since the front tire of the bike had halted itself, but it felt like an eternity. He unsuccessfully tried to move his broken legs, the effort only hurting more. He screamed for help, fully knowing that no one could hear him.

After two terrifying and interminable minutes of immobile panic, his breathing gradually returned to normal. He managed to push himself up on his elbows and sucked in great lungfuls of damp air, so thankful to be alive, promising from then on that he would be a good kid, always do his chores, study for all his tests, and kiss his mother good-bye every day when she dropped him off at school, even when his friends were watching.

After wriggling from side to side for a few seconds, he found that his hands still seemed to work completely normally, but he wasn't able to roll onto his back; the pain in his legs was too agonizing. It was best to lie still, taking deep breaths and trying not to cry.

His right leg was splayed to his side, the tibia and fibula shattered. It looked so far away from where it rightfully should be that he briefly thought it couldn't possibly be his leg. Seriously, for a split-second he thought he'd landed on top of someone else's body, but it turned out he was the only idiot out there that day.

The blood gradually stopped rushing in his ears, and he no longer heard the thudding of his own heartbeat. After another minute, he became aware of two birds calling back and forth to each other. It sounded like one bird was on the restricted side of the moat and the other bird was on the safe side. He wondered vaguely if the bird in the Rad Zone had an extra leg or two heads or whatever.

When Sam was a kid, there had always been stories about the damage done to the animals in the Radiation Zone. These stories had been around for as long as he could remember, passed down from the older kids at school. The most alarming story was the one about Jimmy Bryson, an eight-year-old boy, who had gotten lost the year before Sam jumped the moat. Jimmy's family was camping in the northern section of Cutter County, along the edge of the Rad Zone, where the land was covered in thick forests and hiking trails.

Jimmy was said to have left the family tent sometime overnight, maybe to go out to pee, or maybe because he had a penchant for sleepwalking. No one knew; no one could ask him. Jimmy had gone missing for three days. Search parties had scoured the area, on foot and in the air, and had finally found him in the muddy water of the moat on the third day, almost two miles from his campsite, conscious but not communicative.

Theories zoomed around about what had happened to Jimmy, ranging from the completely logical to the absolutely ludicrous. Some people thought he had been kidnapped, others thought he had been attacked by a roving band of feral dogs. But this speculation had never made sense to Sam. Kidnappers would have demanded a ransom and would not have just dumped him, and dogs would have done some serious damage, or even killed the kid. Jimmy had been found with only a few small scratches that looked to be from thorns or rocks, not teeth.

The most intriguing version (and Sam's favorite story of all time) was that Jimmy fell into the moat in the dark and accidentally climbed out the wrong side, stranding himself inside the Radiation Zone. There, he was found by a great wolf that had been trapped in the Rad Zone after the moat was built, exiling the unfortunate creature to live in toxic waste forever. Over the years, the radioactivity had changed the wolf into something ghostlike, a wraith that attacked its victims without leaving a single mark on the body, allowing them to go about their lives as if nothing had happened, as if they were still whole.

But something did happen to the wolf's victims. The wolf stole something from them, something that could not be swallowed or seen; something that did not even have a physical weight. The wraith-wolf stole its victims' voices, taking the one thing from them that sets humans apart from the animals. This story certainly explained why Jimmy never uttered a single word again after he was found.

The theory was that the ghost wolf still lived on, roaming wild in the Radiation Zone, using different sounds and calls it had stolen from animals or other unfortunate trespassers to lure its next victim into its territory.

While Sam was lying in the dirt with two broken legs, he thought, *Well, I guess the wolf won't have to travel too far to get its dinner tonight.* He shuddered at the image of a looming and hairy werewolf-type creature pulling his voice box out of his throat. Also, in Sam's mind, the creature had two heads, one that looked like Jimmy and the other, a white, shimmering wolf.

A wave of exhaustion settled over Sam as he lay in the damp soil. He wished he were in his bed, safe and whole, his body healthy and strong again. He had seriously screwed up.

He finally was able to slide his hand into the back pocket of his jeans, his fingers weak and partially numb, and was surprised and thankful that his phone had stayed put through his spectacular crash landing. Feeling as though he were moving through sludge, he pulled the phone out of his pocket but couldn't really feel it. Everything was going numb, starting at the back of his head, spreading like warm chocolate fudge drizzled on a sundae, moving down his arms and spine. *What is happening to me? Am I having a stroke? Can I move at all? Can I speak? Oh, no, has my voice been stolen already?* The dire thoughts whizzed through his head.

To this day, Sam doesn't remember pressing the CALL button, but he does remember mumbling to his mother about what he had done. He remembers the helicopter landing in the Rad Zone, and the silt swirling around his broken body. He doesn't remember being strapped into the chopper, nor does he recall the flight to the Cutter County hospital.

After the pain medication took effect, he passed out for a few hours. The next thing he vividly remembers is waking up in the hospital, six hours later, with both of his legs immobilized in casts.

CHAPTER 6

Jessie

A squirrel runs out of Jessie's range, alarmed and chattering, and now Jessie can't hear a thing. The forest is eerily devoid of life. A large boulder sits close to the trail, the sprawling green boughs of a hemlock tree splaying over the top. As quietly as she can, she creeps over to the rock and hides behind it, keeping low among the branches.

After a few seconds, a glossy black crow flies through the trees, coming from the same direction as the squirrel, cawing, "Intruder, not predator. Most likely not a threat." Jessie finds some comfort in the crow's words but knows that what isn't a threat to a crow could still very well be a threat to her. Mountain lions spring to mind.

She forces her breathing to slow and tries not thinking of kidnappers and mountain lions, though that is really all she can think about.

She listens intently, holding her breath. Still nothing. She slowly lets the stale air out of her lungs, and then she hears something. Footsteps, light and quick, and steady, measured breathing. Someone is coming toward her on the same little path she's using. She ducks farther behind the boulder, careful not to touch any of the hemlock branches. Some of the limbs extend out past the rock and hang over the trail. A moving branch in the absence of wind would be a dead giveaway of her position.

The footsteps get louder but are still soft overall. They do not sound like the steps of a full-grown person. Now the footsteps are right next to the boulder; they are right on top of her! Jessie squeezes her eyes shut and clenches her jaw just as tightly. She cowers behind the rock, her forehead nearly touching her knees. The footsteps grow fainter, receding farther down the trail.

Jessie peeks around the boulder and sees a familiar mop of pale-yellow hair and Sam's black T-shirt and blue jeans. He seems to be running easily, like he isn't in any great hurry. No one is chasing him. Jessie laughs in relief.

"Hey! Birdseed!" she calls to him, nearly choking on her words as she climbs out from behind the rock.

"Jessie!" Sam whirls around, his blue eyes huge when he spots her under the hemlock branches. He stumbles toward her, his legs weak with relief. "Oh, thank God, thank God, thank God," he whispers, taking her hand in both of his to help her out onto the trail. "Where is everyone else? Where did Hannah go? Are you alone?"

His eyes are worried and taking in every inch of her. He quickly pulls her against his firm chest, his chin resting on top of her head. She leans into him, a single silent tear leaking down her cheek.

Jessie is so relieved to find one of her friends. Maybe there is some hope now, a chance they will all find each other, one by one. She wants to stay hidden against Sam, with his arms wrapped protectively around her, and let this nightmare be over. Sam slowly rubs her back for a minute as she sobs, the terror of the past few hours overwhelming what little composure she had.

Taking a deep breath, she pulls away from him, his hands still wrapped around her shoulders. "I'm alone," Jessie replies shakily. "I've been walking for probably an hour ... maybe more. ... I don't really know. I haven't seen anyone else. I just woke up in the woods ... on a road, but I was too scared to stay on it. I felt too ... exposed, I guess." She scrubs her face with her hands, wiping the tears away. "A pickup truck went speeding by, but ... it didn't seem like a rescue party. More like they were trying to escape from something ..." It crosses her mind again that they are stuck in the Rad Zone, and their captors wanted to leave them for dead and get away as quickly as possible before they sprouted a third arm or something. "I ran into the woods and found this path and ... and ... I just followed it." She is glancing around as she rambles, her eyes not focusing on anything.

Sam nods and looks around too, surveying the path in both directions. "We have to go this way," he says confidently, gently sliding his hands down her arms and taking her left hand in his to turn her back in the direction he had been going. He is pointedly *not* looking at Jessie's face, and she has the suspicion it is for fear that he will start crying, too. His eyes are rimmed with red.

"I already came from that way. There's nothing down there. I've been walking for an hour, I think. At least." She wipes her eyes with her free hand. Sam is still holding her other hand, which is getting awkward, but she lets him have it for a few seconds, since they almost just died.

"Yeah, that's okay. ... I think you may have gone the wrong way," Sam says gently. "I don't know why ... I mean, I'm not certain, but I think we have to go that way." He hitches his thumb over his shoulder, indicating what he obviously thinks is the correct direction. "Hopefully, we'll find Alex and Hannah soon. Hannah was with me ... before ... but I must have passed out. She said something about you and Alex, but I really don't remember. I'm guessing he is somewhere around here, too. Come on." He begins his easy jog again and turns back to look at Jessie, who isn't following.

"But how do you know it's that way? I have a feeling we need to go this way," she points up the trail, jogging to catch up to him, her headache lingering with the fast movement.

Sam doesn't reply but jogs away from her again, clearly agitated.

"Hey! Leucocephalus!" Jessie tries his favorite nickname when he doesn't answer her. "Don't you dare tell me you've been here before!"

Jessie will be furious if she finds out Sam has made a habit of exploring the Rad Zone. How else could he have this unexplainable feeling of which way is correct? And if Sam has been in here before, that means Alex has surely been in tow. Illegally trespassing in a radioactive wasteland. Great.

Sam still doesn't answer but does slow his pace.

"Sam," Jessie says softly, his name practically foreign to her. She cannot remember the last time she actually used his given name. But this situation is way too serious to use a silly nickname. She needs the truth. Right now. He is hiding something from her. He has to be.

Hearing his name finally makes Sam stop and turn around. He pushes his hair out of his right eye. "You've never used my name before. Are you mad at me or something?" His usual sly grin tugs at the corners of his lips. He takes a few steps backward, not wanting to stop, hoping Jessie will follow him.

"No, not mad ... but how do you know where we are? Have you been here before? Tell me the truth! And don't make up some ridiculous story. I know how much you love to lie." Jessie catches up to him, hands on her hips, demanding answers. It feels a little awkward, a little funny. They've been friends for years, and she never really gets *too* upset with him over anything. The last time she had to be this stern was when she caught him sneaking out his bedroom window while she was babysitting a few years ago.

Jessie really hopes Sam isn't tricking her. *He doesn't usually go to this level of pranking me. Could he really be that much of a jerk?* Her lips tremble as she holds back more tears.

"I don't know ... I mean, no, I haven't been here before. Not exactly. But I *feel* like I've been here before, you know? I feel like I've seen this trail in a dream or something, and I can feel how to get back to, like, a main road or something. But I don't know, like, *exactly* where we are. Does that make sense?"

"Nope," Jessie replies flatly and starts walking again, disappointed, but now going in the direction Sam wants. She brushes past him, and he falls into step behind her. What little hope she has is diminishing rapidly. *I'm pretty sure he has no more of a clue than I do, and he just doesn't want to admit it. Idiot! Why can't he be honest for once?*

"Hey, maybe that will be my Gift," Sam says excitedly. "Maybe my dreams will come true, or maybe I will be able to predict the future or something."

"Ooh … handy," Jessie replies sarcastically. She is getting scared again, and it is slightly comforting to fall back into her usual banter with Sam. After walking another minute, Jessie asks hesitantly, afraid of the answer, "Hey, do … do you think this is the Rad Zone?"

"Oh, no, definitely not," comes his confident reply from a few feet behind her.

"Are you absolutely sure about that? Or is that also just a *feeling?*" She involuntarily rolls her eyes. *I should have known better than to ask him a serious question.*

"No, I'm pretty sure," he says, grabbing a branch that Jessie hasn't bothered to hold back for him before it slashes his face. She is pretty annoyed with him now and really wants to go home. She can't shake the suspicion that he is behind this whole ridiculous thing.

"How can you be sure? How can you possibly have *any* idea?" Jessie demands, walking faster. She needs to escape from him … from his lies.

"Because … it just doesn't, you know … look right." Sam stops and surveys the area, his hands on his lean hips, turning from side to side and gazing intently into the thick forest on all sides. Jessie glances back but doesn't stop. "I mean, really," Sam continues, jogging to close the gap between them. She is stalking away at a brisk pace. "Have you ever seen trees this tall anywhere around Cutter County? No. And you know I've been to the border of the Radiation Zone. … Alex was there. … That's no secret. Now, you can't see across twenty-five miles of the Rad Zone, but I can tell you, from what I saw, there was nothing this … I don't know … *alive* out there. It was all low and scrubby, like marshland and things that had died and were now just starting to come back to life …" He trails off, thinking. Jessie notices he is careful not to admit he had first seen the dead expanse of the Rad Zone several years before he and Alex ventured back there together. She knows the truth. He is such a liar.

Jessie turns around and catches his eye, Sam giving her an almost imperceptible shake of his head. "No … no, I don't think we need to worry about radiation poisoning," he finishes confidently and falls into step behind her again, forgetting to watch for the branches she's going to let fly at his lying face.

Jessie continues in silence and decides not to point out that it would be fifty miles from any point on the border of the Rad Zone to see across to the opposite border, not twenty-five. Sam has never been very good at math, even after the countless hours she has spent helping him with it.

But now she worries they could be in the northern portion of the Rad Zone, furthest from Cutter County, in a place far removed from anything they have ever seen. Sam's confidence does nothing to quell her fears. Jessie is certain he is either in on some big prank or has absolutely no idea what is going on. There is no middle ground.

Jessie lets another branch slide through her hand and whip back at him and hears him mumble, "What the heck?"

Good. I don't want him enjoying any part of this. Maybe if he knows I am mad at him, he will 'fess up and we can get out of here.

Jessie doesn't respond to Sam's mutterings, but she quickly realizes she probably shouldn't take her terror out on him, especially if he really *isn't* playing a trick on her. *Maybe I should be nicer to him. We are in this together, after all.*

The sun is disappearing below the horizon, making the long shadows of the trees even more forbidding. Jessie's thoughts are reeling between fear for herself, fear for Alex, and wondering if Sam actually knows what he is doing. He seems to be fairly confident, and he hasn't given anything away yet about this being a prank, but he can throw lies around like it's his job. Jessie knows she can never *really* trust him.

"Jessie, turn right here," Sam says quietly. His voice is low and subdued, but it breaks Jessie out of her thoughts.

"There's nothing here," she replies flatly, peering through the dense hemlock branches trailing the ground.

"I know, but I think we need to make our own path for a while, try to find some shelter for the night. We can't keep going once it gets dark. Want me to lead?"

"Have at it, Bird Dog," Jessie stands aside, theatrically waving her hand as if introducing Sam onto a stage.

"That's better." He gently puts his hand on her arm as he squeezes past her through the trees. "You using my real name before made this whole situation much worse than it is. That was just weird." He tips his chin toward her as he passes but quickly looks forward, taking the lead through the dense trees. She recoils slightly, having the fleeting thought that he was going to try to kiss her. *What is he up to?*

She feels nervous around him now, like he isn't the same boy she has babysat and befriended all these years. He is different out here, less obnoxious, less cocky ... less like a kid and more like ... someone who is very capable of hurting her.

She tries pushing these suspicions out of her mind. She has never felt nervous around Sam before. *This is weird. Maybe I feel this way because I was kidnapped by a man and for the first time in my life, I realize I am completely helpless. Or is this kidnapping thing just the story Sam is telling me?*

"So, seriously, how bad do you think this is, exactly? I mean, we could die tonight from cold ... or dehydration. We don't know where we are. Alex and Hannah might be dead. Why are you taking this so lightly? Do you know something I don't? Please just tell me." Her voice is high and bordering on frantic. This is not good. She's older than Sam. If anything, *Jessie* should be the one taking charge, making a plan, figuring out where to go, what to do. But she can't think. She has *no idea* what to do.

She watches Sam's broad shoulders slump as he squeezes between the skinny trunks of two close maple trees. She wonders if maybe she struck a nerve.

Sam bows his head, carefully picking his way through a patch of large rocks. He stops and looks back, holding a long branch so it doesn't smack Jessie in the face. She feels a nanosecond of guilt as she remembers the branches she let fly in anger.

He sighs and admits in a tired voice, "No, I don't know anything. I don't know why we were kidnapped. ... I mean, if I had to guess, I would say there is a ransom out for us, being the kids of high government officials and all. But it doesn't make sense that we were let go. I mean, when our parents pay the ransom, how will they take us back? I don't remember what Hannah said. ... I was pretty out of it." He pauses and rubs his forehead, the remnants of the headache still hanging on tenaciously behind his eyes.

Sam continues, not looking at Jessie. "But I guess maybe we escaped? I don't know ... Hannah said something but then she was gone ... I'm sorry for being so ... I don't know. ... What do you call me all the time? Cavalier? I mean, inside, I'm *not* taking this lightly. Honestly, Jessie, when I was alone this afternoon, I started reliving some of the worst days of my life inside my head. I'm sorry it seems like I'm not taking this seriously, but trust me, I am. I feel like if I don't joke around with you a little bit ... I think ... I think I might lose my mind. And I would prefer not to let that happen. ... I don't want you to see that."

"Well, thank you for sparing me your mental breakdown," Jessie shoots back testily, somewhat taken aback by his speech, not really knowing what else to say. On one hand, she's glad he is being so open and honest. It is an interesting side of him. It makes him seem more mature; apparently, he is not just the mouthy show-off kid she has come to love like a brother over the years.

But on the other hand, Jessie has still been holding onto a glimmer of hope that Sam sort of knows how to get out of this mess, and now she fully realizes this is not the case. They will be in big trouble if they don't come up with some survival skills soon.

"I guess we should find someplace to camp for the night," Jessie says, speaking more gently. She feels kind of bad for getting short with him, especially since he just admitted how scared he is, something she knows is not typical of him. "It will probably get pretty cold. ... Maybe we should gather leaves to use as blankets."

"Yeah, yeah ... that's a good idea," Sam replies distractedly. He runs both hands through his hair and looks up at the quickly darkening sky. Jessie guesses he needs to not look at her for a minute. He seems to be on the verge of crying. He *is* just a kid, and Jessie can't blame him. She's been crying all day.

Sam clears his throat and says, "It looks like there is an uprooted tree over there with some branches over the top. Might provide some shelter for the night."

They slowly make their way around the trees and rocks, having to really take their time now that it's getting dark. It would be easy to twist an ankle or break a leg on this terrain. "Careful on these rocks here," Sam says, turning around and extending his hand to Jessie to help her through.

"Yeah, I can see them," she replies tersely. *What is he doing? Does he think I'm an idiot? I can see just as well as he can.* She doesn't take his hand.

The overturned tree is a thick oak with gnarled roots reaching toward the sky. When the tree fell, a large wall of dirt had come up with it, creating a dry burrow shrouded almost entirely by moss and branches. It is well covered on three sides, which will help keep them out of the elements. Jessie can't remember there being rain or snow in the night's forecast, at least not in Cutter County, but then she remembers that maybe they aren't in or even near Cutter County anymore.

"This looks like a pretty good spot." She kneels in the dirt, clearing the leaves and sticks away to sit down.

"Hey, keep those dry leaves and stuff. They'll be good for a fire," Sam says, also kneeling a few feet away and pushing more leaves and twigs into a pile.

"Yeah, okay," she scoffs at him. "And how are you going to make a fire?"

"You know, smash two rocks together or rub sticks together really fast to create friction. ... I pay attention in science class, contrary to popular belief." He gives her his slyest of smiles, and Jessie again has the feeling he is hiding something.

"Well, have fun with that." She sighs and turns away, fighting the urge to roll her eyes, though he probably wouldn't see her too well even if she did. She hears a vaguely familiar clicking noise.

"Or," Sam continues dramatically, "I could use this handy little lighter I happen to have right here in my pocket."

"Are you serious?" Jessie turns toward him, jaw dropping involuntarily, a flutter of hope dancing in her chest. "Why do you have a lighter?" She has never known anyone who carries a lighter. Leave it to Sam.

"I smoke occasionally," he replies casually, gathering larger twigs to feed the bright new flames. Her heart sinks at this news.

"Do you really." It isn't a question. Darn, she should have known. Of all the kids she knows, it *would* be Sam Starling who bends the rules and does something society frowns upon, just to be cool or whatever. Of course, Jessie knows there are worse things he could be doing than smoking as a teenager, but her worry isn't entirely about him. "Does Alex know?" she asks quietly, watching the flame grow brighter. "You know he idolizes you."

Sam sighs and crouches near the fire, gouging a circle in the dirt with a sharp rock to create a firebreak. Jessie has the fleeting thought of *Where did he learn all this?* as she watches him. His tanned face glows in the light as he leans back on his heels, tossing the rock slowly from hand to hand.

"I know he does," he admits softly. "And no, he doesn't know I smoke. No one knows. It isn't often. A pack lasts me weeks. Honest."

Jessie is pretty sure he isn't being honest. She suddenly feels like she doesn't know anything about him, as though he is a stranger she just met. Her heart races. She really doesn't know if she can trust him. At all.

"Well, whatever. It's your health and your life. But please don't let Alex know, and please don't ask him to try it."

"I swear."

"I do have to say, your fire-making skills are admirable." Jessie kneels across from him, pulling her jacket from around her waist and tugging it over her arms.

He gazes at her as she warms herself, then he leans back against a fallen log, his feet stretched toward the blaze.

"Thanks," he says simply. He has no sarcastic comment for her. That's unusual. Apparently, he will take the compliment and leave it at that.

They sit in silence, lost in their own thoughts. At one point, Sam gets up and gathers an armload of larger sticks and branches to feed the fire overnight. Jessie feels like a complete idiot for not thinking of gathering more fuel. Of course they will need to keep the fire going overnight! She quickly helps gather sticks, stacking them in a pile.

When they finish their task, they settle in the dirt again, staring at the flames. Finally, Jessie has to find out what Sam knows. "So, you think there's a ransom for us?" she asks quietly.

Sam doesn't answer right away and instead picks up a large stick, poking it at the small embers of the fire to rekindle the blaze. He shrugs. "Sure, why not? Our families have money. Seems like a good plan."

Jessie makes no reply. So, Sam doesn't know the big secret about politicians. She wonders why his parents have never told him, especially since Sam's father was one of the senators who spearheaded the Switch. Sam is certainly old enough to understand it. He is fifteen, practically sixteen. Her parents had told her about it last year when she was fifteen.

Jessie's parents had forbidden her to speak to anyone about the Switch and how politicians don't actually make a salary anymore; instead, the luxuries they enjoy are all on loan to ensure future "good behavior" from the country's leaders. Sometimes, it amuses her that the public hasn't seemed to catch on to the fact that something has changed with their elected officials. Do they just think the country suddenly stumbled upon a crop of morally upright politicians? Have they ever wondered why there has been such a marked decrease in scandals involving their community, state, and national leaders in the past few years?

But Jessie thinks it makes sense overall. The public is usually oblivious to the personal lives of politicians unless there is corruption. They don't really care what kind of car her father drives or where her family goes for vacation. The public has no idea that all of those trappings of wealth can be taken away in an instant. Politicians are on a leash that is completely invisible to the public eye.

Her butterflies flutter faster as her heart races. She doesn't know why she hadn't given the possibility of ransom money more serious thought earlier. Of *course* the kidnappers wouldn't know there is no money. They are probably regular citizens, kept in the dark about what really goes on in the government.

Jessie swallows her panic. Even if her family sells their few (but still fairly expensive) possessions, she doesn't think it would add up to the ransom-money level. But really, it doesn't matter. They are still stuck out here, whether their parents can scrape together a ransom or not—Sam and Jessie in this cold dark forest, and Alex and Hannah who knows where. Her anxiety is quickly replaced by a slight feeling of nausea as she thinks about Alex and Hannah. Are they even alive? Are they being tortured somewhere?

She tries to listen carefully, thinking she could hear a distant scream if she concentrates hard enough. She shivers. *I really need to think about something else ...*

She toys with the idea of telling Sam the truth about their families. How could it hurt out here? They might not make it out alive anyway. There is no one to reprimand her for blabbing about confidential government secrets. Sam is old enough now to understand. She assumes his parents haven't told him yet because he is too immature to handle learning about his family's lack of money, and he most certainly wouldn't be able to keep it a secret if he knew. The boy talks almost constantly.

She decides not to tell Sam about the Switch. Why burst the last bubble of hope he has? If he learns his parents aren't actually rich, he will also realize, like Jessie has, that they might never get out of here. Without getting ransom money, their captors for sure won't tell the families where their kids have been dumped. There will be no search parties out in these mysterious woods.

Sam peers past the fire, his legs stretched out, and puts one hand behind his head, the picture of relaxation. "Do you hear anything?" he asks Jessie, closing his eyes.

"No," she replies vaguely, still thinking about ransom money. Then she becomes more aware of what he just asked, and fear jolts down her spine. "Why? Do you?" She glances around her into the inky blackness stretching menacingly in every direction. Terrifying images flash through her mind, images of being hunted by men and mountain lions alike. She shudders and pulls her jacket closer, keenly aware that they really aren't protected at all by the fallen tree and sputtering fire.

"Nope." Sam shakes his head. "I thought there might be some animals around for you to, you know, commune with or whatever."

"Oh. No. Well, there are two owls nearby, but they aren't really saying anything important. Looking for mice. They see the fire but decided it isn't scary. They are keeping an eye on it, though."

"Mmm." Sam barely responds, staring unblinking at the fire. He picks up the stick again and swirls the end of it into the embers, catching new leaves on fire. Then he says glumly, "Your Gift is so cool."

"It has its moments." Jessie watches his face, the flickering fire dancing across his smooth skin. He seems sad, or maybe he is just tired and scared like she is. "Actually, I knew you were coming down the trail because of my Gift. Well, not *you* specifically, but I knew I had some company." She explains about the family of squirrels that had alerted her to Sam's presence. "I was terrified it was one of the kidnappers coming back to capture me again. I was so relieved to see you."

He glances up and gives her a quick and wicked smile, his teeth flashing in the orange light. "First time for everything, right?"

She laughs. It feels good to finally laugh, especially with Sam. It's as though they are having a picnic near the duck pond, something they have done a thousand times when they all fished together, staying out well past dark, only running home when the mosquitoes joined them for dinner, and barely making it inside before curfew.

Some of the tension drains from Jessie's neck and shoulders as she laughs, but the relief is short-lived. Sam casts his eyes down toward the fire, his familiar smile vanishing quickly from his handsome face. It's an unusual look for him. He rarely frowns.

"You okay?" Jessie asks tentatively.

"Alex is right." Sam sighs heavily and leans forward, pulling his feet up and resting his elbows on his knees. "What if he and I aren't Gifted? Or what if he gets his Gift and I never do?"

She fights the urge to tease him, but he seems so down that Jessie doesn't have the heart to do that to him. She tries to choose her words carefully. "It's okay. Lots of people don't get a Gift. It doesn't mean there is anything wrong with them."

"I know. It would just be so ... sad, I guess. Like, you couldn't ever live up to your full potential because you just ... can't."

Jessie doesn't reply right away. That's actually an unusually profound thought, coming from Sam. This is the first time she hears that Sam cares whether he becomes Gifted. He has always blown it off as no big deal—as though he is totally awesome the way he is.

"Well, give it some more time. You're not even sixteen yet." She gives him a reassuring smile and says, "What brought on this sudden change of attitude? Surely this near-death experience didn't change your perspective on life, did it, Sam Starling?" She can't help teasing him a little.

He leans back against the tree trunk again and doesn't reply. A mischievous smile dances on his lips, and he quickly covers his mouth. Jessie gets the impression he is laughing at her, though she doesn't really know why, and she whips a small pebble toward his feet. Sam reflexively pulls his feet away, his sudden movement causing him to fall over onto his side, into the dirt. He laughs, and a wave of welcome relief washes over her. This whole thing *must* be a joke.

"Oh, my God, Pigeon, what is wrong with you?" Jessie asks, standing up and taking a step away from the fire. She still doesn't totally trust him, especially not alone. What is he up to? She is acutely aware they have never been completely alone before. Someone else was always with them, acting as a buffer, either Alex or a parent, or even Sam's little sister, Violet. It has kept their relationship casual, or more accurately, professional, since she had been Sam's babysitter for so many years.

He sits up and slowly brushes the leaves and twigs off his shirt, shaking slightly with laughter. Jessie is suddenly very aware of how the curve of his biceps stretches the thin sleeves of his T-shirt as he brushes himself off. He could so easily hurt her ...

Her mind reels in an entirely new direction. His arms are kind of nice to look at. Definitely not scary. She shakes her head and looks away. *What is wrong with me? He's a kid! Why am I noticing how amazing his arms look? I've never paid attention to his arms before. ... I mean, those gorgeous eyes, yeah, but his arms? Okay, get a grip. ... Oh, no, what if he tries to sleep with me tonight? I knew all this was just some elaborate ploy he cooked up to get me alone! I have to get away from him!*

Terror again brews inside her, but this time the villain is right in front of her, not something faceless and soundless lurking among the trees, out of sight.

No, calm down, it's Sam. He's harmless, right? We're friends. He would never try to take advantage of me. Would he?

Jessie is not at all sure of anything. Her mind flashes back to his cigarette lighter. There seems to be so much—*so* much—she doesn't know about him.

She furtively takes a step away from him, moving around the fire, keeping her distance, the blazing circle between them. She tries to think of anything she can do to defend herself against him. *If he comes at me, I'll kick the sticks in the fire at him and make a run for it. Oh, my God, there is no way I can outrun him. I mean, the guy is huge. ... When did he get so tall and muscular? How did I not notice that?*

Her brain whirls, and all that whirling eventually settles in the pit of her stomach, a cascade of the worst butterflies in her life.

She crouches near the fire and reaches toward it, pretending to need warmth. Really, she doesn't want to clue him into her suspicions about him in case he *is* going to try to make a grab for her or something. *Maybe if I stay calm, he won't make any sudden movements.* Jessie has the jarring realization that she would use this same technique if a large carnivore hunted her, though she would know its thoughts. She has no clue about Sam's.

Sam runs both hands through his hair and chuckles, completely oblivious to Jessie's distress. "I just remembered the stupidest thing." He stretches his feet out again and leans back on his palms, gazing at her with his trademark devious smile. "I'm kind of curious to get your opinion on it, actually."

"Oh, God. What?" Jessie takes a tentative step toward the over-turned tree and kneels again.

"Okay, so do you remember when we were kids, like, I don't know ... maybe six or seven years ago now?" Sam begins conversationally, throwing in his usual "likes" and "I don't knows" as his way of thinking when telling a story. It is so classically Sam that Jessie immediately feels better about him. He has a way of sounding intelligent and cultured when it really counts, like at all those political dinners they've attended, but when he is telling a silly story, or reminiscing, he sounds like his usual goofy self. Like Sam.

He continues, "Yeah, it must have been about seven years ago, because it was before you and I really knew each other. But anyway, there was this kid, I don't know, I think his name was Jimmy Bryson, and—"

Jessie gasps and jumps up again, completely shocked. "Samuel Starling!" She barely chokes the words out, holding both hands up to her mouth in horror. "Why on *earth* would you bring that up *now*? Out here?"

"What is your *problem?*" Sam asks slowly, clearly also shocked but for a different reason, his smug look quickly changing to one of bewilderment. "It's just a stupid story."

"Sam, that poor kid. ... Don't you realize no one really knows what happened to him? He couldn't speak for, what? A year? And then he couldn't remember anything about it ... or was too scared to admit what happened. Don't you ever wonder what *actually* happened to him? I mean, like, is there something out there we don't know about? Something that did that to him?"

"Well, yeah, but it obviously wasn't some stupid ghost-wolf thing that steals voices!" Sam stands up and places larger branches on the fire. The flames lick greedily at the new fuel. He gives Jessie a quick glance, his brow furrowed.

"I know. That's not what bothers me about it ... but ..." Jessie's voice trails off, and she sighs, staring at the fire, not really knowing what to say. Finally, she sits down in the dirt, not looking at Sam. She is curious to see how this will play out. Is he really up to something? Or is he legitimately just telling ghost stories around a campfire? She really can't tell with him.

She sighs and continues. "It's just that we also don't know what happened to us. Today ... I mean, yeah, we can still talk and everything, but we're also a lot older than Jimmy was when he went missing. Maybe he was kidnapped, too, and whatever was done to him caused, like, PTSD or something. ... And also, why did you have to plant the idea in my head that there might be something out here? Something we don't even know about? I'm already terrified the kidnappers are going to come back for us. And I'm *really* worried there might be hungry mountain lions around. Thanks a lot! I'm not going to sleep at all tonight because of you and your big, fat mouth." She huffs, annoyed.

"Hey, I'm really sorry. I honestly thought it was kind of funny. I mean, just now. It wasn't funny when it, like, happened. ... Sorry, that came out wrong. It wasn't funny. I mean, it *isn't* funny, not even now," Sam stammers. Then he mutters in a quiet voice, almost to himself, "Maybe I should stop talking."

"Yeah, why don't you try that?" Jessie retorts, trying to sound upset. He seems so taken aback by her outburst that she actually does find it kind of funny. She's not *that* upset with him.

"Look, I used to think about that stupid ghost-wolf thing all the time when I was a kid and being out here made me remember it again. It's funny I remembered it all these years later, you know? I'm not gonna lie, I was terrified of that thing when I first heard the story years ago. It kept me within curfew for like, months. Then I realized I *wanted* to find it. I mean, seriously, how cool would that be? There are so many people out there looking for Bigfoot or aliens or whatever, and they come up with nothing. I want to find the talking ghost-wolf of the Rad Zone!" He places one last stick on the blaze and with an apologetic smile, sits back down in the dirt, hunching close to the fire, looking a bit chilly in only his T-shirt. "I honestly didn't mean any disrespect to Jimmy."

"Well, it was disrespectful," Jessie snaps, folding her arms across her chest. "You shouldn't laugh at people's disabilities like that. You're a spoiled rich kid who never had a tough day in your entire perfect life. And you're a bully, too."

Now it is Sam's turn to be shocked. Jessie has never spoken to him like that, and he can't tell if she is teasing or not.

"Jessie, I didn't mean … Are you serious? I honestly don't even know what to say right now."

She laughs and throws another pebble at his feet. "No! I'm just trying to get you back for scaring me. Trying to make you feel bad. Is it working?"

"Uh, yeah, a little. Yeah." He shakes his head, and Jessie gets the impression she rattled him. *Good. He needs to have absolutely no idea what is going on for once,* she can't help but think.

"So, anyway …" He glances up at her, eyebrows raised, and says conversationally, "What's new with you?"

She laughs. "You are so weird sometimes."

"Thanks." He shoots her his sly smile. "This whole situation is weird."

"Yeah …" Jessie agrees vaguely. After a minute, she quietly asks, "Do you want to know who I thought about today?"

Sam scoffs and says, "Um, I'm gonna take a wild guess and say definitely *not* Jimmy Bryson."

"Nope. Guess again."

"Me?" He raises his eyebrows, his voice comically high and hopeful.

Jessie rolls her eyes. "You are so pathetic."

"Okay. … Seriously, who?"

"No, I'm not going to tell you now; you'll laugh at me." She suddenly feels very self-conscious.

"I promise I won't," Sam says, no hint of sarcasm in his voice.

Jessie quickly concedes. "Okay. But definitely promise you won't laugh?" She has never told anyone how much she admires Christie Cutter. Most people idolize famous athletes and movie stars, not security guards who sacrificed themselves for coworkers. *Sam is going to make fun of me so bad for this …*

"I promise," Sam replies solemnly. "But just so you know, I have never once kept a promise in my entire life and actually revel in breaking them with reckless abandon. So, you know, fair warning."

Jessie sighs and shakes her head resignedly. "Christie Cutter." She braces herself for the heckling that is sure to come. To her infinite surprise, Sam remains silent for a few seconds. His mouth doesn't even twitch up in his almost ever-present smirk.

"Wow, Jessie …" He looks away and pushes some branches into the center of the fire. He definitely sounds disappointed.

"What?" Jessie spits out defensively.

"You really think we're in the Rad Zone, don't you?"

"Well, yeah … I mean, mostly earlier today … when I was alone. Now, I don't really know … I mean, really I think I was trying to channel some of Christie's bravery or something. Like, *What would she do in this situation?* You know what I mean? What's wrong with that?"

Sam continues playing with the branches in the fire, pushing them into a neat pile. "There's nothing wrong with that. Thinking of Christie just shows how mature you are."

"What? What do you mean?" Jessie asks uncertainly.

"Well, I don't know … I guess, like … you know, we were both in the same situation today … both stranded in the woods, alone … not knowing where we were." They lock eyes. "Not knowing where to go for help or whatever."

"Okay …"

"And you thought of an actual real-life hero and tried to view the situation from her eyes."

"Okay, so?"

"Jessie, I literally thought about a mythical ghost-wolf thing that haunts the Radiation Zone. Like a little kid or something." He drops the branch he is holding and hunches up, wrapping his arms around his drawn-up knees, looking somewhat defeated.

"Sam, come on ..." Jessie laughs but tries not to. He is not usually like this. He must be feeling pretty vulnerable out here, too. "Technically, you were thinking about Jimmy Bryson getting lost in the woods. The ghost-wolf thing is part of that story. A stupid part, mind you, but they go together." She gives him an encouraging smile.

"Mm-hmm ... okay. I guess I just feel like such a little kid compared to you," Sam admits in a quiet voice.

"Well, if it makes you feel any better, you definitely don't *look* like a little kid."

"Hey, are you calling me fat?" he teases, flashing his crooked grin.

"Well, I mean, yeah." She shrugs and smirks at him. "You *do* eat an awful lot of ice cream."

"Mmm ... I could go for some ice cream right now ... gallons and gallons of it." He leans his head back against the fallen log and stretches out again, looking more like his cool and relaxed regular self.

"Yeah. Me, too." Jessie tries not to think about how hungry and thirsty she is. She resumes the previous conversation. "But, seriously, back to Christie. I mean, could you do what she did?"

Sam has a surprisingly profound answer to her question. "How could I possibly know?"

"True ..." Jessie mutters. She realizes she is definitely *nothing* like Christie Cutter. She was a blubbering mess today. She suddenly feels ashamed of herself.

They fall silent, lulled into a trance by the crackling flames. Other than the popping of branches, the night is completely still. Not eerily silent, just peacefully quiet. Jessie is exhausted from the crazy events of the day, and soon her head begins to nod. "Wow, I cannot keep my eyes open," she says, stifling a yawn.

"So don't," Sam replies, his eyes closed. He is leaning back against the log, hands behind his head. Suddenly he leans closer to the fire and fidgets, running his hands up and down his bare arms, not looking too comfortable anymore. "Man, it's cold," he says. "We're going to have to feed this fire all night with these little branches. How come there's never a stack of firewood around when you need it?"

"Hey, I'm sorry, I'm really not all that cold. Here, do you want to wear my jacket for a while? It's kind of big on me. It might sort of fit you," Jessie says uncertainly, her eyes locking again on his thick shoulders and biceps as she walks over to him, unzipping her jacket. She kneels in front of him, sliding it off her arms.

"I have a better idea," he says softly. He slowly tugs the jacket out of her clenched hands and takes both of her hands in his to pull her gently onto the ground next to him, smoothly lying down right behind her. He spreads the jacket over them both and puts his arm around Jessie's shoulders, holding her close to his chest.

It all happened so fast, and Jessie is surprised to find herself lying on the ground, wrapped in Sam's arms. *Jeez, how many other girls has he pulled this move on? He has obviously practiced it.* A moment of panic rises in her throat. *This is it. This is what he has been planning.*

For a split-second, she worries he might take off her bra or pants. But he simply holds her, completely still, his right arm splayed on the ground as a pillow, his left arm held protectively around her ribs.

"What are you doing?" she asks, quickly squirming away and turning around to face him. She is surprised he lets her go so easily, but she really doesn't like having her back to him. She can't shake the feeling that he is up to something, though he has already passed up a bunch of opportunities to make a move.

His left hand is resting lightly on her ribs, still under her jacket, but otherwise he doesn't try to move any closer to her.

"Keeping us both warm. ... You know, surviving," he murmurs, his voice barely above a whisper. Their faces are only a few inches apart, and Jessie scoots her hips farther from him, toward the fire. Sam pulls his hand back. He doesn't make a move toward her but continues to look straight into her eyes. "Jessie ... please kiss me," he says softly.

"I-I don't think it's a good idea," she replies just as softly. "Sam, you know I love you. But it's more like … like you're my brother." She sits up to face him, legs crossed in front of her. He needs to know she won't ever fall in love with him. She has never thought of him in that way.

"Mmm, that's what I thought you would say," he says, closing his eyes briefly. He doesn't sound disappointed or upset, just makes the statement as if he is talking about the weather. He rolls onto his back and looks away from her, left hand under his head. He throws her jacket back to her. She takes it but doesn't put it on.

Sam sighs and closes his eyes. "When I was all alone today, running through the woods, I didn't know what to think. I had no idea where any of you were or if anyone was even still alive. But I thought about you, Jessie. … A lot. I knew I had to find you … to make sure you were safe. Thinking of you, thinking of finding you … I don't know … I felt like you kept me going. Like finding you was the last thing I ever needed to do …" His voice trails off, and he glances at her. "I want us to be more than just friends, you know? Can you, like, I don't know … maybe think about it?"

Jessie stares at him for a few seconds, a little shocked but also relieved. He is being so sweet and caring. Maybe she *doesn't* need to be afraid of him.

Finally, she says as gently as she can, "Sam, I have thought about it. I've known for a while you've had a crush on me … years, actually. But I'm sorry … I just … I don't feel that way about you."

He sighs heavily. "Okay. I guess I was … hoping … I don't know." He trails off uncertainly and looks back at her. "I'm sorry if I, um, scared you just now. I should have said something first."

Jessie shrugs. "That's okay. Talking first would have spoiled it." She gives him a tentative smile and throws her jacket to him. She crawls on her knees to where he is stretched out and lays on her side next to him. When he doesn't turn toward her, Jessie reaches across his chest to his left arm and pulls him until he, too, is on his side, lying face-to-face with her. She spreads the jacket over their arms. "I don't mean to give you mixed signals here or whatever, but I think I'm okay with this," she whispers.

Sam gives her a sweet but tired smile and wraps his arm over her shoulders, their noses nearly touching. He raises his head and gently kisses her forehead. She doesn't kiss him back but instead burrows her face into his chest.

"Can I ask you one question?" Jessie mumbles softly into the fabric of his T-shirt.

"Sure," Sam whispers.

"Do you smoke so you won't get fat?" She smiles as she teases him, feeling better about this strange situation—really, about this entire strange day. It is nice just being with Sam.

He makes no reply, but Jessie likes the way his low laugh rumbles in his chest against her face. He rests his chin on top of her head and curls his strong arm completely around her back, pulling her into him a tiny bit more. The sweet smell of dried sweat on his T-shirt reminds her immediately of long summer days. They have spent so many summers together. She wonders how much more time they have. *Will we ever make it out of here?*

CHAPTER 7

Hannah

Hannah wakes with a start and knows immediately she must have been knocked out for a while this time; the sun is much lower in the sky and there is a deeper chill in the air.

The man and truck are gone. Hannah is alone, on a gravel road, not sure if it's the same gravel road she was on earlier. The surroundings look the same, with tall trees on either side and otherwise no descriptive landmarks. It looks more or less like the same road, with a gradual slope downward into the trees. She remembers the truck going slightly up hill when they were all in the back of it, so she assumes she needs to go downhill to get out of here. *That makes sense, right? God, I can't think.*

Her hands are still bound in front of her, but she is able to move her legs and stand up, only slightly dizzy. She walks down the road, hoping she's going in the direction of her friends, but she's not sure. It all looks the same, but somehow different. Even if this is the right road, there is no way she will remember where she dumped Sam. She *might* be able to recognize Jessie's rock ... and will definitely recognize the brown building where she left Alex, but he also may be the farthest away. She doesn't know what to do.

She decides to stick to the road rather than trying to find an alternate but more protected path through the woods. The masked man shouldn't come back now, already having left her for dead once. She hopes. The road should be safe. She does wonder why he didn't kill her, though.

After walking a few minutes, Hannah feels well enough to try an easy jog. She soon spies a bend in the road, maybe the bend the truck had curved around when she and Sam had escaped together. It sort of looks like the same bend. And some of the rocks look familiar. Maybe she recognizes the spot where she ran into the woods with Sam. But she can't be sure. It's not like she was paying much attention to the trees and fallen branches as they scrambled away from the truck. She investigates quickly and calls for Sam, not really expecting an answer. There is none.

If this is indeed the spot where she left Sam, Hannah does some calculations in her head, trying to figure out how much ground she has to cover. But she can't quite remember how fast the truck was moving, how quickly she got her friends out ... everything is a blur.

Doing some math in her head calms her zinging nerves. It is a logical distraction, something that makes sense. Otherwise she can't coherently think about what is *actually* going on. *We have been kidnapped! And our parents can't pay and have no idea where we are. How am I going to get out of this? Maybe I shouldn't have gotten us out of the truck. Maybe I should have waited to see what would happen.*

Feelings of doubt shroud her, inhibiting all productive thought. She blindly runs; not a hard run, just an easy lope over the loose gravel, her body working almost involuntarily, her muscles feeling fresh and strong. This is good. This is what she is used to—physical activity with little or no pain—for a while.

A wave of relief washes over her as Jessie's rock comes into view. Hannah immediately recognizes it, a large triangular rock with lichen and moss growing up the sides, very near the road.

"Jessie!" Hannah calls as she gallops to the rock, only slightly winded. She frantically searches around it, peering into the dense trees stretching endlessly beyond.

No one is here. "Jessie!" She listens intently for almost a minute. Either she has gotten away, or the masked man has captured her again.

Realizing there is nothing more she can do, she takes off running toward Alex, more hopeful now that she knows she is definitely on the right track. But she can't help feeling worried. In a few minutes, she will either find one of her friends or have to face the fact that she is completely alone out here.

After about half a mile, the brown structure comes into view. Hannah feels relieved, though she doesn't know yet if Alex is there. It is so nice to see something *familiar.* An actual structure, a shelter for the night. She is getting pretty concerned about the possibility of having to sleep in the middle of the woods tonight. *No, thank you.*

Suddenly, a shrill scream pierces the still evening air. Her heart nearly leaps out of her chest, and she tumbles to the side of the road, taking cover in the shallow ditch, her bound hands throwing her off balance. Who screamed? Was that Alex? It sounds like someone is being tortured!

She huddles in the ditch for a few seconds, the night going completely silent again. Maybe it's some kind of animal. She desperately hopes it isn't a predator. Taking a deep breath, she resumes her sprint. She can barely discern the structure's outline in the darkness. From what she can tell, nothing is stirring around the building. She runs all the way around it, scanning the darkening woods on all sides, looking for Alex.

"Alex?" she calls, though not loudly. She really doesn't want to alert anyone else to her presence. What if she's not alone? *Is someone watching me? This is so creepy.*

Halting in front of the doors, she finds the men's room door slightly ajar, stuck on the gouged concrete in the entryway. She tugs on the door, only able to open it another inch or two, but the gap is wide enough for her to squeeze inside. The door scrapes along the rough concrete as she pulls it closed.

It is even darker inside, and it takes a few seconds for her eyes to adjust. There is a whitish mound of something in one corner, a big pile of toilet paper and paper towels. "Alex?" she calls again. She shrieks as a figure lurches out of the pile toward her. She jumps back, trying to squeeze out through the doorway.

"Hannah! Stop! It's me!" Alex sheds his blanket of paper, and they stumble toward each other, collapsing on the dusty tile floor, sobbing hysterically.

CHAPTER 8

Sam and Jessie

Twice during the night, Sam got up to rekindle the fire. That kind of sucked. As soon as the fire burns down, it gets pretty darn cold pretty darn fast. Jessie had stirred once, but Sam didn't think she fully woke up. That's good. She must be going crazy worrying about Alex. Sleep gives her some peace.

Sam is still wrapped around her and really, *really* doesn't want to get up. But the fire is dying down again. Sitting up, he tucks the jacket carefully around Jessie and surveys the dim outlines of the nearby trees. There is a faint dusting of snow on the ground. It has to be near freezing, if not below. Thank goodness Jessie had the good sense to bring her jacket. And thank goodness Sam had his lighter. He makes a mental note to thank Violet for always making him carry a lighter. He never knows when she might ask him for it, and it has just become a habit to always carry it.

Sam smiles as he thinks of his six-year-old sister. He really misses her. He wonders what his parents told her last night when he didn't come home. Is she wondering where he is? Or did they make up some story to keep her from worrying? His parents keep everything bad from Violet. She doesn't even know the truth about herself.

He stokes the fire and steps over to Jessie, kissing her on the head without waking her. He has to admit, this is practically a dream come true for him. Well, aside from being kidnapped. Sam and Jessie are completely alone for the first time in their lives. He always enjoys being with her, even when it is something stupid like Jessie helping him with homework.

He gazes at her, admiring the curve of those perfect pink lips and the way her dark hair gleams in the bright firelight, framing her face. Then he quickly stops staring because he doesn't want to be an absolute creep, though no one can see him out here.

Though he wants nothing more than to curl up with Jessie, he has work to do. It is light enough to see reasonably well through the trees. It is time to find water. He doubts he will find food. Sam only knows two edible plants, dandelions and some kind of mushroom he only knows by sight, but he isn't the kind of guy who is going to wander through the woods and "forage" or whatever. Seems like a lot of work for not a lot of calories. If he could have his way, he would have a constant supply of pizza and ice cream at the ready all the time. Foraging at this time of year is pretty pointless anyway. There is nothing much growing out here. Except maybe despair.

Sam picks his way slowly through the rocks and underbrush, glancing back twice to make sure Jessie is still back there, cozy and safe by the fire. He lost her once. He can't let it happen again.

He feels foolish for confessing his feelings to her last night, especially since she hadn't reciprocated, but what is that old saying? Desperate times call for desperate measures? Something like that. He doesn't know if this is a "desperate measure," but it certainly is a desperate time.

He hopes his sense of direction will kick in better today now that some of the fear and adrenaline has worn off. The feeling of vague familiarity is still with him, as though he has been here before, but things are really not much clearer than they were yesterday. He feels as though he visited these woods a long time ago, maybe when he wasn't yet fully aware, but his brain managed to suck up some information, holding onto it for when he would need it. Too bad he can't do that with algebra.

His footsteps meander to the path they had used yesterday. Out here on the trail, the ground is less covered by leaves and sticks, making it easier to find some clean patches of snow. He collects some snow off the ground and from the smooth trunks of fallen trees. It is only a light dusting of snow, and he has to be careful not to scrape up too much dirt. He knows not to drink mud. That would totally suck if they made it this far and then died of diarrhea or something equally embarrassing.

After fifteen minutes, Sam has collected about two cups of fairly clean snow on a wide piece of birch bark. But since he's wearing only jeans and a T-shirt, he can no longer feel his feet, arms, or fingers. He's thoroughly frozen. Every muscle is locked in place, and even moving his jaw is difficult. He stumbles back to the fire, shivering uncontrollably, his spine involuntarily curving forward, tightening his abdominal muscles into a painful knot.

Jessie is standing over the fire, adding more leaves and branches to the flames, the snow on the branches hissing as it evaporates. She attempts to gather snow on her jacket, but there isn't enough clean ground that deep in the woods to get a decent amount. Most of the snow has landed on the canopy of pine branches high above their heads.

She turns around when she hears Sam's footsteps.

"There you—" Relief turns to alarm when she sees him. "What is wrong with you?" she yells. Sam is nearly bent double and can barely cling to the birch bark, the pile of snow teetering on top. He stumbles the last few feet into their campsite and falls to his knees, pushing the birch bark toward Jessie.

"I w-w-went back to the tr-trail to f-f-find clean snow. I didn't realize how cold I was until I st-started coming back." He huddles near the fire, drinking in the warmth. Jessie grabs her jacket off the ground, quickly shakes out the bit of snow she had collected, and throws it over him.

"Oh, my God, you are ice," she says as her hand brushes his shoulders. "Why didn't you wear my jacket?" She pulls the hood over his head and rubs his back, which is working miracles on his frozen muscles. Before he admits he didn't have the heart to steal her jacket from her while she slept, she adds, "This isn't the brightest thing you've ever done."

"Noted," Sam replies, shivering and sliding his arms through the sleeves, which are two inches too short and more than a little tight in the shoulders. "Hey, drink that snow before it melts into the ground," he orders, wiggling his fingers at the fire. "I almost died for that! You can have all of it. I had some already."

Jessie does as she is told, looking grateful as the icy particles slide down her throat.

"Thanks, Robin. That was really good ... but now I'm really cold. You couldn't warm that up for me first? I'd like a vanilla latte," Jessie teases in a falsely haughty voice, kneeling next to him. He starts taking off her jacket to give it back to her.

"Here ..." he says, but she puts her hand on his arm to stop him.

"No, it's okay," she says gently. She pulls the sleeves of her light sweater down over her hands. "You can wear it for a while. I'm okay. You can just ... hold me again for a while." She glances at him, a small sheepish smile on her face.

Sam gives her a surprised and somewhat tentative smile and rearranges himself in the dirt, still shivering. He pulls Jessie onto his lap and wraps his arms around her. She reaches for his bare wrists and massages his icy skin, pulling his hands closer to the fire. His hands are still shaking, and he is sure she can feel the muscles in his torso shuddering periodically as she leans against him. That's manly. He takes a few deep breaths, letting the warmth from the fire and the warmth from Jessie dissolve into him.

"Do you want to move closer to the fire? I feel like I'm blocking the heat." Jessie shifts to get out of his lap. "You poor thing. You are absolutely freezing." She speaks to him as though he is a dying bird that had slammed itself into a window.

"No, don't move ... this is helping," he mumbles, holding her tight against his chest, his shivering dissipating. They sit together until the sun comes up fully, shards of light cutting through the hemlock boughs above them.

"How did you sleep?" Sam asks after a while, disappointed that she will probably want to get moving soon. After all, she doesn't love him, and this is getting a little intimate. But he's not ready to let her go quite yet. He tightens his arms around her, his hands clasped in front of her, and leans his forehead into her back. He hopes she doesn't mind. Maybe he can say he is still trying to get warm if she asks him to stop. To Sam's surprise, Jessie reaches her hands up and takes his, drawing his arms even tighter. She absently massages his wrists and hands again, keeping him warm where her jacket doesn't reach.

"Amazingly well. You?"

"Ditto," he mumbles, his face buried in her hair. "Can't we stay here and wait for someone to find us?" He really just wants to be alone with her, kidnapped or not.

"No, you lazy bum!" Jessie laughs. "No one knows we're here. We have to get moving."

"I know ... but this is like, I don't know ... nice. You know?"

"Wow, you really have a way with words," she teases. "Are you really the same kid who used the phrase 'witty repartee' as a ten-year-old?"

Sam laughs and leans back, loosening his hold. "Alex told you about that, huh? That's funny. ... That was the day we met, I think." He knows perfectly well what day it was. That day is cemented in his brain for all eternity.

"Yeah, he asked me later what it meant."

"Well, what can I say? Your presence utterly vanquishes my characteristic scintillating humor and debonair charm ... or, like, you know, whatever." They are falling back into their usual silly banter.

Sam sighs and rests his cheek on Jessie's back again, giving her shoulders a gentle and, he hopes, comforting squeeze.

"You're right, you know," Jessie says quietly, leaning back into Sam's chest. "This really is nice."

"I'm always right," he whispers in her ear. Jessie elbows him gently in the ribs.

They stare at the fire, mesmerized, lost in their own thoughts. Last night, and even now, Jessie realizes she likes Sam's touch, his strong arms around her. With Sam wrapped around her all night, it really hadn't been a bad night. Not a bad night at all. She wants to tell him how safe and warm she felt all night, but it is awkward telling him that. Especially since she had refused to kiss him. Why give Sam false hope that she might someday love him? All they need is to survive this ordeal, and then everything will go back to normal.

Jessie's anxiety mounts like a volcano ready to erupt. She focuses on Sam's steady breathing, willing herself to slow her own breathing to match his and hoping some of his confidence and calmness will steady her nerves. But they really need to get moving. She needs to find Alex.

She will give Sam a few more minutes to warm up near the fire. He is being so sweet and so ... mature ... about all of this, like he grew up overnight. *I'll give him another minute ... but I can't stop thinking about Alex.*

Jessie reaches toward the flickering fire and pushes more branches into it. The blaze catches again, giving them an excuse to sit awhile longer, waiting for the fire to burn down. Neither wants to say they really should move on, but finally Jessie can't take it anymore. Her brother is out there and needs her help.

She sighs and stands up, disentangling herself from Sam's viselike grasp. "Come on, Blue Jay, we really need to go."

"Fine." Sam sighs theatrically but bounds to his feet, brushing his hands off and shaking his legs out. "I was losing circulation in my feet anyway."

"Oh, no, we can't let that happen. We won't be able to tell if you get frostbite."

"Hey, why is frostbite so expensive?" Sam gives Jessie his typical mischievous grin.

"Oh, my God, are you seriously telling jokes right now? I don't know. ... Why?"

"Because it costs you an arm and a leg!" Sam claps his hands together and laughs, delighting in her eye-rolled response. "Come on, that's a good one!"

"No, just ... please stop talking." She feigns annoyance and picks up the birch bark tray. "This was a good idea. Let's collect more snow on the way out. Who knows when we'll find actual water?"

"Why, Jessica Cox," Sam says, pretending to be taken aback. "Are you actually complimenting one of my ideas? I'm flattered."

"Well, collecting snow to save our lives is still pretty dumb compared with trying to jump your bike across the moat to the Rad Zone," she replies sarcastically. His blue eyes narrow at her, the smile disappearing from his face.

"Hey, how did you know about that? I thought my parents kept that all hush-hush so I wouldn't have to go to boarding school or jail or whatever."

"Where else would you try to do a stupid bike stunt? And there were no witnesses, so it couldn't have been out in the neighborhood. Also, you were taken to the hospital in a helicopter."

"Excellent points," Sam concedes. "And just so you have all the facts, I didn't *try* to jump the moat. I *did* jump the moat. It was the landing that got me."

"Oh, well, I guess that makes it all okay. Good job."

"Thank you." Sam gives her sarcasm right back and flashes his row of perfect teeth.

She gazes at him and tries to find something about him that isn't gorgeous. Even after sleeping all night in the forest, he looks like a model. Jessie tears her eyes away. *Okay, I need to think about something else ...*

They slowly pick their way through the rocks, both of them longing for the deer path from yesterday. It was so much easier and faster than this. Sam has the vague impression that they should stay off the trail for a while, but he doesn't know why. Jessie gives him no argument about not keeping to the trail; she is too worried and exhausted to even think at this point.

But what if he's taking them in the wrong direction? What if Jessie was right yesterday and had been going in the correct direction all along, and then he screws things up by going in completely the opposite direction? She is way smarter than he is. He should have let her be the adult, and he should have followed along. What was he thinking?

He isn't too surprised that she figured out he jumped his bike into the Rad Zone. She's smart. He is pretty sure he could have gone to prison for that, minor or not, and he always guessed his parents paid people off to keep that from happening, but he doesn't have any solid proof.

Sam rubs his eyes as he remembers lying on the ground in the Rad Zone, almost positive he was going to die. Instead, he spent a week in the hospital, had two full leg casts for two months, and was grounded for a year. He got really good at playing computer games. Thank goodness his parents allowed him to play computer games, even while he was grounded. Otherwise he probably would have gone absolutely insane. Instead, he went partially insane.

He wasn't allowed to ride his bike, play school sports, or stay out after dark, even after he had completed physical therapy, for a whole year. He spent most of his time holed up in his room, alone, long after the casts came off. What a mess he had made of his life. His parents were so angry. They were only ever that angry at him one other time.

Sam turns his thoughts back to their current predicament but finds they are no more productive. He worries he seriously messed up and is taking them in completely the wrong direction.

He finally decides all these worries jamming his brain are from lack of food, and he tries pushing the doubtful thoughts out of his mind. He daydreams of his usual Sunday morning breakfast of waffles or French toast with his family, Violet and he whining to go watch TV instead of having to sit in the stately dining room, using the "good china." His mother insists they all have Sunday breakfast together as a family, no matter how lame Sam thinks it is. What he wouldn't give to be in the bright, warm mansion right now, safe and loved, sipping hot chocolate and dumping extra syrup on a hot, doughy breakfast. *Mmm, syrup.* His stomach clenches painfully.

The last time his stomach hurt this much was when he almost drank himself to death on his father's Scotch. *That* was the angriest Sam had ever seen his parents. It was a few summers ago, when he was thirteen, and he had been begging his parents to let him stay home alone without a sitter one night when they went out for dinner. Violet was sleeping over at a friend's house, and Jessie and Alex were away on a business trip with their parents. Of course, the whole situation would have been avoided if Jessie was available to stay with him; he *never* turned down a chance to see her.

His parents finally gave in, allowing him to stay home alone without any adult supervision. There were two conditions, however:

he was not allowed to invite friends over, and he had to answer his phone when his mother called, which she planned to do every hour on the hour.

"I am seriously not enjoying this stomachache," Sam complains to Jessie as they slowly make their way through the underbrush.

"Try not to think about it," she replies from a few feet behind him. She had also been thinking about how hungry she is.

"It still isn't the worst stomachache I've ever had, though. ... Have I ever told you about the time I almost died from drinking my father's Scotch?"

"No. And I don't think I want to hear about it now." Jessie rolls her eyes, but Sam doesn't see her. "You're such an idiot."

"I know."

They walk in silence for a while until Jessie, who needs to think about something other than hunger and maybe finding Alex dead in the woods, finally says, "Okay, actually, I kind of want to hear about the Scotch. I'm curious to see just *how* dumb you are."

"Oh, I'm like, *dumb* dumb," Sam replies confidently. "It's award-winning–quality stuff. ... My parents had gone out to dinner, and they finally let me stay home alone. I was super excited about it, but like, I don't know ... I got super bored, like, fast. At first, I entertained myself by playing computer games, but that only lasted about twenty minutes. Being home alone in a huge empty house was *way* more boring than I had anticipated. I don't understand how kids look forward to staying home alone. It's really lame, isn't it?"

Jessie makes a noncommittal reply, thinking about how she loves to stay home with a good book and Puffin curled in her lap. But Sam would never understand that.

"So, I scrolled through my phone for a while, but that got pretty monotonous. I eventually wandered into Dad's home office. I don't even know why I went in there. ... Anyway, there was a huge bottle of Scotch on his desk. I mean, I knew I shouldn't try it. That was a 'grown-up' drink or whatever." He makes air quotes with his hands. "I seriously stared at that bottle for, like, a whole minute, having an internal argument with myself. But, I mean, who was gonna know? I was only gonna taste it."

"Yeah, right," Jessie scoffs. "You know you have no self-control."

"Shut up, I'm trying to tell a story!" Sam teases, glancing back and flashing his devilish grin. "So, at first, I took this tiny little experimental sip, you know? I mean, it was like a quarter of a teaspoon. Man, it was horrible! Almost hurled right there. I didn't see how Dad could drink that stuff, to be honest. But after a few seconds, it wasn't so bad. It was like everything was going numb. It was *really* weird ... and interesting. Way more interesting than playing dumb computer games that I play all day anyway; you know what I mean?"

"No. But go on."

"So, I took another sip, and I don't know, it wasn't too bad. I ended up taking the whole bottle back to my room, completely forgetting my plan to only take one taste. I'm kinda dumb like that."

"Yes," Jessie agrees, deadpan.

"Okay, I deserve that one. Anyway, I answered my phone when Mom called, and I let her know that everything was fine. I was just playing computer games. Which are way more fun with a buzz, by the way. You should try it. By the second hour, though, I had almost finished the bottle. I totally couldn't answer my phone when Mom called to check on me. I could hear it ringing, like, really far away. It sounded like it was under water or something. Ugh ... so stupid ... I was lying sprawled out on my bed. Couldn't even sit up. Couldn't even really open my eyes. I remember groping blindly for the phone because I knew I was gonna get into *so* much trouble if I didn't answer, and then ended up dumping the rest of the bottle down my shirt. That's pretty much the last thing I remember before I passed out. My parents found me twenty minutes later when they got no answer from me. I was barely breathing. My parents were livid. They were all like, 'This is why you can't be left alone!'"

"That actually sounds pretty accurate. I thought you would embellish it a bit more."

"What do you mean?" Sam turns around to face her and furrows his brow.

"That lines up pretty well with what your mom told me," Jessie replies smugly.

"What?"

Jessie relishes catching Sam off guard. It rarely happens. "Seriously, think about it. After that happened, I still needed to babysit you. Your mom told me what you did. She told me to make extra sure you stayed away from your father's stash of alcohol. It was for your own safety."

"Oh, my God ..." Sam moans. "That is the most embarrassing thing ever."

"I can't say I was really surprised, to be honest."

"Glad I can live up to your very low expectations of me." Sam's teasing, but there is a note of disappointment in his voice.

"Well, it isn't difficult."

They fall silent for a few seconds, then Sam says defiantly, "Hang on! You said you didn't know I did that!"

"No," Jessie disagrees. "You asked if you ever told me about it, not whether I knew about it."

"Good God."

"Oh, come on. You love telling your stories. Besides, you wouldn't have brought it up if you didn't want me to know."

"I guess ..." Sam sighs. "I'm so hungry I don't know what I'm thinking."

They continue walking for almost an hour, Jessie becoming more anxious as she thinks about Alex alone in the woods. Or maybe dead in the woods. She is glad Sam is staying quiet. She might start crying if she has to keep up a conversation. Listening to his stupid story helped take her mind off her fears, but only for a few minutes.

They clamber over a large, fallen tree blocking their way. Without looking back at Jessie, Sam off-handedly says, "Think it made a sound?"

"Oh, brother," Jessie replies. Sam can tell by her tone that she is rolling her eyes. He doesn't even need to look at her. "That's the oldest joke in the book. Get some new material."

"Hmm, annoyed with me already, I see. Want me to 'leaf' you alone?" Sam silently congratulates himself. That was good.

"Wow, do you *work* at being annoying?" comes Jessie's quick reply. She sighs in exasperation, but Sam knows she's kidding.

"Oh, no, honey. This is all natural talent."

"Well, you could teach a class."

He glances back with a devious grin to see her staring right back at him, her big hazel eyes a little red, but not so red that it looks like she has been crying. Maybe on the verge of crying. And Sam doubts crying from laughter because he's so hilarious.

"You okay?" he asks, turning around, brow furrowing with worry.

"Yeah, awesome. Thanks for asking." Her words sound flippant and sarcastic, but her tone is flat, and Sam catches a slight waver in her voice.

"Jessie ..." He whispers her name, now feeling like kind of a jerk for joking around so much. *Man, I'm such an idiot. Her brother might be dead, and I'm making tree jokes!*

He gives her his best smile and reaches his hand out slowly to take hers, not entirely sure if he should. "We'll be okay. We'll get out of here. I promise." He pulls his hand back.

"You're such a liar," Jessie says, but she wears a faint smile on her lips.

Her perfect lips. Her perfect kissable lips. ... Jeez, focus, Sam.

"Well, that's true." He laughs softly and caresses her fingertips. He tucks her long hair behind her ear, something he has never done before, but something he immediately likes. He so badly wants to kiss her.

Jessie looks away from him but doesn't pull her hand out of his. He inches closer to her. She massages his hand the way she had done earlier near the fire, then suddenly glances down, mild alarm written on her face.

"Sweetie ...?" Jessie stops kneading his hands and inspects his palms.

"Mmm?" Sam doesn't want her to stop. He hovers over her, head bent above hers.

"What happened to your hands? They are all scraped and bruised. I didn't notice that earlier." Jessie's big sister/babysitter instincts are kicking in.

Aw, man, now she's all worried about me. She probably desperately wants a box of Band-Aids and some triple antibiotic ointment for me.

"Oh, it's nothing," Sam says casually. "Really, it's no big deal." He tries to take her hands in his again, but she immediately grabs his palms and turns them toward her for a more thorough inspection, their moment of tenderness clearly forgotten. "I fell on the gravel road with Hannah yesterday …" Sam concedes, quietly explaining what he remembers. Jessie is obviously not going to let this go. "Actually, I think she pushed me … I don't know. It's no big deal." He pulls his hands away, not wanting her to see his frailties.

"She pushed you?" Jessie asks uncertainly, trying to wrap her brain around this new information. She slowly follows him through the underbrush.

"Jessie, I don't know." Sam sighs, getting annoyed with her. This detail doesn't matter at all. "It was right when I was waking up, and I just don't remember much. I remember her being …" He stops speaking before he says the word "terrified." He doesn't want Jessie to have that image of her best friend in her head.

He picks his way around another fallen tree, trying to fabricate a story that might not make Jessie feel too scared and vulnerable. "Being, like, angry with me or something. She kept yelling at me to move and pushed me to the side of the road."

"Huh, okay," Jessie says, skeptical.

"Why?" Sam asks. *Really, who cares? It makes zero difference.*

"I don't know … do you think Hannah was, like, in on it?"

"What?" Sam turns to face Jessie, utterly shocked by her accusation against Hannah. "Jessie, no, she was telling me to run. Screaming at me to get away from the road, to hide."

"Okay …" Jessie's thoughts whirl.

"Jessie, how can you possibly think Hannah had anything to do with this?"

"Because …" she stammers, trying to formulate her crazy paranoid thoughts into something comprehensive for Sam. "Because how was Hannah completely awake while the rest of us were totally comatose? I mean, were you supposed to be asleep, and you accidentally woke up too soon? You are, like, way bigger than me and Alex … maybe they didn't give you enough sedatives? I never actually *saw* the kidnappers take Hannah. She yelled, but then I passed out … but maybe you woke up too soon, so Hannah had to resort to violence, then cover up her true plan as you became more aware of what was going on. So, she told you to keep running or whatever."

Sam looks confused. "When did Hannah 'resort to violence'?"

"She pushed you!" Jessie cries, exasperated. *How can he not see this?*

"Oh ... yeah ... Jessie, seriously. Hannah has nothing to do with this. She was as terrified as me." Sam says this last part quietly and furtively looks away.

"Why wasn't she sedated like us, though?" Jessie asks, barely above a whisper, as her suspicions against her best friend mount uncontrollably. Tears sting her eyes. She loves Hannah. *How could she do this to us?*

Sam heaves a deep sigh. "I don't think that's it. I've been wracking my brain since I woke up in the woods yesterday. Everything is such a blur, even now. I remember she said something ... something about blurry vision. I couldn't see well ... and she said ... she said something about it clearing in a minute ... yeah, I'm pretty sure she had been sedated, too. I think she had the same side effects; you know?"

"Well, if she was the one who sedated us, she would probably know the side effects, right? She does all that EMT stuff. Maybe she got her hands on some of those street drugs that knock people out almost immediately."

"But Jessie ... why?" Sam stops walking and looks at her. Jessie thinks he looks tired and maybe a little annoyed with her.

She has to admit that Sam has stumped her with his simple question.

"Because," she finally replies. "Because maybe you just can't trust anyone."

Sam has no idea what to say. *What is she thinking? Is she having a mental breakdown or something? She is literally accusing her best friend of being in on this kidnapping thing! How can I get her to feel better? Should I tell her a joke? Ah, no, don't be an idiot.*

She is not meeting his eyes, and Sam gets the feeling she is trying really hard not to cry. He slowly edges toward her, closing the two footsteps of distance between them very tentatively. It really hadn't even occurred to him that one of their friends could be one of the bad guys. Anything is *possible,* but really it doesn't make sense to him.

"Jessie ..." Sam reaches out to her again and gently touches the side of her arm, fully expecting her to pull away. Her face crumples as she looks at him. She is trying mightily to hold back the tears.

"I'm sorry," she whispers and lets Sam pull her close to his chest. He doesn't speak. He isn't sure how tightly to hold her and has no idea how to comfort her when she can't even trust a lifelong friendship.

Then finally, almost inaudibly, he whispers, "You can trust me." *Darn, that sounded kinda creepy.*

He starts to let her go, hoping she doesn't get all paranoid about *him* next. To Sam's surprise, she wraps her arms around him and squeezes him, her head pressed into his chest.

"I know," she whispers, wiping her eyes. "I'm sorry, I'm just so scared ... especially for Alex. I don't know what to think anymore. Oh, God, Sam. What if he is out here freezing to death? Or is already dead? No one will ever find his body ..." She steps away from him and wipes her eyes. "I've been thinking about him all morning, worried that we'll ... just come across him frozen to the ground or something. I'm still worried about an animal or something getting him ... I mean, we had a fire ... there's no way Alex could have ..." Jessie rambles. "How could he have possibly made it through the night? You were away from the fire for only a few minutes, and you could barely speak this morning. There is no possible way he could have survived the night, is there? Sam, we need to find him!" Jessie sobs, her shoulders shaking. "He must be freezing ... he only ... he only had a light ... a light jacket." She hiccups.

"Shh ... he's okay, Jessie, I promise." *Wow, I'm a terrible person. I've been daydreaming about kissing her, and her brother is probably dead. Sometimes I hate myself.*

Sam really wants to hug her again and hold her as tightly as he can to protect her. He has never seen Jessie this upset about any-thing before. And thinking Hannah was in on the kidnapping ... that's just nuts.

He wipes a tear off her cheek with his thumb as she raises her head, more tears falling from her long lashes. Her lips tremble, and she falls into him.

"Sam, there's no way he's alive out here ..." Jessie sobs. She wraps her hands around his waist and presses her head hard into his shoul-der, like she is trying to give herself a really slow concussion and may-be forget about all of this.

"He's a smart kid, Jessie," Sam whispers, slowly running his hands up and down her back, hoping he is offering some comfort. "I'm sure he figured something out." But Sam knows that, intelligent or not, if Alex didn't find some place warm to hide for the night, he is most assuredly an icicle by now.

"Shut up. You don't know. Stop making promises you can't keep," Jessie whimpers. "And I still don't understand how you know where you're going ..." She abruptly pulls away from him and harshly wipes her eyes, ashamed that she is completely losing it in front of him.

"I don't," he says simply, but wishing he really could promise her that everything will be all right. "I told you yesterday, I have this strange feeling ... like, an instinct, you know? This just seems right to me." He tries taking her hand again, but she pushes him away, actually shoves both of her hands into his chest. *Whoa, who's resorting to physical violence now, hmm?*

She really only succeeds in pushing herself away from Sam, as he really hadn't moved at all, but still her intent is quite effective. He is about to ask her what he did wrong, because he's pretty thoroughly confused, when she lays into him.

"Of course it seems *right* to you! You're probably loving every minute of this! You probably planned all this, didn't you? Just to show off. Getting to come to my rescue, and leading me around, acting like you know what you're doing! And then you randomly have a *lighter* in your pocket? Where did that even come from? You probably planned all that so you could swoop in and save the day! And then you tell me scary stories around the fire ... and ... and ... and keep me warm all night like I'm a little kid who needs to be protected!"

Sam stares open-mouthed at Jessie for what feels like ten minutes. She has never *ever* yelled at him before. Not like this. And when she did get upset with him in the past, he definitely deserved it. Since he's usually doing something stupid.

Finally, he stammers, "Wow, Jessie ... that's not what I meant ... like, at all ... I mean, like ..." Then it dawns on him. *Of course.* "Wait, is this your way of trying to make me feel bad or something? Like how when I mentioned Jimmy last night or whatever? Are you only pretending to be scared or paranoid or whatever?" He folds his arms over his chest, feeling pretty accomplished with his assessment of her. She's totally kidding around. That has to be it.

"Are you *freaking serious?*" Jessie explodes. "Oh, my God! How can you be such a child?"

"Hey, everyone has to be good at something!" Sam quips, desperately hoping his sarcasm will calm her down. This is getting kind of scary. A minute ago, they had been sharing a tender moment of hand-holding and hugging. What happened? How did things get so bad so fast? He had been trying to say and do all the right things. *What is her problem? Five minutes ago she was grabbing onto me like I was a long-lost best friend, and now she's, like, pissed at me. Girls.*

"You're impossible," Jessie mutters under her breath as she stalks past him. He leans away from her, slightly worried she might try to push him again. He knows she can't actually hurt him, but still, he doesn't want to invite more physical violence.

She marches away from Sam, who is not entirely upset to see her from this angle. He follows her, a small smile playing on his lips. He is slightly mesmerized (okay, more than slightly) as her wavy dark hair bounces down her back, catching the rays of the morning sun. He can't ever get mad at her, no matter how angry she gets with him. It simply isn't possible.

CHAPTER 9

Jessie

The sun is taking the chill out of the morning air, and Jessie feels a tiny glimmer of hope once again. She knows she is being kind of ridiculous about Hannah. But she really doesn't know what to think, she's so scared. She is grasping at straws—crazy, paranoid straws—trying to figure out what is going on.

She also knows she was wrong to take out her fear and frustration on Sam, and that she shouldn't have fallen into such despair. But she can't help it. Thinking about Alex and Hannah and the danger they are all in is too much to handle right now.

They trudge on in silence, Jessie lost in thoughts of her brother when Sam pipes up from quite a few feet behind. "Jessie, please turn right there. And before you ask, 'Why?' I am going to honestly tell you I don't know. It is literally a feeling I've had for the past couple of minutes, and I can't shake it." Sam stops and looks off into the forest, his eyes distant, like he is trying to see for miles. Jessie hears him mutter under his breath, "This is too weird."

She doesn't utter a word; she doesn't have the energy to ask him what specifically is "too weird," but promptly makes a ninety-degree right turn and marches off again, not following anything that resembles a path.

A minute later, a sizzle of shock races down her spine, and she stops short. Ahead, a brown, rectangular shape is visible through the trees. Some kind of structure? Or is her mind playing tricks on her?

"Hey," Sam says, his interest also piqued. He sees it, too!

Elation courses through her, and she forgets she is supposed to be worried about Alex and mad at Sam.

"What's over there? A house?" Jessie's voice is tinged with excitement.

"I don't think so ... too small." Sam shoots her down pretty fast.

They rush over to the squat building, a new spring in their steps, to find an abandoned restroom—the kind you find in parks and picnic areas. It is a brown, cinder-block structure with two doors, one for men and one for women, the metal signs barely visible, situated next to a gravel road. They wander up to the doors.

"Oh, goody," Sam says. "Now I don't have to hear a girl complain about peeing in the woods." He smiles at her, trying to lighten the mood with his dumb humor.

Jessie rolls her eyes and shakes her head at him.

"I'll see if there is anything useful inside." Sam pulls the door open only a few inches before it halts, and he can't quite fit his muscular frame through the narrow opening. He tugs on the rusted metal door, trying to force it open another inch or two. Then he tries to wriggle into the opening to push the door from inside with his full weight behind it, but he almost immediately gets stuck.

"Um, maybe you should go on a diet," Jessie quips, amused, watching him wrestle the old rusty door. It is so easy to fall back into their usual silly banter, like nothing is wrong, like their lives aren't at stake right now ... and like she hadn't just shown him a side of herself she didn't even know existed. He really didn't deserve her anger. She knows without a doubt she would be a huddled ball of tears and snot by now if Sam hadn't found her. Everything she said earlier about Alex dying overnight could have been said about herself.

"Oh, man, I was thinking the same thing! Too much of Paul's ice cream, I guess. I really should've had a salad," Sam replies, smirking and running his hand down his flat stomach.

It takes some effort, but he eventually bullies the door enough to squeeze himself through. The door holds fast on the rough concrete and doesn't close. He tilts his head back out the doorway to peer at Jessie and says slyly, "No peeking," and disappears inside.

"What an idiot," Jessie mutters under her breath, but she feels herself smiling. She tries the women's room door, but it won't open at all. It is rusted shut.

Suddenly, Jessie hears a familiar voice scream her name from a few hundred feet away. She whirls around.

"Alex!" Jessie shrieks, spying her brother and Hannah crashing through the trees toward the restroom. "Sam, get out here!"

Jessie sobs at the sight of Alex, who also has tears streaming down his cheeks. The siblings hug each other. Hannah comes in for a hug as well, and Jessie throws one arm around her best friend.

"Alex! Hannah! Are you all right?" Jessie can barely speak through her tears.

"Yeah, we're fine. Cold, but I think otherwise good," Hannah replies.

Sam suddenly stumbles out of the doorway, alarmed by Jessie's scream, and nearly crashes into the group. "What's going on?" he sputters as his eyes adjust to the bright day and he regains his balance.

"Sam! They're here! We're all safe," Jessie cries. She wipes the tears from her eyes and Sam gives her a quick hug, then high-fives Alex.

"Dude!" Sam exclaims to Alex. "You made it! You are a tough little guy, aren't you?"

Alex quickly sobers and shakes his head. "No," he admits quietly. "Not really. I never would have made it without Hannah."

"Were you together this whole time? You weren't alone?" Jessie's mind reels, her previous suspicions about Hannah immediately forgotten. She feels a flood of gratitude toward Hannah now.

"We started out alone. But I knew Alex was here. I put him here," Hannah explains.

"What do you mean?" Jessie asks, uncertain again. Maybe Hannah *was* in on the plan. Jessie stares at Hannah for a moment before she realizes that Hannah's hands are bound together at her wrists by a thick rope.

CHAPTER 10

When Hannah finishes the tale of how she had orchestrated their escape, Jessie and Sam stare at her, mouths hanging open in disbelief.

After a moment, Sam recovers his ability to speak. "Hannah, you are amazing. ... That sounds terrifying. I barely remember you with me. ... Man, I wish I could have woken up sooner to help you." He shakes his head in wonder, then asks, "Why didn't you two just run like escaped convicts down the road this morning? This isn't exactly a vacation resort."

"We barely slept overnight in the restroom. We were so cold and scared," Hannah admits. "We finally fell asleep when it started getting light. I have no idea how long we slept. Do you have any idea what time it is?"

"If that's a test question, I'm gonna say 10:17 a.m.," Sam replies.

Hannah rolls her eyes. "Can't you ever be serious?"

"Actually, Hannah, I was going to say it's probably around ten o'clock," Jessie says, pushing Sam's elbow to try to get him to be serious. She knows he is just happy they are all safe, though.

Hannah continues, "Well, we were just out looking for water when we saw you two. We were planning to leave soon. There's a creek just through the trees over there," Hannah raises her bound wrists to point to the stream she and Alex had discovered.

"Oh, darn, where are my manners?" Sam says. "Hold out your hands." He fishes his lighter out of his pocket, then sifts a thin piece of bark from the leaves on the ground. "Here, slide this between the rope and your wrist. I'm sure I'll never hear the end of it if I burn you." Sam smirks at Hannah, who does as she is told.

"Hey, thanks," Hannah says, surprised that Sam carries a lighter. "The knot's too tight for Alex to untie."

Jessie observes Sam as he carefully burns the thick rope. Her mind wanders to the previous night when she was impressed with the fire he made. "That's actually kind of brilliant. How do you know stuff like this?"

"Um, I really like playing with fire," Sam replies seriously.

"I have never seen you play with fire," Alex inserts, laughing. "Why do you even have a lighter?"

"Actually, it's for arts and crafts," Sam replies instantly with his usual smirk. He glances quickly over at Jessie, who gives him a small smile and nods her head slightly, as if giving him a silent "well done" or something. Hannah is about to ask what is going on with that but then realizes she really doesn't care. They need to get out of here.

The ropes fall away from her hands, and she rubs her palms together, flexing her wrists. "Thanks, Boy Scout," she says to Sam. "You're more useful than I thought. Come on, we'll take you to the creek and then we can get out of here."

They walk back toward the creek, Hannah and Alex picking up the paper cups they had dropped in their excitement upon seeing Jessie by the restroom.

"Luckily there were cups in the restroom, but that was about it," Hannah says.

"Well, we can be eternally thankful for that. God forbid we scoop water with our hands!" Sam teases.

"Please shut up for a second!" Hannah playfully scolds Sam. "The adults are trying to figure things out!" Though, truth be told, she actually missed his silliness overnight when things were particularly cold and dark.

"Any idea how far it is to a main road?" Jessie asks. They all stoop at the creek's edge and fill the small paper cups with clear, freezing water.

"We drove on this road forever before I got up the courage to drop Alex here," Hannah admits. "It has to be seven or eight miles ... maybe more. It will take us half a day to walk out to the main road. And there is nothing down there that I could see from the truck bed."

They ponder this predicament in silence. Their earlier elation at finding one another is now completely deflated. They really are no better off than they were an hour ago, other than knowing they are all safe, alive, and unhurt. The thought of walking all day into who knows what is daunting to all of them. The four friends traipse back to the gravel road, not speaking, eyes downcast.

Jessie's feet already hurt from walking all morning and yesterday. She doesn't know if she has the strength to keep walking all day.

Suddenly Alex peers down the road, alarmed. "Guys, I hear something coming. ... It sounds like a truck I heard yesterday ..."

"Oh, no! That's him!" Hannah screams. "He's come back for us! Hide!"

They all hear it—the roar of a big engine and large tires crunching over gravel. They dive behind the shelter of the restroom, all knowing it really isn't a good hiding place. If someone is looking for them, the first place they would check would be in and around shelters and structures. But the woods here aren't as dense as what Sam and Jessie had walked through this morning. There are taller trees here, with fewer large rocks and less underbrush. There is nothing to give all four of them quick cover from the road.

Jessie's heart pounds in her ears as she presses her spine against the back wall of the restroom. She leans her head back and closes her eyes, trying to steady her breathing. Alex takes her left hand, his skin warm on hers. She opens her eyes and rolls her head toward him, ready to give her little brother a reassuring smile. But instead of finding Alex's hazel eyes, she meets Sam's blue ones. Her smile falters as she feels a stab of guilt for screaming at him earlier. But he doesn't appear to be holding any grudges. Jessie squeezes his hand and closes her eyes in terror as the truck engine calms to an idle hum on the road.

Jessie's heart thuds even faster as Sam pulls her arm gently toward him. His lips softly caress the back of her hand, and she wrenches her eyes open and looks at him. He is leaning straight-backed against the wall, feet wide apart, his own eyes closed. He is breathing slowly and steadily, her hand held tightly to his chest.

"Blaze, check inside," a man's gruff voice says from out on the road. Then heavy footsteps scrape through the gravel along the side of the restroom. Sam lets go of Jessie's hand and moves toward that corner of the building. Before she can stop him, he creeps to the edge and flattens himself against the wall.

A man appears around the corner. He is dressed in blue jeans and a thick work coat. A black ski mask is pulled over his face. Before the man can even see his prey cowering behind the wall, Sam punches him hard in the stomach. The man grunts and doubles forward but is quickly upright again. He is a big guy, even bigger than Sam, and Jessie doubts Sam stands much of a chance in hand-to-hand combat against him.

"You stupid punk!" the man screams as Sam aims a kick at his right knee. Sam's blow lands, and the man goes down on his backside. Hope surges through Jessie. Apparently, Sam has some pretty good fighting skills.

Jessie is about to push herself away from the wall to help, though she really doesn't know how she can possibly detain a grown man. Maybe throw a rock at his head? Before she can decide if this is a feasible idea, Hannah rushes in, holding the length of rope that had bound her hands.

"Sam, I have the rope! Can we tie him up?" Hannah dashes to Sam's side but then hesitates, also unsure how to restrain someone. Sam tries to grab the man's hands as the stranger lurches up from the ground.

"Yeah, great idea," Sam says, panting. "Can you get his other hand?"

"Oh, no you don't, sweetheart." The man's low voice sounds like shattering ice, gruff and cold, and if anything could sound "deadly," this is it. Jessie shies away from them, overcome with fear. How can Sam and Hannah have enough wits about them to formulate any kind of plan? This is insane. She has never felt so useless in her life.

Before Hannah and Sam can grab hold of the bigger man's hands, he is back on his feet and pointing a pistol straight at Hannah. Sam sees it and dives for the man's arm.

"*Run!*" Sam screams at his friends. "Get into the woods!"

Jessie sees the gun, then looks back along the wall for Alex. He isn't there.

"Alex!" Jessie shrieks. Where did he go? Has he already started running? She realizes that she never actually saw Alex come back behind the restroom with the rest of them. She had closed her eyes pretty quickly. And then she'd been so distracted by Sam ...

She glances back at Sam and Hannah. Sam now has the man's shooting arm in both of his (Jessie has no idea how he managed that), but the bigger man is too strong. The gun is still pointing at Hannah, who suddenly grabs Jessie's hand and pulls her around the side of the restroom, then across the loose gravel of the road, and into the woods. Before Jessie realizes what is happening, Hannah pushes her to the ground, forcing Jessie to take cover.

"We can't leave him!" Jessie sobs, trying to pull Hannah's hands off her shoulders. She needs to find Alex and get back to Sam. "We can't leave!"

"Shh! There's nothing we can do, Jessie. He'll kill us all. Our parents didn't make the ransom. You know that. They are asking for $20 million. They could only get $7.8 million." Hannah's voice is cold and harsh, with a note of finality that stops Jessie's struggling. She stares at Hannah. Is this Hannah's way of giving up? Jessie knows she isn't a quitter, and out of everyone, it will most likely be Hannah who comes up with a solution to their predicament.

Suddenly, a single gunshot pierces the otherwise still air, and Sam lets out a howling scream that seems to last for a century. Jessie's world tips sideways as new terror strikes. Her vision blurs and she is instantly dizzy.

They peek between the trees and intently study the front of the restroom. Jessie's breathing is an uncontrolled stutter of wheezy gasps, sparks flashing in front of her eyes as she hyperventilates.

Sam is dead. He must be. And where is Alex?

Hannah keeps a strong arm on Jessie's shoulder, pushing her into the dirt, keeping her from doing something stupid, like bolting out into the open. Jessie knows they need to stay hidden. It will do them no good if they are all shot, one by one. Hannah's breathing is slow and steady, her eyes unblinking.

A lanky figure leaps out of the doorway of the restroom, struggling to haul a large black duffel bag through the tight opening. He appears to be a teenager but is also wearing a ski mask, so it is difficult to tell his age. He looks bigger than Alex, but not much. "Stop!" he screams desperately, his voice high, as he runs around to the back of the restroom. "He had it! Alex had the rest!"

The big man suddenly appears at the front of the building, grabs the duffel bag from the boy and throws it in the back of the truck. They both hop into the cab and speed off in the direction they had come, spitting dirt and gravel into the trees. Jessie and Hannah duck to avoid the spray, then blindly tumble out onto the road, cross over it, and nearly crash into Alex as he springs out from the doorway.

"Oh, God, thank God, I had no idea—" Jessie stammers as she hugs her brother. "What happened? What did that kid mean when he said, 'Alex had the rest'?"

Alex turns his pale face toward her. He looks stunned, confused, his eyes wide. "I guess ... my Gift ... I always have exact change."

The duffel bag contained exactly $12.2 million—the balance of the ransom.

Alex and Jessie hug each other but know they can't linger. They must help their friend. They run behind the restroom and find Sam lying on the ground, curled almost completely into a ball, breathing heavily, with a pool of crimson blood widening out from the bullet wound in his upper right leg. Bile rises in the back of Jessie's throat. *That's a lot of blood.* She throws herself onto the ground at Sam's head. He rolls onto his back, gasping, and looks up at her, his eyes glazed and red. "Jessie," he whispers hoarsely. "Is everyone okay?"

New tears spring to her eyes. Sam is lying here, his life literally draining onto the dirt, and he is asking about his friends, making sure they are safe. She regrets even more how she had treated him this morning.

A harsh, ragged gasp suddenly escapes Sam's lips, and he propels his chest and shoulders off the ground, as if doing a sit-up, his bloodied hands reaching helplessly toward his injured leg. Then he collapses back into the dirt, exhausted.

"That hurt worse than the gunshot!" he says through gritted teeth. After a few seconds, he relaxes a bit, his breathing becoming steadier.

"Get over it. It's a tourniquet, and it's probably going to save your life," Hannah says as she finishes tying her jacket securely around Sam's injured leg. Jessie hadn't even noticed she was there. Thank goodness Hannah has been a volunteer EMT since last year—something to add to her college application. She had said she's "seen some stuff." Jessie wonders if she has ever seen anything as gruesome as this.

"Probably?" Sam huffs and groans, rolling from side to side, trying to find a more comfortable position to dissipate the pain.

"Well, you know, margin of error," Hannah stands up and puts her hand out to Sam. "Can you sit up?"

Sam stops moving and gives Hannah a defeated look. "I don't ... I can't ..." he whispers.

"Come on, Sam, you can do it," Hannah says encouragingly, extending both of her hands to take his.

Jessie watches, feeling completely useless and sickened by the huge amount of blood that had drained from Sam's leg. She has no idea how to help.

Sam extends his bloody hands for Hannah to pull him upright, his head lolling forward. She props him against the back wall of the restroom and shakes his shoulders. His head drops onto his chest.

"Stay with me, Sam," Hannah says in a wavering voice as she lifts his head by his chin. His eyes roll up. He gasps and manages to look at her. "It hurts. It's too tight ..."

Jessie watches in horror as Sam writhes in pain, fussing with the tourniquet. She has never seen him get hurt before. Even as a kid, he would wipe out on his skateboard almost daily, doing his stupid stunts, and every time he would laugh and leap up, completely unscathed. And now, years later, he is so big and strong ... and seems invincible.

His head drops to his chest. It occurs to Jessie that he might pass out, and she sits against the wall next to him, ready to cradle him if he falls to the side.

"Stop it," Hannah says sternly, batting his hands away from the tourniquet. "It's stopped the bleeding. Leave it."

"Jessie ...?" Sam whispers, unable to lift his head to look at her, slumping down the wall toward her shoulder.

Jessie doesn't know if he knows she's here, but she turns to him and gently eases his head and shoulders into her lap. He starts shaking, and she takes her jacket off to cover his bare arms. *Oh, my God, he really might die.* She cups one hand under his chin and uses the other to smooth back his hair, cradling his head in her lap.

"I'm here. ... I'm here," she whispers, not at all sure he can hear her.

CHAPTER 11

Hannah and Alex stand over Sam and Jessie. Hannah has her hands on her hips, light trails of blood staining her khakis. She surveys the two of them on the ground.

"Jessie," Hannah says briskly. "Alex and I can go back to the creek to get water for him. Just sit tight, okay? We'll be quick." Her voice wavers as she speaks. Even Hannah is losing her nerve. But Jessie is glad she is coming up with any kind of plan. She can't think … at all.

Hannah stares at Sam's leg. She's not sure if he has lost so much blood that he will need a transfusion. She has seen people in accidents who lost what was probably less blood than this and ended up needing a transfusion. Maybe this seems way worse because she knows Sam. Maybe it *isn't* as much blood as it looks like. *If the tourniquet holds, he should be okay, right? I think the bleeding stopped. … Wait, was there that much blood on my jacket before? Wow, it seems drenched.*

Hannah is glad she thought of something to do. She wishes she had a bag of medical supplies … all she can do now is get water. Walking to the creek will give her a few minutes to clear her head and try to come up with a way out of here. The only option, it seems, is going for help. Running as fast as possible down the road.

"Come on, Alex. Let's get the cups and go to the creek," Hannah says, trying desperately to keep the waver out of her voice.

Jessie absently nods at Hannah and gently strokes Sam's hair, her hand moving as though it belongs to someone else. She puts her other hand on his chest, feeling his body shudder under her fingertips even through the fleece lining of her jacket. Alex peels off his own jacket and places it over Sam.

"Thank you," Jessie murmurs to her brother. Silent tears stream down his face. Then he and Hannah disappear into the trees, each holding a few small paper cups.

Oh, God. How could I ever think Hannah was part of this whole mess? What's wrong with me? Of course Hannah's Gift was the reason she didn't stay asleep as long as we did. Without her Gift, who knows what would have happened? We could all have been shot by now.

Jessie thinks about how Hannah saved them. She must have been terrified, jumping in and out of that truck, knowing she could have been caught at any moment. She shudders. At least she got to speak to her mom on the phone. Their parents must be going absolutely insane.

Jessie cries silently over Sam, tears splashing softly into his hair. "I'm sorry, I'm sorry, I'm sorry," she whispers over and over to him, though she is certain he can't hear her.

After a minute he stirs and reaches up with his bloodied right hand, groping for hers.

"Are you there?" he mumbles. "I can't … feel anything …"

Jessie clasps his hand, and he relaxes, his trembling abating slightly. "I'm here, sweetie."

"Jessie," Sam whispers. "My leg hurts …"

"I know. It'll be okay soon … I promise." Tears stream down her cheeks, and she knows the only way Sam's pain will go away is if he dies.

"Were we just talking ... talking about ... ice cream or salad or something?"

"Yes, honey, that was a few minutes ago." Jessie strokes his hair, taking some comfort in knowing he can hold a conversation, though he clearly has no idea what happened to him. "Do you remember that we found Alex and Hannah? Everyone is okay."

"I don't ... want any ice cream. I'm too cold," Sam mumbles in a barely audible whisper, not replying to her question. Maybe he didn't hear her. Jessie desperately hopes he doesn't have brain damage or something from the blood loss.

"That's okay ... you can have hot chocolate instead, okay?"

Sam makes no reply. His breathing slows until Jessie no longer hears it. She watches his chest, searching for the rise and fall, but it is difficult to see with two jackets on top of him. Is he still breathing? She has never seen anyone die before. Is this it? This silence? This can't be all there is. How can someone like Sam, always so full of life and full of antics, just be ... still?

She cries harder and shakes his shoulder. "Sam," she pleads. "Come back to me. ... I need you with me."

"Mmm?" he moans, only briefly fluttering his eyes open. She breathes a sigh of relief, wishing he would fully open his eyes and maybe give her one of his devilish grins. She craves seeing those sparkling blue eyes, the color of the sky on a clear summer day.

"Sam? Can you hear me?" she whispers. He remains still, his face relaxed now in sleep, or maybe he passed out. She's not sure. "Sam, please don't leave me ... I can't get through this without you. Please wake up." Her tears fall faster as she leans over his face, her hands frantically pushing down on his shoulders and chest, trying to get him to open his eyes. He doesn't stir.

Her frantic hands eventually slow to a rhythmic caress, and she remembers how she had held his hands earlier this morning ... keeping him warm, then finding the scrapes on his palms. She had thought their predicament was bad then. That was nothing compared with this.

Jessie is getting cold without her jacket. It is cool in the shade of the wall, and a breeze has picked up. She buries her hands under the jackets stretched over Sam's chest, feeling the warmth of his skin through his shirt. *That's a good sign, right? He isn't freezing, and he hasn't lost so much blood that he can't regulate his temperature or whatever.* Jessie doesn't know if that makes sense medically, but she feels better knowing he is somewhat warm.

The tree branches stir above them, squeaking and rattling in the March breeze. Her thoughts drift back to the night and morning they had shared, wrapped up together by the fire. ... The fire! She can make a fire! Feeling a glimmer of hope, she says loudly, not bothering to whisper this time, "Sam, can you give me your lighter?"

He makes no reply. She hadn't expected one. Feeling a little embarrassed, she slowly slides her hands into the pockets of his blood-soaked jeans and gropes for the lighter. Now she's kind of glad he is asleep. This is awkward.

She stretches her fingers deep into his pockets, not wanting to disturb him. But quickly she wishes he would make some kind of sarcastic comment like, "Oh, sure, now you're ready, when I'm on my death-bed." That would help her know he'll be okay. Like if he could crack a joke, all would be right with the world. But he remains silent. It is so strange to see him completely still and quiet, without the corners of his mouth turned up in a carefree smirk. His smooth face is ghostly pale; all remnants of his vacation tan have disappeared.

Jessie finds the lighter and takes her time drawing her hand out of his pocket, letting her fingers linger on the ridges of his abdomen. *What is wrong with me? The kid is literally dying and I'm feeling him up.* His shirt had ridden up when he reached over for her hand, and Jessie hastily pulls it down, covering his exposed skin, tightening the jackets around his arms and chest.

She scrapes together a pile of leaves and twigs without disturbing him, making a firebreak in the dirt and flicking the lighter. The leaves easily catch the flame. She leans back and grabs some fallen branches, trying to be as quiet as possible as she breaks them into smaller pieces. But Sam doesn't stir. He breathes more easily, and Jessie is reassured by the gentle rise and fall of his chest. Tightening the jackets around him helped monitor his breathing better. And now they are too tight for her to get her hands under them, which is good. She doesn't want Alex and Hannah to find her caressing Sam's chest. Super awkward.

Sam's eyes flutter open, and he spots the fire next to him. "Hey," he drawls in a low voice. "Look at you, Girl Scout." He wiggles his shoulders from side to side, feeling like he is suddenly confined in a straitjacket.

Jessie laughs quietly, reassured that he doesn't seem to have suffered any brain damage. He is remembering the conversation from earlier. He tries to look up at her but can't tip his head back any further in her lap. She shifts to his side, keeping his head in her lap. "I thought you died," she whispers.

He narrows his eyes at her and scoffs, then grimaces in pain, tensing up and taking a deep, ragged breath.

"You can't get rid of me … that easily." He gasps, finding it difficult to speak in full sentences. "Besides, I've been hurt worse than this." Another breath. "At least this time it's only one leg … and I'm not alone."

Jessie has the urge to roll her eyes and say, "Oh, please. Sappy, much?" But she is so relieved he is still alive and sporting his usual arrogance that she thinks she will cry if she speaks. Now it is her turn to remain silent. She is having difficulty swallowing the lump in her throat.

Sam slowly and clumsily frees his right hand from the tight confines of the jackets, a motion that makes Jessie smile, as she has never seen Sam do anything clumsily before. Even when he wipes out on his bike or skateboard, he does it with a grace and agility that looks like he *meant* to fall. He reaches over to hold her hand again, caressing her fingers gently. *Oh, my God. He is comforting me! And he was just shot!* Tears fall down Jessie's cheeks as she gives him a watery smile, but his eyes are closed again, and he doesn't see it.

CHAPTER 12

Alex and Hannah walk back to Jessie and Sam, balancing the cups of water. Hannah sees smoke.

"Oh, wow! How did you make a fire?" she asks, shocked.

"Sam's lighter," Jessie replies, cradling Sam's head in her lap.

"Oh, yeah, I forgot about that." *Arts and crafts. Mm-hmm,* Hannah thinks skeptically. *He's such a liar.* It occurs to her that maybe she should think a little better of him, since he is probably going to die in the next few hours ... *Nah. He's still a jerk.* She kneels beside them and surveys the tourniquet on Sam's leg. Seems to be holding. Sam stirs, and Hannah says to him, "Sam, we have more water. Do you want to sit up?"

Sam slowly opens his eyes, and Jessie shakes his shoulder gently. "Come on, sweetie, you can do it," she says.

Sam groans as he shifts onto his side. He immediately tenses with pain as he moves his injured leg. Jessie keeps a close eye on him as he eventually gets himself into a seated position. She kneels next to his left shoulder, careful to avoid his bloodied right leg, and holds him up, her hand across his back. He glances over at her, his mouth turned down in pain, or concentration, or maybe both. He looks a little angry.

"Sorry, did I hurt you?" Jessie asks, quickly taking her hand off his back.

He scoffs. "Like to see you try. ... No, there's nothing you could do that would make me feel worse." He takes a cup of water from Alex and greedily drinks, leaning back on one palm.

"We'll go back for more," Alex says, collecting the empty cups. "And get some more sticks for the fire. Jeez, Sam, it's a good thing you carry a lighter. We could have used that last night. But I've never seen you do arts and crafts." He turns toward the trees and begins scooping up branches and leaves, making a pile near Jessie so she can feed the fire. Hannah realizes she's not the only one who doesn't believe Sam, but if he is trying to keep a smoking habit from Alex, that's a good thing. Alex needn't know about that.

"Well, what can I say? I'm a man of many talents," Sam says weakly but manages a wink at Jessie, who looks like she is ready to melt into him. *Oh, brother.* Hannah rolls her eyes at Sam's arrogance. *Even after getting shot, you are still an annoying little brat.*

Sam draws the two jackets closer around himself and shifts toward the fire with some difficulty. Jessie tries to help move him but doesn't have much success. He's pretty big. Hannah thinks back to how much she had struggled with him in the truck bed. ... *I should have left him in there. Things are so much worse now because of him. ... Okay, that's kind of mean.*

"I apparently need to start carrying a jacket wherever I go, though ..." Sam pauses to take a breath, finding it difficult to speak. "Do you want these jackets while you're out in the woods? I'm warm by the fire."

"No, that's okay. Maybe later. It's warm enough right now," Hannah replies, gathering branches. She thinks maybe he has some color back in his cheeks, but it is hard to tell. He had been deathly pale before she and Alex went to the creek. And he is sitting up by himself now, which

Hannah thinks is a step in the right direction. "Are you feeling better?" Hannah asks, dropping her branches on the pile.

"Oh, much." Sam smiles up at her. "Look at you being all concerned. ... I knew you loved me!"

"Wow, seriously?" Hannah's reply comes with an eyeroll. *Annoying little jerk!* Hannah scolds him silently but is secretly elated that Sam feels well enough to be his typical arrogant self. Maybe her tourniquet will get him through this after all.

Sam's reply is a quick shrug at her, another wink at Jessie, and a lopsided smile at Alex. But Hannah thinks his eyes look terrified.

Alex and Jessie spend a few minutes gathering more branches around their campsite, Sam jokingly finding some "excuses" not to help. "Sorry, I got a pebble in my shoe; can't walk," and "I got too close to the fire, and my feet melted off," to which Jessie replies, "Okay, that's actually more disgusting and horrific than getting shot. Please stop!"

Hannah is sitting on the ground, lacing her sneakers tightly. "I'm going to run down the road for help," she says, bounding up from the dirt.

Jessie stares at her, mouth partially open, and says quietly, "You most certainly are not."

"Why not?" Hannah retorts.

"Hannah, we are finally all back together! I can't let you leave! You don't even know how far it *is* to the main road ... and what if the main road is just as desolate as this?" Jessie waves her arms at the dense trees. "You don't know! What if you can't make it out before dark? You have no idea where you're going! Besides, aren't you supposed to stay in one place when you're lost?"

"That's when people are actually *looking* for you!" Hannah throws her hands up in frustration. "I doubt anyone knows we're here!" She takes a steadying breath and says quietly, "Jessie, it's not a big deal. I'll stick to the road ... I'll eventually come to *something*," Hannah takes a step toward the road, exasperated by her friend.

"How can you possibly know that? What if you get hurt, too?" Jessie demands, waving her hand at Sam. "What if that man comes back? You can't fight him alone!"

Hannah is fed up. "Look!" she almost screams at Jessie. "You're not the one who was awake and alone in that truck! You're not the one who came up with a plan to get us out of there! Would you have preferred to stay in that truck, Jessie? Do you think that would have been better? Did things not turn out exactly how you wanted?"

Jessie shakes her head. "No, Hannah ... that's not ... that's not what I'm saying ..." She is taken aback by Hannah's outburst. Hannah is usually calm and collected and never loses her temper. Of course, they have never been in a situation as dire as this. "I just feel like ..." Jessie stammers, not sure what else to say to convince Hannah to stay until morning, when there will be more hours of daylight for Hannah to run for help.

"I don't want to hear it, Jessie! Grow up and let me do this! Sam needs to get to a hospital, like, *now!*"

Tears stream down Jessie's face. "I know ... I know he does. ... But you'll be all alone ... what if—"

"I'll go with her," Alex says. He has been standing near the fire, slowly moving branches into the center of it, trying not to intrude on the girls' argument.

"Absolutely *not!* You will *not* be running through these woods in the dark." Jessie's voice becomes sterner as she turns to face her little brother. She dries her tears.

"Jessie, we have *hours* of daylight left," Alex insists. "It's probably only a little after noon."

"But you don't know how far it will be until you actually find help! You are *not* leaving!"

Hannah doesn't want Alex with her, either. He will only slow her down. With her Gift, she can go awhile without tiring. She knows it could be seven or eight miles to the main road. They were in that truck forever before she got up the courage to drop Alex here.

She has to admit there is some logic behind Jessie's fears. Who knows how many more miles she will have to go on the main road before finding someone who can help? Feelings of doubt creep in, puncturing holes in Hannah's confidence. She takes a tentative step toward the road, not sure she can really do this.

"Jessie, get a grip!" Alex yells at his sister. "We can do this! Hannah and I will go together. We will be okay. We *have* to get help!"

"Alex, you're just a kid! You cannot run that far before it gets dark!" Jessie cries.

"Jessie, please let me do this!" Alex is on the verge of tears himself. He doesn't think their captors will be back, now that the ransom has been paid, but his usual low-level anxiety is ramping up.

"Alex, shut up! Just *shut up,* okay?" Jessie shrieks at her brother, immobilizing him with her anger.

"Jessie, I have to do this!" Hannah screams back at her friend.

"Please don't leave me alone with Sam! What if he dies?" Jessie wails, shoulders shaking as she sobs.

Sam finally pipes up from his spot on the ground. "Jeez, come on, guys, stop!" He massages his eyes with his hands, trying to lessen his headache, which is worsening as he listens to his friends argue. "Can I make an executive decision as my last dying wish?" he tries to joke.

No one replies. Alex and Hannah turn away from Jessie, kicking the gravel in frustration, and Jessie buries her head in her hands, refusing to look at Hannah.

Sam takes this as his cue to continue. "I think I will be okay until tomorrow. I think if I was gonna bleed out ... I mean, it probably would have happened already, right?" He looks questioningly at Hannah, who shrugs at him, not sure how long it takes for someone to bleed out from a bullet wound.

Sam takes a breath. "I don't want anyone risking their life for me, okay? I mean, thank you, but ... Jessie's right. Once it gets dark ... I can't have you running through the woods, not knowing where you are."

"There's a *road.*" Hannah gestures impatiently toward the gravel track.

"Hannah ... please stay ... okay?" Sam sighs and sits up slowly to survey his friends. "I have a bad feeling ... about this road ..."

Jessie kneels beside him. "You've had a feeling about the trails and where to go since yesterday. I mean, you got us here," she gestures at the restroom building. "What do you mean you have a bad feeling?"

Sam furrows his brow, not sure what he is trying to say. "I don't know, exactly. I feel like ... this road ... it isn't safe or something."

"You just said we should have run away like escaped convicts! Now you're changing your mind?" Hannah glares at Sam.

"I just have a really bad feeling about it," Sam says quietly, trying to convince her. "I know I joke around a lot, but I'm serious about this, okay?"

Jessie exchanges a worried look with Hannah, who sighs and walks back to the fire. She stretches her hands over it, warming her fingers.

Sam glances up at her. "Hannah, I think you should wait until morning ... and go alone. Okay?" He gives Alex an apologetic look, hoping he hasn't offended him by making him sound useless.

Hannah and Alex nod, though they don't fully agree with Sam. Sam sighs and stretches out on the ground, hoping he really will be okay until morning.

CHAPTER 13

Alex and Jessie wander back to the creek in silence, tension hang-ing in the air between them. They fill their cups with water, also in silence, and deliver them back to Sam. Then they go back into the woods, collecting more branches for the fire. Alex doesn't say a word to Jessie the entire time, but he seems especially distraught.

"Wanna talk about it?" she asks Alex, getting ready to apologize for freaking out on him and Hannah.

Alex answers with his own question. "Did you recognize them?"

"Who? The ski-mask bandits?"

"Yeah," Alex replies, eyes cast downward.

"No, I didn't. ... But look, it really doesn't matter. Don't worry about them. They got the money, thanks to you! You definitely saved us all!" Jessie tries to find some way of encouraging him, but feels a false confidence as she speaks, as she isn't entirely sure their captors *won't* come back. Maybe with reinforcements next time. With more guns ...

Alex doesn't seem to hear her praise. He remains subdued and doesn't look at his sister. Then he mumbles, "That was Blaze Givins and his older brother, Scott."

Jessie drops the armful of branches she's carrying. "Are ... are you sure?" she stares at Alex, her mouth agape.

"Yeah. I heard Scott call him 'Blaze' when we were hiding, and I knew it had to be him, so I ran back out to the road to try to stop him ... but Blaze had already gone inside ... and Scott was already ... you know ... back there ..." Alex waves his hand in the direction of the restroom building and swallows hard, fighting the urge to cry. "And Blaze saw me and said, 'I'm sorry, Alex. Scott made me do it. He isn't in his right mind.' Then he saw the duffel bag in the corner and looked inside and ran out, yelling for Scott to stop. But it was ... it was too late."

"Oh, my God," Jessie stands still and puts her hands on her forehead, feeling like she will fall over if she takes even one step, not sure what to think. She is stunned. *Blaze?* He always seemed like a good kid, quiet and a little shy, like Alex. Not a careless daredevil like Sam. ... Scott, on the other hand ... Scott had a bad reputation, one he started developing years ago when the boys' father, Senator Givins, was killed by a car bomb. Jessie barely remembers the actual incident, but she vividly remembers the entire county mourning for practically an entire year. It was awful.

Mrs. Givins committed suicide a few months after her husband's death, leaving Scott and Blaze in the care of her elderly father, who died himself less than a year later. The boys bounced around for years from family member to family member. Blaze was quite young when it all happened, and he doesn't seem to remember much or be too traumatized by the ordeal. But Scott was old enough to understand why his father died. He knew it wasn't an accident. He knew it was a politically motivated assassination. And he knew his father wasn't the real target. And now he is out for revenge.

"Wow, Alex, I'm so sorry," is all Jessie can think of saying to her troubled brother.

They continue gathering firewood in silence and traipse slowly back to camp, both exhausted under the weight of their despair. The forest is darkening quickly, but their little home is somewhat cheery with the crackling fire and the last rays of sun sparkling in patches between the trees. They each sip a cup of water and sit around the fire, not speaking.

Sam is propped up against the wall, his injured leg stretched out. He looks maybe a bit better, a little more like himself. Jessie sits on his left side, ready to help him if needed.

"Okay, forgive me for being slow on the uptake …" Sam rubs his eyes. "I mean, it's been kind of a rough day … but … Alex, your Gift is … what, exactly? Always having money when you need it?" Sam inquires, looking at Alex, who is warming his hands over the flames.

"I think it's more like I always have exact change. I mean, that explains the money for Paul's ice cream and the duck food, too. I'm pretty sure I didn't have all those dollar bills in my pocket when we were there … I thought I had a twenty. And then I randomly have exactly $12,200,000 right when I need it? I mean, I didn't actually count it, but somehow, I know that's what was in that duffel bag."

"Yeah, Mom said she could get $7,800,000 … and they needed $20 million," Hannah stares wide-eyed and unblinking at the fire, clearly amazed by Alex's new Gift.

"Magic trick, indeed." Sam nods slowly.

Jessie remembers Sam's comment at Paul's Patio when Alex randomly pulled the exact money he needed out of his pocket. She hadn't thought much of it at the time.

"I just wonder where the money came from …" Alex muses quietly. "I mean, I *did* have money in my pocket when we went for ice cream …"

"What, you mean you *don't* carry millions of dollars around with you wherever you go?" Sam asks, putting a note of skepticism in his voice that almost sounds like he isn't joking. "Seems careless. You never know when you'll need to buy an aircraft carrier."

"Oh, my God, I would like to buy a small private island right now so I can get away from you!" Hannah teases Sam.

"Oh, sugar, if you get your own private island, I will *never* leave you alone!" Sam replies, sounding more like himself than he has in quite a while. Hannah rolls her eyes but laughs with him. Apparently, it took a few near-death experiences to make them bond. Jessie smiles.

Jessie looks over at Alex, who is not joining in with the corny banter. "Alex, honey, don't worry about where the money came from, okay? It doesn't matter. We are safe now, thanks to you."

"Yeah," Sam replies seriously. "Don't worry about it. You're awesome. Maybe don't look a gift horse in the mouth." He stares at the flames for a second, then his eyes widen as a shocked but triumphant expression crosses his face at the exact moment Hannah says, "Wow, really? That's lame."

"Okay, I did *not* mean to say that! Seriously, okay?" Sam sounds sincere, and Jessie believes him. It *was* kind of funny, and she chuckles softly. She leans into his side, letting him know at least *she* appreciates his fortuitous puns. He takes her hand and gives it a gentle squeeze.

Alex manages a smile and says to Sam, "I hope *your* Gift horse is that you can't make stupid puns anymore."

"He would literally never be able to speak," Hannah chimes in.

"That would be fine," Alex quips.

They all laugh, feeling some of the fear and tension drain away.

"Seriously, man, it was amazing," Sam says to Alex. "The ransom money could have come about a minute sooner, though." He gingerly pats Hannah's makeshift tourniquet around his thigh.

"Speaking of which, we should probably take that off to make sure you get some circulation to your foot," Hannah says. "Just for a few minutes." She moves over to him and gently tugs at her jacket. "Sorry ... this is gonna hurt."

"Yes, I'm aware." Sam sighs theatrically, then in a low voice, says, "Just do it." He grimaces as Hannah tugs the knot out of the jacket and eases it off his leg. The amount of blood that had accumulated on the material is unreal. Jessie can only watch for a few seconds before needing to look away, nauseated.

Sam holds his breath, lips pressed into a thin line, making a heroic effort to stay silent. Finally, he lets out a gasping groan that turns Jessie's stomach. She squeezes his hand tightly while Hannah shakes out her jacket and inspects his leg.

"Is there anything I can do?" Jessie asks uncertainly, still clasping Sam's hand. She wants to reassure him that everything will be okay and tell him he is being so incredibly brave through all of this. But she knows she can't say many words without vomiting.

She's also unsure if she can look at Sam's face without crying. She chances a quick glance up at him and immediately wishes she hadn't. Sam's face is red and taut, blue eyes tear-filled and blood-shot, lips trembling.

"Sam ..." Jessie whispers, tears springing to her eyes. She has no idea what to say. This is unbearable, seeing him like this, in so much pain, knowing she can't help him. *I should have let Hannah go! He needs help!*

Sam looks at Jessie, then quickly looks away, and she thinks maybe he seems angry, but she can't be sure. His expression had changed so quickly that maybe she imagined it.

"It's okay," Sam gasps. "I'm okay." He closes his eyes and takes a deep breath. He pulls his hand away from Jessie and splays both palms out to either side, bracing himself against the pain, his back pressed into the wall.

"Well, there's no fresh blood," Hannah says, surveying his jeans. She can't see the actual wound under the material, but she's guessing any fresh blood would have soaked through by now. Hannah reassures herself by saying, "That's good. ... Can you feel your foot?"

"What foot?" Sam jokes, but his voice is tight and strained.

"I'll take that as a yes."

"Yeah." Sam nods. Then he gasps and says, "It's good." He wiggles his right foot to show her and leans back against the wall, his entire upper body tense with pain, the muscles in his shoulders and arms bulging. Jessie looks away. She can't stand seeing him like this.

She is so glad Hannah is here, taking charge of the situation. There is no way Jessie would have known what to do by herself; no way she would have had the courage to remove the tourniquet. And she would *definitely* never be able to put it back on.

"Okay, we can leave the tourniquet off for a while, but if the wound starts bleeding again, I'll have to put it back on," Hannah says.

"Okay, thanks, Hannah," Sam says, stretching his leg and wincing. He eases himself down the wall, trying to find a more comfortable po-sition but not having much luck.

"Try not to move too much," Hannah instructs.

Sam glances up at her, his eyebrows raised, giving Hannah the most adorable and innocent look Jessie has ever seen from him. "Uh, yeah, not a problem."

"Well, I need to make sure you don't do anything stupid," Hannah replies, only partially teasing. "You're good at stupid, aren't you?" She gives him a small smile.

"I could teach a class," Sam says slyly, quoting the gibe Jessie had used on him earlier. A quick bark of sharp laughter escapes from Jessie.

Hannah looks at her, mildly disappointed. "He's not that funny."

"I'm just glad he's not dead!" Jessie replies, still smiling, but she knows Hannah has always been annoyed by Sam and is not entirely surprised that she still does not appreciate his humor, especially given their current circumstances.

"Well, whatever. I'm going to get more water, before it gets completely dark. Alex, do you want to help me?" Hannah picks up her cup.

"Yeah, sure," Alex jumps up and grabs the rest of the paper cups, glad he is given a job to do.

Jessie is finally alone again with Sam, and she chews her bottom lip, trying to work up the courage to apologize to him. After getting shot, it seems like kind of a small thing, her completely going insane on him earlier. But still, she feels bad. He didn't deserve it.

Before she can speak, she realizes Sam has fallen asleep again. Or maybe he passed out. She still really has no idea. He is propped against the back wall of the building, slumped over toward his left side, blond hair falling over his forehead into his eyes. *I am so sorry, you beautiful, crazy kid,* she thinks to herself, gently pushing him back against the wall.

"Mmm ... what's going on?" Sam mumbles, straightening himself up.

"You were all bent over, sweetie. I didn't want you to hurt your back. Here, can you lean against me?"

"Jessie ..." Sam whispers, allowing her to guide his head onto her shoulder. "Do you need your ... your jacket?" He seems to be having trouble speaking again. Is he losing more blood? The tourniquet is still off.

"No, honey, you can rest now." *Stop being so NICE! You were literally just shot! Be a selfish brat like usual!* Tears spring to her eyes again, a fresh wave of guilt washing over her.

CHAPTER 14

Hannah and Alex quickly scoop up more water and each drink a cup, refill, and then begin the slow journey back to camp, careful not to spill a drop. They won't dare venture back to the creek again until morning.

Sam is asleep when they return, and Jessie motions for them to be quiet as they settle back into camp. They stare at the fire, listening to the branches crackle. Alex's eyelids droop. He is listening to Sam breathe, very aware that any breath could be his last. They all eventually drift off to sleep but are rudely awakened by the screech owl once again proclaiming his presence.

"Damn it! That stupid owl!" Alex hisses as he jolts from his slumber. Hannah jumps up on high alert. Jessie subconsciously recognizes the sound as an owl and doesn't get quite as much of a fright.

Sam laughs at Alex's outburst. It's a weak, wheezy laugh, as though it takes all his effort to expel the air from his lungs. But it's a laugh, and Alex instantly feels better.

"Okay, that really made my day," Sam says, giving his friend a tired smile as he gazes across the fire.

"What, that I am apparently terrified of a stupid *owl?*" Alex throws branches on the fire, with feeling.

"No, just your reaction to it. That was good."

"Well, I'm glad I can, um, make your day better."

"It pretty much had to get better at some point," Sam jokes. He gives another weak laugh, then coughs and gasps as fresh pain shoots through him. "Is there any water left? Or is it reserved for honest, hard-working people?" He tries to keep joking but he is getting weaker by the second. He struggles to sit up as Jessie takes his hands.

Alex passes two cups of water to Sam, who drinks all of it and says, "Thanks, man. You're awesome."

"I try to be," Alex replies lamely, wishing he could come up with sarcastic comments on the fly like Sam. *Jeez, even after getting shot and nearly bleeding to death he is still cooler than me.* Alex sits down again, feeling anxious and exhausted, worried about what the cold, dark night may bring.

He has been feeling completely useless today, and has to keep reminding himself that Hannah has EMT training and of course she is the best one to help Sam. But Sam is *his* friend, and he has helped Alex through some tough times. Alex feels like he owes it to Sam to be here for him now and help him get through this. But he has no idea what to do.

Alex is broken out of his thoughts when Sam says, "You know what I could go for right now? A hot dog, a dozen s'mores, and some morphine."

They all laugh, though it is a bit forced. They had solved the problems of warmth and hydration, but it has been over thirty-six hours since they have eaten. How long can they go without food? A few days? Maybe a week? How much extra energy do they need to walk out of these woods? Will Sam even be able to walk? None of them have any answers.

They sit quietly, lost in thought and worry. Finally, Hannah says she would like to put the tourniquet back on, so Sam's wound won't bleed overnight.

"Yeah, I was hoping you would fall asleep again before you realized that. ... Darn," Sam says, shaking his head dismally at her.

"Can you go even one minute without making a sarcastic comment?" Hannah rolls her bloodied jacket up to cinch down onto his leg.

"Definitely not an entire minute," Sam answers, smiling at her and shifting himself back on his palms to give Hannah room to work. He yelps in pain as she tightens the tourniquet.

"Jeez, Hannah!" Sam sputters, sprawling on his elbows, rocking his right leg back and forth to ease the pain. "Is that really necessary?"

"It is if you want to live," Hannah replies.

Yikes, Alex thinks to himself. *Hannah sounds kinda pissed. Maybe someone should tell her she needs to work on her bedside manner.*

As if reading Alex's mind, Sam mutters, "Your bedside manner is deplorable." He pushes himself up and leans back on his palms, carefully arranging his injured leg into a more comfortable position.

Hannah wipes her hands slowly on her khakis, hoping she didn't do more damage with the tourniquet. "Sorry ... I'm just ... I'm not exactly sure what I'm doing, you know?"

"That's okay." Sam shrugs and gives Hannah a tired smile. "None of us does ... but we seem to be doing okay so far... well, you know, aside from me getting shot."

This brings a ghost of a smile to Hannah's lips. "There is that one pesky detail."

"Seriously, thank you so much ... for helping me, Hannah," Sam says, all sarcasm lost from his voice, his blue eyes wide and earnest, glinting in the firelight.

"Thanks, I guess. And, um, you're welcome ... I guess." Hannah is grateful the darkness is nearly absolute as her cheeks flush.

"Honestly, Hannah ... I wouldn't have blamed you if you'd left me in that truck by myself."

Hannah's eyes widen. She hadn't told her friends *anything* about leaving Sam in the truck when she recounted her tale of escape. She sits down near the fire and shrugs. "Actually ... I thought about it ..."

Sam gives her an understanding smile. "I thought you might ... I can be a pain in the butt, can't I?" He sighs and says, "Thank you, Hannah. You truly are amazing."

Hannah shrugs again and thinks about Sam's sincere compliment. *Maybe he isn't such an idiot.*

"Anyone want to tell ghost stories?" Sam asks, his moment of seriousness obviously forgotten. *Nope, still an idiot.*

"I absolutely forbid you from talking about the wolf thing again!" Jessie nearly shrieks at him. She had taken Sam's hand after he settled down from the pain of the tourniquet and now she pushes it away as if it has burned her.

"Oh, God," Alex pipes up. "Were you going on about your ridiculous ghost-wolf buddy last night? I would have thought you'd forgotten about that stupid thing by now."

"No! Never! I can't believe you guys don't like that story. Didn't you ever want to go look for it?"

They all shake their heads in unison, thoroughly uninterested in the old tale.

"It's so dumb," Hannah says. "It doesn't even make sense. Like, even if there was a wolf that got stuck in the Rad Zone, it probably wouldn't live very long with the radiation."

"The radiation made the wolf *immortal!*" Sam explains, pretending to be exasperated.

"Okay, but where did it even come from?" Hannah asks flatly. "I don't think there were ever wolves around Harrisburg. I mean, it was the state capital for hundreds of years. It wasn't like, out in the middle of nowhere."

"Wow, you all are absolutely no fun. I need to find new friends."

"No one else would put up with you," Alex teases.

Good one, kid, Hannah agrees silently. *I wish I had thought of it.*

"Well, not for free," Sam concedes.

CHAPTER 15

Jessie

Jessie crawls to Sam's left side after he falls asleep. She lies next to him, reassured by his steady breathing. He seems to be doing well, even joking around, which she thinks is a good sign.

She spreads her jacket over them both, Hannah and Alex sharing Alex's jacket closer to the fire. Jessie can't believe only twenty-four hours ago she was sure Sam was pranking her. Things really went downhill fast today. Never in a million years would she have guessed they would be in this situation tonight. Getting kidnapped and lost in the woods was bad enough. And now ... Jessie shivers, and not entirely from the cold.

Sam is stretched out on his back, hands at his sides. Jessie longs for him to roll onto his side and pull her tightly to his chest like he did last night. She inches her way closer to him, tucking her arms against his ribs, trying to get a little further under the jacket, which she had placed mostly over his chest and shoulders.

He stirs at her movement, lifting his head to find Jessie nestled against him, burrowing her arms into his shirt.

"Hey, come here," he says softly, raising his left hand so she can snuggle against him. She gently lowers her head onto his shoulder, left arm slung across his broad chest. He wraps his arms around her, arranging the jacket over them both. "Better?" he asks, rolling his shoulders back and forth to seat his arms tighter over her back.

"Much," she sighs against him and squeezes his ribs, wishing she could dissolve into him. He is so big and warm and ... comforting. "Let me know if I'm hurting you, okay?"

"Not possible, sweetheart," Sam mumbles as he drifts off to sleep again. "Not possible."

Jessie lies awake a long time, listening to Sam breathe, her head rising and falling with him. Either she or Hannah get up every half hour or so to rekindle the fire, awakened from their light fitful sleep as soon as the chill becomes more noticeable. Jessie marvels at how the boys remain sleeping through the entire night. She is pretty sure she has been awake for 90 percent of it, and she doesn't think Hannah is faring any better.

At some point, Jessie remembers she slept the entire previous night through without stirring, and that Sam must have diligently fed the fire all night. Why hadn't she realized that? Why hadn't she thanked him? *How could I have been so oblivious? He took such good care of me, and I didn't even notice!*

She squeezes his ribs and presses her head into his chest, wishing he would hold her tight. His hands have fallen to his sides as he sleeps, and they are no longer wrapped around her shoulders. She feels extremely vulnerable without his arms around her.

Waves of anxiety roll over her, and she quickly stands up. She needs to move and do something, anything, while waiting for the dread to pass. She warms her hands and places more branches on the fire, purposely not being too quiet about it.

She huddles near the flames, watching them dance, feeling more alone and hopeless than she has ever felt in her entire life. She vaguely wonders if Sam ever has thoughts of doubt, or loneliness, or fear.

Probably not, she decides. *He doesn't seem like the type to dwell on stuff.* Jessie wishes she could be carefree like him and not worry constantly about classes and tests, the future, a career, and just ... everything.

Maybe Sam is a good influence on her. He always has a way of cheering her up. His stupid jokes and goofy personality are sometimes the only things that make her smile.

She cautiously creeps over to his supine form, knowing he won't wake up, as he didn't the previous two times she got up to stoke the fire. She lies down again, her head on his chest, left hand slung across his ribs. She tugs her jacket over her shoulders.

Her heart nearly pounds out of her chest when she feels Sam's hands interlace over her shoulders, creating that comforting and secure weight on her that she never even knew she needed.

"You awake?" she whispers, not expecting an answer.

"Mmm, not really," comes his sleep-muddled reply.

"Okay, sorry. Go back to sleep."

"Why? Do you need something?" he asks, sounding more awake.

Jessie thinks it's funny he asked that, since he really can't move. It isn't like he can get up and actually go get something for her.

"No ..." she whispers. *I have everything I need now.*

∗∗∗

Jessie wakes as the sky lightens, having no idea if she slept for six minutes or six hours. She's lying next to Sam, her jacket mostly over herself and not him. She is a little disoriented but fully wakes up when she hears a soft moan next to her.

Sam appears to be asleep but is trembling from head to toe. Is he having a nightmare? A seizure? Is he freezing?

She scrambles up and places her hand on his face to gently wake him. A thin sheen of sweat slips under her fingers. He's burning up. He has a fever, and probably blood poisoning or something. Jessie never even thought about something like that. *I should have let Hannah go!*

She shakes him harder, watching his eyelids. "Sam, wake up ... Sam!"

Hannah scurries over, alarmed. "What happened? What's wrong?"

"He's burning up." Jessie's voice cracks, her mind racing, but she knows there is nothing more they can do. A lead weight drops into her stomach. She can't control her thoughts. Sam is going to die. She takes a deep breath and looks at Hannah, who also has her hand on Sam's forehead. "That wound must be getting infected. Do you think he has blood poisoning?" Jessie asks her friend with blatant fear in her eyes.

"I hate to say it, but that occurred to me overnight. I honestly don't know what else to do other than try to clean the wound. But cleaning it with dirty creek water is probably not going to help much."

"Well, dirty creek water is all we have." Jessie grits her teeth. "And we have to get his fever down. ... Do you think we can carry him to the creek? Let the water run over his legs for a minute? Maybe buy him some time?"

"I have no idea ..." Hannah whispers, staring at Sam. "I don't know if that will cause, like, hypothermia ... or shock or something ... but I don't think we have any other choice. I doubt dribbling a cup of water over the wound will really do anything ... but I don't know for sure." The two friends stare at each other, and then Hannah says with new resolve in her voice, "Let's do it."

By this time, Alex is peeking around Jessie's shoulder at Sam. He doesn't say anything, but he knows his friend is in serious danger. He backs away as Hannah and Jessie stand, assessing their situation. Sam stirs and groans, slowly rubbing his eyes with the back of his hand.

"Sam?" Jessie asks tentatively, kneeling beside him. "How are you feeling? Can you sit up, sweetie?"

"Mm ... I don't know ..." Sam's voice is hoarse, barely above a whisper. He slowly turns onto his left side, having extreme difficulty moving even half an inch. He tries to sit up but is too weak to make much progress. Hannah and Jessie reach down and grab his shoulders, propping him against the back wall of the restroom. He clearly has trouble staying upright on his own. He looks terrible. Pale cheeks, eyes rimmed with red, chest heaving with the effort of breathing. The thought crosses Jessie's mind again: he is going to die.

"I-I don't feel—" Before Sam can finish, he coughs and retches into the dirt, but there is nothing in his stomach to vomit up. He gasps in pain, his breathing more ragged and wheezier than yesterday. He leans his head against the wall, eyes closed, hands braced in the dirt to keep from falling over. "Everything is spinning," he manages to whisper.

"Sam, we need to clean your wound," Hannah says, again taking control of the situation, to Jessie's relief. "Can you stand at all? We want to take you to the creek. Okay? Get you cleaned up a bit." Hannah surveys the tourniquet, looking for fresh blood.

Sam nods weakly. The girls each take one of his arms and slowly haul him to his feet. He puts all of his weight on his left foot, his right leg hanging uselessly. Hannah is on his left side and steadies herself under his arm.

"Alex, grab the cups," she says, aligning herself under Sam's thick shoulder. Jessie stands on his right side, terrified of bumping his wound as she fumbles to get his arm over her shoulders. She doesn't think Sam can help her at all. His head lolls forward, and Jessie has the feeling he wouldn't react much even if she did hurt him. He seems completely exhausted.

Sam groans and shifts onto his right leg, Jessie feeling the pressure spread across her shoulders as he leans into her. *This is going to be a slow journey.*

The creek is only a few hundred yards away, but it feels like ten miles. There is no path, and Sam struggles to navigate the rocks and tree branches strewn everywhere, unable to lift his foot over the obstacles. He moans in pain whenever his foot is accidentally pushed sideways by a rock or tree root, which happens frequently.

"You're doing great, honey," Jessie mumbles, though she's on the verge of panic.

"Wish I could say the same for you." He tries to tease her, but his voice is raspy and wavering. Then, almost inaudibly, he mutters, "Oww ... *damn it.*" He doubles over in pain. Jessie lays her hand on his taut stomach and pushes him upright to continue their journey. She is sure they will never get him up if he falls. *He's gonna die, he's gonna die, he's gonna die ...*

Alex runs ahead of them, doing his best to remove any loose debris from their path and breaking off low-hanging branches that would hinder them.

It takes about twenty minutes to get Sam to the edge of the creek. Well, it *feels* like twenty minutes to Jessie. She has no idea. Could have been anywhere from three minutes to seven hours.

They stand in the loose sand and gravel near the clear, rippling water, all gasping and sweating, Sam hanging limply between the girls' shoulders, barely able to stay on his feet. Jessie is beginning to think this was a very bad idea. How will any of them have the strength to get him back to camp?

"Okay, Sam, we need to put your leg in the water. It will probably be best to take your shoes and pants off, so you have dry clothes to get into," Hannah instructs. "And I have to take the tourniquet off again." There is an apologetic note in her voice.

Sam merely nods and allows the girls to lower him onto the sand and loose rocks at the water's edge. Jessie wishes he would make some kind of sarcastic comment as she unties his shoes. *We're literally undressing him! He should be having a field day with this!* She chances a look at his face, afraid of what she might see, afraid he will mirror the fear and despair she's feeling. Does he think he is going to die?

But Sam makes no sarcastic comments, and his expression is almost blank, his red eyes vague and cast downward. *He's gonna die, he's gonna die ...*

The girls pull off his sneakers and socks, doing the same for themselves so they can wade into the icy water with him. Sam momentarily passes out when Hannah unties the tourniquet. His eyes swim and roll up, head lolling in the dirt. Jessie is kind of glad about that. It is a tiny relief to know he isn't feeling the pain anymore. But it also terrifies her; she knows people have to be really sick or really in a lot of pain to pass out. She wants to scream. This is so hard to watch!

They quickly undo the button and zipper of his jeans, then slowly ease the pants over his wound. His leg is a mess. Angry red flesh pulses around the bullet hole, a gaping black inkwell that oozes fresh blood as they move him. Red lines radiate from the wound, traveling up the skin. Blood poisoning. Jessie doesn't know much about medicine yet, but she knows that can be fatal.

Sam regains consciousness and screams as the freezing water rushes over his legs. Jessie thinks she might faint, but she knows she has to stay strong for him. She *needs* to do this.

He writhes in the icy water and then suddenly grabs Jessie's wrist with both hands and tries unsuccessfully to climb up her arm to escape the freezing knives of the rushing creek. *This was a stupid idea,* Jessie thinks as her eyes well up. She bends against Sam's weight, clawing at his arms with her free hand.

"I can't do this, Hannah, please stop!" Sam screams. He falls backward into the water, splashing them all with the freezing spray. He gasps uncontrollably, his eyes red and wild.

Oh, Sam, Sam, Sam, I'm so sorry. Jessie puts a hand on his shoulder, trying to steady herself as much as him. It occurs to her that they should have stripped off his shirt and boxers as well. *He is completely soaked. He will never get dry out here. He's going to freeze to death.*

"It's okay, we're finished," Hannah says softly. "You did great. Let's get you dry."

"Oh, my God," Sam moans, covering his eyes, the water rushing over his legs. "I can't do this ..."

"What are you talking about?" Hannah asks a little gruffly. "You're doing it. We needed the water to wash out your wound, and look, wound washed. All done."

Sam makes no further utterances as the girls pull him back onto the sand. He lies flat on his back, shivering violently.

Something crashes through the trees nearby and Jessie looks up in alarm, certain she will soon catch the thoughts of a blood-thirsty mountain lion moving in for the kill. A wave of relief washes over her as she spies Alex running toward them.

"I brought these!" he calls, holding up what looks like fifty paper napkins from the restroom. "This was my bed the other night. I think it should be enough to dry him off."

"Good thinking, kiddo," Jessie says tightly, working hard to keep the bile from rising into her mouth, taking a few towels to sop the water off Sam's good leg. She'll let Hannah work on his injured one.

Sam

Sam raises his head and gazes at the girls as they dry him off, his vision blurry. *Okay, I'm no doctor or whatever, but I think I'm pretty well screwed.* His legs are completely numb, which is actually better than the excruciating pain. But he worries he may be too far gone at this point. *Maybe I should have let Hannah take her chances on the road yesterday ...*

It wasn't exactly fun getting dumped in the freezing water, but he knows that Jessie and Hannah were only trying to help. *This vacation is getting worse by the minute ...* Sam groans as he tries sitting up, only managing to prop himself on his elbows, hands splayed out, chest heaving from pain and exertion. Attractive.

He watches the girls work, feeling more helpless than he did even when he had both legs in casts. This is humiliating.

"You missed a spot," he quips, his voice much hoarser and higher than what he considers manly, but he hopes his stupid jokes will make the girls not think of him as a complete invalid.

What are they thinking right now? That I'm a total moron for getting shot? As if getting kidnapped and lost weren't bad enough. I had to go and get shot. Idiot! What was I thinking? Why did I try to fight off that guy? We should have just run into the woods and not looked back. But no, I had to be dumb. And now look at the mess I've created. Thoroughly screwed ... medically speaking.

Jessie catches Sam's eye and gives him a quick smile, reacting to his stupid joke.

"You're such a jerk," she says quietly, working her way up his left leg with the towels.

"Yes, I've been telling you that for years, Jessie," Hannah adds, also giving Sam a quick smile. "But you don't listen to me."

Sam glances at his bullet wound, seeing it for the first time. Medically speaking ... it looks kind of awesome. And if it weren't *his* leg, he would probably be like, *"Cool."* But since it happens to be a new feature on one of his four favorite appendages, he's definitely not feeling too proud of it right now. *Maybe I'll get a cool scar or whatever.*

Jessie moves to his hip and gently puts her fingertips on his left hand, still splayed in the dirt. The remnants of dried blood on his hands look like paint chips on his skin. He doesn't move as she washes him, not sure if he should be completely humiliated or kind of enjoying this. She gingerly scrubs each finger with the towels, and even coaxes some of the dirt and blood out from under his fingernails. That's nice.

She places his left hand on the ground, and Sam reaches over to give his right hand to her. Before she can start scrubbing, he encloses her hand, giving her a soft squeeze. She gathers her courage to look at him, and their eyes lock.

Sam feels moisture on his cheeks but isn't sure if it is creek water that has splashed up or tears that have run down. He's trying really hard not to cry but is not having much success. Jessie blots his face with the towel, his hand still holding hers. Finally, his eyes well up and the tears spill over. He pulls his hand away and wipes his eyes.

"Jessie, please don't let me die out here," Sam whispers. He can't keep the waver out of his voice. His teeth chatter.

She moves to his other side and silently dries his right arm, then does her best to sop the water out of his T-shirt and boxers. She doesn't say anything. She doesn't want to lie to him and tell him everything will be okay.

Hannah begins replacing Sam's socks. "You're not going to die," she says, a little gruffer than what Sam thinks is necessary. But maybe it's good she is acting like this. It does give Sam the encouragement he needs to keep going. Like if Hannah gives up, they will all give up. "You need to help me put your pants back on. I can't stand seeing your ugly legs much longer." Hannah gives Sam a rare smirk.

Sam pushes his palms into his eyes to stem the flow of tears. With some difficulty, the girls manage to shimmy the jeans back onto his legs. The right pant leg is stiff and cold with dried blood, and he wishes they could rinse it off, but he knows jeans will take forever to dry out here, even close to the fire. His shivering subsides only slightly, and they all know he must get back to the warmth soon.

But now Sam feels like there is something *really* wrong.

"Let me know when you want to start walking back," Hannah says. She gives Sam a reassuring smile and picks up the towels. Sam rests on a large rock with his head bowed almost to his knees. He looks *so* bad. Jessie surveys him as she also gathers the sopping paper towels.

"Give me a minute ... I don't feel ... right," he says, voice tinged with concern.

"What do you mean? Are you going to pass out?" Hannah asks, kneeling beside him. "Sit on the ground if you're going to pass out. Just don't puke on me."

Sam shakes his head. "No, it isn't like that ... I feel like ... like I forgot to do something really important. But I can't remember what it is. It's like there is something stuck in my brain, clawing to get out." He peers at the rushing water, a distant look in his red eyes.

Alex glances at Sam and says flatly, "Huh," like he is thinking hard about what Sam said.

Jessie is concerned there is something wrong with Sam's brain. Maybe he has lost too much blood. Maybe they shouldn't have put him in the freezing water. Maybe it was too much of a shock to his system or something.

She sits beside him on the rock and strokes the damp hair off his forehead. He closes his eyes at her touch. She massages the tight muscles of his back in slow circles.

"Just take a minute," Jessie whispers to him. "You're doing great. ... Alex, why don't you go back and put more branches on the fire so we can all warm up?"

Alex does as he is told and runs toward the campsite. He is glad he has something to do but has a nagging suspicion Jessie wanted him out of the way. Something is up. It's weird, what Sam said. Unsettling, actually ...

Like something very important is trying to claw out of his brain. Alex had that same feeling only a few days ago ... when he and Jessie were going to get ice cream. He had been walking down the hallway at home and felt like ... hmm, he never actually remembered what it was he was supposed to do. That seems like so long ago now.

Back at the fire, Alex tosses the largest branches onto it, worried about Sam. He really thought Sam was going to be okay when he was joking around last night. He almost seemed like his normal self, just a little weak. And now, today, he is so much worse. Alex realizes he needs to mentally prepare himself for the worst.

He stands in the smoke from the roaring fire, tears streaming down his face. He really wants to be home, playing baseball with Sam, or fishing at the park.

Suddenly, a thought crashes over him. That feeling he had Saturday morning, that Sam is having now: It doesn't mean something is trying to get out of his brain. ... Something is trying to get *in.*

✳✳✳

Jessie wipes Sam's face with a paper towel as fresh tears leak from his eyes. He is staring at the rushing water. Hannah stares at him. *He looks terrible. I think putting him in the water was the dumbest thing we could have done,* Hannah thinks bleakly. *I don't know what to do now.*

"This really sucks, Jessie," Sam says quietly, his voice cracking on her name.

"I know, but you're doing great." She gently dries his neck, massaging his muscles. Hannah watches them, slightly perplexed. *That seems oddly intimate. I mean, I know Jessie is trying to take care of him and everything, but ... Oh, no. They're falling in love!*

Hannah rolls her eyes. Jessie does not need a troublemaker like Sam Starling to mess up her future. She may as well kiss her dreams of college good-bye. Sam will have her skipping class—or worse—with him by this time next week. Or he might be dead by this time next week ... then Hannah won't have to worry about him screwing Jessie up too much.

She feels a brief pang of guilt when she realizes that Sam being dead is better than Sam being with Jessie. Well, she doesn't think she *actually* feels that way, but Sam is definitely not good for Jessie. Jessie has goals and plans and a bright future ... and Sam doesn't.

Hannah secretly hopes Jessie is only being nice to Sam because he is on the brink of death.

"I'm so glad you're here with me," Sam whispers to Jessie, gazing at his newly cleaned hands.

"Me too. ... You always need someone to take care of you, don't you?" Jessie teases, not wanting to get too personal with him, since Hannah is standing so close by. She hastily removes her hand from his neck and places it in her lap. She hadn't really realized she had been massaging him. It just seemed like a nice thing to do for the poor guy.

A flicker of a smile plays across Sam's chapped lips. "Well, I guess I'm in trouble, since you can't even take care of a houseplant." He glances at Jessie through half-closed eyes. She doesn't know if he is keeping his voice low to share a quiet moment with her or if he is too weak to speak any louder. He holds her gaze, then looks back at the rushing water. "I just need another minute ..." He bows his head to his knees, looking thoroughly beaten. She ruffles his hair playfully, not liking how defeated he looks. He still needs to get back to camp, and she worries he won't have the strength to move at all.

"Don't let yourself get too cold, Hummingbird. We need to get you back to the fire soon." He is wearing her jacket, the front open. "Here, can we zip this up for you?" Jessie attaches the bottom of the zipper and slides it up only about three inches before it gets stuck. "Can you suck in a little?" she teases, amazed once again at how big he is. *How have I not noticed how much he has grown? He is not a kid anymore.*

"Sure, let me crack a few ribs." Sam wheezes breathlessly. At first, she thinks he is kidding, pretending she has squeezed all the air from his lungs with the tight zipper, but when she catches his eye, she knows immediately that he is not joking.

"Sam ... what is going on?" Jessie asks. She opens the zipper, as if that would help anything. "Are you okay?"

"Yeah ... yeah ... I need a minute," Sam answers vaguely. His mind is clearly somewhere else. Suddenly he tenses and sits up straight, performing the fastest movement Jessie has seen him do in a while. "Oh, my God," he says so quietly she can barely hear him.

"What? What's the matter?" she asks, frantically searching his face.

"I feel like ... like ... oh, my God. Guys, I know exactly where we are!"

Sam bends his legs to get off the freezing rock he's planted on. Something bizarre just happened. He can't explain it. He tries standing, feeling like he is moving involuntarily, his body going through the motions and his brain not keeping up. *I think maybe I'm having a stroke or something. That's fun.*

"Okay, take it easy," Hannah says as he wobbles to his feet. His injured leg is less painful than it had been, but he is also the weakest he's been since their jaunt to the creek began. Hannah steadies him on the loose pebbles. Sam sways, leaning heavily on her shoulders. "What do you mean you know exactly where we are?" she asks.

"I've had this feeling ... since I woke up in these woods on Saturday ... like I had sort of been here before, you know?" Sam speaks slowly, partly because he's so frozen he can barely get his mouth to work, but mostly because he's not entirely sure how to describe what is happening. He's had a fuzzy idea of his location since waking in the woods—nothing definite. But now everything is crystal clear.

His teeth chatter. "I s-suddenly just realized we are 147 m-miles north of Cutter County, in an old Pennsylvania state p-park that shut down. I don't know what the park was called, but the restroom f-f-facility is 9.2 miles from the m-main road, which is called Old Mine Road." He speaks as if the words are coming from someone else's brain but through his mouth. "And the park office is six-tenths of a mile f-farther up this road. ... What the heck? How do I know this?" He stares wide-eyed at the girls, incredulous and confused, mouth agape in bewilderment.

"Happy birthday, Sam. Welcome to the Gifted Club." Hannah smiles happily, clapping him on the shoulder. He buckles under her hand but regains his balance quickly. He stares at her, not fully understanding what she means. She further clarifies, "It appears you are a human GPS."

Suddenly they hear Alex running through the woods from the campsite, yelling, "Sam! Sam! You are going to get your Gift!"

Sam tries thinking of some sarcastic comment (something cleverer than, "Well, golly gee. Ya think?") but he is still too confused and shocked to process words coherently.

His brain suddenly has a map of a forty-mile radius from where he's standing. It's as if he has studied a detailed map of this area or lived here all his life. He thinks of home, the street he lives on, the school, the community park. He can only remember what he already knows about the area, not a forty-mile radius of Cutter County. *Hmm, I wonder if the radius will change as I move. Jessie can only hear animals' thoughts within about fifty feet or something. ... Weird.*

Sam whispers, "Oh, my God ... I know where we are. I can get us out of here!" He is getting excited, feeling warmer, more energized, and more alive than he has felt in a while.

"Sam!" Hannah shrieks, breaking him out of his partly confused and partly elated thoughts. He had involuntarily taken a few steps toward camp and immediately pitched backward, his right leg unable to support him at all. Hannah grabs his arm before he goes down on his butt, and Jessie jumps to his other side, taking his left arm and slinging it across her shoulders.

"Oww, I forgot I can't walk," Sam mumbles, hanging from the girls' arms as his reality crashes around him. He sighs. It is going to be a long, painful trek back to camp. Something tickles his right leg, and he says resignedly, "Hannah, you better get that tourniquet back on." The wound is bleeding again.

***

Twenty minutes later, Hannah and Jessie have Sam back at the fire. Alex had done a splendid job of building it up nice and high, and Sam could feel the heat from a distance of sixteen feet and four inches. *Hmm, I don't know if I'm going to like this Gift. Seems like a lot of math is involved. Maybe I can return it.*

His skin had returned to its usual ice-cold ambient temperature as he slogged through the woods, and he is shaking worse now than when he was submerged in the water.

"Oh, God, Sam, your lips are turning blue," Jessie says, sitting next to him.

Jeez, don't tell me that, sweetheart. Blue lips can't be good. He vaguely wonders if he will die. The thought has been fleeting in and out since last night, depending on how horrible he feels at any moment.

He's suddenly very tired, bordering on exhaustion, his earlier elation over finding himself Gifted completely sapped, and he can barely hold his head up as he rests near the flames. He's hunched up as close to the fire as possible, Jessie's jacket wrapped around him, but he can't really feel any of that. Everything is numb. He is vaguely aware of Hannah standing over him, hands on her hips.

"This park office. It's half a mile away, right?" she barks at Sam.

He only manages a slow nod in response to her question and physically can't pick up his head to look at her. "Six-tenths," he whispers hoarsely. "Further up the road ... away from the main road. Then make a right turn ... the office is only a few hundred feet ..." His voice trails off weakly.

"I can run there and back in probably twenty minutes! How about if I go there, see if there is anything useful? I'll stop back here and then go to the main road. There's plenty of daylight left."

"Sounds great!" Jessie agrees readily this time.

"Here," Alex says. "Take my jacket to carry stuff back in. I'm going to hope there is food or something to bring back."

"Thanks, Alex. That's a good idea. It would be awesome *not* to have to run over nine miles on an empty stomach," Hannah says, taking the jacket.

Sam can see her out of the corner of his eye, his head still too heavy and his neck too weak to look up at all. Hannah's shoes point in his direction.

"Okay, GPS boy," she says. "I hope you're right." She turns to leave.

"Hannah ... wait!" Sam manages to pick his head up but is still having trouble speaking. "I have to tell you ... now ... in case I'm not ali—umm ... awake." He glances quickly at Jessie, hoping she hadn't caught on that he thinks he will be dead soon. She is putting more branches on the fire and isn't paying attention to him. "Um, in case I'm not awake when you get back ..."

"Yeah?" Hannah asks, walking toward him.

"This road ... it's a good thing you didn't risk it yesterday ..." He stops speaking to concentrate on breathing.

"Okay ...?" Hannah kneels next to him.

"There's like ... seven different turnoffs to abandoned cabins and trails that you need to watch out for."

"Are ... are you serious?" Hannah mutters under her breath.

"Sorry ... the way out is not straight ..." Sam speaks slowly and explains how to navigate the old gravel tracks of the state park, trying to be clear, hoping Hannah is understanding him. There are no road signs left to guide travelers to the exit. Hannah must remember which of the seven turns to take and when. For nine miles.

Her pale-blue eyes are wide with fear. "There's no way ... there's no way I can remember all that. I can't go. I don't even remember what you just said. Left, left, right, straight?"

Sam shakes his head. "No, left, left, straight, right—"

"Okay, okay!" Hannah leaps up, furious. "We will have to think of something else. I can't remember all that!" She had been *sure* she could run to safety. She only needed enough time and daylight. Now, all hope is lost. Tears well in her eyes.

"Hannah, go to the park office," Jessie says sternly. "Maybe there is a park map, or a pencil and paper. Sam can write the turns down for you ... if he's still ali—I mean, awake, when you get back."

Sam glances at Jessie and can't help but scoff, giving her a sly smile. *Man, she doesn't miss a trick with me ... must be from all those years of babysitting when I was up to no good.* He turns his attention back to the girls. Hannah is wiping her eyes.

"It's okay, Hannah," Sam says gently. "We'll figure something out. Let's see what you find at the office. It's really close!"

Hannah nods silently and turns away from the group, disappearing around the corner of the restroom.

"Good luck!" Jessie calls after her friend.

CHAPTER 17

Hannah

Hannah sprints along the road toward the park office, her long legs quickly settling into an easy lope. She prays she will find something useful but knows there is no way there will be a working phone. *I really just need a map.* Her mind reels with the directions Sam rattled off. She can't remember any of them.

This short section of road is easy to navigate ... six-tenths of a mile, then a right-hand turn ... then a few hundred feet. *There it is!* The little building is nestled in a stand of birch trees. Sam was right.

She dashes to the front porch, a rustic wooden railing encircling a picnic table and bench. The front door has been smashed in and is barely holding on haphazardly by the upper hinge. Her heart sinks. The place has been looted, probably years ago.

Hannah creeps through the doorway and finds a countertop to her right. Old pamphlets about wildlife, the park trails, and events at the park litter the surface. She quickly flips through them, blowing dust and dirt off the glossy paper. It takes a minute for her eyes to adjust to the dark interior; the windows are grimy, and the weak sunlight barely filters through.

Hannah gasps. One pamphlet is a map! She unfurls it, her eyes frantically searching the squiggly lines of the trails and roads that meander through the park.

She has no idea where she is. The tiny icons all run together, and she is too overwhelmed to even look for the park office on the map. *Whatever, Sam can read it later. What else is here?* She pockets the map and scans the small room.

Her eyes fall upon a familiar shape at the back of the room—an old vending machine. She doesn't dare wish for something to still be inside. Even from here, it is obvious the front panel has been smashed in. She investigates anyway and laughs when she finds one Little Debbie Oatmeal Creme Pie at the bottom of the machine. She scoops it up and pockets it.

There is a door in the back corner of the office, probably a storage closet. It hasn't been smashed in, and it easily opens when she turns the dusty door handle. It is pitch black inside; there are no windows.

As her eyes adjust, she makes out the shapes of cartons and boxes. The boxes only contain a few sparse office supplies, and there is nothing immediately useful. Other boxes are wrapped in tight cellophane. She scratches at one desperately, hoping it isn't more park pamphlets.

As she works away at the packaging material, her thoughts turn back to her friends. It is truly amazing that Alex and Sam got their Gifts right when they needed them most. And something so incredibly useful, too. She wonders if maybe some of the Gifts work like that; like if the Change knows you have a special need, it will provide. After all, Jessie has wanted to be a veterinarian since she was a kid, and her Gift helps her communicate with animals. Hannah vaguely wonders if her own Gift will somehow make her a better doctor one day. Maybe she will be able to work extralong shifts without getting tired or something.

The cellophane is difficult to rip through, and there is nothing sharp enough to cut it. She toys with the idea of giving up on this mission. But what if there is food in this box? Running all that way won't be so bad if she isn't completely starving.

She wonders if Sam will survive long enough for her to run for help. He wasn't looking so great when she left him. On the other hand, he is probably too arrogant to let himself die from this. He'll have to make it back home so he can brag to the whole town about what he's been through, and how his Gift saved them all. He'll probably conveniently forget that Alex got the money. *He's such an arrogant jerk sometimes ... most of the time, actually ... What does Jessie see in him, anyway? If they become a couple, I'll have to find new friends.*

Her thoughts turn to Jessie and how they had first met as four-year-olds in swimming class. Hannah had jumped off the diving board and gotten a nose full of water. She came up sputtering and choking, her sopping hair covering her face and mouth, making it even more difficult to breathe. She panicked, but before the instructor could reach her, Jessie had thrown a pool noodle right onto Hannah's flapping hands, allowing her to catch her breath and calm down. They became fast friends that day.

A tearing noise brings Hannah out of her reverie. She has gotten through the cellophane! The thick plastic falls away, and she quickly tears through the cardboard flaps, almost screaming with delight as the box opens. Everything she could hope for is in here!

The box contains a variety of on-the-go snacks, including granola bars, nuts, and single-serving bags of potato chips. She digs through it. A separate, smaller box underneath contains first-aid supplies, including pain relievers, bug repellant, itch relievers, and alcohol wipes. The box is too big and awkward to carry, but she can wrap almost all of the food and the first aid supplies in Alex's jacket. She finds a small watering can on another shelf and stuffs the rest of the food into it, then sprints toward camp, wolfing down a stale granola bar.

Elated and much more rejuvenated, Hannah runs as fast as she can, her mind continuing to wander to her friends. She wonders if Sam is feeling any better yet. His wound looked much worse than she had expected, though she's not really sure what she should have expected, having never seen a gunshot wound before. There has been *nothing* like that in her EMT training. Knowing how to place a tourniquet sure came in handy, though.

As she runs, Hannah thinks back to one experience she had last September.

It was a late Wednesday afternoon, and Hannah was curled up on her bed, finishing some biology homework. She loves biology and is fascinated by the human body and how all the various parts work together to create one amazing whole.

Suddenly her cell phone rang on the bedside table. Jessie was supposed to call to go running later that evening. But she felt a flutter of excitement when she read the phone display. It was her neighbor, Phillip King, head of the local EMT unit, calling to see if she was available to get some real-world medical experience.

Hannah had been volunteering with the EMT service for a few months, since summer, when she had told Phil in passing about her dream of becoming a doctor.

"Hey, Phil, what's going on?" she asked, sliding off her bed and quickly lacing up her shoes. There was no time to waste when Phil was on the line.

"Car wreck on the interstate. You home?"

"Yeah, I'll be out front in one minute."

"See you really soon." Phil disconnected. Hannah ran down the stairs, crossed the stately dining room of the governor's mansion, and hurtled out the front door.

Phil, in the next driveway over (which was still almost a quarter mile away, due to the expansive yard surrounding the Buckley residence) was backing his pickup truck out of the garage. Hannah sprinted down her driveway to meet him on the road, barely winded as she flung open the door of the black pickup, the blue light on the roof flashing. *This Gift is amazing,* she thought as she slid into the seat and buckled up.

"Hi Phil, thanks for calling," she said as Phil peeled up the road, siren blaring.

"You bet. I wasn't interrupting anything, was I?" He turned onto the main street and expertly wove around the cars that were pulling to the side to let him pass.

"No, nothing really. I was finishing my biology homework."

"My favorite!" Phil beamed and turned slightly toward her, keeping both hands on the wheel. Phil himself was a senior in college and had recently been accepted to Harvard Medical School.

"I need to text Jessie to let her know I might not be able to meet." Hannah pulled her phone out of her shorts pocket.

"Make sure you take some time for yourself. You'll burn out quickly if you always make yourself last priority," Phil said wisely as he sped down the interstate ramp.

"I do ..." she said uncertainly, but his comment made her ponder the past few months. Every waking moment had been spent at school, doing homework, researching colleges, or at some after-school activity or club. Maybe she was pushing herself too hard. Nah, her Gift made her immune to things like exhaustion and fatigue, right?

She didn't have long to dwell on that question. A thick plume of black smoke was rising in front of them, tendrils of soot curling into the breezy September air.

"There it is," Phil said, jutting his chin toward the sinister warning sign of the wreck ahead. The two lanes of traffic on the interstate were completely stopped. Phil shot his truck onto the shoulder and bounced along, the stopped cars nothing more than a blur.

This was the part Hannah hated; the final few seconds before arriving on a scene, not knowing what grisly mess would greet her. She had seen some awful things in the past few months. The worst was a baby who had flown through a windshield from not having the proper car seat. *I'm not thinking about that,* she scolded herself, leaping out of the truck and grabbing Phil's bag from behind the seat.

They rushed to the smoking car, a small, turquoise sedan on its roof in the ditch on the right side of the road. Hannah couldn't see any flames coming from it. Whatever was on fire must have burned out. She desperately hoped there wasn't something smoldering inside that would ignite while they were working to free the driver. Most cars were electric, but some of the older models, like Phil's pickup truck, were hybrids, and still used some gasoline.

"Hey, man, you okay?" Phil knelt at the driver's window, or rather, the empty space that used to be the window. A bloody hand protruded from it. "You alone in there?" Phil stretched out onto his stomach and gazed into the car to determine if the owner of the bloody hand was conscious, or even alive. Hannah knelt next to him and unzipped the medical bag, pulling out large rolls of gauze, splinting materials, and the intravenous catheter kit. She expertly laid everything out in a neat pile, the way Phil had shown her months ago.

"Yeah," the driver of the wrecked car said. Hannah felt a wave of relief. The man was coherent enough to answer questions.

"What's bleeding, pal?" Phil asked.

"My ... my arm. The windshield broke and fell in on me ... I think ..."

"Okay, pal, what's your name?" Phil quickly donned the medical exam gloves Hannah held out to him; then she put on a pair herself.

"Danny," came the faint reply as the bloody hand disappeared.

"Okay, Danny, I'm Phil. Do you think you can move at all? Are you pinned down?"

Danny's bloody right hand and a much cleaner left hand appeared in Hannah's field of view.

"Uh, yeah, I can move," Danny said with a grunt, wriggling toward the window space.

"Okay, great job. I'm going to help you out of there, okay?" Phil stretched his arms into the car and firmly grasped the man under his armpits. Within a minute, Danny was kneeling in front of them, but barely. He was doubled over in pain, a steady stream of crimson blood cascading from his right arm.

"Danny, sit back on the ground, keep your head between your knees," Phil instructed. "Hannah, get the tourniquet."

Hannah removed the tourniquet from the bag while Phil expertly wrapped thick bandage material around Danny's arm. She gazed at the man, who was holding his knees up to his chest, with his chin down, eyes closed.

"How old are you, Danny?" Hannah asked, putting a hand on his shoulder.

"Nineteen. I ... I must have fallen asleep while driving. I go to college during the day and work at night. Don't sleep much ..." Danny's voice was wispy, as if he were remembering a dream.

"Here, Hannah, let me show you how to apply the tourniquet," Phil said. "Place it directly over the wound and bandage ... really cinch it down, as tight as you can." Phil let her apply the tourniquet, double checking its tightness. "There you go. Great job! Danny, how does that feel?"

"Okay, I guess. ... I can't really feel anything ..."

"Sit tight. I'm going to do a quick exam, check your vitals," Phil pulled a penlight from his pocket and checked Danny's eyes. Hannah handed him the stethoscope. The scream of the approaching emergency vehicles filled her ears.

They worked together in silence until the ambulance and a police car pulled up. This part was always a blur to Hannah. There was such a flurry of activity that she tended to melt into the background and observe, taking in as much as she could for future reference.

Hannah watched, mesmerized, as the medical professionals strapped Danny to a stretcher and deftly loaded him into the ambulance. She gave him a thumbs-up before the doors closed and was relieved to see him return the gesture with a tired smile.

Suddenly she felt a warm trickle on her leg below the knee. She looked down. To her shock, a rivulet of bright blood oozed into her sock. Her blood? Why was she bleeding? Or had she knelt in Danny's blood?

"Hey, Phil, can I have some gauze? I got blood on my leg." She ambled over to Phil's truck, where he was packing up his bag.

"Uh-oh. Yeah, here you go." He glanced at her and handed his bag over.

"Oh, no ... I must have gotten cut on someth—Oh, shoot! There's glass in there!" Hannah dabbed at her leg, thoroughly annoyed with herself. This was her greatest fear; she worried she would be a nuisance to Phil and cause more trouble than what she was worth.

"Let me take a look." Phil gently probed the skin below her knee. The wound was bleeding freely. "Oh, Hannah, this is pretty deep. You might need a stitch or two in that, but it should be fine. Come on, let's take you to the hospital. You might want to get a tetanus shot, too. Who knows what's in that dirt?"

To Hannah's relief, Phil did not seem upset at all. On the contrary, he seemed genuinely concerned, like a parent or big brother.

"They can flush it out really good for you. Here," he held out another pack of gauze. "Put some pressure on it. ... Well, you know." He gave her a big reassuring smile. They climbed into the truck and Phil drove in silence.

"I'm sorry to be such a pain in the butt," Hannah said as the Cutter County hospital came into view. The hospital was situated almost in the middle of Cutter County, in the downtown section. Everything was relatively new in that area, having been constructed after the power plant meltdown. The city planners had done a fine job of making the town feel old-fashioned, with a wide, tree-lined boulevard through the center of town, and two streets dedicated to small shops and cafes. Hannah and Jessie frequently rode their bikes to the cafes after school to do homework together.

"It's really no trouble, Hannah. Don't worry about it. ... Maybe just wear long pants next time." He gave her a friendly smile. "Besides, I have some schoolwork to finish while I wait for you, and I'll be less distracted sitting in my truck than at home. My teenage brothers are always bugging me to play computer games with them. You're actually kind of doing me a favor."

An hour later, her leg freshly cleaned and closed with two stitches, Hannah walked out the double doors of the hospital and caught sight of a familiar boy strolling in from the parking lot. *Must be a kid from school,* she thought, not paying much attention. As she neared Phil's truck, she recognized the boy as Sam Starling, whom she really didn't know but knew she didn't like. She had hung out with him only a couple of times with Jessie and Alex over the years, but the kid was always so loud and obnoxious that Hannah always found an excuse to be somewhere else.

"Hey, Sam," she said casually, not breaking her stride and not planning to exchange any more words than that.

"Oh, hey," Sam replied, taken off guard. He had been looking at something in his hands and glanced up quickly. Part of what he was holding fell to the pavement with a dull clatter. Hannah saw that he held a stack of children's books, four or five of them, their brightly colored covers glittering in the last of the sun.

"Jeez, remind me never to ask you to carry my books at school." She picked up the book he had dropped. He put it on the bottom of the stack and met her eyes, a smirk on his face. She had expected him to look embarrassed; the always cool and suave Sam Starling had fumbled his books. But Sam didn't look embarrassed. Instead, he looked completely at ease, as usual, and casually pushed his blond hair out of his right eye.

"Yeah, you'd better not. I'd pretend not to know you. You'd be all ashamed. It would be awkward." He tucked the books under his arm and said, "Well, I guess you caught me."

"Yeah, what are you doing here? Taking reading lessons?" she quipped, a note of cruelty in her voice, which surprised her. She never made fun of people, but she *really* didn't like this kid.

"Well, you know, court-ordered community service." Sam grinned slyly.

This admission surprised Hannah. *Court-ordered? What did he do to deserve that punishment?* She decided she really didn't want to know and said quickly, "Well, have fun with that," and strode away toward Phil's truck.

Sam laughed and uttered a low, "Thanks, I'll try," but she wasn't paying attention to him anymore. She wondered if Jessie knew what Sam had done to warrant being sentenced community service at the hospital. *I guess it's better than going to juvenile detention or whatever.*

She always knew Sam was kind of a bad kid, but he mostly just seemed high-strung and annoying, not really capable of criminal behavior. She had never heard he had been arrested for anything, either. Well, his parents did a good job of covering it up, whatever it was. The kid obviously couldn't be trusted ...

Hannah is dwelling on this memory as she spies the brown-painted cinder blocks of the restroom facility. The smoke from the fire fills her nostrils, and she sprints the last few hundred feet to their campsite, her worries about Sam's delinquency temporarily forgotten.

CHAPTER 18

Back at their camp, while Hannah is half a mile away and hopefully finding something useful, Alex and Jessie wander into the woods to collect more firewood. They make an ever-widening perimeter around the fire, since they are using quite a bit of wood keeping it going nonstop.

They gather armloads of sticks and branches, making slow trips back and forth. Finally, they end up near the creek. Both sit on the rocks, dizzy from lack of food.

Jessie sighs deeply and rests her head on her drawn-up knees, then rubs her eyes. Alex wonders if she is sick or hurt. Suddenly he sees an alarming stream of tears flowing down her cheeks.

Alex is surprised by his sister's sudden breakdown and wonders if something else is wrong. He had thought there was *some* hope now, since Sam knows where they are, and Hannah should be able to run for help.

"Jessie?" Alex speaks tentatively, barely keeping his voice from wavering. "What's wrong? Are you okay?"

Since Sam got shot, Alex has been having visions and nightmares of Jessie lying motionless on the hard ground with a pool of blood around her. He realizes this is ridiculous, and he's pretty sure Jessie is not physically injured, but he fears something terrible will happen to each of them, one by one, until they are all dead in the woods, never to be found.

Alex nestles himself on the rock next to his sister and puts his arm around her shoulders. "Please tell me what's wrong. Is it something I did?"

Jessie shakes her head. "No, sweetie, of course not. I'm just so ... so tired. God, I wish I had let you and Hannah go yesterday. I was so terrified that you would get hurt, or captured ... and that Sam was going to die, and I'd be alone with him ..."

"It's better we stayed, Jessie. You heard what he said about the way out. We never would have made it."

"But now I'm really terrified that Sam ... that Sam isn't going to make it. He looks so bad. I'm sorry, I shouldn't be telling you this. I don't want you to lose hope ... I don't know if we will really be able to get out of here ... it all seems so ... so impossible. I'm sorry ..." Jessie trails off miserably.

Alex is silent for a minute, then says, "It's okay. You're not telling me anything I haven't already thought about myself. I know he might die. I'm pretty sure he thinks he is going to die, too, with how he was talking earlier." He gives her a small smile and quietly asks, "Do you love him?"

"What? Yeah, of course I do!" Jessie says firmly. "He's like another little brother, just like you." She cups his cheek.

"That's not what I meant ..."

Jessie sighs and turns away from him. "Yeah ... I know what you meant. Honestly, I don't know. He's done some things out here ... I mean, we've always gotten along really well ... but he has such a terrible reputation. I can't see myself getting involved with someone who does the things he does. He's always getting into some kind of trouble, you know?"

Alex shrugs. "But does he really?"

"What do you mean? He is *always* getting into fights at school ... he mouths off to his parents ... his mom just kicked him out of the house Saturday morning. And Hannah told me she caught him doing court-ordered community service at the hospital a few months ago. What was that about? I didn't even know he had been arrested. There's so much I don't trust about him. I'm pretty sure he sneaks into the Radiation Zone. He does some stupid stuff, you know?" Jessie dries her eyes.

She looks sheepishly at Alex, who doesn't reply. She continues, "I just don't think I should be, like, romantically involved with someone like Sam." Jessie looks uncomfortable as she utters the words "romantically involved" to Alex about his best friend. This is an awkward conversation.

But Alex knows he needs to tell Jessie the truth about Sam because Sam never will.

"I don't think his reputation is as bad as you think," Alex replies slowly, picking up a handful of pebbles and casting them one by one into the rushing creek. "A lot of what he says is a joke, stuff he makes up because he is bored or whatever."

"I don't know, Alex ... I've *seen* him do stupid stuff or heard about it from other people. It isn't all talk with him."

"You used to babysit him. Has he ever done anything really bad? Like, other than stupid bike stunts in the driveway? And don't count the time he broke his legs. He told me later he did that because he was angry about something at school and admitted it was the stupidest thing he ever did." Alex continues to toss pebbles.

Jessie laughs mirthlessly for a second. "Okay, so taking *that* particular screw-up off the table, no, he never really did anything bad *while I was babysitting*. But that's different. I get the impression he was always on his best behavior with me. ... He never drank an entire bottle of Scotch while I was around, anyway ..."

Alex chuckles. "Oh, yeah, I forgot about that. Yeah, that was pretty dumb. Again, he did that because he was bored. He wasn't *trying* to be bad."

"Bored or not, he should still know right from wrong. I mean you and I know never to do that! I don't know, Alex, sometimes he makes me nervous. Like, I can't really trust him. I feel like he's always up to something or trying to hide something. It's just a feeling I have. I can't explain it."

"Yeah, that's true. He does like to keep his secrets."

Jessie continues without asking him to clarify his comments any further. "I honestly can't picture myself with him. Anyway, I'm sure he has plenty of other girls he can choose from, besides me."

"He does. ... But he hasn't chosen them."

"Really?" Jessie asks skeptically. "I always assumed Sam had a whole host of girlfriends who willingly lined up to be his next conquest."

Alex shakes his head. "Nope. I have seen him turn girls down. He's been in love with you since the first time he met you at the baseball field that day ... and he's been waiting for you all this time. He's been asking me for years to find out how you feel about him. It's really kind of annoying."

"So why are you telling me this, Alex?"

It is Alex's turn to sigh deeply, and when he speaks his voice wavers. "Because," he says, but his voice breaks and he has to start over. "Because he really might die. I mean, he's in bad shape, Jessie. Even I can see that. And I think he has a right to know how you feel about him, if you really do love him ... like it's only fair to tell him the truth in case he really does ... you know. ... And after he saved us from Scott. ... I guess I feel like if you really *do* have feelings for him, you need to tell him. You know what I mean?" He glances at her quickly, then reaches down and slowly sifts another handful of pebbles.

"Okay, first of all, *you* saved us from Scott. You got the money. Don't put yourself down, and don't let Sam tell you anything different. He'll probably try to steal the credit when we get out of this. You know how he likes to show off. And stealing credit from you would be too easy because you are too nice, and he knows you won't argue. I can't fully trust him. And neither should you."

Alex is almost offended that Jessie basically called him a pushover, but he's too tired and hungry to defend himself—which only proves her point, but whatever. He's more irritated that Jessie isn't giving Sam *any* credit for fighting Scott.

"But Sam is the one who tried to fight Scott off!" he retorts. "I really didn't do anything, at least not on purpose. I just happened to get my Gift. How could Sam possibly know Scott would have a gun?"

"Because Scott is a *criminal!* It was stupid of Sam to try to overpower him anyway. He only got himself into more trouble. ... As usual!" Jessie angrily leaps off the rock.

"Please don't be mad at him, Jessie. He really does always try to do the right thing." Alex clambers off his rock and drops the pebbles he had been playing with. Jessie turns away but not before he sees the tears welling in her eyes.

"Yeah, right. Name one time," she scoffs. "This should be good. Let's see how that idiot warped your mind over the years."

Alex's anger flares. She is insulting his dying best friend! Luckily, Alex has years of stories to change Jessie's mind.

"Well, literally the day I met him ... Chris and Justin were ready to beat me up. I mean, Chris had his fist pulled back and everything ... Justin was holding me down ... I couldn't move ... I was all alone. They really could have hurt me." Alex looks up at her, but she is walking toward the camp. He can't tell if she is even listening to him, but he continues anyway. "And then suddenly, Sam was there. I don't even know where he came from. He was just ... there. Then he made fun of them the way they were making fun of me, and, I don't know, basically told them off, and we left. He didn't throw a single punch. Like, I don't think he was actually *looking* for a fight. He just wanted to help me. Then when we were playing catch, he tried to make me feel better by missing the ball after I missed it ... every time. He didn't want me to feel like too much of a baby or whatever."

"Really?" Jessie asks skeptically, but she stops and turns around. "Did he tell you that?"

"No. I caught on months later, after we became better friends. I mean, he could literally catch almost anything I threw at him, bad pitches and all. But every time I missed the ball, he would make sure to miss the next one. I asked him about it, and he tried to deny it at first, saying he was no better than me. But I figured it out. I mean, I always did feel inferior to him ... how could I not? And he knew that."

Alex pauses, thinking. "I think he really does have a big heart, Jessie. You should give him a chance. ... I'm not the only kid he saved from bullying, either. There were six others I could name over the years. And guess how many fights Sam has been in at school? Six. Every time, he only got involved because some kid was bullying someone else. He came to their rescue." Alex shrugs. "He's not a bad kid."

Jessie slowly wanders back to the edge of the creek and perches on another rock. Alex sits next to her, hoping he has changed her mind.

"Okay, what about the time he tried to walk off school property?" She is still not convinced.

"Do you remember Kat Fisher?" Alex asks. "She was in the year between us, but she used to live down the street from us. She moved away about three years ago, I think."

"Oh, yeah. I do remember her." Jessie is confused as she searches her memory, wondering what Kat has to do with anything.

"Well, I guess she got a bad grade on a test or something, and some of her friends were making fun of her. So, she got really upset and tried to leave school during gym class. Sam was also outside since they were in the same class. This was before he got held back a year ... but anyway, he saw her sneaking off the grounds, and he went running after her. When they got caught, Sam said he was the one who was trying to sneak away, and Kat ran after him to get him to come back."

"Okay, but why would he do that? What was he trying to gain by doing that?"

"Nothing for himself. He genuinely didn't want Kat to get into trouble. She was a good student, and her parents would have been furious with her. And she probably would have been suspended if she'd actually left school. She didn't need to be punished just because she had a bad day. I think Sam felt like he really had nothing to lose. It really didn't change *his* reputation at all. Anyway, it's not like they actually *left* school property. What was the worst that could happen to him? By that time he had his reputation, he was used to being grounded. He knew his parents would just ground him for a week or whatever, and life would go on. Besides, I think he liked having a bad reputation. He liked to see what people thought of him."

"So he's a fake," Jessie says flatly. Under her breath, she mutters, "God, what an idiot."

"He's not a fake. Well, I mean, maybe he is, sort of ..." Alex stumbles over his words. "But Jessie, you don't get it. Think of it this way; you know how there are some people who you think are good, and they end up doing something bad, or dishonest, or something that sort of ruins your perception of them?"

Jessie half-heartedly agrees. "Mm-hmm."

"Okay, so Sam is, like, the opposite of that."

Jessie gives Alex a blank look.

"He wants to be all cool and act like he doesn't care about anything, but really he watches out for everyone. I think it's something his father taught him. 'Always help those who can't help themselves.'"

"Hmm ... that *does* sound like something Senator Starling would say," she muses. "But what about his court-ordered community service at the hospital last year? Spin *that* so he's a saint."

"Fine. I will," Alex responds defiantly. "But that involves telling you a big secret about Sam and his family, one that he asked me never to discuss. ... I guess maybe it doesn't really matter now. But if I tell you, please promise not to tell anyone."

"I promise," Jessie whispers, thoroughly intrigued.

"I bet Hannah saw Sam at the hospital on a Wednesday night, right?" Alex asks, already knowing the answer.

"Yeah, I think so. It was after one of her EMT calls. She usually does that on Wednesdays."

"Well, Sam has been going to the hospital every Wednesday for the past five years."

"What? Why?" she blurts, alarmed. She immediately fears the worst. Is Sam sick? Is his big secret that he is hiding a chronic illness? *But, man, the guy looks amazing for someone who needs to go to the hospital every week.* "Is he okay?" Jessie asks, barely more than a whisper.

"Oh, yeah. He's fine. He reads to the kids in the cancer ward."

A wave of relief rushes through her, and she is more than a little annoyed at Alex for scaring her.

"Why? Is it court-ordered or whatever?"

"No." Alex shakes his head. "It's his way of giving back."

"Giving back for what?" She suddenly wonders if maybe Sam *had been* sick and is now cured. She really wants Alex to get to the point already.

"Okay, don't tell anyone this. The Starlings have kept it a secret for six years, but Violet was born with some kind of blood cancer."

Jessie gasps. "Oh, my God! Is she okay? Like, in remission?"

"Yeah, she's been in remission since she was three. All her tests come back clean every six months, and she's doing great."

"Why do they want that kept secret? That's great that she beat it!"

Alex shrugs. "I guess because they never told Violet she was sick. She doesn't really remember any of it. I guess there is always a chance the cancer could come back, and they don't want her to live in fear of it. Every six months, she gets bloodwork and a bunch of other tests done, and Sam goes with her and, like, pretends to go through the same tests so she thinks it is routine for everyone. He gets his blood drawn and everything with her. Actually, I think he ends up donating his blood."

"Wow." Jessie finds she really doesn't know what to say but realizes her previous anger and mistrust toward Sam is suddenly gone. Well, maybe not all of it. "Is that why Violet is so small? Did the cancer stunt her growth or something?"

"Yeah, I guess so."

"Huh, and here I thought it was because Sam always steals food off her plate when she isn't looking."

"Yeah, well." Alex laughs. "He does do that."

"Jeez, Alex ... you have certainly given me a lot to think about. Thanks for telling me. And I promise I won't tell anyone." Jessie shakes her head. Sam *is* a liar. She always knew it. But maybe that isn't such a bad thing. She has a sudden urge to get back to him as quickly as possible and give him a big hug ... and maybe kiss him. Maybe. She quickly brushes away the fresh tears glistening on her cheeks. "Come on. We really should get back to him."

***

Alex and Jessie had just gotten themselves settled on the ground next to the fire when they hear Hannah's quick steps on the gravel road. She runs behind the restroom, barely winded, and skids to a stop.

"Guys!" she yells too loudly. Sam had been dozing and wakes up with a start, tensing up as new pain surges through him.

"Jeez!" he complains. "This better be good, Speedy," he slowly sits up, tentatively stretches his legs, and massages his lower back. He looks extremely uncomfortable. Jessie wishes she could do something to help him.

"Oh, don't worry. It is!" Hannah replies, undoing her bundle. Alex and Jessie crowd around her, peering excitedly into the fabric of Alex's jacket and at the plastic watering can. "I did find a map!" She grabs it from her pocket and hands it to Sam.

"Yay!" Alex exclaims. He sits next to Sam to study the map with him, fully knowing he can't contribute at all to the rescue effort.

"Oh, wow!" Jessie says as she spies the food. "Look at all that!"

They sort through their new treasure, the piles of food stacking up like gold coins. They agree to eat slowly to avoid shocking their systems and losing what they eat.

After they each finish a granola bar, Hannah pulls the oatmeal creme pie from her back pocket.

"And now, ladies and gentlemen," Hannah says, holding the pie away from them, "I present to you: the one and only ... perfect snack."

It is the most delicious thing they have ever tasted.

"Mmm ..." Sam says, licking cream off his fingers. "I could use about a hundred and twelve more of these."

"Same," Alex says.

"Hey, don't get that pristine map all grimy with your gross fingers!" Hannah teases Sam.

Sam pretends to lick the full length of the map.

Jessie and Alex laugh, and Hannah rolls her eyes. "You are *so* disgusting."

"Disgusting or not, you needed me to get you out of here. Who knew that office was so close?" Sam gives her a smug look. "Come here. I'll show you where we are ..."

***

Hannah feels good about getting out of here. The exit road is clearly marked on the map. There are numerous turns, but she knows she can mark her progress as she runs down the road. *I got this,* she thinks, tightening her shoelaces.

After slowly savoring a few more bites of food, Hannah suddenly jumps up. "Oh, I almost forgot!" She goes back over to Alex's jacket and pulls out the small first aid kit. "Sam, I found some Advil, but it expired five years ago."

"Sold!" Sam says, reaching his hand up to grab the foil packet of medicine from her. He greedily opens it and swallows both pills without water. "Oh, yeah, much better." He stretches out a little, the way someone might on a sandy beach. They all laugh at that, feeling better than they have in a long time.

CHAPTER 19

Hannah pockets four more granola bars and three bags of peanuts and drinks her fill of water. She has a long journey ahead of her. She and Jessie hug, not certain when or if they will see each other again. Jessie swallows the lump in her throat as Hannah disappears again on the road.

The morning slowly passes into afternoon, and Jessie worries nonstop about Hannah. She has no idea how long it will take her to run nine miles. She knows Hannah isn't especially fast. Stamina is her skill.

Jessie is sitting near the fire and distractedly pushes the embers around with a stick. "Would you two mind if I go for a walk? Just up and down the road ... I won't go far. I just need to move a little."

Alex and Sam nod noncommittally, both stretched out by the fire, slowly sipping from cups of water.

Jessie stands up and brushes her pants off. "I can't sit here and worry about Hannah." She raises her eyebrows at her brother. "Are you sure you're okay to stay here and keep an eye on Sam?"

Alex shrugs. "I guess. What do I have to do?" he asks uncertainly.

"Don't let me die," Sam pipes up, trying not to move at all. Everything hurts.

Jessie and Alex exchange an awkward laugh, neither of them sure that Sam *won't* die on their watch. She leaves for the road, and Alex disappears between the trees as he walks a widening radius around camp, collecting more firewood.

Sam idly stares at the stash of food next to him. They had all been slowly munching on the snacks, Sam not able to eat much without feeling sick. He still has a fever. The Advil didn't help much with that, but the pain in his leg does seem to have lessened.

He grabs a bag of potato chips and tries to pass the time by reading the small print on the back. It is not an easy task. His vision blurs, and his head swims, and potato chips bring back a lot of bad memories for Sam. *I wonder how many of these little bags of chips I ate when I was recovering from my bike accident. Ugh ... probably hundreds.*

After his casts came off, part of Sam's physical therapy was walking a little farther every day. The concession stand at the community park is about a half mile from his house, and he used that as his goal. There and back; a full mile of walking. It was an agonizing task, not exactly physically painful after he had gotten through the first week or so, but it was painful in other ways. Like, emotionally or whatever.

He would slowly hobble to the park, his muscles and joints stiff and sore after months of being jailed in those stupid, horrible casts. But it felt good to be out moving again, especially on summer evenings.

His friends would usually interrupt their various activities to sit with him for a few minutes as he rested, fatigued, on a park bench. Of course, everyone wanted to know how he was doing—was he in pain? Was he bored at home? Sam answered them all, doing his best to sound upbeat and optimistic, regaling them with tales of how many levels he had conquered on their favorite computer games.

Quickly, though, his friends went back to their sports and fun, leaving Sam on the bench all alone, near the concession stand. He would buy a bag of chips while he rested, wishing one of his friends would sit with him the whole time, and then maybe walk home with him. But no one ever did.

He spent so many hours alone, wishing that someone, anyone, would help him get through another day.

If he does survive this, it is going to be another long, lonely, miserable few months. What if he gets held back in school again? He decides he can't let that happen. He's six years older now and can handle the pain and confinement and set his mind to his school tasks. When he was ten, he was upset with his situation and not old enough to fully understand that it was entirely due to his reckless behavior. He had just been so angry.

Often, Sam would go two or three nights in a row without sleeping. He would scream in his room all night, and even his mother couldn't console him. His father started coming home from Washington a few nights a week to spend some quality time with his struggling son.

But nothing helped. Sam only became angrier and more unreachable. Finally, his doctor prescribed sedatives for him. They definitely helped him sleep, but they also made his brain too fuzzy to concentrate on schoolwork. He hated how the drugs made him feel, sluggish and heavy, but it was better than screaming for hours at a time, pounding the walls, pounding his casts, trapped inside the prison he had created.

Will that happen to him again? Will he sink into a depression that robs him of sleep and his friends and his entire personality?

Sam shudders. When had he become such a deep thinker?

He throws the bag of chips to the side, pretty sure he has eaten enough of them to last his entire lifetime. He reaches for another granola bar and slowly munches it, but he isn't feeling quite well enough to finish it. He wraps the rest and stuffs it in his pocket, his hand brushing his lighter. Tears spring to his eyes.

His lighter makes him think of his little sister, Violet. Will he survive to see her again? Violet has been through so much and has always been so strong. Of course, it probably helps that she doesn't really know she's sick. Sam and his parents have tried to pretend over the years that all the doctor visits and blood tests she endures are part of normal, everyday life. Luckily, she is still too young to ask a lot of questions about it, even now. The time is coming, Sam knows, when she will learn the truth.

He remembers donating blood for Violet, a half a pint at a time, when she was a tiny baby. They were perfect matches. And now, ironically, Sam is the one needing the blood transfusion. Maybe it won't matter anyway. Will Hannah even be able to get help in time—before his blood is poisoned beyond the limits of medicine?

For lack of anything better to do, Sam grabs the bag of potato chips again and pulls the corner open. The salty scent reminds him of loneliness, helplessness, and shame. His memories of sitting alone on the park bench wash over him.

"Whatever. Might as well get this party started," he mutters and tips the bag into his mouth. Not bad, considering they are five years outdated. He slowly works his way through two more bags, throwing the trash on the fire, trying not to think about his uncertain future.

He becomes vaguely aware of Alex piling sticks next to him. Alex is silent and seems moody, which is unlike him, especially since now, maybe, they have a greater chance of being rescued.

"Hey, man," Sam says to his friend, struggling to sit up and only managing to prop himself on an elbow. "Are you okay? You seem really upset, like, more than usual. You know you saved us, right? I didn't mean what I said about you getting the money a minute too late."

"It's not that." Alex prods some of the embers around in the dirt. "You don't know who those people were, do you?"

"No, I was too busy getting shot." Sam regrets this comment as soon as it slips from his lips. He meant it to be funny, but he realizes it sounded kind of accusatory. Alex doesn't seem to notice and continues playing with the charred sticks at the edge of the fire. "Why? Do you?" Sam asks, tipping the remnants of another bag of chips into his mouth. *Yeah, these are pretty darn tasty. I should contact the company and let them know their potato chips should be in underground bunkers for the next nuclear meltdown. "Our chips are apocalypse-approved! Stock up now!"*

Silent tears slide down Alex's dirty cheeks, and Sam listens quietly as he learns about the recent felonies committed by Scott and Blaze Givins. *Jeez, I'm really glad I didn't voice my potato chip advertisement before he told me this devastating news. Insensitive much? Idiot.*

Sam desperately wants to sit next to Alex and wrap a brotherly arm around his shoulders, but he knows he can't get up. He sighs and says quietly to his friend, "I'm really sorry I got you all into this."

Alex looks up and wipes his eyes. "What do you mean?"

Sam has a feeling Scott's intended target was only supposed to be him; Jessie, Alex, and Hannah were probably innocent bystanders who got caught up in Scott's plan for revenge. They happened to be in an opportune place at the same time, giving Scott a chance to collect even more ransom money.

Sam massages his eyes. "Scott has always been gunning for me. ... No pun intended." He shrugs and gives Alex a tentative smile. "Okay, maybe a little pun intended. He beat me up the day I jumped the moat. The only injuries I got from my bike accident were my two broken legs. The cuts on my face, the bruised ribs, the black eye ... all that was courtesy of Scott. He said it should have been my father who was assassinated."

"What? Why?" Alex asks, never having heard this story.

"It was my father's limo. Senator Givins was only borrowing it for the weekend. He was coming home to Cutter County on a Friday afternoon. My father worked late and planned to come home Saturday morning. The car bomb was meant for my father."

"Wow! I didn't know that. Do you know why someone wanted him dead?"

Sam shrugs. "Not exactly. I know he had a few enemies in Washington back then. ... That seems to have died down in the past few years, though."

Alex raises his eyebrows. "Pun intended?"

Sam gives his friend a small smile. "Anyway, I have a suspicion this kidnapping is pretty much all my fault ... or my father's fault ... and I'm sorry."

"I've been thinking it's my fault because I'm friends with Blaze, and my family is rich and his isn't. I figured he and Scott are jealous."

"Oh, okay." Sam feigns relief. "Let's go with your theory. Whew, I really dodged a bullet there."

Alex shakes his head. "You are really too much sometimes."

"I know." Sam sighs and stretches his leg gingerly, then says somberly, "Unfortunately, I think this goes way beyond petty jealousy. I've always wondered what would have happened to my family and me if it had been my father ..." Sam is unable to continue.

"What do you think will happen to them?" Alex asks, his voice wavering. "Do you think they'll go to jail?"

"Well, that depends," Sam says slowly, pondering his answer. He picks up another bag of chips and absently opens it. He really has no idea how many he's eaten, and he's not really hungry, but focusing on these chips is easier than thinking about the mess he caused with Scott. "Are we going to turn them in?"

Alex looks up with disbelief in his eyes. "You ... you don't think we should?"

Sam munches thoughtfully. "I don't know. I mean, they've had it pretty rough. I had it pretty easy, and I've done illegal stuff."

"But you never *kidnapped* and *shot* someone!"

"Desperation makes people do some crazy things." They sit in silence for a few minutes, Alex wearily holding his head in his hands and Sam finishing his chips and throwing the bag on the fire. He reaches for another.

Before he can open it, Jessie screams from the road, "Build the fire! Build the fire high!"

Alex jumps up, both boys momentarily confused why Jessie sounds so terrified. Then Sam catches a movement in the forest, off to his left. Three coyotes have taken off, deeper into the woods, also startled by Jessie's screams.

"Go! Get out of here!" Alex yells, throwing rocks in the general direction of the coyotes. Jessie appears at the corner of the building, scanning the campsite, clearly alarmed.

"Are you okay?" Jessie asks, her eyes huge with terror.

"Yeah ... fine," Alex says. He is a little dazed, not quite sure what happened. Jessie is breathing hard from her sprint back to camp, and Alex hands her a cup of water.

"Thanks," she gasps, guzzling the water in a long swallow. "The coyotes smelled the blood. They had their minds set on lunch." She glances at Sam as she speaks, noting the huge amount of dried blood staining his pants. She kneels next to him, trying to steady her breathing, the new elevation of her heart rate having nothing to do with her recent exertion. *God, he looks bad. He isn't going to make it ...* She tries to push these thoughts away as she hovers over Sam, her long hair dangling in his face.

Sam managed to sit up during all the excitement and slowly eases himself flat on the ground again, hands splayed out, chest heaving with the effort of moving. His cheeks are pale, eyes glassy and rimmed with red.

"There is no shortage of excitement out here," he mutters quietly, voice wavering as his head falls back in the dirt. Jessie gives his shoulder a gentle squeeze. He slits his eyes open, and her pulse quickens again.

"Sam ..." Jessie whispers but trails off. His eyes close again, his breathing ragged and shallow. They somehow need to get him out of here, or at least find a safer place. "Maybe we should build another fire right outside the doorway in the front? At least we can go into the restroom if the coyotes come back." She looks at the boys for approval. Alex nods, and Sam twitches his lips, silently letting Jessie know he will do whatever she suggests.

Alex sorts through the remains of the fire. "That's a good idea, Jessie. I'll start a fire near the front door." He grabs the ends of some of the larger sticks, their tips still ablaze, and carefully takes them to the front of the restroom. "Ah, darn ... these aren't really staying lit. Sam, can I have your lighter?"

"Fifty bucks," Sam replies flatly as he tosses his lighter to Alex.

Alex reaches into his pocket and comes up empty-handed. "Nope, nothing. My Gift knows you're an idiot."

"Ah, well ... still worth a shot." Sam gives his friend a devious but somewhat forced smile.

"Okay, you really need to stop," Alex says, feigning exasperation as he disappears around the side of the building again.

Jessie kneels beside Sam.

"Do you hear the coyotes?" he asks, eyes flickering with the tiniest bit of fear.

Jessie shakes her head. "No, all is quiet out there." For now.

Sam sighs. "Good. That was an interesting feeling. Being hunted." He lies back in the dirt and laces his hands over his stomach.

Jessie is about to tease him but stays quiet, deciding not to mention that Sam had already technically been hunted down and shot like an animal. That might be a little too cruel, even for him.

She cups his cheek with her hand. He seems cooler. Maybe his fever is gone. "How are you feeling?"

Sam reaches up and grasps her wrist, turning his face into her palm.

"Oh, absolutely fantastic," he replies sarcastically, the corners of his mouth twitching up. Jessie searches his face. His brow is furrowed, eyes bloodshot and glassy. She knows he will never admit the true extent of his discomfort to her. It will be one sarcastic comment after another. As if proving her point, Sam adds, "I feel like I could run a marathon."

"You couldn't run a marathon even when you had two good legs," she teases, speaking softly, letting him caress her wrist, her fingers still resting gently on his face.

"Hey, is that another fat joke? You're so mean," Sam whispers just as softly, taking her hand in both of his and laying it on his chest, playing with her fingers.

"I think it was more an insult to your willpower, or lack thereof. But I'm telling you, you really could stand losing some weight. I'm getting tired of hauling your fat butt around."

"Wow ... the ugly truth comes out at last. I see how it is. And I've been trying so hard to be perfect for you," he says, flashing one of those smiles that immediately makes her feel like everything in the world is right and wonderful. It isn't his usual devilish smirk, or the movie-star smile he uses when showing off. This smile is genuine, one Jessie has seen rarely over the years, but it is her favorite. She now realizes what is so different about it: it shows how much he cares.

His eyes come alive, hiding the pain and fear Jessie had seen there all day. She catches herself involuntarily thinking, *He is perfect.*

She chuckles softly at his corny banter but can't think of anything funny to say to him. She feels a little thrown off, like Sam is a stranger she is only now getting to know.

"You have the best smile," she finally whispers, almost inaudibly. A lump forms in her throat, and she's having some trouble speaking around it. She disentangles her fingers from his and reaches her hands up to massage his shoulders. She whispers close to his ear, "I've always loved your smile, ever since I first met you ... before I met you, actually. Sometimes, when we were stuck at those stupid dinners when we were kids, I would watch you from across the dining room, hoping to catch a glimpse of that smile." Her voice wavers, tears quickly filling her eyes.

"Hmm ... maybe the truth isn't as ugly as it first appeared," Sam muses. "I'm not hating this massage, by the way." He closes his eyes and rolls his head from side to side.

"Oh, good. My goal was to give you an unhateful massage," Jessie retorts, squeezing his shoulders harder, internally thankful that he hadn't made a big deal out of her confession. "I'm actually only doing this to warm up my hands."

"Oh, man, you are full of insults today, aren't you?" Sam laughs. But then he grimaces as pain shoots through his leg and lower back. He gasps and tenses his upper body, causing Jessie to pull her hands away in alarm. She sits up quickly, not realizing how closely she had been hovering over him.

"Oh, my God, I'm sorry! Did I hurt you?"

"No, no," Sam says with a moan, putting one hand behind his back to ease his spasming muscles. "I told you before, you can't hurt me." His lips twitch, and his face relaxes as the wave of pain dissipates. He gazes at her through half-closed lids, having some difficulty focusing on her. "Sometimes, there are these random bolts of pain, you know? Like everything is seizing up at once. Man, this sucks."

"Jessie," Alex sternly interrupts. "Let's move."

"Oh, yeah." Jessie leans away from Sam and looks at Alex on the other side of the fire. She had actually kind of forgotten he was there.

"Come on, Jessie, pay attention," Sam teases, his voice raspy and weak.

"Well, you distracted me!" She slaps him gently on the chest. Before she can take her hand away, Sam grabs it and squeezes her fingers, completely enveloping her little hand in his big one.

"Mm, yes, well, I am pretty distracting," Sam replies, eyes closed, the corners of his mouth turning down as he grimaces in pain. He lets go of her hand and puts both of his behind his back. He doesn't look like he has any interest in getting up.

"Come on, lazy bum," Jessie says, shaking his shoulder. "We need to move."

"Do we really have to?" Sam whines. "Seems like a lot of work." His eyes are still closed. He doesn't have the typical teasing lilt in his voice, and Jessie worries he might actually be serious this time. Is he giving up? Is he too exhausted and in too much pain to even care anymore?

"Sam, seriously ..."

"We'll be fine here."

"Why risk it, sweetie? The coyotes might come back."

"I'll risk it."

"Sam, you're being an idiot." Jessie glances at Alex, who shrugs, also not sure why his friend is suddenly uninterested in moving to a safer place.

Finally, not knowing how to convince him, Jessie simply says, "Please."

That gets Sam's attention. He opens his eyes and looks right at her. "You're lucky you're pretty," he whispers.

"Come on. I'll help you up."

Sam is right about one thing. It *is* a lot of work to get him up. He can't stand, even with Jessie pulling his arms. Alex rushes over to help, but Sam groans and falls back onto the hard ground, his chest heaving.

Oh, my God, he is getting weaker and weaker! Jessie's thoughts whirl. *I have no idea what to do without Hannah. Maybe moving him isn't a good idea. Maybe we should just take our chances ...*

"Oww." Sam moans as he lies flat on his back. "Can you ... can you give me a minute?"

Suddenly, Jessie tenses next to him as unwelcome thoughts stream through her brain. She hears it. Or, more accurately, she hears *them*. They are being stalked.

"Crap," she whispers, peering into the darkening forest. "Those three coyotes are still right there ... about fifty feet away. I can only catch a few words as they go in and out of my range. But they still want to eat—" She almost says "eat you" to Sam but stops herself just in time.

Sam is feeling pretty horrible. He's been feeling worse and worse throughout the day but doesn't want his friends to know that. They are scared enough and already think he's going to croak at any second. He has been doing his best to sound "cavalier," but it is getting increasingly difficult to keep up the act.

Jessie kneels next to him, listening to the coyotes in the forest, but also in her head. Sam is glad she stayed with him for a minute but really just wants to sleep. Or, better yet, slip into a nice, comfortable coma and never have to move again. No matter how hard he tries, he can't take his mind off the horrors waiting for him when he gets out of here. *If* he gets out of here.

He tries not to think about it, but the more he pushes those fears away, the more they press in on his thoughts. Turmoil rages in his head.

Jessie turns back to face him, then peers into the trees, trying to catch a glimpse of their furry stalkers. "I wonder if they would eat the snacks we have and maybe leave us alone? God, I wish my Gift allowed me to speak to animals so they could understand me." She whispers under her breath, "Please, please, please leave us alone."

Sam can't stand seeing Jessie this scared. This may be the final straw for her. Something that he can't even begin to understand. Well, he understands that being hunted by a pack of starving coyotes can never be good.

He can't imagine being inside the thoughts of this band of coyotes right now. Jessie knows exactly what they are thinking ... knows exactly how they will slice up his leg in equal thirds. He wonders vaguely what wine they will pair with him. *I will probably be super salty from all those stupid potato chips. Okay, I think maybe I'm getting delirious now.*

Sam knows he is completely helpless and will definitely not be able to fend off three coyotes if they all attack at once. He has been lifting weights for years, but he knows his strength won't much matter in his current state. It will probably only take one bite, to his neck or the bullet wound, and he'll be done.

He shudders, tremors of pain and fear wracking his body. He so badly wants to be sitting on the bank of the duck pond with Jessie, fishing and watching birds, warm and content. With his arms around her.

Alex hauls huge portions of their sticks and branches to the front of the restroom for the new fire, leaving Jessie alone with Sam while he catches his breath after moving two inches. They lock eyes, their hands clasped tightly together, both terrified and exhausted.

"Jessie, I ..." Sam whispers, trying to raise himself into a seated position again. He's too weak to do so and falls back into the dirt on his elbows. "I need you to know, if I don't make it out of here ..." His voice cracks.

"Shh, Sam, please ... please don't talk like that." Jessie sobs quietly. "You're gonna make it."

"Jessie ... listen ..." He's breathing hard after making another unsuccessful attempt at sitting up. "Damn it ..." he mutters, thoroughly frustrated with himself.

"Here." Jessie grabs his other hand and gently pulls him up.

"Jessie ... I want you to know..." Sam inhales sharply and gazes at her, their eyes gleaming with tears. "When we were kids ... at those dinners ... I would always look for you, too. And ... and I feel like I'm still looking for you. There's never been anyone else ... only you, Jessie. And I need to know ... if you love me."

Well, darn. He definitely had not meant to say that. *Idiot.*

"Oh, okay ... okay." Jessie whispers, not at all sure what she is supposed to say. "Why are you telling me this?" she blurts. She knows she sounds callous, but she *really* can't focus on what Sam is saying right now. Her brain is whirling with her own thoughts and those of the coyotes. They won't get out of her head. They continue lurking within her range, focusing on their next move.

"Because ... I don't know if I'm gonna ... Jessie, I love you." Sam's voice cracks, and he stares at her questioningly, eyebrows raised.

She can't look him in the eye for long. Her thoughts swirl with what Alex has told her about him, how he held her that first night out here. *Am I falling in love with him? Or am I just desperate for protection right now?*

"Sweetie, we can talk about this later, okay? We need to move." Jessie absolutely cannot think about this.

Sam's reply is a slow nod, lips set in a firm line, eyes sliding away from Jessie's. She thinks maybe she really screwed up.

Alex strides around the back corner of the restroom. "Jessie, are you ready to—holy crap, those coyotes are right there!" He kneels beside his sister, ready to help pull Sam to his feet, keeping one eye on the three coyotes prancing between the trees. "Are they still thinking about lunch?"

"Yeah. Our movement really piques their interest. They are feeling more curious now."

"Oh, good. Less homicidal, then?" Sam groans as he shifts his weight, allowing Jessie and Alex to take his arms. They haul him to his feet with some difficulty. Another wave of pain and nausea is rolling over him. He is seriously regretting stuffing himself full of chips, as they're threatening to come up and splatter his shoes. He feels awful. He is dizzy and hot and cold at the same time. His vision is swimming, and his stomach is churning. The pain in his leg is searing. *Oh, and let's not forget that Jessie has basically just rejected me, right to my face. Things cannot get much worse.*

Sam moans in pain as he stands unsteadily between Jessie and Alex. He can't straighten his back; his muscles are so mangled from lying on the ground for days. He can't take even a single step. The pounding in his head blurs his vision, and he pitches forward, but luckily, Jessie and Alex have a good hold of his arms and shoulders.

"Sorry," Sam mutters, not really sure what he's apologizing for. *Maybe for saying all that stuff to Jessie. Man, I'm stupid. Why did I have to put that on her? She has enough to worry about.*

He mostly feels like he needs to say something—really, anything—to fill this empty void of fear and silence. *Think about something else.* His mind slides back into its usual banter for a second, and he says, "This is a great team-building exercise, isn't it?" But then he has to fight hard not to vomit.

"We've got you," Alex says encouragingly, chuckling at Sam's stupid joke. Jessie makes no comment, but Sam thinks she may have given his arm a tiny squeeze. Maybe it was to make him shut up, though. He can't be sure.

Sam steadies himself between his friends and slowly hobbles around toward the front of the building. His right leg drags. He can't lift his foot at all anymore.

Suddenly there is a loud commotion in the woods, a great crashing of branches and leaves.

"Alex, they're coming!" Jessie screams.

They make it around the front corner of the restroom, the life-saving fire in view. It is small though, not nearly as well-fueled as their other fire, and Sam prays it will be enough to deter the hungry coyotes. In only a few seconds, they will be in the relative safety of the doorway, behind the fire. He hopes they can fend the coyotes off as a united front from there.

"No! No! Nooo!" Jessie screams, hearing unwelcome thoughts that are not her own. She suddenly whirls around, dropping Sam's right arm as she does so, leaving him to fall heavily to the ground, Alex going down with him.

Sam wails in agony as his injured leg hits the packed dirt and gravel. Sparks flash in his eyes, quickly dissolving into gray and white pixels of confetti. *I'm gonna pass out. Oh, God, don't pass out here,* he thinks desperately, nearly biting his tongue as he sprawls on the ground, too stunned with pain to move.

He turns his head to look over his shoulder and sees Jessie out of the corner of his eye, though blurred with tears. She did the right thing. She had to let him go. Two of the coyotes had rushed in, ready to launch themselves at their prey. Their paws are alarmingly close to Sam's feet, and he sees Jessie and Alex doing their best to defend all of their lives, throwing rocks and waving sticks, screaming and crying.

"Oh, God, Sam." Alex is suddenly at his side, pausing his onslaught of rocks to help his friend. "Are you okay?" he asks breathlessly.

"Fantastic. You?" Sam mumbles.

"Eh, kind of bored by all this," Alex replies, deadpan. Sam smiles at his friend's wit under these desperate circumstances. *I have taught you well, my friend.*

Suddenly Alex jumps up and grabs a handful of gravel, hurling it into the forest.

Sam rests his head in the dirt, tears leaking down his cheeks. He smells smoke from the new fire. They are so close, but he has the fleeting feeling that he just wants to die. Right here, right now. *I'm ready. There is no way I'm ever coming back from this. Get out the wine, coyotes. Please put me on a silver platter.*

The image of meeting his demise quickly morphs into a realistic scene, with sharp edges and crisp lines. A crystal-clear aerial view of himself lying in the middle of the forest, being torn apart by bloodied teeth, takes a solid shape in Sam's mind. He is not fighting back, his pain is gone, his life is draining away, he is relieved of his earthly responsibilities. *Stop thinking about this ... you promised ...*

Jessie screams at the coyotes as she and Alex throw great handfuls of gravel and sticks at them, keeping Sam out of reach of those snapping jaws. He thinks maybe he should try to make himself smaller, less of a target, rather than stay sprawled out like he is, his fingers an inviting entree, reaching toward the tree line. *Maybe I should try to get into a fetal position or something. Nah, screw it. I don't even want to move. I could lie here for the rest of my life ... which won't be long.*

"They aren't sure about the smell of the smoke," Jessie says, panting, from somewhere behind Sam. She reaches for a large branch and pokes in the general direction of the coyotes. There are only two now to fend off; the third one, the smallest one, has retreated into the woods and is running back and forth, watching her packmates intently but is too timid to join in the fray.

"Alex, can you get some of the burning branches from the fire?" Jessie calls to her brother without looking at him. There is no way she is taking her eyes off these two relentless coyotes. Their hunger is overpowering their fear, and she hears them planning another attack.

She has never been in the collective minds of a pack before; it is extremely frightening but also fascinating. How different the thoughts of a predator are from those of prey animals. The coyotes simultaneously work with each other to plan their next moves, keep an eye on the small female who has retreated, and are acutely aware of their own placement of their feet and how they interact with their surroundings. It is incredible. Jessie is stunned almost into inactivity by listening to them, by *feeling* them. Being in the minds of these fierce creatures that also show care and concern for their own is not an experience she will soon forget. The streaming thoughts of the coyotes are nearly ... human.

Alex appears with two large, flaming branches, and he brandishes them valiantly, stepping quite close to the coyotes to wave the orange tongues of fire right in their snouts.

"Get out of here!" Alex screams at the top of his voice, which is becoming shrill with fear. He and Jessie are both getting tired. Jessie is losing hope ... *We can't do this.*

Sam continues to watch all the excitement unfold out of the corners of his tear-filled eyes. He's still lying on his stomach, having managed somehow to move his hands underneath his chest. He doesn't remember doing that. Suddenly he feels like he is falling through a chasm as his body lurches involuntarily. For a split-second, he thinks the coyotes are on top of him, pulling his arms apart. He eventually realizes that Alex has grabbed his right shoulder and literally flipped him over onto his back, his right leg turning over painfully. Sam's head swims, his vision blurring with pain and tears.

"Ahhhh!" A macho shriek escapes Sam's lips as Alex pulls him up by the armpits, his butt and legs dragging painfully on the ground. His stomach heaves and he almost vomits down his shirt. He manages to keep his chips down, and Alex hauls him behind the fire, onto the concrete entryway of the restroom. Sam's leg is killing him.

Both boys are breathing heavily; Alex is muttering, "I'm sorry, I'm so sorry," his head bent over Sam, one hand on his shoulder. "I needed to get you out of there." His face is streaked with tears. "Can you speak? Are you okay? Don't pass out on me, buddy."

"Yeah," Sam croaks between taut lips, not really able to open his jaw, which is still clenched, making his teeth feel soft and nearly non-existent as he bites through the pain. *This vacation is getting worse by the minute.*

"I have to get back to Jessie." Alex gives Sam an apologetic look and disappears to help his sister.

He and Jessie scream as they throw handfuls of gravel at the retreating coyotes. The coyotes yip constantly, their feral voices high and agitated, but they are falling back into the safety of the forest. Trying to fight off the two-legged creatures with the orange heat that tickles their noses is not worth the energy they are expending. The two larger coyotes have rejoined the small female, but all three keep looking at their prey, their thoughts an equal mix of confusion and interest.

"Alex, get back here," Jessie instructs. Alex is partially in the woods, uncomfortably far from either fire, and Jessie worries the coyotes will change their minds and attack him next, since Alex alone does not pose much of a threat. Together, the three coyotes outweigh him, for sure.

Alex's lit branches have dwindled to charred spears sputtering only the slightest wisps of smoke. He steps back to join Jessie, who sinks to the ground, kneeling on the gravel near the restroom wall.

The full adrenaline of the last few minutes hits her like a cartoon piano dropped from the sky. Her entire body shakes, and she finds it difficult to breathe. Finally, she holds her breath to listen intently for the coyotes. There is nothing; they have retreated beyond her range.

Alex puts a steady hand on Jessie's trembling shoulder. "Jessie? Are you hurt?" he asks, new concern rising in his voice.

"No, I'm fine. It's just that their thoughts ... they were so ... calculated. Oh, God, they were going to kill us!" Her voice cracks, and she sobs into her hands.

"Yeah, but they didn't."

"I've never heard anything like that from an animal before. Working as a pack. That was amazing ... and terrifying."

"Hey, we make a pretty good pack, too," Alex says, giving Jessie a timid smile, trying to snap her out of whatever mental state this is. He doesn't like it. "Except for Sam. He's useless." He takes Jessie's hand and gives it a quick squeeze. He is pleasantly surprised to find he doesn't feel like breaking down and crying for a change.

"Oh, no! Sam!" Jessie whirls around and runs to the front of the restroom, where she finds Sam curled on the ground, biting his lower lip between clenched teeth, rocking his raised right leg from side to side in pain. When Jessie dropped him a few minutes ago, he fell with his full weight on his wounded leg, tearing the delicate flesh even more.

Jessie can't think of anything to do to ease Sam's pain, except try to reassure him that everything is okay. But she knows they are far from okay.

"Sam, I'm sorry. I'm so sorry." She kneels next to him, not sure if she should touch him or not. He must be furious with her. He is in agony.

"It's ... okay ... Jessie," he says, gasping. "Alex, it's okay. You did ... good. The pain's temporary ..." He tries to look up at Jessie and give her a reassuring smile but fails miserably. All he can do is grimace, hands balled into trembling fists. Finally, he manages to say, "But being eaten is forever."

Normally, Jessie would have rolled her eyes at that stupid comment, but right now Alex and Jessie give feeble laughs, feeling marginally better. Jessie puts a hand over Sam's forehead and gently pushes back his hair, though it doesn't really need pushing back. She needs to do this one thing, this one familiar motion, to ground them again. Everything is spinning out of control. What hope she had earlier today is now lost. She isn't sure if any of them will make it through the day. The coyotes might come back, maybe with reinforcements. And Sam really looks awful. Jessie can't even comprehend how bad he looks, but the phrase "on his deathbed" comes to mind.

Sam turns his head toward her and rolls slowly onto his left side to lift his chin over her knees. He sobs into her lap and covers his face with his hands, as though trying to hide. Jessie knows he can't take much more of this. Neither can she.

She gently strokes his hair, picking out scraps of leaves and twigs.

"I don't want to do this anymore, Jessie." Sam is sobbing. "I can't do this."

"Shh ..." she coos. "I've got you ..." He cries softly. Jessie is not sure what to say. She has never had to console him like this. She stays silent for a moment, then whispers, "Is the pain subsiding at all? Do you need anything?" She quickly realizes the last was a dumb question, since there is literally nothing she can do for him. *Please say something sarcastic*, she silently prays.

Jessie nearly begins crying when Sam simply replies, "No," and rolls his head off her lap to lie flat on the concrete, eyes closed, both legs splayed out. She doesn't know if his terse answer is in response to her first or second question, but she doesn't want to ask anything else. She notices his jeans are glistening in the firelight with fresh blood.

Sam sighs and says curtly, "Jessie ... tourniquet ..." and waves his hand vaguely at his leg.

Jessie does her best to wrench the tourniquet onto Sam's leg, hoping she is doing it correctly, Sam gasping and sobbing anew with the pain.

Alex appears around the corner, holding the watering can, which is still nearly full of water.

"Good thinking, kiddo." Jessie beams at him to let him know she is okay. The poor kid must be freaking out. "And you were right before, we do make a pretty amazing pack."

"Yeah, we do. Except for this freeloader." He grabs Sam's left foot and gives it an affectionate tug.

Did he just call me a freeloader? That's mean ... but fair. Before Sam can come up with a sarcastic reply, the coyotes begin howling a high-pitched eerie song. Sam shivers, and not because he's cold. The coyote howls are spooky.

Alex and Jessie jump up and face the forest, keeping Sam out of harm's way. Sam rests his hands over his eyes. *My God. Please kill me already.*

"Okay, I think we're good," Jessie says after a few seconds, the tension in her shoulders draining away as she relaxes. "I caught the thoughts of one of them. They are moving off, going back to the den. Let's maybe build the fire up some more ... but I don't think they'll be back." She says this last part uncertainly, not knowing for sure if the coyotes will regroup and try again to kill them later.

***

They huddle around the new fire, settling under the narrow aluminum awning of the restroom. They are all shaky and not speaking, trying to get their breathing and their thoughts under control. Sam tries to come up with some kind of sarcastic comment while he lies flat on the concrete being useless, but his brain is still preoccupied with just being alive.

Jessie chances a trip behind the restroom to get their food supply. She hadn't eaten much before taking her walk, and then things got crazy. She digs into a bag of peanuts and sits down quietly beside Sam.

"Do you hear anything?" he asks her.

"No, the coyotes aren't very close. My brain is silent for the moment ... except for my own terrified thoughts." She smiles and glances at him out of the corner of her eye. He makes no reply but is glad she feels comfortable enough to sit with him. *I guess maybe I didn't scare her off with all the crying and "I love you" garbage.*

Alex also settles down by the fire with a few bags of nuts and chips.

"You should try to eat something," Jessie instructs Sam. "Try to keep your strength up."

"He ate like five bags of chips while you were out for your walk," Alex says, munching on his peanuts.

"It wasn't five," Sam says a little defensively. "It was more like … four. Actually, it could have been six. You know I can't count that high."

"Oh, good. I'm glad you felt well enough to eat," Jessie says, sounding reassured that he is apparently doing better.

"Yeah, I'm good," Sam lies, trying to sound cavalier, lacing his fingers behind his head to make a pillow for himself. He stares at the fire, hoping he looks calm and comfortable.

"Remember when you would walk down to the park and get chips when you were recovering from your bike accident?" Jessie asks him.

"Oh, no, I don't remember that," Sam replies, not meeting her eyes. *Oh, my God, those stupid chips!* He didn't know Jessie had noticed that.

"That must have been a terrible summer for you," she says.

Jessie, sweetheart, I love you; but seriously, please don't mention that summer ever again.

"Mm-hmm …" Sam barely responds, not wanting to completely ignore her. He closes his eyes, trying to push away his old memories and new apprehensions. "Can we please talk about something else? I mean, really, like, anything else."

CHAPTER 20

Jessie stares at the fire, her eyelids getting heavy. Alex sighs and says, "I really miss Mom and Dad."

Jessie nods. "I can't wait to get home and give Puffin a big hug."

"Wow," Alex says with a note of disdain in his voice. "You're going to hug your dumb cat before you hug Mom and Dad?"

"Oh ... I mean, well ... *obviously* I would hug Mom and Dad first," Jessie stammers, feeling guilty.

"I'm not surprised, Alex," Sam pipes up. "Jessie has trouble showing any kind of emotion toward humans. She can only connect with animals."

"Yeah, she's been that way her whole life. You'd think I would be used to it by now." Alex laughs and gives Jessie a brotherly punch on the arm. She doesn't laugh.

"Mm-hmm, me, too," Sam agrees.

Jessie glances at Sam, not really sure if he is joking. He has his hands behind his head, eyes closed, lips pressed together in a taut line. For once, she has no idea if he is teasing her. He doesn't have that familiar lilt in his voice, and there's no sly twitch of his lips.

"What will you do when you get home, Sam?" she asks.

"Lie down and die," he replies flatly.

"You can do that right now," Alex teases.

"Wow, Alex. All this time, I thought you and I were best pals. I guess I'll just have to be alone forever," Sam replies.

Okay, is that another thinly veiled insult to me because I didn't tell him I love him? Jessie wonders, butterflies waking up in her stomach. *Why is he being so immature about this all of a sudden? Things need to get back to normal before I can figure out how I feel about him. Why can't he understand that?*

Jessie eventually drifts off, exhausted. Her previous night of near-sleeplessness has finally caught up with her.

Alex quietly places more branches on the fire and stands, staring at the orange flames, his eyes unblinking. Sam watches him, his thoughts slipping back to Jessie. *Why did I tell her I love her? Definitely not a good time to do that. She was going crazy, listening to those coyotes, and then I go and make everything awkward and really throw her off. Why am I so dumb? Ah, maybe it's for the best. She is probably better off without me anyway.*

"Hey, Alex, can you get me some water?"

"Sure." Alex throws down the stick he is holding and dutifully pours a cup of water out of the plastic can. "Do you need help sitting up?" He kneels next to Sam.

"Uh, yeah ..." Sam admits, annoyed that he can barely move without help. Every part of his body is screaming in pain. He extends his hands, and Alex pulls him up gently.

"Thanks." Sam rests his head in his hands and rubs his eyes. "Wow, I never thought I would get so dizzy just by sitting up. This really sucks."

"Um, yeah. You can say that again," Alex mutters. He hands Sam the cup of water.

"Thanks." Sam takes a deep breath and says, "Hey, listen. I really need to thank you for saving my life." He slowly sips the water, meeting Alex's hazel eyes briefly and then quickly looking away.

"I think you would have been able to go a few more hours without a cup of water," Alex says, smirking at Sam, who doesn't have the energy to smile back. Alex sobers when he realizes his friend is not kidding. "Seriously, man, I think we all sort of saved each other, in some way," he says, sitting down on the concrete.

"I'm not talking about now." Sam finishes the water and holds the empty cup out to Alex, who quickly refills it. He continues in a halting voice, not entirely sure he wants to talk about this, but plowing ahead. Alex has a right to know the whole truth. "You remember ... you remember when I broke my legs, right?"

"Of course. That was crazy."

"Yeah, I know, I was there." Sam's voice catches in his throat as he thinks about what he is about to tell his best friend now. He glances at Alex, who has a slightly amused expression on his face. Sam knows he isn't going to be laughing after he finishes telling this story.

Alex gazes at his friend, still worried that Hannah won't find help in time to save him. Sam's eyes are almost completely red, with dark blue-black circles under them. His lips are cracked, and there is dirt and dried blood on his cheeks. He looks frail and weak, like he's lost all his substantial muscle in the past twenty-four hours. His normally perfect hair has bits of dried leaves in it. The typical carefree glint in his eyes is extinguished.

Alex's usual low-level anxiety creeps up as Sam fidgets with his water cup. It is very unlike Sam to hesitate when telling a story. *What is going on? Is he in some kind of trouble? I mean, other than probably dying soon?*

"I've never told anyone about this, except my doctor. I didn't even tell my parents. So please don't tell anyone I told you, okay?" Sam looks around past the fire to Jessie, making sure she is still asleep. Alex squirms, thinking about how horrible he is at keeping Sam's secrets. And now Sam is confiding in him again.

"What illegal stuff did you do this time?" Alex teases, trying to lighten the mood.

"Promise you won't tell anyone about this?" Sam gives him the sincerest expression Alex has ever seen.

"Um ... okay," Alex agrees slowly, afraid of what Sam is going to tell him.

Sam sighs and brushes some dirt off his T-shirt. Then he squints at the fire and leans back on one palm. Finally, he says in a soft voice, "It was a really bad summer for me after my accident. Actually, the whole year was kind of awful. You remember Violet had blood cancer as a baby, right?" He glances at Alex.

"Yeah." He nods solemnly, not sure where Sam is going with this. He never speaks of Violet's illness.

"Well, my parents were, like, beyond stressed that whole time. They were fighting constantly, always away at different doctors and hospitals with Violet. And my father was working away a lot in DC and could only come home once or twice a week. It was really stressful for everyone. I didn't even know what was going on with Violet at the time. ... I guess Mom and Dad didn't want me to worry about her or whatever. I don't know. I remember... I remember feeling angry a lot—most of the time, really—and I wasn't sure if they even loved me. God, then I go and stupidly break my legs." He whispers this last part.

He takes another deep breath to steady himself, physically and emotionally, then buries his head in his hands. This is a side of Sam that Alex has never seen before. He never talks about the past, never seems to feel guilty for the stupid stuff he has done.

He continues. "I was stuck in those casts for what, two months? Those two months were awful, let me tell you. And then the months after I got my casts off were actually worse. ... Violet was still really sick, no one was telling me what was going on, my parents were still fighting, I got held back in school. There was just nothing good left anymore, you know? And I was still ... I don't know ... angry ... all the time. None of my friends wanted to hang out with me because I couldn't play sports or anything. Man, I could barely make it to the park and back." He shakes his head, trying to rid his mind of his memories.

"Sam," Alex whispers, wanting to say something to help him feel better, but having no idea what to say.

"I was literally an invalid. Anyway, my mom had gotten me a prescription for sleeping pills while I was recovering. I would go *days* without sleeping ..." His glassy eyes widen, as though he is surprising himself with what he is saying. "So, there was one day when I decided I didn't want to deal with it anymore. Just didn't want to be here anymore. You know? I was done. I was sitting on the bench in the park and suddenly felt so ... like, *relieved* that I finally knew what to do. I had gotten my sleeping pills refilled the day before, and I was gonna go home and take the whole bottle. I mean, it was like a hundred pills."

Alex gasps loudly and makes a whimpering sound that he's not too proud of. He's stunned. Completely shocked. He cannot believe what Sam is telling him. How could Sam Starling, the coolest kid he knows, even *consider* killing himself? Alex is shocked into total silence, not sure how to process what his friend is admitting.

Suddenly, a thought strikes Alex. Sam lies *all* the time. He lied to Hannah about reading to the kids in the cancer ward. He lies to everyone about why he gets into fights at school and about lots of other stuff. He *must* be lying about this.

"I don't believe you," Alex says in a voice that is not as firm as he'd hoped.

"Well, it's the truth," Sam replies flatly, not concerned about Alex's doubts. "The point is you saved me. And I need you to know that." He catches Alex's eye. "That day, when I was sitting on the bench, after I decided to go home and end it all, you showed up at the park and sat down right next to me, like we were best pals. I didn't invite you over, you were just there. And you seemed happy to see me."

"I was happy to see you!" Alex defends himself. "We're friends!"

"Right, but we still barely knew each other at that time." He gives Alex a tentative smile. "You said I still owed you a game of catch ... and you wanted to meet up the next day."

"Okay, yeah. So?" Alex is more than a little confused by Sam's story. "I still don't understand."

Sam laughs softly, a laugh that shakes his shoulders and makes the tears he is barely holding back spill onto his cheeks. He quickly stifles it, not wanting to disturb Jessie.

"You're so cute and innocent sometimes," Sam whispers affectionately, then grimaces as pain shoots through his leg. He gasps and takes a second to regain his composure. Alex pours him the last of the water, and he takes a sip.

With a ragged and wheezy breath, Sam says quietly, "Alex, don't you get it? You gave me something to look forward to, like I finally had something to live for. You made me realize that maybe there was some point to all this, you know? Like I could get through all that crap," Sam waves both hands in the air, "if I just kept going. Besides, I had already let you down by not showing up for our ball game once. I couldn't let it happen again."

"Hmm ... I think I remember that day. You seemed kind of weird, like distant and less of an arrogant snob than usual. ... But you're right, I didn't really know you very well yet and I thought it was your regular type of weirdness."

"Oh, man. I have a regular type of weirdness?"

"Well, you know what I mean. You were always a little different, maybe a little sketchy sometimes. I mean, honestly, I don't know what lies you've told me over the years."

"Yeah, sorry about that ..." Sam says sheepishly, giving Alex a crooked half-smile and a sidelong glance, his blue eyes only partially open.

"That's okay. I think it's part of what makes you so much fun. Like I never know what you're going to say next. Remember the skydiving story? You totally got me out of a fight with that bogus story, and Chris and Justin never picked on me again after that. You made *me* cool with your lies. And that's pretty difficult, since I'm super uncool." Alex smirks at Sam, still not sure what he is supposed to believe.

The boys are silent for a minute, lost in thought. Sam tries not to cry as he remembers too vividly the torment he had felt while lying trapped in his room all alone, even without the casts anymore, day after day and night after night. For years.

After he finishes his story, he can't rid himself of the old feelings of guilt and loneliness that haunt him. They're closer to the surface of his consciousness now than they have been in a while.

"So, is that the only time you ever ... you know ... thought about it?" Alex asks tentatively.

Sam toys with the idea of not telling him everything, but he's pretty deep into this now. He shakes his head almost imperceptibly. "No," he admits quietly. "There was one other time, when I was twelve." He leans back and stretches his legs, deciding right now to tell Alex everything. No more secrets. "I was in my room, working up the courage to write a note ... I had my sleeping pills all spilled out on my desk, ready to go ..." His voice cracks as he thinks about that night. "Violet came running into my room, all happy about something. I don't remember what. But I thought, *She has no clue she's been fighting for her life since the day she was born ... and here I am, planning on ending mine.*" Sam sighs heavily and massages his forehead. He glances over at Alex, whose eyes are welling with tears. *He must be so disgusted with me.*

Sam looks away, fighting back his own tears. After taking a sip of water, he continues. "She asked me what I was doing, and I told her. Oh, God, Alex! I *told her.*" His voice cracks. "She was barely three years old!" Sam is so ashamed of what he did to his little sister. He prays every day of his life that she doesn't remember it. She didn't deserve all that. "I didn't think she would understand ... she was so young." A sob catches in his throat.

"Did she?" Alex asks quietly. He fidgets next to Sam.

Sam eyes his friend, trying to gauge what Alex is thinking. *He must realize his best friend is a monster.* "I honestly have no idea. And I'm terrified to ask her." Sam begins crying, thinking about that night, and continues in a halting whisper, "I remember the look of *pure love* on my sister's face as I calmly explained to her why some people have the feelings I have, and that it isn't her fault. I just kept ... kept talking to her ... about all these thoughts in my head that I couldn't explain at the time. I have no idea if she understood any of it ... but I guess she understood enough. When I finished speaking, she kinda looked up at me, like with all this wisdom, you know? And she held my hand with her little, tiny fingers and said, 'Promise you'll always be with me.' And I didn't know if she meant, like, physically or spiritually or whatever, you know?"

Alex nods slowly, hanging on Sam's every word.

At least he hasn't run away screaming yet. I guess that's a good sign, Sam thinks.

"She was so young, Alex!" he says. "I never thought she would understand any of what I said. But it seemed like ... like maybe she did. I don't know. Part of me felt like she was giving me permission to just ... let go."

Alex doesn't say anything, and Sam isn't sure if he wants him to.

"I chose to take her proposition at face value, which is another reason why I'm still here, I guess. ... Playing catch with you and not wanting to break a promise to my three-year-old sister kept me going, I guess." He glances at Alex again, who has tears falling freely down his cheeks. Alex jumps up suddenly, and Sam can't help but think, *Yep, this is where he runs away horrified into the forest, never to be seen again.*

Instead, Alex falls into Sam, crumpling himself against his chest, his skinny arms completely wrapped around Sam's back. It is the biggest and tightest hug anyone has ever given Sam in his entire life.

Sam leans back on one palm and wraps his other arm around his best friend. They sit there holding each other and cry silently for a minute. Then Alex slowly disentangles his hands from around Sam's back and wipes his eyes. "And here all this time, I felt like *I* owed *you* my life for taking that bullet for us."

Sam runs his hand through his hair, not really sure what to say. "Maybe we can call it even?"

Alex settles on the concrete again and draws his knees up to his chest. "Deal," he says.

Sam scoffs quietly and then sobers. "I got professional help after that night with Violet. Turns out I have a mild to moderate case of bipolar disorder with hypomania, but it will probably get worse as I get older." He pauses, waiting for Alex to ask a bunch of questions about his mental illness.

To Sam's surprise, Alex says, "Ohhh ... that explains a lot, actually."

Sam glances at Alex, who kind of shrugs and says conversationally, "We just learned about bipolar disorder, like, two months ago in psychology class ... Man, I should have known!"

"That's the one test I passed in my life without having to study too much." Sam laughs quietly. "I just checked all the boxes that described me." He scrubs his face slowly with his hand. "Oh, buddy ... it feels really good to talk to you about this ... I was afraid you would hate me or something."

"Nah, it would take a lot more than that."

Sam chuckles. "Good to know. ... So, you know those week-long 'vacations' I take in the middle of the school year?" he asks, making air quotes with his hands.

"Mm-hmm."

"Half of those are really just me stuck at home, physically not able to get out of bed," Sam admits.

"Huh, I never would have guessed." Alex pauses and asks tentatively, "So, was Cancun ...?"

"Cancun was real." Sam leans back on both palms and gives him a crooked grin. "I highly recommend you go there, actually."

CHAPTER 21

Sam drifts off to sleep a few minutes later, feeling as though a great weight has been lifted from his shoulders. He is weak and shivering, but his mind is more peaceful than it has been in years.

Jessie stirs and raises her head, checking on the boys. They both appear to be sleeping soundly. Her thoughts immediately fill with worry. Has Hannah made it out to safety yet? She has been gone for hours. She must have run nine miles by now. What if she got hurt? Or made a wrong turn and is now even farther away?

Images of Hannah fill Jessie's brain. She is being chased by men wearing ski masks, tying up her hands, shooting her ... Jessie tosses and turns, unable to find a comfortable spot on the hard-packed gravel. She lies awake, staring at the deep-blue, cloudless sky.

At some point, she realizes she must have fallen asleep again, because she is disoriented when she hears a vaguely familiar rumbling sound down the road. She bolts upright. Something is crunching along the road toward them. A car is coming!

She jumps up and peers down the gravel track. A police car is speeding toward them, lights flashing. Alex is awake, too, and he jumps up, happily yelling, "We're saved! We're saved!" Alex and Jessie hug each other and dance in a circle. They are going home!

The police car slows to a stop, and Hannah leaps out the passenger side. "How is he?" she immediately asks, giving Jessie a quick hug.

Jessie glances at Sam, who is lying motionless on the concrete near the restroom door, not even a little disturbed by the commotion.

"I don't know ..." Jessie's voice wavers. "We've all been asleep ..." *Why didn't I think to check on him immediately after waking?*

By this time, the police officer is out of the car, carrying a duffel bag over her shoulder. She is a sturdily built Black woman with a kind face and a warm smile.

"This is Officer Ripley," Hannah says, introducing her to Alex and Jessie.

Officer Ripley says, "I'm going to check your friend first, okay? The medical helicopter is on the way—it should only be another few minutes. But I'll see if I can help him in the meantime." She rushes over to Sam, who still hasn't moved.

"The main road was crawling with police cars," Hannah explains. "They were able to trace the phone signal when that man called my mom and knew he was in this general area. The police have been searching houses, thinking we were being held hostage somewhere."

The police officer looks back at the group and says, "Do you know how long he has been unconscious?"

Jessie shakes her head, tears sliding down her cheeks. Hannah takes her hand. "No," Jessie says, barely above a whisper. "He's been asleep for a while ... I didn't ... I didn't try to wake him up or anything."

Officer Ripley shakes Sam's shoulder. "Son, can you hear me? Son?" She checks his wrist for a pulse and silently counts his heartbeat. "His pulse is a little weak."

Jessie watches and covers her mouth with her hand, silently crying. Hannah walks over to see if she can help Officer Ripley with anything. Alex leans into Jessie's side, and she wraps her arm around his shoulders.

By this time, they hear the medical helicopter in the distance. Within a minute, it is landing on the clear patch of road in front of the abandoned restroom, dirt and dry leaves swirling in the air under the thundering propeller.

Sam lies motionless, and Hannah reaches down to pull Jessie's jacket over his exposed face. Jessie stares at Sam, willing him to wake up, but she quickly turns away. *He looks like a corpse.*

A paramedic springs out of the chopper, and he and Officer Ripley quickly strap Sam's limp body onto a stretcher. Before Jessie knows what is happening, Sam is inside, and the chopper is lifting off. It occurs to her that this is the second time Sam has been airlifted in his short life. Tears stream steadily down her cheeks, and Hannah wraps an arm around her.

"He'll be okay," Hannah says, though a bit uncertainly.

"He looked dead!"

They watch the chopper vanish above the trees, then gather the watering can, paper cups, and the remains of their food. Alex douses the fire, grinding some of the stray embers into the dirt with the toe of his shoe. They pile into the police car, and Officer Ripley drives as fast as she safely can down the rutted gravel road.

CHAPTER 22

The next few hours are a complete blur for Jessie. She sleeps on the ride to the hospital, her exhaustion overtaking her worry. She has no idea how long they traveled, but her mind finally clears as she is ushered into the hospital emergency department in an unknown town. They are immediately taken in together for physical exams, bloodwork, showers, hot meals, and questioning. Jessie glances at a clock on the wall in the exam room. It's 3:15 p.m.

The doctor, an upbeat young man by the name of Steve, marvels at how lucky they are to have survived so long with only minimal health effects. Other than being slightly dehydrated and sleep-deprived, they all check out fine.

Dr. Steve is very interested in their Gifts, being unGifted himself. Pennsylvanians have known for a while that most Gifted people are concentrated in and around Cutter County. It is rare to find a Gifted this far north.

"You're lucky you didn't get frostbite," Dr. Steve says. *We're lucky we had Sam and his lighter,* Jessie muses. *Hey, Doc, do you know why frostbite is so expensive?*

A pang of dread washes over her as she thinks about Sam.

***

Jessie, Hannah, and Alex are allowed to stay together in one room for observation.

"Your parents are all on their way. They should be here in about an hour," Dr. Steve says as he leads them down the hallway to their room. "A nurse will be in shortly to check your vitals again. Do you have any questions?"

"Have you heard anything about Sam Starling?" Hannah asks. "He was the boy with us who was airlifted."

"Ah, yes." Dr. Steve suddenly looks somber, and Jessie's heart sinks through the floor and into the morgue, where it may remain cold and dead for the rest of her life, depending on what Dr. Steve says. "He needs quite a bit of blood before he can be taken to surgery. Using that jacket as a tourniquet saved his life. Once he is in more stable condition, he will be taken into surgery, probably sometime overnight. It's still too early to tell if the septicemia—blood poisoning—can be treated quickly. He is strong and otherwise healthy, though. We should know for sure within twenty-four hours." Jessie notices he doesn't say anything about a "grim prognosis," but she expects he isn't really allowed to divulge that kind of medical information to nonfamily members.

"Is he awake?" Jessie asks, trying to picture Sam's twinkling blue eyes and genuine smile—the one she had discovered while out in the woods. She needs to get a new vision of Sam in her brain; all she has been seeing in her mind is him lying motionless as the helicopter landed.

"I'm sorry, but no, he hasn't regained consciousness since arriving." Dr. Steve turns toward the door. Then he turns back and says, "I'll let Sam's surgeon know to give you access to him when he's awake.

Usually, we only allow immediate family into the ICU, but we can certainly make an exception in this case."

"Thank you, Dr. Steve, " Hannah says, sounding just as professional as he does.

Alex and Jessie echo Hannah's words of thanks, then settle into their room for the evening, picking at their lukewarm hospital food. No one has an appetite. No one speaks. The nightmare is not over.

Tremors quiver through Jessie's legs and stomach, a wave of anxiety cascading over her as she thinks about Sam. She breathes deeply, calming the turmoil rolling through her.

They sit on their beds, wrapped in soft blankets, surfing through TV channels, not able to focus on anything. Their parents arrive thirty minutes later, and they are enveloped in hugs and tears. Sam's parents linger in the doorway, not yet allowed to see their son.

"Sam really saved us!" Alex says to Senator and Mrs. Starling. "He got his Gift, too!"

"Oh, really?" Mrs. Starling says, wiping a tear from her cheek. "What is it? No, wait!" She holds up a frail and trembling hand. "Don't tell me. He can tell me himself." Her voice wavers.

Hannah and her parents sit on her bed in the corner, all chattering excitedly. Jessie and her family decide to take a walk down to the cafeteria for tea and ice cream. Alex is excited to tell their parents all about his new Gift. Mrs. Cox sobs as Alex tells them about getting the ransom money.

"We felt so helpless. Even when we all pooled our resources and cashed in our life insurance, it still wasn't enough. The kidnappers called after the first night and told us they had killed you all," she says. "Oh, God, we have all been a wreck. The Starlings didn't even tell Violet what was going on. They said Sam was on a camping trip. They haven't told her that he got hurt."

"Oh, that's good," Jessie says in a low voice. *The Starlings have been right to keep so many secrets from Violet. It is better not to know.*

Jessie suddenly feels very tired and halfheartedly eats a spoonful of ice cream. Sam's lilting voice echoes in her head. *"Too much of Paul's ice cream, I guess."* She envisions Sam standing in the doorway of the restroom, strong and whole, his blue eyes glinting, making stupid jokes as he wrestled with that old rusty door.

Tears well up, and she quickly wipes her nose and eyes with a napkin, trying to pass her distress off as a yawn. She keeps her gaze down, closely watching the last few globs of ice cream melt into a puddle in the dish.

Alex talks excitedly for another ten minutes, telling their parents how he and Jessie fought off three coyotes. Mrs. Cox goes pale and asks her son to please stop talking about the coyotes. Mayor Cox puts his hand on his wife's arm and gives his son an encouraging clap on the shoulder.

Eventually, a nurse comes by to tell Alex and Jessie they need to get back to their room for the night. Their parents give them big hugs and promise to be back first thing in the morning. They will be right across the street in a hotel. That still seems too far away.

***

Jessie has a fitful night, as she knew she would. Every noise puts her on edge. She waits for the door to open, for someone to come in with news about Sam. Good or bad. But no one comes. She finally falls asleep around 2:00 a.m. and wakes up around 7:00 a.m.

Alex is already awake in the bed next to hers, or maybe he never fell asleep. He is staring at the ceiling. Jessie can see the sheen of his open eyes in the early morning light. "You awake?" she asks, knowing he is.

"Yep."

"You scared?"

"Yep." He turns onto his side to face his sister. He bunches his hands under his pillow and stares at her, blatant worry clouding his eyes. "He's my best friend, Jessie. He can't die."

"We don't know anything yet." Jessie gets out of her bed and crawls into Alex's. They used to hide together under the blankets during thunderstorms, and twice when their parents had really terrible arguments, but it has been years since they consoled each other like this. She strokes Alex's hair off his forehead and immediately wishes she hadn't. *Oh, God, what if Sam dies?*

She blots her eyes with the sleeve of her sweatshirt, her favorite one, which her parents had brought from home. She doesn't know

240

what else to say to Alex. They lie awake, silent and staring at the ceiling, shrouded in fear.

Their parents arrive promptly at 9:00 a.m. when visiting hours begin. They come in carrying a tray of cut fruit and bagels with cream cheese. The kids dig into the food, excited to eat something fresh and juicy and not from a dusty box in a broom closet in an abandoned park office. And it is much better than last evening's rubbery hospital food. Jessie feels guilty that Sam is missing it. He could eat this entire feast himself.

Senator and Mrs. Starling had gotten to see Sam overnight, before he was taken into surgery. He was semiconscious but was not able to hold a conversation due to the pain medications he had been given.

They chatter for a few minutes, all trying to be happy and think positive thoughts, but a cloud of dread hangs over them. Eventually they all fall into silence, occasionally strolling through the hallway or wandering outside into the small courtyard.

Finally, Mrs. Starling's phone rings at 10:24. Sam is out of surgery.

They all run up to the surgery wing, none of them wanting to wait for the elevator, and they are quietly but efficiently ushered into Sam's room. He isn't awake yet, and the nurse tells them it may be a while before the effects of the anesthesia wear off. Extra chairs are brought in to accommodate Sam's parents, Alex, Hannah, and Jessie.

Jessie tries to prepare herself, mentally and emotionally, before entering Sam's room. But nothing could have prepared her for what she sees when she walks in. Sam lies, frail and ashen, on the hospital bed, a thin sheet covering him. He looks so small; his muscular arms and shoulders appear to have shriveled, and he seems to take up only a tiny portion of the narrow bed. His chest barely rises and falls as he takes shallow breaths. His skin is the same color as the sheet. The swell of a large, bulky bandage is visible on his right thigh.

Seeing him like this flares Jessie's anxiety again, and she has an uneasy feeling that Sam is going to waste away to a dry husk, his strength, his humor, and his charm stripped from him before she can even appreciate him and all he wanted to give her. *Why couldn't I just tell him I love him? I had so many chances! I'm such an idiot!*

Sam's parents stand close to him, whispering how much they love him and how proud they are to have him as their son. Jessie desperately wants to tell them about Sam's Gift and how he used it to tell Hannah how to get out of the forest, but Mrs. Starling was right. It will be better coming from him.

Jessie hesitantly takes one of the chairs near Sam's feet, feeling as though she is intruding on something private between Sam and his family. Hannah gives her a questioning look and motions for Jessie to take the chair next to Mrs. Starling, who is sitting near Sam's head and stroking his hair. Jessie doesn't know if she can sit that close to Mrs. Starling without becoming a blubbering, teary mess, but she slowly sits down and hunches in the chair, staring at Sam's right hand a few inches from her face.

Should I take his hand? Will his parents think that's weird or something? God, this is so awkward. Her mind races. She wishes she were in the waiting room with her parents. Or, better still, here in Sam's room, but completely alone with him. But what would she say? They really hadn't spoken much after he insulted her about her inability to love, and she is not sure if he is upset with her or not. *Will anything more happen between us? Or were our feelings for each other simply the result of desperation, fear, and survival instinct? Warmth, water, food ... and companionship. Warmth, water, food ... companionship. ... Companionship.*

Finally, Jessie takes Sam's hand and caresses his calloused but limp fingers, not caring what the Starlings think of her, but she is relieved when Mrs. Starling puts her hand on Jessie's shoulder and gives her a reassuring smile.

"Jessie, thank you for taking care of him," Mrs. Starling whispers, tears in her eyes. "You, too, Hannah ... and you, Alex."

Jessie looks helplessly at Hannah and can't help but think, *Sam is the one who took care of me!*

They sit in silence, Sam's father somberly sitting with his hands folded in his lap, Mrs. Starling still stroking her son's forehead, her thin, pale hand robotically moving back and forth. Jessie watches her absently while holding onto Sam's hand, but it isn't the same. She desperately wishes he would cover her hand with his, squeezing her fingers reassuringly, a devilish glint in those irresistible eyes. But he remains still and lifeless.

Jessie can't take this waiting another minute. Sam has to wake up—and soon. She chokes back a sob, stands up, and walks out of the room.

***

Sam still isn't awake by the time Jessie's parents say they need to get back on the road. She pleads with them to let her stay, and the Starlings even say it would be no trouble; they can bring Jessie home in a day or two.

"But, sweetheart, we just got you back," her mother says, making Jessie realize her mom is right, and that Jessie is being selfish, asking to stay away from her own family even longer.

She pushes Sam's hair up to say good-bye. His skin is cold and clammy under her fingertips. She gives him a soft kiss on his forehead, disappointed that he doesn't stir at all. After giving his parents quick hugs, Jessie rushes out of the room behind her family.

Hannah and her parents are in the waiting room. They will be visiting Hannah's grandparents in New Jersey for a day or two and will not be heading back to Cutter County with Jessie's family. They are bunched together, saying their good-byes to one another.

"We'll have to do this again soon," Jessie says, hugging Hannah, tangling her hands in Hannah's long hair.

"Yeah, best birding trip ever," Hannah replies. Then she whispers in Jessie's ear, "He'll be okay."

"Don't lie. ... He was never okay to begin with," Jessie jokes, but tears sting her eyes.

Hannah hugs her tighter and softly kisses her ear. To Jessie's surprise, Hannah whispers, "You're good for each other."

Jessie realizes that coming from Hannah, this is as close to an approval of Sam that she will ever get. "Thank you," she whispers back and adds, "Thank you for saving him."

"I hope I don't regret it," Hannah jokes, pulling away from Jessie and giving her a teary smile.

"Me, too."

***

The ride home is interminable. Jessie sits in the back of the limo, her parents getting down to serious conversation. Alex learns the truth about politicians and their monetary facade. Jessie only half listens. She knows all this already, but she does feel bad for Alex. He is shocked into silence for a few minutes.

Jessie tries to remember how she felt when she was first told that her entire life was a lie. She mostly remembers not trusting anyone for a long time, not even her parents. After all, if adults can lie about something that momentous, what other secrets are they keeping? It is an uncomfortable feeling, like there is really never anything or anyone you can truly rely on.

You can trust me. Sam's words from their first morning in the woods float back to Jessie. She thinks about how, only a few days ago, she viewed Sam as kind of the "class clown" of the neighborhood, the kid who probably would never amount to much, the black mark on an otherwise well-respected family.

After these past few days, Jessie realizes maybe Sam isn't such a black mark after all. He *is* a liar. But not in a bad way.

CHAPTER 23

After the news of the safe return of the four Cutter County kids, everyone in the neighborhood wants to hear the long version of their adventure and how the kids survived the northern wilds of Pennsylvania. Alex, Hannah, and Jessie all explain that it was a team effort, that in some way, they had each saved each other's lives.

By now, Sam's parents know of his Gift, and pretty soon the whole county will know. One thing the kids didn't know, until their return, was that the government had released information about the politicians' "honor system" in an effort to prevent kidnappings from occurring in the future. Some people don't believe it, saying it was a cover-up designed to make politicians less of a target for extortion.

Most people, however, do seem to believe it now that the message has had a chance to sink in. Jessie thinks most citizens remember how frequent news reports of political corruption were in the past, and how, in recent years, there have been none. Things are slowly making sense.

For three days after their return, Alex and Jessie have been agonizing over whether or not to tell the police about Scott and Blaze Givins. But they needn't have worried. Blaze had already turned his brother in, but he asked that Scott be put under the care of a psychiatric facility rather than go to prison. The Starlings, Coxes, and Buckleys all agreed to those terms and did not press charges for the kidnapping of their children.

Alex's $12.2 million was found to be missing from a charitable fund set up for the search for and rescue of missing children. The director of the fund had reported it stolen, having no idea that it was Alex's Gift that had drained the donations. Blaze and Scott returned the money, untouched and still in the duffel bag, to the Cutter County police.

Blaze comes to visit Alex, mostly to apologize, but also to say goodbye. He will be moving to California in a few days to live with his cousins. He can't stay in Cutter County, knowing his friends will always hate him. Alex and Jessie plead with him, saying that of course they don't hate him—that they know he had no control of the situation. They ask him to please, please stay. But there is no changing Blaze's mind.

Blaze had written an apology to Sam and asks Alex to give it to him when he gets out of the hospital. It's in a sealed envelope, and when Blaze hands it over, he says to Alex, "I hope you don't mind, but this isn't the kind of thing I can write to Sam in an email."

Alex and Jessie hug each other as they watch Blaze walk down their driveway and out of sight, knowing they will never see him again.

✱✱✱

A week after returning home, Jessie gets a call from Hannah.

"My parents told me that Sam is coming home tomorrow! His parents are throwing a huge party at their house for him, and the whole town is invited," Hannah says excitedly. "But get this. Now that the world knows our families aren't rich, everyone who has RSVP'd is insisting on bringing food and gifts for us. Like, they think we are completely poor or something. Our parents said it isn't necessary, but we're all, like, heroes or something."

Jessie wonders briefly if she and her family will be treated differently by the public. Maybe like outcasts? Or more like equals? It is interesting how nothing in her day-to-day life had actually changed, only the public perception of it.

After Hannah's phone call, Jessie finds it difficult to concentrate on anything. She debates calling Sam but loses her nerve even before drawing her new cell phone out of her pocket. She hasn't spoken to him since that last day in the woods. Will he be mad at her for not calling? She feels guilty and a little panicky.

The past week had been so busy with press conferences, visiting relatives, celebrating Alex's fifteenth birthday, and catching up on schoolwork that she hadn't really had time to call Sam. Besides, she really doesn't know what to say. "*I'm sorry*" is definitely something she needs to tell him in person, not over the phone.

She scrolls through Sam's social media, checking for updates. Sam has been posting daily progress reports about his recovery, mostly complaining that he misses playing baseball and eating his mom's home-cooked meals. Jessie sent a message almost two days ago, but he never replied.

Unsettled, she puts her phone away and passes the evening in her room. She brushes Puffin, who is starting to shed out for the spring. "A little to the left ... yeah ..." Puffin purrs as he presses his head into her hand.

She searches through her closet for the perfect outfit to wear for Sam's reception tomorrow, with little to no help from Puffin. It is supposed to be a celebration for all four kids, but she feels it is really Sam's victory. His mother had called shortly after Hannah did, personally inviting Jessie's family to the party.

Jessie's nerves zing as she rifles through the rack of clothes in her closet. This is weird. She has never once worried about what clothes to wear. *Why does it matter so much what I wear tomorrow? Will anyone really care? Will Sam care?* She smiles. Knowing Sam, he will either like anything Jessie wears or take absolutely no notice of it at all.

"Okay, this is silly," Jessie says to Puffin, taking a seat on the floor of her room and picking up his brush, absently grooming him again. Eventually, she is sleepy enough to go to bed, never having picked an outfit.

The next morning drags by. The party will begin at 4:00 p.m., but Sam is coming home around two o'clock. Alex, Hannah, and Jessie walk to the Starling mansion together to meet him. Jessie has butterflies in her stomach the whole way. She has no idea what to expect.

"You're awfully quiet," Hannah observes as they walk up the tree-lined street. The new spring buds smell fresh in the light breeze.

"Yeah, sorry," Jessie replies vaguely, following the antics of a darting goldfinch in a nearby tree, yet not really able to focus on the little yellow bird.

"What are you worried about, sis?" Alex asks. "Sam's fine."

"Yeah, I know ... I just haven't spoken to him. I don't know what to say."

"Well, knowing Sam, he'll be doing all the talking," Hannah says, shaking her head but smiling. "You know him. He never shuts up."

"Yeah, I guess ..."

"What do you mean you haven't spoken to him?" Alex asks. "You didn't talk to him while he was in the hospital?"

"No. Why? Did you?" Her butterflies flutter faster.

"Yeah, every day ... sometimes twice a day. You didn't even wish him a happy birthday?"

"Oh ... darn ... I actually forgot what day it was." Another layer of guilt wraps around her. She stammers, "I-I didn't know if he would feel much like talking. He never called me, either. ... Do you think he wanted me to call?"

Alex shrugs in reply. "I don't know. He never mentioned you."

The butterflies suddenly morph into a lead weight, and she feels dizzy. She stops walking involuntarily and has to run a few steps to catch up with Alex and Hannah, who are onto a different subject entirely.

Oh, my God, I knew this would happen! Sam hates me now. Why didn't I call him? Why didn't I just pick up the phone and call him?

***

The day is the warmest they have had all year. The afternoon sun streams down, washing the budding landscape in a warm glow. Alex, Hannah, Violet, Mrs. Starling, and Jessie sit on the marble front patio of the mansion, eating and drinking light refreshments. They have a clear view of the long driveway from here, and they all stand and cheer when a black limo turns in from the road.

Violet hops excitedly from foot to foot. She has been told that Sam hurt his leg while hiking and that he will be fine, but she can't jump and climb all over him like she usually does.

Jessie notices Violet is holding a bouquet of brightly colored strings in her hand, their long ends trailing from the bottom of her small fist. It is a bunch of paracord bracelets she has made, and there are three or four others on her arm.

"Those are pretty," Jessie says, touching the bracelets in Violet's hand, admiring the array of colors and patterns.

"I need Sam," Violet responds.

Yes. We all need Sam.

After another minute, the limo pulls up close to the marble steps, and Senator Starling exits the car, waving to his family with both hands, a huge, dopey grin on his face. He walks around to the other side of the car, where Sam is slowly emerging. Jessie's breath catches in her throat as she glimpses his pale hair. He is carefully unfurling his long legs, his right leg obviously stiff. He's wearing a crisp, white, button-down shirt and new jeans. Jessie can barely discern the bandage under the fabric on his leg.

Sam glances up at the group gathered on the porch, gives them a quick wave, and walks slowly, without crutches, from the car. He does take his father's arm to limp up the two steps to the raised patio.

His mother is sobbing uncontrollably as she gently hugs her son. Violet clings to Sam, her arms wrapped tightly around his waist, still bouncing on her tiptoes. Jessie sees Sam wince as Violet's small hand brushes his right leg when she lets him go.

The family disconnects from their hug, and Sam's father, tears in his eyes, motions for Alex, Hannah, and Jessie to come over.

Sam gives Jessie the briefest of nods and the faintest of smiles but is quickly enveloped by Hannah and Alex. Jessie hangs on the edge of the group, standing behind her brother, not sure if she should give Sam an individual hug. *This is so incredibly awkward.* She finally decides to lean into him from the side, around Alex, and wraps her arms around his shoulders.

"You look great," Jessie whispers in Sam's ear before quickly letting him go. Sam doesn't reply but instead gives her an almost sad smile. His eyes are tired, the usual glint faded out. In her head, Jessie hears his lilting voice reply smoothly, *I always do,* his typical dumb joke after someone compliments his appearance.

She gives him what she hopes is an encouraging smile but really does not like this silent and subdued side of him. What if this whole experience changed his feelings for her too much? Jessie can't help thinking the worst.

After a few minutes of chatting and catching up on the events of the past week, Sam's parents invite them to move to the more spacious back deck, where they can all sit down together. Hannah and Alex help gather the food and drinks to move to the back of the house, leaving Sam and Jessie alone for a minute on the sun-drenched porch.

Well, not completely alone. Before Jessie can take Sam's hand (she is really trying to work up her courage), Violet runs back to them, waving her handful of brightly colored lengths of paracord.

"Sam! I forgot! Will you please help me?" she asks sweetly, stopping in front of her big brother, pale blond pigtails bouncing.

"Sure thing, kiddo." Sam slides his lighter out of his pocket and kneels in front of her, his left knee on the ground, his injured right leg bent but not taking much weight. He takes the strands of cord from Violet's hand one by one, expertly burning the ends together to form bracelets. He works the cords slowly, meticulously, his hands steady.

"Thank you!" Violet chirps happily when he finishes, grabbing her new bracelets. Then she pulls two out of the bunch and holds them out to Jessie. "Here, Jessie. Sam said these are your favorite colors!" Before Jessie can thank her, Violet skips back into the house. Sam remains motionless on the patio, watching her go.

"Arts and crafts, I see," Jessie says, standing at his shoulder.

"Yeah ... I wasn't being totally honest with you. I have never even tried smoking," he admits and looks up sheepishly, giving her a shrug that plainly says, "It seemed important to lie at the time."

"Yeah, I think I figured that out eventually." She gazes down at his upturned face, his blue eyes squinting against the bright sun.

His eyes cloud as he shifts his right leg to stand up. He pitches forward and groans, "Damn it, Jessie ... I can't move." He splays his hand on the unforgiving marble, trying to maintain his balance. "I can't believe I've been through all this and now can't even walk into my own house." He stares coldly at the ground, not looking at Jessie. She stoops beside him.

"It's okay; I'm here," she says, slinging her arm around his back.

He remains silent. She gives him a few seconds.

"Sam," she says quietly. He refuses to look at her. His shoulders heave as he takes a deep, shuddering breath. "Sam, please ... let me help you." She doesn't like seeing him like this, so defeated, so sad, so unlike himself.

Jessie has been daydreaming for the past week about their reunion, always envisioning Sam scooping her up in his strong arms and kissing her. None of her happy scenarios had him looking like this. It's as though the week in the hospital has done nothing for his recovery, but instead has made him weak and subdued.

She wants to kiss him, right here, but decides now isn't the best time. *When is the best time? Will there ever be a good time?* Her thoughts are back to racing, which is all they do now, and she desperately tries to think of some corny joke that might cheer him up.

"Come on, let's get you up," she whispers, her hand tracing slow circles on his back. "We have a party to get to. And it isn't a party without you."

"You do make a good point," Sam mutters and finally looks up at her with a tentative smile. Then in a louder, teasing voice, he says, "Hey, you'll be happy to know I lost some weight in the hospital." He allows Jessie to pull him upright. "Even their ice cream tastes like cardboard." His leg is stiff, and he has to lean into her, holding her shoulder to keep his balance. "I'm all set to run that marathon." His breath tickles her ear as he leans on her, his solid weight familiar and comforting.

"Mm-hmm. You would stop for food after running a hundred feet."

"Oh, thank you so much. I was going to say fifty." He removes his hands from Jessie's shoulders, feeling a little awkward. He so badly wants to wrap her in his arms and never let her go.

But apparently Jessie has other ideas. She clasps his hand and gently pulls him toward the house. Clearly, she has no intention of lingering out here with him on the porch, alone.

"Jessie, wait." Sam says, tugging her hand back. She spins around, and he wraps his hands behind her back, pulling her in. Their eyes meet. "Wait a minute, please."

Sam is about to kiss her when the front door opens, and Violet calls out, "Come on, Sam! I miss you! Come inside! Don't you miss me?" She skips over to them and of course hangs onto Sam's bad leg, so that pretty much kills the moment.

"Ow, Vi. Not that leg, okay?" Sam disentangles her tiny hands and swings her effortlessly up into his arms. He turns back to Jessie and gives her a tired smirk. "Darn. Missed opportunity." He sighs and limps into the house, his little sister hanging happily around his neck.

CHAPTER 24

Later that night, Sam finds himself sitting on the edge of his bed, slightly winded after navigating the sixteen stairs up to his bedroom and changing into sweat pants and an old T-shirt. It has been an exhausting day; practically everyone in the county had stopped by to hear the tale of the four kidnapped Cutter County kids. Sam was almost constantly barraged with questions about their adventure and was forced to repeat his story over and over again for five hours. He won't mind if he never has to do that again.

He tried to make it a good story, but as the night wore on and he got increasingly exhausted, the telling got shorter and more abrupt. Sam's last statement was, "We were kidnapped; now we're home." He said this with a sly smile and a wink at his audience, who all laughed, most of them knowing he possesses a good sarcastic streak. He then made a show of barely being able to stand up from his chair, pretending the throbbing in his leg was much worse than it was. *Seriously, people, please go back to your regularly scheduled lives.*

His mother, who had been checking on him a few times every hour, saw his discomfort and efficiently brought the party to a close. Thank God. Now, he hunches on his bed, thinking over the events of the past ten days, his mind whirling, one hand pulling absently at the edge of the comforter.

He feels so lost, even with a newly installed, foolproof, internal GPS. Nothing makes sense anymore. His family isn't rich; apparently no politicians are. Everything they have can be destroyed in an instant. One mistake by him or his parents, and his whole life could be different. He finally understands the truth of the words his parents have screamed fairly frequently over the years: *"We could lose everything if you keep this up!"* He always thought they were being dramatic—or maybe lying to get him to behave better or whatever. Now he realizes their angry scolding was actually a warning.

How many other secrets are his parents keeping? They obviously excel in the secret-keeping department. Violet's illness has been kept hidden from her for her entire life. And almost no one knows Sam jumped the moat into the Radiation Zone. Sure, Jessie figured it out, but it isn't public knowledge.

Jessie. She's another mystery. Sam still has no idea how she really feels about him. There was that awkward exchange earlier on the front porch, but it really didn't clarify anything. She still didn't seem too eager to be alone with him.

Heaving a deep sigh, Sam eases himself farther onto the bed, carefully adjusting his injured leg. His leg really isn't too painful anymore, mostly just stiff; still, it took him almost five minutes to get up the stairs. That's ridiculous. It used to take five seconds.

He slowly rolls the new bottle of pain pills back and forth in his hands, the gentle rattle lulling him into a trance. He sets the pill bottle on the bedside table, then eases open the drawer and pushes aside his various old cell phones, watches, and cuff links, searching for the one thing he knows is hidden far in the back. His fingertips find the familiar curve of the old pill bottle, and he cautiously draws it out.

The prescription is six years old, and he has no idea if the pills' potency has worn off by now. But he knows there are eighty-two pills still left inside. He used to count them repeatedly, sometimes six or seven times in a row, unable to bring himself to throw them away. He had to know how many were left in case he needed them. He always wondered if it was courage or cowardice that made him keep these pills. Maybe a little of both.

He unscrews the cap and gazes down at the eighty-two pills. They are so tiny. Almost insignificant. He dumps out a handful, about thirty pills, jostling them into a neat pile. He stares at them in his palm for a solid minute. "Whatever. Might as well get this party started," he mutters and raises his hand to his mouth.

A soft knock on the door startles him from his trance. "Crap," he mutters, quickly tipping the pills back in the bottle. He shoves both bottles into the drawer and closes it. "Come in," he calls, expecting his mother. His voice is raspy from talking so much this evening. A pang of guilt jolts through him when Jessie quietly creeps around the door.

Sam knows he has kind of been ignoring her this evening. "Oh ... hey. What are you still doing here?" He gingerly slides farther back on the bed and swings his legs up, stretching out and turning to face her. She looks especially beautiful tonight.

"I just wanted to say good-night," Jessie replies, coming into the room, lingering at the foot of the bed. "I feel like I really didn't get to see you much at the party."

"Yeah ...," he says vaguely and looks away from her. "That was a lot of people, right?"

"You seemed like you were having fun telling our story."

"Oh, yeah? Okay, good."

Jessie gives him a quizzical look. "You weren't having fun? But you love telling stories."

Sam shrugs. "I mean, yeah, I guess. I'm so ... I'm just tired, you know?"

"Okay, I'm sorry, I won't bother you then." She gives him a tiny smile and turns to leave.

"Trust me, you're not bothering me. You're keeping me out of trouble." He reciprocates her smile and leans back on the pillows.

"Is it okay if I stay for a few minutes?" She tentatively puts her hand on the edge of the mattress, indicating that she would like to sit down.

"Absolutely," he replies softly. "It's not like I'm doing anything important anyway."

"Yes, you have my permission to take the night off from being important," Jessie teases, sitting at the end of the bed.

"I can't. It's a full-time job," he quips without a trace of a smile. He tries to sound "cavalier," as Jessie would say, but he doesn't think he's pulling it off. It is getting more difficult to keep up this act. He's exhausted. He wants to sleep for a week ... at least. Or maybe never wake up. "I, um, I really like your outfit, by the way ..."

"Oh, thanks." Jessie blushes and glances down at her black skirt and gray leopard-print blouse.

"You make me feel like a fat slob." Sam pulls at the frayed hem of his old T-shirt.

"Sweetie, you would look good in a plastic bag and duct tape."

He laughs softly but makes no reply.

"I've missed you so much, Sam," Jessie whispers. "And I'm ... I'm sorry I didn't call you while you were in the hospital. I didn't even wish you a happy birthday." Jessie leans forward and looks down at her hands, then glances around Sam's room. She needs to look anywhere but at his face. She studies the sports trophies he has won over the years on one shelf. Then she looks at the other wall, which contains a whole mess of computer gaming equipment she doesn't understand.

"It's okay ... it wasn't really one of the happier birthdays." His voice wavers. He really doesn't want to think about the past week ... or the next few months. He takes a deep breath and glances at Jessie, having great difficulty summoning his best devious smirk. "Of course, maybe it would have been slightly better if you had called me."

Jessie's eyes widen, and Sam worries he may have offended her with that dumb remark.

"I'm sorry," she repeats, her voice barely more than a whisper.

Sam gets the feeling she is apologizing for much more than not calling him on his birthday. "It's okay. I honestly didn't feel much like talking anyway."

"That's a first," Jessie teases, her face brightening.

"I know, right? People usually beg me to shut up." He runs both hands through his hair and manages a tired smile.

"Sam? Can I ask a favor?"

He raises his eyebrows but doesn't reply.

"Will you hold me again?"

Sam keeps his eyebrows raised, not sure he heard correctly. Maybe this is a dream? A fantasy inside his head? Or maybe he really did swallow all those pills and is now in a coma?

Jessie fidgets. "I mean, only if you want to. ... I understand if you're tired or whatever ..." Her sentence trails off lamely, and Sam worries she is regretting her decision to visit him.

"No, no, I'm okay ..." Sam shifts himself on his pillows, doing his best to smoothly slide to the center of the bed to give Jessie some room. His leg twinges, and he hopes Jessie doesn't see him wince.

She stands up, nervously smoothing her skirt, and walks toward the head of the bed, looking like she is not quite sure what to do. Sam feels the same way.

He scoots down, so he is almost lying flat, with his head and chest propped up on the pillows. He doesn't say anything. *Talking will spoil it,* he thinks, recalling Jessie's words from their first night in the woods. That seems like so long ago.

Jessie snuggles into his left side. She leans her head against his shoulder and turns into him, her hand slung across his chest. "Hmm, not as romantic without the fire," she mumbles into his T-shirt, her eyes closed.

"Do you always have to make a joke of everything?" He takes her hand carefully in his, trying to enjoy the comforting warmth of her skin.

"I learned from the best. You really should teach that class ..." She takes a deep breath against him, then says quietly, "Sam, can I tell you a secret?"

"Sure," he replies, distracted by the drawer full of his own secrets less than two feet away.

She answers by not saying anything.

"Hello? Anyone home?" he teases gently. He trails his hand through her long hair, then rubs her back in a slow circle, remembering all the times she comforted him while he was trying not to die out in the forest.

"Actually, no ... I don't want to tell you."

"Oh, come on. I'm all intrigued now. Is it something about Christie Cutter? I'm not gonna make fun of you. I promise ..." He quietly adds, "Seriously, Jessie ... I want you to be comfortable enough to tell me anything." *I'm such a hypocrite. There are things I will never tell you.* He thinks of the eighty-two pills, the letter he was trying to write all those years ago, and Violet running into his room. Tonight, it was Jessie.

She raises her head off his chest and looks up at him, their eyes meeting briefly. Then she says, "Actually, I'm worried I might offend you, to be honest ..."

"Try me."

"Okay, but please remember I was pretty much out of my mind when we were lost that first night, all right?"

"Mm-hmm," Sam vaguely agrees. She can't possibly tell him anything worse than the secrets he is keeping from her.

Jessie rests her head on him again. "Okay, I don't mean to be mean to you or whatever ... but ... when we were lost in the woods that first day—I mean, I guess mostly that first night when I was alone with you—I thought ..." She trails off, not entirely sure what she wants to say.

"That I was gonna hurt you?" he supplies for her, thinking back to when he woke up in the woods, alone and confused and feeling more vulnerable than he had ever felt in his life.

"Yes!" Jessie snaps her head up. "I thought you were playing a prank on me or something, just to get me alone with you. I didn't ... I couldn't, like, you know ... trust you, entirely." She tries to choose her words carefully. "And I pretty much thought that almost the whole time ... up until you were ... you know."

"Yeah, I could tell you were suspicious of me." Sam sighs and looks at the ceiling, remembering how Jessie had pointedly kept her distance from him right after he started the fire. "I honestly don't blame you. I mean, I don't think we'd ever been completely alone before, had we? Not for any length of time ... I really thought it was all a giant joke. Like, I seriously didn't know what was going on. God, that would have been an epic prank, though, right? I do kind of wish I had thought of it. I'll have to remember to bring fake blood next time."

"Shut up! Don't even joke about that!" Jessie slaps him hard on the arm, chuckling at his stupid comment. He was really hoping their tender moment would end in a kiss, but they seem to be getting further from that possibility, what with the physical violence and all.

They are silent for a minute. Jessie is not really sure what else to say, now that she has confessed to Sam that she was afraid of him that first night. She squeezes herself closer to his side. She's not really sure how long she should stay with him and thinks she should probably get home now that the party is over.

But she can't leave him yet. He is finally back, safe and warm—and right here with her. She thinks about the nightmare they endured together. She will never forget him lying curled on the ground in a pool of blood, the life draining from him. And he had asked if everyone else was okay. Silent tears well in her eyes. She had been so wrong about him. For years.

"Sam ..." Jessie whispers, raising her head off his chest to look at him. His eyes are closed.

"Mmm?" he responds sleepily.

"Sweetie, I have another secret to tell you."

"Oh, goody." He opens his eyes and gives her a crooked but tired smile. "Can I make fun of you for this one?"

She laughs quietly and shakes her head, then pulls herself up to eye level with him, cupping his cheek in her hand.

"Sam." Her voice wavers as she gathers her courage. "I need to tell you ... when we were lost out there ..." She swallows the lump forming in her throat. "You were absolutely amazing."

He searches her eyes and tucks her hair behind her ear. "I could say the same thing about you, sweetheart." He says this so sincerely she thinks she might start crying before she can finish the speech she had prepared.

"No, I wasn't ... I wasn't like you. You were so *brave* ... and selfless ... and I feel like ... like you make me want to be a better person."

"Whoa! That's a twist," Sam twitches his lip up. No one has ever said that to him before. It feels good.

"Sam, I feel so stupid. I don't know why I just couldn't admit this, but ... I love you. And I think maybe I always have."

His eyes widen with a sudden spark she hasn't seen for quite a while, though it is gone just as suddenly.

"But Jessie ... I'm not ... I'm not good for you. Everyone knows that."

"That's because no one knows who you really are. You have done too good a job at hiding it all these years. But I see who you are. I see the real you. You showed him to me out there. You are perfect for me, Sam. And I don't mean to rat out my brother, but Alex told me what you have done over the years ... saving kids from bullying, keeping Kat from getting suspended ... reading to the kids. You are truly amazing."

"Aw, that little weasel," he whispers, but she can tell from his tone that he isn't upset with Alex.

"I realize now that you are one of the kindest and most selfless people I have ever met, or probably will ever meet. I want to be with someone like that."

"I don't know, Jessie. There are other things about me ... things you don't know ... and probably won't like." He glances at his bedside table, his brow furrowed. He really should throw all those pills away before someone finds them.

"So what? No one can possibly know everything there is to know about someone else. You can't know everything about everybody."

Sam looks up at the ceiling and closes his eyes. Jessie really didn't think he would be this resistant to her. She doesn't know if his feelings toward her have changed, or if he is just exhausted and overwhelmed and can't think about a relationship right now.

"Can you repeat that? Maybe a little slower?" he teases, but he still doesn't look at her.

Jessie props herself up on her elbow and leans onto his chest. She isn't sure what he is going to do, but she has to take her chance now. "Sam," she whispers. "Please kiss me."